Diary of an
Engaged
Wedding Planner

VIOLET HOWE

www.violethowe.com

Cover Design: Robin Ludwig Design, Inc.

www.gobookcoverdesign.com

Published by Charbar Productions, LLC

(p-v5)

ISBN: 099649684X
ISBN-13: 978-0-9964968-4-1

Dedication

For Bonnie.
For lifelong friendship.
For unconditional love & acceptance.
For unwavering support & understanding.
For laughter & tears.
Here's to security blankets.

Books by Violet Howe

Tales Behind the Veils
Diary of a Single Wedding Planner
Diary of a Wedding Planner in Love
Diary of an Engaged Wedding Planner
Maggie

The Cedar Creek Series
The Ghost in the Curve
The Glow in the Woods

The Cedar Creek Family Collection
Building Fences

Short Story Anthology Contributor
Pieces of the Heart

Acknowledgments

I feel like this list grows with every book. I am so blessed to have such a huge support system. Many people I have thanked before, and they still have my gratitude and appreciation. Specifically for this book, I'd like to offer my sincerest thanks to:

Bonnie and Sandy: For all the reasons you already know and a few you may not realize.

Lesley: Thanks for continuing to be my audience, through rain, snow, sleet and children.

Heather: I don't know there will ever be a book I publish that I don't need to thank Heather. You're like my guru. I think I'm going to put a poster of you on my wall. Here's to Tina and Amy.

Beth: You are such a bright spot in my life, and I enjoy you so much. Thanks for being such a great sounding board and creative reference. Oh, not to mention, a pretty awesome friend.

Donna, Lisa, and Melissa: Thank you for your careful eyes and detail to attention.

Annie: You are the best! Thanks for everything, especially your patience on this one!

Alexis: I'm so glad we met! You inspire me and uplift me, and you also make me laugh. Thanks for your support, your encouragement, and your willingness to share your knowledge and your friends.

My Knight & Dr. Smooth: This was the hardest labor & delivery yet, and I can't thank you guys enough for being so supportive, so patient, so forgiving, and so loving. My biggest dream is to make you both proud.

And finally to the best street team ever, the Ultra Violets! I am so honored to have your support and your input. Thanks for taking the ride with me!

June

Saturday, June 7th

I want to go on record as saying I told them it was a bad idea.

They didn't listen to me. Obviously. If they had, I wouldn't have been standing there, dripping all over the restaurant carpet. Seaweed tangled in my hair, green and brown sludge smeared over my once-white dress, and blood oozing from cuts on my knees and hands where I'd crawled across the rocks to get out of the water. I looked like something the cat drug up and the kittens wouldn't have.

Of all the weddings for a bride to request that everyone wear white.

Thank the Lord above I'd opted for granny panties this morning and not a thong. Something told me that spending all day on a yacht might pose a wind and water wardrobe risk. Of course, had I known that risk would involve full submersion in Tampa Bay, I'd have worn a swimsuit underneath my dress.

I must say, the life jacket didn't make much of a fashion statement, but it did at least cover my boobs and bra. Below the jacket, the water had plastered the thin white material to my skin and made the dress pretty much transparent. Granny panties ain't pretty, but they do provide full coverage.

My hat's off to the poor restaurant manager. He actually maintained eye contact for *most* of the conversation with only a few downward glances. I wish I could say the same for the restaurant patrons who sat there gaping openmouthed in their fancy dresses and suits.

If only Reverend White had actually read his itinerary and realized we wouldn't be docking until after the reception ended. Preacher Man had booked another ceremony just two hours after the yacht wedding, so he needed to get back on land pronto.

Bringing the boat back in would have compromised the entire event schedule, so together, Lillian and the boat's captain came up with the brilliant solution that I would drive Preacher Man back to the dock on a Jet Ski.

Never mind that I'd only driven one once before, and that was on a calm lake with Cabe sitting right behind me telling me what to do. Nothing like the busy traffic and waves I encountered today. Not to mention how unladylike it is to straddle a personal watercraft in a short dress, especially when escorting a man of the cloth.

My protests fell on deaf ears, though. Lillian wasn't going to hike her British arse up on a motorized ski to drive Preacher Man back to shore, and none of the crew could be spared to make the trek.

"See that white building in the distance?" The captain pointed to a minuscule white dot on the far horizon. "The dock is just to the left of that. Head straight for it and then turn and head straight back. You'll be able to find us, no problem."

Yeah, right. No problem. Except that no one had checked the fuel level before we departed. Preacher Man and I were halfway to our destination when the engine suddenly cut off.

No coughing.

No sputtering.

Just one minute we were flying across the waves, and the next we were stopped, bobbing up and down in the middle of the bay.

"What happened?" Reverend White asked.

"It stopped." I stated the obvious as I jiggled the key and mashed every button I could find.

"Did you try turning it off and back on?"

I nodded but then tried again, just in case.

"Is there a power switch, or only a key?" He leaned around me just as the waves from a nearby boat hit us, throwing him against my shoulder and nearly unseating us both.

"Whoa!" The Reverend threw both arms around my waist in an effort to stay onboard. The black garment bag between us slid toward the water, and he quickly let go of me to catch it.

I tried the key again, but the engine didn't even attempt to make a noise.

"The lights on the handlebar thing come on, so I don't think it's the battery," I said, trying to sound more knowledgeable than I felt.

Preacher Man leaned around me again, this time with one hand firmly on my shoulder and the other hand tightly clenching the garment bag. "Maybe it's out of gas? Open the gas cap," he said.

I unscrewed the lid on the gas tank between my legs, struggling to keep my dress from giving out a crotch shot. Black nothingness stared back at me from the depths of the tank. "It's possible," I said. "I can't really tell."

Two Jet Skis roared by, close enough to nearly turn us over as their wake hit us. I dropped the gas cap in my haste to grab the handles, but luckily it landed beside my foot on the running board. I had just bent to pick it up when another wave hit us, and my head bashed into the left handlebar as my body lurched forward. Preacher Man slammed into my back, grabbing onto me for dear life before regaining his balance and sitting upright.

"We obviously can't just sit here. We gotta do something," I said as another wave knocked us all cattywampus.

Preacher Man unzipped his black garment bag and dug around to find his phone beneath the folds of his robe. He couldn't get a signal, though, so he put the phone back in the bag and held it up to zip it just as a large boat passed by. I braced for the boat's wake, but Preacher Man had one hand holding up the garment bag and the other on the zipper. The wave knocked him off balance and he toppled sideways, dropping the bag in the water as he struggled to hold onto me.

"My bag!" He half-stood behind me, leaning precariously over the edge to fish the garment bag from the water before it sank. He dove in without hesitation, gripping the black plastic bag and holding it as high as possible above his head as he treaded water. I took the bag from him and slung it sopping wet across the back of the seat.

"Is it waterproof?" I asked.

"I'll find out soon. How should I proceed?" He looked up at me from the water, and then back toward the seat behind me.

Visions of him toppling both of us in the water played out in my head as I threw my hands up in protest. "No! Don't even try it. You'll turn it over for sure!"

"Well, what do you suggest? You want me to swim to shore?"

Weighing the options of me being thrown in the water against him swimming, I leaned heavily in favor of staying dry, but Reverend White didn't strike me as the athletic type. I looked toward the shore in the distance and knew he'd never make it. Hell, I didn't even think I could make it, and he had a good fifty pounds on me.

We tried for several minutes to get him onboard—pushing, pulling, tugging, praying—but nothing worked. Any time he put his weight on one side to lift out of the water, it would lurch that direction and nearly pitch me over. At one point I stood with all my weight on the opposite side from him, but solid as I am, my mass was no match for a soaking wet Reverend White pulling up out of the water.

The poor man gasped and heaved, red-faced and exhausted from the effort. "It's no use. I can't get back on."

Water-goers zipped past us in all directions, but no one so much as glanced our way. I waved my arms overhead to try and signal distress, but evidently we were invisible.

"Okay, we seem to be drifting toward that bridge, so I'm thinking if you hold onto the side and I try to paddle somehow, the current will carry us that way."

The Reverend nodded as he wiped his hand across his face, the top of his shiny, bare head already turning pink in the blistering sun. "I'll try to push and you steer."

While I appreciated his gallant offer, I could see the man was clearly struggling to breathe. I think the life jacket was the only thing keeping him afloat. No way did he have the stamina to push me anywhere.

"Maybe I could paddle with my life jacket." I unsnapped the cumbersome orange jacket and extended the largest piece toward the water.

"That's not a good idea," Reverend White said. "You're not supposed to take that off. It's a law. If you're on a watercraft, you're supposed to wear the life jacket."

I rolled my eyes at the absurdity of his comment. "Well, if some marine patrol officer wants to stop and give me a ticket, I'd happily pay it just to be off this thing and somewhere dry."

I caught sight of a boat approaching and waved the bright orange life jacket as I yelled to catch their attention. No use. They flew past, leaving behind a wake large enough to tip us over.

"Watch out!" I grabbed both handlebars, my wrist threaded through my life jacket so it hung there, useless but within reach. The wave rocked the craft hard to the left, directly into Preacher Man, who grunted and disappeared under the water.

Panic set in quick, and I nearly dove in after him. The last thing I needed on my karma record was killing a preacher. Not that it's okay to kill anybody, but I'm thinking a preacher's got to be pretty high on the list of points deducted.

He popped right back up—Thank the Lord—coughing and spitting as his life jacket bobbed around his ears.

"Are you okay?"

His eyes met mine with a glare that conveyed choice words, but he simply cleared his throat and spit them away with the foam in his mouth. "What are we going to do? We can't stay here. We're quite literally sitting ducks. You mentioned paddling for shore?"

I tried to use the life jacket again, but I might as well have been trailing my fingers in the water. The cold, hard truth settled over me even as I resisted it, certain I could find another way. In the end, only one solution existed. I had to get in the water so we could both push the stupid thing to shore.

The sun blazed down hot, but its heat in no way prepared me for the chill of the water as I let go of the handlebar and plunged in. Wet cold took my breath as the water flooded through the thin layers of my dress. I kicked hard at first, panicked to stay afloat in such deep water, but soon I relaxed and allowed the life jacket and the waves to carry me.

It took us an eternity to reach the bridge. Every time we looked up, it seemed further away. The current, the waves, and the wind nudged us sideways pretty much every other kick-stroke. My legs ached and my muscles burned, unaccustomed as they were to any real physical exertion. My lips stung from licking them too often under the constant assault from the sun and salt water. The life jacket chafed my skin under my arms and around my neck.

I had begun to wonder if we'd ever reach shore. I did a mental recall of any movie I'd ever seen regarding shipwrecks or being stranded at sea, hoping some kernel of survival wisdom would come to mind.

All I could remember was Tom Hanks sporting a massive beard and being fixated on a volleyball and some dude named Pi sleeping under psychedelic stars in a boat with a tiger. Neither of which helped my present situation.

Then, just when I thought I may end up a statistic in my own Poseidon adventure, we reached shallow water. I kicked hard, encouraged by the sight of the bridge getting closer. Big mistake. Slimy, cold tentacles wrapped around my foot and calf. I kicked with all my might as I yelped and shoved away, certain a piranha or shark had taken my leg in one bite. I think it's possible I may have even levitated above the water for a minute, but I don't know for sure because Preacher Man couldn't see me from his side.

He poked his sun-reddened bald head around with eyes wide as he yelled, "What happened?"

Embarrassment warmed my cheeks even as the sun burned them. "Seaweed," I said as I gingerly put my feet back down. "Sorry. It freaked me out."

It got worse the closer we got to shore. The tall stalks reached almost to the surface, tangling in my feet and legs and wrapping around my waist like tentacled creatures engulfing me and pulling me under. My kicks increased in intensity as I fought imaginary monsters, and the Jet Ski got heavier as the water shallowed out and our exhaustion intensified.

If I had been directing our disaster movie, I would have had a white sandy beach with swaying palm trees to welcome us ashore so we could lie down and catch our breaths.

Instead, we encountered a virtual barricade of sharp rocks lying in wait under the bridge. We'd both stubbed our toes and split our shins before we realized how far into the water they extended. I clung to one of the larger rocks, too tired to lift myself up out of the water. Preacher Man climbed onto the barricade and past me, but his heaving chest showed his state of exhaustion and revealed the redness of his face was in part due to exertion and not just sunburn.

I prayed he wouldn't pass out because there was no way I had the energy to run up the hill and get help. Plus, I needed his help to get the useless tub of metal out of the water.

"How are we going to get it past the rocks?" I asked in his general direction, squinting from the prolonged exposure to the constant glare of the sun combined with the ever-present splash of salt water.

"I don't really care," Preacher Man said as he spat sea foam. "He sent us out on faulty equipment, and *he* can deal with it however he chooses. I have a wedding to get to."

I almost laughed at the curtness of this gentle man who had never so much as raised his voice or said a cross word in my presence. I guess our adventure had pushed him to his limits. Then, when he realized the black garment bag was no longer laying across the seat where he'd left it, it pushed him farther.

He kicked at the rocks and then picked up an empty bottle and threw it. The poor man probably came as close to cursing as he ever had in his life. I crawled further up onto the rocks to where I could stand and scan the lake with my blurry eyes, but the water had certainly claimed his bag. Who knew when it slid off? We had both been so focused on reaching the shore that neither of us had seen it fall.

"My keys! My phone! My robe! This is a disaster. My watch is filled with water. I have no idea what time it is. I'm probably already too late for the next wedding, and I have no way to call them or get to them." He plopped down on a flat rock and removed his sopping wet canvas sneakers and socks to reveal stark white feet, wrinkled and puckered.

"We can't just leave it in the water. We have to try to get it on the rocks somehow and go for help." I stared at the Jet Ski with contempt. I think I was trying to convince myself as much as Reverend White.

It took a bit of searching, but I found a low point in the rocks that I thought we could leverage the machine against enough to get it up out of the water. The amount of effort it took was Herculean, and we both collapsed on the rocks when we finally had the damned thing banked enough so it couldn't float away.

What a pair we made as we hobbled up to the highway above. The cuts on our arms and legs made us look like we'd been juggling knives. Unsuccessfully. Reverend White had put his wet shoes back on without the soaked socks, and his feet were already starting to blister. I had sliced my right foot open on one of the jagged rocks, the pain of which had made me curse with complete abandon and disregard of Preacher Man's presence. He'd simply looked at me with understanding and asked if I was okay.

We reached the road and set out for the restaurant on the other side. One step on the scorching hot pavement in my bare feet was all it took for me to channel Flo-Jo. I crossed that road in record time, thankful there was no traffic at that moment.

The clock in the restaurant lobby chimed five times as we entered, and Preacher Man and I looked at each other in disbelief. We'd been gone almost three hours, and he'd missed his second wedding.

Little Heidi Hostess didn't even attempt to hide her disgust when we sloshed into her foyer and asked to use a phone, dripping water and reeking of seaweed. She reluctantly handed it to Preacher Man before leaving to find her manager.

The manager returned with Heidi Hostess hot on his heels. "Swimwear is not allowed…" he started, but then stopped as soon as he saw my white dress clinging to my skin in all the wrong places. He glanced from me to Preacher Man, who was having a heated conversation with someone on the other end of the phone as water dripped from his shorts. Manager Guy looked back to me. "We do have a dress code here."

Really? Seriously? Did he think I was actually showing up for dinner soaking wet and wearing a life jacket? I'm sure my expression clearly conveyed the utter ridiculousness of his declaration, but I clarified our purpose just to be sure.

"We got stranded. Our Jet Ski ran out of gas, and we climbed up by the bridge. We just need to call for help."

The manager swallowed hard, and I could see his struggle to keep his eyes above my chin.

"Why were you wearing a dress on a Jet Ski?" Little Heidi Hostess asked as she stood there chewing her gum like a cow eating cud. The manager cleared his throat and motioned for her to be quiet.

"We were at a wedding on a yacht, and Reverend White here needed to get back to his car. I was supposed to bring him, but we ran out of gas."

"So someone will be coming to get you? Soon?" Manager Guy looked like he wanted that to happen just as much as I did.

Preacher Man hung up and turned back to me. "The file's in my car, to which I have no keys. Their number's in my phone, which is in the water with the keys. I have no way to reach the bride or groom."

"So who did you call? Is someone coming to get us?" I asked.

"That was my wife," he said. "She's in Orlando. She can't be here for an hour at least."

Manager Guy cleared his throat and twisted his hands together. We had arrived during prime early bird dinner hour, and patrons filled the lobby, gaping at us in amazement.

"Johanna?" he called out to Little Heidi Hostess, who popped a big bubble across her face in response.

"Try and get everyone seated as soon as possible. And spit out that gum." He ushered us into the kitchen and out of sight of the paying customers.

"I can have someone drive you wherever you need to go," he said as he pulled a linen tablecloth from a shelf and handed it to me.

I accepted his offer wholeheartedly, shedding the bulky, wet life jacket and fashioning myself a tablecloth toga to hide my lacy underthings from the openmouthed stares of the kitchen staff.

"Can I try to call my boss?" I asked. "I'm sure she's worried about me, and I don't feel right leaving the Jet Ski under the bridge without at least letting someone know."

"Sure, sure."

I got Lillian's voice mail on the first ring, which meant her phone was turned off. I left a message explaining what had happened, the name of the restaurant, and the location of the abandoned watercraft.

"I've got someone driving Reverend White home. Is there any place we could drop you?" Manager Guy looked hopeful that soon he'd be rid of us both, but I didn't really have a place to go. I'd ridden to Tampa with Lillian, so I didn't have my car.

I shook my head. "I'm not local. I think I'll head back down under the bridge. I don't want to leave that thing unsupervised, and I have to think they'll come looking for me at some point. If I could use your phone for one more call, though?"

I dialed Cabe's number, unsure of what he could do to help me, but needing to connect with him after all that had happened.

"What's up, Buttercup?"

At the sound of his deep, rumbling voice my tears started flowing. I poured out the day's events between sniffles, assuring him I was fine and just needed to hear his voice and know he was there on the other end of the line.

"I'm on my way," he said. "I'll be there in an hour."

"No, don't come. I'm sure Lillian will be looking for me soon. There's no sense in you driving all the way over here."

"Babe, you need dry clothes. You need shoes. Even if she comes and gets you, what are you gonna do? Go back to the wedding bleeding, barefoot, and soaking wet? Let me come get you. Lillian can handle the rest of the day on her own. She's a very capable lady."

There was nothing I wanted more in that moment than for my handsome prince to come and rescue me. Well, I wanted a shower, clean clothes, and something to eat, but Cabe coming to get me would solve all that *and* allow me to collapse in his arms. Win-win.

Lillian got my message and called the restaurant before I went back under the bridge. She said the boat captain would send a truck and trailer to meet me so I could be absolved of duty and go home.

I've never been so happy to see Cabe. I don't know that he could say the same, especially since I reeked of seaweed. We had to ride home with the windows down because of the stench.

I pretty much went straight to the shower when we got back to my place, ignoring my sunburned skin's protests as I cranked up the heat of the water and tried unsuccessfully to scrub away the fishy smell.

Cabe welcomed me out of the shower with a warm towel he'd fluffed in the dryer.

"Thanks for rescuing me."

He smiled and picked a strand of seaweed from my hair. "Any time, milady."

The dinner he'd prepared smelled delicious, but I only managed a few bites before I fell asleep on the couch. Cabe picked me up and carried me to bed at some point, tucking me in with a sweet kiss on my forehead. Probably not the weekend he had in mind when he proposed last night.

Sunday, June 8th

Talk about bad timing.

It had only been two days since the love of my life rode in on—and fell off of—a white horse to ask me to marry him. The bruise on his derriere looked pretty painful this morning as he left the bedroom headed to the shower. Should be a crime to mar such a perfectly sculpted specimen.

Lillian had picked me up to go set up the yacht in Tampa less than an hour after Cabe popped the question Friday night. Then I'd come home sunburned and exhausted after my castaway experience last night, definitely not in a mood to celebrate our engagement.

"I'm sorry. If I had known, I might have been able to move things around," I said as we stood at the airport departure curb this morning saying goodbye.

"No worries," he said. "I knew before I proposed that you had to work this weekend and that you were flying to Chicago to get your certification. I just didn't want to wait until you got back."

I figured that might have something to do with the last time we parted at an airport, when he got arrested for shoving a TSA officer and I flew to Paris without him and ended up in someone else's arms.

"You're not worried about me going out of town, are you?"

He shrugged and smiled. "Should I be?"

I laughed and held up my left hand, watching the diamond sparkle in the sunlight. "Little different circumstances this time."

Cabe's blond curls lifted in the early morning breeze. I'd never seen his hair so long before, tousled and unruly as it framed his face and dusted his collar. It only served to make him more attractive, and the butterflies in my stomach swarmed lower as I reached up and ran my hands through those curls, lacing my fingers behind his head and pulling him to me.

Our lips met and held. I inhaled deeply, breathing in his masculine scent and memorizing every aspect of the moment to carry with me on the plane. His tongue brushed across my bottom lip, and I opened up to him, welcoming his slow exploration. I couldn't resist twisting my tongue against his, and the kiss deepened as we pressed to each other and tried to savor the minutes we had left.

"I really wish I didn't have to go," I whispered against his cheek when I pulled away.

He stroked his hands up and down my back and hugged me to him with a sigh.

"Deacon and I will be right here waiting for you." He nodded toward the goofy dog hanging his head out the back seat window. Strings of drool oozed from his jowls and dripped down the side of the car door. He cocked his head as Cabe said his name, his ears twitching with excitement.

"See? Deacon misses you already. He's salivating over it."

"Nice. Deacon salivates over everything, though. Don't you, buddy?" I ruffled the fur between his ears and tried to avoid being slimed.

The security guard made eye contact with me as he approached us for the second time.

"Okay, Cable. He's coming back around. We better wrap this up. The last thing you need with your appearance before the judge next week is another altercation at the airport."

Cabe scowled in the guard's direction but released his hold on my waist and picked up my carry-on bag. "Here you go, Buttercup. Safe travels. Call me when you land?"

I nodded and stretched onto my toes to kiss him again.

"I'll miss you."

He smiled. "You too, my *fiancée*."

He emphasized each syllable of the word, and we both laughed at the newness of it.

"Wow. I like the sound of that."

Our lips met again, this time hungry and impatient, as we resisted saying goodbye. The security guard blew his whistle near us, sending Deacon into a barking fit.

We pulled apart abruptly, my heart racing as I smoothed my skirt and took a deep breath, stealing a glance back up at Cabe smiling down at me.

His normally translucent blue eyes had deepened into a much richer hue. His sexy grin hinted at naughty thoughts, and I clearly wasn't the only one who wished we had more time alone.

"We'll continue this…*conversation*…later?" I tugged at the front of his shirt and pulled him down for another quick kiss before turning to walk away. I could feel Cabe's eyes on me, and I knew he'd watch me until the guard made him get in and move the car.

"I love you, Tyler Warren!"

I turned back as he pulled away from the curb, Deacon still barking and wagging his tongue out the window. I laughed and ignored the burning hole in my chest as my heart left with them.

It's not that I don't want to go on this trip. I do. I've looked forward to getting my certification and fulfilling the terms of my promotion. I'm also pretty excited to see Chicago since I've never been, and based on their bios, the instructors of the course should be interesting to learn from.

But I feel like Cabe and I just found each other again, and I don't want to leave him.

It's so different flying this time. Last time I buckled into a plane seat, I flew to Paris and back without Cabe, wondering what the hell had happened to make him leave me. This time I'm still flying without him but as his fiancée.

Wow. *Fiancée*. Still sounds odd to me. Foreign, somehow.

With everything that's happened this weekend since he proposed, I haven't had a chance to really process it.

I'm getting married.

I'm going to be someone's *wife*. Cabe's wife, so I'm pretty freakin' happy about it, but still. A *wife*.

Holy crap. That's some pretty grownup stuff.

Oh, wow. I have to plan a wedding. *My* wedding.

Oh, wait a minute. Oh, dear Lord in heaven.

I have to tell my mother I'm getting married.

I've dealt with many mothers of brides in my career, but something tells me my mama is going to be the Mack-Daddy Mother of the Bride of all time.

I have to plan *my* own wedding. With *my* mama.

Oh, heaven help me.

We gotta elope.

Tuesday, June 10th

"How's the course going?" Cabe asked when I called him tonight. "You learning a lot?"

"Yeah, it's cool to hear the instructors' ideas and see things from a different perspective. You'd be amazed at how star struck these other girls are about being a wedding planner, though. Some of them are fresh out of high school or community college and have no clue what they're in for."

"Are you giving them some truth?"

'Ha! No. Who am I to disillusion dreamers? There's two of us in the class who have already been working weddings. The others flitter around us like flies on honey. '*Oh wow! It must be so glamorous. All the dresses and flowers. Everybody must be so happy all the time. You must looove your job.*' Aargh. I do love my job, but they are in for such a rude awakening."

Cabe chuckled. "I'm sure they'll do fine. Have you told your mom we got engaged yet?"

I spewed Diet Coke all over the paperwork in front of me. I think I even inhaled some based on the burning fire that lit up the inside of my nose and made my eyes water. "What?" I coughed out.

"You okay?"

"Yeah, just choked on my drink. Abrupt topic change, Cable."

"So, have you?"

"Um, no. I haven't talked to her. I don't think she even knows I'm in Chicago right now. Why do you ask?"

"I was just wondering if you'd told her and what she said."

I shuddered against the dread rising up within me. "No. I haven't yet." Nor did I plan to anytime soon. I wanted to hold off on that announcement as long as possible.

Cabe was silent for a moment. Did it bother him that I hadn't told her?

"I just haven't had time to talk to her, you know? I left for Tampa right after you proposed, and then I certainly didn't have time to talk to her Saturday with the wedding and the whole Jet Ski fiasco. It's been such a whirlwind since I got here that I've barely had time to talk to you and keep up with messages from brides."

He was still silent.

"Cabe, what's up? Why aren't you saying anything?"

"I don't know."

I sighed. "What's wrong?"

"I was just thinking. We've known each other six years, but I've never met your family. When we get married, they'll be my family, too. So I dunno. I was kind of thinking, you know, if you wanted to, that maybe we should make a trip to meet your mom and tell her in person."

My stomach turned inside out as my brain silently screamed, *"Nope. Not a chance. No way in hell."*

I hadn't even had time to fully process that I was *engaged.* That I was getting *married.* I knew I needed to tell Mama at some point, but I wasn't ready. Not now and maybe not ever.

I love my mother, and I know she loves me. But that woman drives me absolutely bonkers. She can take the most simple thing on earth and twist it into torturous drama. I had no desire to set those wheels in motion before I had to. Better to delay the inevitable.

"Ty? You still there?"

"Yeah. I'm here."

"Well, it was just an idea."

I winced at the disappointment in his voice. "I know, and I appreciate it. It's a great idea. I just don't know if I'm ready for that."

More silence on his end, but I chose to ignore it. It wasn't a subject I wanted to delve into further.

"I gotta go, okay? We'll talk about this more when I get home."

"Okay. I miss you."

My heart clenched, and I longed to be curled up next to him.

"I miss you too, Cabe. Bunches."

"Ya know," he said, his voice a little lower and more seductive, "we could indulge in a little long-distance playtime. Whaddya say? Wanna talk dirty to me?"

"Um, as enticing as that sounds, I'm sitting in a hotel bar waiting for the Polly Planner wannabes to come down for a drink and discuss glamour and such. Rain check?"

"Most certainly. Wanna call me later?"

I chuckled. "How about I cash in that rain check in person Thursday night?"

"We could do both…"

I grinned at his playful tone and considered blowing off the girls at the bar to have phone sex with my fiancé. I might have done it, too, if Deacon hadn't interrupted.

"What's up with him?" I asked as Deacon barked incessantly in the background.

"He wants to go for a walk. Deacon, buddy, come lay down."

I sighed and redirected my thoughts back to work mode. "You go walk him, I'll go entertain my groupies, and we'll continue down this path another time."

"If you're sure. Because I could put him in the backyard."

I laughed at his insistence. "Good night, Cabe."

"G'night, Ty. Love you. Miss you."

I bit down on my lip as I put the phone down, thinking about his request to meet Mama.

Obviously he's going to meet her eventually. It's not like I can get married and not tell her.

But not yet.

I kind of want to keep the news just between us for a while. Like a magical secret that only we share. Once I tell Mama, I know it's going to develop a life of its own and become a living, breathing thing that quickly grows beyond my control. So for now, I want to protect this little kernel of joy and keep it all to myself. For as long as I can, anyway.

Friday, June 13th

It was tough being back in the office today. If I hadn't already had a planning session on the calendar, I probably would have just slept in and dragged myself out of bed just in time for my rehearsal tonight.

My flight home yesterday was delayed coming out of Chicago, which meant I missed the connecting flight in Atlanta. So by the time I got home and in bed, it was well after midnight.

Cabe and Deacon seemed to be deep in sleep minutes after they hit the bed, but my thoughts were racing with the information overload from the week plus going over everything in my head for this weekend's wedding and today's meeting.

By the time I met with my bride, Angie, today, I was on my fourth cup of coffee and searching for any reserve of patience that might be lurking in the corners of my mind. A search that proved for the most part futile.

It's not that Angie isn't a sweet girl. She is, really. But this is our third planning session, and we still have nothing set in place for her wedding other than the officiant and the location.

She has a clear vision of how she wants her wedding to look. She's spent no telling how much time flipping through magazines and poring over wedding web pages to find pictures of every detail she wants to incorporate. She carries around a binder filled with clippings and screen shots of every single aspect of her dream wedding. No stone has been left unturned.

White chair covers. Red satin bows. White silk draping from the rafters. A canopy of twinkle lights suspended over the dance floor. Lush arrangements of Casablanca lilies in cylindrical vases. An orchestra. A monogrammed custom vinyl dance floor. Arrival in a vintage Cadillac and departure across the lake in a decorated pontoon boat.

But we're talking champagne tastes and beer-belly budget. Cheap beer.

Angie has five thousand dollars to spend and a guest list of two hundred.

It ain't gonna happen. It's mathematically impossible.

Champagne Angie refuses to hear that.

Both planning sessions so far have ended in a stalemate where she stomps out in tears and nothing gets settled.

When she called to book today's meeting, she assured me she had a plan in place that would make everything work out.

I assumed she'd cut her guest count down to a manageable number or crossed a few dream items off her checklist.

But no. I should have known better.

She launched right into it as soon as she sat down. "Okay, so obviously the biggest expense we have is the food and the bar, right?"

I nodded, somewhat apprehensive to be in agreement with anything until I heard the whole plan.

"So I figure the easiest way to cut the budget is to get rid of the caterer."

Not sure I'd heard her correctly but curious as to where she was headed, I leaned forward in my chair.

"I found a chicken place that can do a bucket of chicken and two side items for each table for six dollars a person. That includes biscuits—one per person—and they're willing to throw in paper plates and wet wipes. So that's *way* cheaper than the caterer. If we ask everybody to throw their stuff in the trash when they're done, we wouldn't need servers to clear the dishes, and people could use their wet wipes to clean off the tables after they finish eating."

She looked at me like she had just handed me a top secret formula that would cure cancer, end hunger, and achieve world peace. With a wet wipe thrown in for free.

"Angie, darlin', I know you're searching for a way to make all this work. You've been real resourceful and diligent in your search, but honey, you can't invite two hundred people to fly into town and sit on chair covers under a twinkle light canopy and feed them buckets of chicken and mashed potatoes with plastic forks. It's just not done."

"Oh, no, no, no. We weren't gonna do the little white plastic forks from the chicken place. Mama said that'd be tacky. She found boxes of clear plastic forks—the real nice, thick plastic—at the dollar store and bought enough for us to use. I already told the chicken place we didn't need theirs."

I panicked as I realized she had already put this harebrain scheme into action. "Angie! Did you already book the chicken?" My brain rejected the notion of *booking* chicken so I mentally searched for the proper term. "Order it? Did you order the chicken? Have you paid them anything?"

Her elated expression wilted a bit at the tone of my question. "We gave them a deposit. Why? Is that bad?"

I rubbed my hands over my eyes and took a deep breath.

"Sweetie, you can't do that. You can't serve buckets of chicken with chair covers and Casablanca lilies. You just can't. We either need to cut the guest list down to where you can afford the caterer, or we need to redesign the wedding to fit your budget."

Her face fell into a frown and tears filled her eyes, but I didn't let it stop me from talking sense.

"Look, I know you don't want to cut anything, but trust me when I say your guests will not be impressed with buckets of chicken. They would much rather have a great meal and no silk drapings or chair covers."

"But it's really good chicken," she protested. "We went and ate there before we gave them a deposit. It's delicious. Not greasy or nothing."

Unfortunately, I had to consider the possibility that if Angie and her mama thought finger lickin' good was an appropriate wedding menu description, their guests might be thrilled, too. But I had vendors to protect and our company image to uphold, so I focused on the other limitations of the budget that chicken didn't solve.

"Let's look again at the decor. If we just nix the silk draping and then—"

"No! I love that silk draping. Look at this," she said, digging through her binder for a magazine clipping. I'd seen it before. Every time we'd met. A concert hall in Manhattan draped with yards and yards of imported silk, uplit with colored gels every few feet so that even the shadows on the ceiling several stories above danced with colors.

In stark contrast, Angie's location was a one-story pavilion on a lake. Tin roof with wooden rafters. A large wooden pole in each corner holding it up. Patio pavers for flooring and palm trees planted in between the poles. Not exactly the same canvas to start with, so no matter how much money she spent on silk draping, it was never going to look like the picture. Which I had explained. Several times.

"Angie, it's beautiful, but as we've already discussed, you can't afford it, and it's not going to look the same as the picture without the lighting and the high ceilings."

Tears rolled through the trail of mascara down her face, and emotion painted vivid red splotches on her cheeks.

"But it's my wedding. I should be able to have whatever I want. It's the one day in my life where everything is about me. It's my day, and I want it to look like this."

She jabbed a bright blue fingernail at the magazine clipping and glared at me, defiance flashing in her eyes.

I sighed and wondered how rude it would be to get up and pour more coffee in the middle of our conversation. Crushing dreams in a gentle manner required more sleep or more caffeine. Or both.

Angie must have taken my hesitation as a sign of me wavering.

"So are you going to give me what I want, or do I need to talk to your boss?" She tucked her chin and raised her brows as she said it, certain she'd just handed me a package sure to make me quiver in my boots.

I almost busted out laughing for sure that time. The only *boss* in the office was Lillian. I had no fear whatsoever that she would be on my side in this argument. Bring it on.

"Angie, my hands are tied. I understand you want your wedding to be wonderful, and it will be, but you have a very limited budget. We have to work within that budget, and I don't have control over the vendors' prices."

She shook her head and put up her hand to stop me. "I had hoped it wouldn't come to this, but you leave me no choice. I will not allow you to ruin my wedding. I need to speak to your boss, and I won't take no for an answer." She crossed her arms and turned away from me.

I wasted no time in getting up and going to Lillian's office to convey the request.

"Is this the twit you told me about before? The one who wants a five hundred thousand dollar event with five thousand dollars?" Lillian raised one eyebrow to a sharp angle and peered at me over her glasses.

I nodded.

"I don't have time for this," Lillian said, removing her glasses with an exhale and shoving back her chair from her desk. "When is her wedding? How many guests? Buckets of chicken, my arse."

Lillian swept into the conference room with all the authority and haughtiness in her possession. A quite formidable entrance that wasn't lost on Champagne Angie, who immediately sat up straight and wiped the tears and mascara from her face.

"Angela?" Lillian's British accent was clipped so sharp it almost stung.

"Yes?" Champagne Angie nodded and sniffled, her gaze darting back and forth between me and Lillian with a mixture of apprehension, confusion, and blatant fear.

"I understand you have an issue with Tyler's handling of your affairs. Tyler has been gracious enough to take on your event, even though it falls far below the budget threshold we deem essential for our clients."

I blinked and tried not to look at Angie. If we had any such threshold, I'd never heard of it before now.

"She did this out of the goodness of her heart because she is passionate about brides and she took a particular liking to you and wanted to help. However, I fear it's become obvious that in order to create the wedding vision you have in mind, you cannot afford our services. The money you are spending to have Tyler's assistance would be much better put toward the trappings of the day to get you closer to achieving your dreams. If you'll just follow me, I'll have my assistant Carmen draw up paperwork to cancel our contract and refund your deposit, which you can then redirect for your silk drapings."

Lillian spun to go as if it were a done deal simply based on her saying so. Angie's mouth opened and closed as she watched Lillian leave the room.

"Wait! I don't want to cancel. I can't do all this by myself. I need Tyler to help me."

Lillian came back and peered at Angie. "Oh, but you can, my dear. You can do all this by yourself. You have been. Just look at all this work you've done." She swept her hand to indicate the clippings spread across the table. "You don't need us. Your money would be better spent elsewhere."

"No. I want a wedding planner. I want Tyler. I need her to help me." Champagne Angie had stopped crying, the distress in her eyes outweighing her earlier defiance. She shrank a bit in her chair as Lillian leaned over the table and braced her weight on her knuckles to tower over the young girl.

"Then I suggest you *allow* her to help. You are hiring Tyler for her expertise and her guidance. If you want to pay for her services, then get the full value for your money and allow her to plan your event to be cost-effective and beautiful. Otherwise, your money is wasted. As is her time. Are we clear?"

Lillian stood back up to her full height and cocked that sharp, fear-inducing eyebrow again.

Angie nodded in an uneven rhythm, her chin shaking but her gaze unwavering. "Yes, ma'am."

I almost felt sorry for her. She had no idea what she'd asked for when she demanded to meet my boss.

"There now," Lillian said with a huge smile that lit up her face but did nothing to ease the eyebrow arch or the set of her eyes. "I'm so glad we got that settled and can move forward. Tyler, do let me know how plans are progressing? I'm anxious to hear what you come up with."

It took almost two hours more, but we nixed the silk draping and decided to talk to the florist about doing a cheaper arrangement with maybe a single Casablanca lily or perhaps another flower similarly striking but less expensive. We also discussed possibly doing away with the chair covers, but I could see the disappointment weighing on her so I tabled that decision for a later date. She left with a promise to cut people from the list and revisit her available funds.

I feel bad for her. I really do. I want her wedding to be everything she wants it to be. I know how much it means to her, and I'll do whatever I can to make it happen. But you can't squeeze blood from a turnip. There's only so much I can do with the money she gives me to work with.

It naturally turned my thoughts to my own wedding. I don't want to go into debt or put anyone out for a huge wedding. It's just not necessary. Besides, where would we have it? If I have it here, most of my family wouldn't be able to come. Not that Mama would let me do that anyway. She'll insist it's in our church back home. But I don't know if that's what I want. I'd kind of like to have it here and hire the vendors I work with and know so well.

We also have to consider Cabe's family. That situation is so messed up right now I'm not sure who would even come. He's still not speaking to his sister after Galen joined forces with the dark side and invited Cabe over to meet their half-siblings with no warning.

He has at least been talking with his mom since they fell out over Maggie taking Galen's side and calling Cabe's father, but they're not as close as they used to be. Every time I ask about her, he's not eager to discuss it.

The more I think about it, the more I think it would solve everything if we just eloped.

Saturday, June 14th

Mama called this morning as I was getting ready for work. I should have let it go to voice mail, but I felt guilty that I haven't talked to her in so long. Even more so since I'm basically hiding some pretty important news from her.

"Hey Mama." I put her on speaker so I could finish my make-up.

"Hey sugar. You having a wedding today?"

"Yes, ma'am. I'm getting ready now." *Oh, and by the way, I'm having a wedding of my own.* I couldn't say it out loud.

"Well, I won't keep you. I was just calling to tell you Marlena's getting married."

Great. Just great. My aunt Marjorie's daughter Marlena is a year younger than me and has always been the gold standard my mother used as a comparison.

Why can't you be more like your cousin Marlena? Why don't you act like Marlena? Why couldn't you just try to do it like Marlena?

Marlena was a pageant queen. Marlena was stick thin. Marlena had perfect teeth. Marlena's hair never frizzed. Marlena made straight As and got a college scholarship. Marlena finished college and got her degree. Marlena took a job as a pharmacist at a children's hospital right out of school and actually helps people for a living. Marlena has been dating a pediatric heart surgeon and the two of them travel to Uganda and Peru each year to provide medical services to the unfortunates of the world.

Now Marlena is getting married. The bar will be set. High. Very high.

Any thought I had of telling Mama about my engagement dissipated.

There is no way I am going to plan a wedding at the same time as Marlena or anywhere within a year after her event.

I might just be moving my date up. I don't even have a freakin' date set yet, but whatever Marlena's is, mine needs to come first.

That's it. I gotta talk Cabe into eloping.

Sunday, June 15th

"I have a surprise for you," Cabe said when I arrived at his place. His eyes were wide with excitement and mischief, and his broad smile made me all tingly inside. "Close your eyes."

He took my hand and pulled me inside the house and down the hallway to his bedroom.

"Okay, open them!"

The smell of fresh paint overwhelmed my nostrils as I slowly took in the transformation. He had painted his walls to match the deep lavender of my own bedroom.

"Do you like it? You like it, right? It's the color of your room."

He was so excited he couldn't stand still, and the grin on his face was echoed in his eyes.

"Yes, it is." I turned slowly again, noticing the different nuances in the color with the additional windows in this room. In my room, the color appeared a bit darker, more gray. The brighter lighting brought out a more delicate variation of the shade. "It's beautiful, Cabe."

"Yes! You like it!" He picked me up and twirled me, kissing me as he put me back on the ground. "I hoped you would. I did the first coat Friday night after you left and finished it up yesterday while you were at work. You said the house looked bare, so I thought I'd add some color."

I nodded. "It looks good."

"You like this color, right?"

"I picked it, didn't I?" Memories of the day I'd picked that color for my walls flooded back. Cabe and I weren't together then. I'd painted over my memories of us as I prepared to move forward without him. Now, here I was, embarking on a completely different journey with him by my side. Did the color still work?

23

"What made you pick this color?" he asked.

"It seemed calm. Serene. I needed serenity. Why'd you pick it?"

He laid across the bed and pulled me down with him. "I wanted you to feel at home here. In this room. This house. Our house. Our bedroom."

I lifted onto my elbow and propped my chin in my hand to look at him. "*Our* bedroom?"

"Yes, *our bedroom*. I always intended for it to be ours."

He meant it. I had no doubt. But it still bothered me that he'd gotten the house while we were apart. I would have liked the house better if we'd picked it out together. Searched together. Bought it together.

"What's up, Buttercup?" He pushed my hair away from my face and tucked it behind my ear. "Does that bother you? For me to say it's our bedroom?"

I shook my head but didn't meet his eyes.

"Ty, I needed to get out of the pool house. I crashed there when I came back from Seattle, but it was past time for me to stand back on my own two feet and get a place of my own. Plus Mom and I were barely speaking, which made it awkward as all hell living in such close proximity."

I met his eyes again. "I know that. I'm not saying anything about it."

"No, but I can tell it bothers you that I bought the house without you. I need you to understand why."

I flipped onto my back, uncomfortable facing him while I pouted.

"I do understand why. You don't owe many explanations. We weren't together then." My heart pricked a little at the memory of our time apart.

He turned my face to his and moved so close we were almost touching noses.

"Ty, I bought this house because I needed to make commitments toward a future. Our future. I needed to establish some roots. Some stability. A place to offer you when I came begging for you to take me back." He kissed the tip of my nose and caressed my cheek. "I never thought of it as just my house. It was always ours for me. I only looked in the neighborhoods near our lake. I purposely searched for a big kitchen with the island so we could work side-by-side when we cook. I made sure it had a fenced-in yard because I knew you wanted a dog."

He motioned toward the large wall of windows above the bed and the other windows on the wall adjacent to it. "I picked this house because it had plenty of windows so we can lay together in the light of the moon. And you always told me how much you missed your front porch back home, so I told the realtor that was a necessity. I even had the swing installed before I brought you to see it. Baby, from the moment I decided to get a house, I looked for *our* house. I always planned for us to live in this house together."

My heart melted a little. I had no idea he'd put that much thought into it. Taken me into consideration. At the same time, it still hurt. Like I'd missed out on something. I didn't know how to just switch that off and stop feeling it. I also didn't know what to say to ease his worried expression, so I chose what was probably the safest thing out of everything swirling around my head. "I love you."

"I love you, too. Probably more than you'll ever know, but I'll keep trying to show you." He kissed me as he pulled my body against his.

I pulled back, unwilling to let it go just yet.

"It just hurts, Cabe. I appreciate you doing all that, I really do. But the house reminds me of our time apart. Painful memories. It's something you did without me. I wish we'd found it together."

"C'mon, Buttercup. We have a lifetime to find houses together. Every place we live from this point forth, we'll find together. But let's start here. Please? Make this house a home with me. Our home?"

It wasn't an offer I really wanted to refuse. I did love the house. It was perfect for us, and it made me feel better to know he picked it *for* me. I could choose to harbor the resentment, or I could let it go and embrace the house and make it ours. Our first house.

I didn't answer him with words, but I think my body told him all he needed to know to understand that I agreed.

Wednesday, June 18th

"So, your mom's birthday is coming up next week. What are we doing?"

I'd debated whether or not to bring it up all day, but the date was getting too close to ignore.

"I don't know." Cabe was tinkering with the secondhand lawn mower he'd bought, trying to figure out why it wouldn't crank.

"When's the last time you talked to her?"

"I dunno. Couple of weeks ago, maybe?"

I plopped down on the back porch steps watching him, trying to decide how deep in the water I wanted to wade.

"Does that bother you?"

He glanced up at me and immediately turned his attention back to the motor.

"I'm serious, Cabe. You guys used to be so close, and now you hardly ever talk. You never have told me exactly what went down. I know you're pissed that she gave your dad your number—"

"He's not my dad. He's basically no more than a sperm donor."

I took a deep breath and reconsidered my decision to wade into this mess. Being abandoned by his father at the age of three had carved deep scars across Cabe's heart, and the recent events with his sister and mom had reopened old wounds.

"Okay, but I hate seeing you and Maggie at odds like this. Y'all need to hash this out."

"It's fine."

I waited a moment to see if he would continue, but he didn't. "Okay. Did you guys talk about everything then? Did she say why she did it?"

"Why she did what?" He continued to focus on the motor, but his jawline tightened. He knew exactly what I meant, and I had to decide

26

whether or not I wanted to push him.

"C'mon, Cable. Cut the crap. Look at me."

He put down the screwdriver and granted my request, disinterest clear on his face.

"She says she didn't give him my number or tell him to call me."

"Then how did he get it?"

He stood and adjusted the position of the lawn mower. "I don't know, Ty. Maybe he looked it up on the internet. It's not that hard to do."

The mower roared to life as I opened my mouth to respond. I glared at the temperamental machine as Cabe wheeled it around to face the lawn.

"I want to try and get the yard done while it's running, okay?" He didn't wait for an answer, so I stood to go back inside and postponed the discussion until after dinner.

Later, when we had cleared the dishes from the table and Cabe was washing the last of the pans, I broached the subject again.

"Did you ask your mom why she called him?"

Cabe sighed and slid the heavy skillet under the water to rinse. "You're not gonna drop this are ya, Buttercup?"

I took the skillet from him and dried it. "No, I'm not. I want you to work it out with her. Talk to her. Look how much time we wasted with each other by not getting things out in the open."

He dried his hands on the towel I held and then encircled me with his arms. "You're right. We shouldn't waste any more time." He bent his head and touched his lips against mine, but I pulled back before he could intoxicate me into forgetting the discussion at hand.

"Oh no you don't, buddy! You think you can start kissing me, and I'll just forget all about this, but we need to talk."

He slid his hands under my shirt and crept them slowly up my back, unlatching my bra with a quick flick of his thumb as I struggled to remember why it was so important to resist.

"Cabe, I'm serious. I don't wanna blow this off. Did you ask Maggie why she called him?" I put both hands on his chest and lightly pushed back against his efforts to kiss me until he sighed in resignation and released me. I followed him into the living room, wriggling my shoulder and elbow through the bra strap and then through the shirt sleeve before repeating the acrobatic movement on the other side so I could pull it from beneath my shirt and toss it across the chair.

"How do women do that? How do you completely remove a piece of clothing that's underneath other clothing without taking off the top layer?"

I flopped down on the couch next to him. "Years of practice. Don't change the subject."

"She called him to discuss what happened at Galen's house. She didn't know he was going to call me."

"Does she call him often?"

Cabe shrugged. "I don't know. You'd have to ask her. He's not something we discuss."

"How could you guys not talk about this? Have you seriously never asked your mom if she kept in touch with him?"

"I don't know, Ty." He rubbed his face and ran his fingers through his curls until they stood out in a snarled mess. "I told you I wanted nothing to do with the man. Asking a lot of questions about him didn't seem to be a good way to pretend he didn't exist, you know?"

"This blows my mind. I don't get it."

"Oh really?" He tilted his head to one side and lifted his eyebrows with a smile. "You don't get families not communicating? How many times a month do you talk to your mom? How many times has she visited here or you visited there since you moved away? And by the way, have you told her yet we're engaged?"

I drew in a deep breath and pinched my nose against the headache just starting behind my eyes. "We're not talking about my family right now. Stay on topic."

"You can't sit there and act like it's so foreign to you that my mom and I wouldn't want to rehash something uncomfortable to discuss. You haven't even shared something that should be happy news. I mean, as far as *I'm* concerned, our engagement is happy news."

"Of course it is. I just haven't really talked to Mama since you proposed. So you've already told your mom, then?" I tried to deflect the line of questioning back to him.

"She knows I bought the ring. I thought maybe we'd tell her it's official when we see her on her birthday."

"So we *are* going to see her on her birthday?"

Cabe cupped my cheek in his hand. "Yes, Buttercup. I'll call her tomorrow and see where she wants to go. Okay?"

I nodded and turned my head to kiss his hand.

"So I don't understand," I said, unable to drop it. "If she didn't give him your number, why are you still mad at her?"

He dropped his hand and laid his head back on the sofa with his eyes closed.

"I'm not mad at her, Ty. There's just been a lot of crap, you know? She and I have both said and done some things that are hard to move past. But we'll work through it. It'll be okay. Can we please talk about something else now?" He rolled his head to the side to look at me. He half-grinned, hopeful I'm sure that I would give in and drop the topic.

It still bothered me, though. I guess maybe it was because there was so much he had kept from me regarding his mom and sister. I still felt like I was in the dark. Like I didn't know everything going on. From the bits and pieces of information I had, it didn't make sense that the two of them would have such a rift between them.

Maybe I'll feel better once I see him and Maggie together next week. Maybe it'll be back to normal and all will be okay.

Saturday, June 21st

A hellacious storm tore through in the wee hours this morning. The thunder woke me a little before four, crashing and rumbling like multiple explosions had been triggered just outside the house. The windows rattled and the old boards creaked as the wind battered us with rain.

Deacon paced and shivered, mumbling and whining like he always does when the weather turns bad. Poor dog. Summer in Florida is not the place to be if you're terrified of thunderstorms. Although I must admit, this was much worse than our standard run-of-the-mill afternoon storm. This was more like Armageddon. I pulled Deacon up on the bed next to me and smoothed my hands over his fur, whispering, "It's okay, baby. You're alright." Even though I wasn't so sure we weren't all going to be blown away.

I thought Cabe was going to sleep through the whole thing. I was sorely tempted to jab him in the side and wake him up to suffer through it with us, but before I could act on those impulses, a dazzling bolt of lightning lit up the whole room followed by a huge clap of thunder that nearly shook the house off its foundation. Cabe didn't flinch at the bright light or the deafening boom, but he certainly woke up when Deacon jumped right in the middle of his chest, barking and moaning as if he was trying to save Cabe from an imminent demise.

The sky flashed again, followed by another splintering crack of thunder, and this time Cabe was awake for it.

"Holy hell! What's going on?" He sat up and tried to push Deacon off him as the dog dug in for dear life.

"Storm. It's really bad. I can't believe you've been sleeping through it. Deacon's wigging out." And so was I.

"Power's out," Cabe said as he looked at the clock on his nightstand.

"Wonder how long it's been out?"

"For about twenty minutes now, but the storm's been raging almost an hour."

He rolled to face me and petted Deacon, who was curled up and shivering between us.

"You been awake?"

I nodded. "I'm hoping this blows over before my wedding. Heather and Sean are such a nice couple. I don't want their wedding day ruined."

The thunder popped again, and Deacon yelped. Cabe looked up at the ceiling as the wind howled across the roof.

"Forget the wedding. I'm hoping it doesn't ruin our house."

It had passed in another half hour, and we finally got Deacon calmed down and got back to sleep around five. I was relieved to see blue skies and sunshine when my alarm woke me at seven.

When I had the pre-ceremony photography going smoothly, I left Heather and Sean in Charlotte's not-always-capable hands so I could drive over to the reception hall to check their progress.

It was an easy set, only fifty guests with a buffet, but since Heather and Sean and most of the guests were professional ballroom dancers, we'd ordered a huge dance floor to accommodate their repertoire of moves. I was a bit nervous about it being set correctly or the tables looking lost at the back of the room.

I was relieved to see that the manager on duty at the Garden Club was Ivan. His laidback personality and easy smile always made for a pleasant event.

"Good day to you," Ivan said as he bowed dramatically. "Your linens and Chiavari chairs have arrived. Haven't seen the dance floor yet, but they've got plenty of time."

I glanced at my watch and frowned. The dance floor had been scheduled for delivery at eleven. It was only twenty after, so they weren't terribly late, but with such a huge installation, I wanted to know the set-up was going well before I headed back to the ceremony.

"We had a couple of huge limbs down with some debris on the patio, so we're clearing that now. I'll be out there if you need me," Ivan said. "Quite a storm, huh?"

I nodded as I searched the wedding file for a delivery contact number. My call was answered with immediate hold music and no person.

Servers were beginning to arrive around me, folding napkins and fluffing linens across the tables as they all discussed the early morning storm and their lack of sleep because of it.

After what seemed to be an eternity but was probably only a couple of minutes, a frazzled voice replaced the hold music.

"This is Shelia, have you been helped?"

"No, Shelia, this is Tyler Warren over at the Garden Club. We have a dance floor scheduled to be delivered for a wedding today. It was supposed to be here—"

"We aren't doing any deliveries today."

I hesitated, unsure I had heard her correctly.

"I'm sorry. Did you say—"

She cut me off again. "Lightning hit our building. Knocked out the computers, the main power, the well. Everything's fried. We can't make any deliveries today."

I blinked and tried to comprehend what she was telling me.

"We have a wedding this afternoon. The dance floor was supposed to be delivered at eleven."

Shelia groaned in exasperation. "Like I *said*, we aren't making any deliveries today."

My mind refused to accept her words. "But, but I have a confirmation. We've booked the dance floor and the wedding's today. I confirmed with Ronnie yesterday." I stared at my handwriting on the purchase order. C/W Ronnie 6/20. Clear as day.

"That may very well be, but we don't have any computers. We don't have any power. We have no way of knowing what orders were supposed to come in or go out. We have no idea what inventory we had or where it was scheduled to be. I'm sorry, but we can't make any deliveries today."

"But I have a wedding." This couldn't be happening. I had a confirmation. A purchase order. I'd confirmed yesterday that the dance floor would be delivered today.

"It's Saturday. Lots of people have weddings. And birthdays and bar mitzvahs. But we can't see inside our warehouse. No lights. We can't tell what was ordered and what was paid for. No computers. *We can't make deliveries today.* Now I'm sorry, but as you can imagine, it's a little crazy here and the phones are ringing off the wall. They're the only thing working it seems since we can't even use our toilets with the well blown out."

Panic spun my brain in circles as reality started to set in. "Wait, can I talk to Ronnie?"

"Ronnie's out back with Jorge trying to get the well going. He can't help you."

"But I confirmed with Ronnie yesterday. We talked about the wedding in some detail. I'm sure he'll remember me."

Shelia sighed again, her patience with me wearing thin on her already frayed nerves. "It don't matter if Ronnie remembers you or not. We aren't making any deliveries. Period."

"But I have a wedding. It's someone's *wedding*. They're ballroom dancers. Like professionals who travel all over the world dancing. The dance floor is probably the single most important thing in the room other than the band. I can't have them arrive and there be no dance floor!"

My voice sounded shrill and high-pitched even to me. The air in the room was suddenly too thick to breathe, and the world seemed tilted a little too far in one direction. I closed my eyes against the dizzy sensation.

Shelia exhaled loudly and restated her position. "I'm sorry. There is nothing I can do. We aren't making deliveries today. Now I have to answer the phones, hon."

"But if I could just talk to Ronnie? He'll remember. I'm sure of it. I have a fifteen by fifteen dance floor for only fifty guests. It's over twice the number of dance tiles y'all would normally send out. We discussed it yesterday at length because I was concerned about it fitting in the Garden Club and he was saying y'all were pretty well booked today and he wanted to know if I could use less tiles but I told him about the professional dancers and that I needed it as big as possible."

My words rushed out without any pause in case she was going to hang up, my Southern accent coming through full and thick as it always does when I'm stressed. Her silence on the other end made me think perhaps she really had hung up, but then she sighed again.

"Look. I'd love to help you. I would. But you have no idea how big of a mess we got over here. I can't just start sending out trucks with tiles and tables and such without knowing where anyone's going and who's paid and who hasn't. We can't make any deliveries today."

I took a deep breath and tried to calm my voice. "I understand, but I have a purchase order right here that shows it's been paid in full. It shows exactly how many tiles I need. Is there some way I could fax it to you or…" I stopped as I realized the stupidity of the question. "Maybe I could just read it off to you, and then show it to the driver when he got here?"

"I'm sorry. Good luck with the wedding."

Shelia hung up, and I hung my head.

How on earth was I going to tell Heather and Sean that the one thing they most wanted for their wedding was not happening? The one feature of their event that meant the most to them and their guests?

My phone buzzed with a text from Charlotte that the pictures were almost done. I had to get back to the hotel to get the ceremony started. But I couldn't just leave without a solution to the dance floor.

I went to find Ivan and passed the first of the arriving band members on their way in to unload equipment. A lot of good the band would do me with no dance floor.

If I had expected Ivan to panic along with me, I had underestimated the calm nature of a man from Jamaica. "It's fine. No worries, no harm. They can dance right here." He gestured toward the commercial-grade carpeting on the floor.

"Ivan. That won't work. They're professional dancers. They need to be able to glide."

He shrugged. "Maybe we can use the patio."

"It's five thousand degrees out there. Besides, it's nowhere near big enough. I need all this space for dancing."

Ivan smiled. "It will be okay. They can dance right here. You have the space. Just not the floor. They will be happy to be married. We will give them a good party."

I had no patience for the optimism I usually enjoyed.

"I have to get to the ceremony. I'll call and let you know what I figure out."

Ivan nodded. "It will be fine. We will be ready for them."

Leo, the band leader, approached as I turned to go.

"What's up? What a storm, huh? We had a tree down on my street. I had to drive through my neighbor's yard to get here."

I nodded and motioned for him to walk with me. "We have no dance floor coming."

Leo stopped. "What?"

I motioned again for him to follow me. Time was short, and I had to get back to the hotel.

"The rental company got hit by lightning. They're not making any deliveries."

"That's not good." Leo rubbed his goatee and frowned. "We got a lot of dancers in this group."

"Yes, I know. I gotta get back to the ceremony site. You guys are good, right? Got all the music? Everybody's here?" I turned to him as I unlocked my car door. "You're gonna have to knock this one out of the park. They're gonna be pissed about the dance floor."

Leo nodded. "Yeah, we're set. Want me to call around? See if I can get a floor?"

"Yeah. If you have time, that'd be great."

I called Cabe on my way back to the ceremony and asked him to do the same. It was all for naught, though. Even with Cabe, Ivan, and Leo all making calls, there was no dance floor to be found. I knew it was a long shot, especially on a Saturday when we weren't the only ones calling to find a replacement and we needed a gargantuan amount of tiles.

There was nothing I could do. The dancers would have to use carpet.

Heather and Sean took it as well as could be expected. Tears, fury, anguish, and then acceptance. Their money would be refunded, of course, but their wedding wouldn't be what they had planned.

Cabe had dinner waiting for me when I got home, exhausted from the stress of the day. He felt bad that he'd struck out on finding a replacement floor.

"How could they just say they're not going to deliver when you had a purchase order clearly stating what you had ordered? And you confirmed it. The guy knew about it."

He put the plates on the table and returned to the kitchen for silverware. He wasn't saying anything I hadn't already said numerous times throughout the day, but I was sick of talking about it.

"Can we please talk about something else?" I asked as he joined me at the table.

"Sure. Let's talk about our wedding."

I rolled my eyes and groaned. That certainly wasn't a less stressful topic.

"Okaaay. Or maybe not." He shrugged and shook his head. "I didn't realize that was a groan-inducing conversation."

Oops. I reached for his hand and smiled, reminding myself not to lump our wedding in with all the others I deal with every day. "I'm sorry, babe. It's not. What do you want to talk about?"

"Have you thought about a location? Where you'd like to have it?"

I shook my head and gulped down a swallow of wine. The dull pain that had started throbbing in my head with the dance floor increased in intensity as he continued.

"Are you thinking to have it here somewhere, or do you want to go back home?"

I closed my eyes and inhaled deeply, trying not to dampen his enthusiasm with my stress and reluctance. When I opened my eyes, he was watching me intently.

"Tyler, I feel like every time I mention the wedding, you get this look on your face like we're discussing going to the dentist. Should I be concerned that my bride doesn't seem the least bit enthused to be marrying me?"

I shook my head, ignoring the pounding behind my eyes. "It's not that. I'm all kinds of enthused to be marrying you. But having a wedding? Not so much." I paused, steeling myself to jump in the deep end and say what had been on my mind pretty much all the time lately. "I was thinking maybe we could elope."

Cabe looked down at his plate and stirred the food around with his fork.

I took it that he needed some convincing. "I'm just thinking it's going to be a hassle trying to get my family and your family together in one place, you know? Plus, the cost of a wedding is just outrageous."

"We have money, Tyler. That's not an issue." He didn't even glance up from his plate.

"I know, but there's no reason for us to spend it on a wedding. We want to do some renovations on the house, and I'm looking at going back to school for my degree. I'm just thinking our money would be better spent elsewhere. Besides, I'd much rather lay out some cash to take a really great trip somewhere and get married while we're there. Honeymoon and wedding in one swoop. Boom! Two birds, one stone. No stress. No hassle.

Whaddya say?"

He took a bite and chewed slowly, still not looking at me. I reached over and rubbed my hand across his forearm. I had an inkling he wasn't going to like this idea, which was why I hadn't brought it up earlier. He swallowed and paused a moment before he spoke.

"Ty, I know this is what you do every day, so it's not that exciting to you. And I get that all the family issues will be tough to deal with. Your mom, my mom. Logistics. I understand why you'd want to go somewhere." He looked up at me then, covering my hand on his arm with his own hand. "But I want a wedding. I want to see you walking toward me in the dress. I want to hold hands with you and walk back down that aisle as husband and wife while everyone cheers us on. I want the first dance, and the toast, and the cake and all that cheesy stuff you see every day. I don't intend to do this again, so I want to do it right? Ya know?"

Without any doubt, we were both thinking that although he didn't intend to do it again, he had done it before. When he married Monica, they'd had a rushed ceremony in Big Sur with only her mother and her sister in attendance. He didn't get the big wedding then, and I was trying to avoid it now.

I swallowed down bitterness at remembering his first marriage and took a deep breath. "We can still do that. I can walk down the aisle, and we can do a first dance and a toast and cake. But with just the two of us on some Caribbean island somewhere. Then we could have a party when we got back. One with our friends and your family here, and then maybe one back home."

"What do you think your mom would say about that?"

A chill ran across me at the thought of her reaction. My two older sisters had each robbed my mother of an opportunity to plan a wedding. Tanya had done a courthouse shotgun wedding when she and Tom got pregnant their senior year of high school, though she'd miscarried soon after. Then Carrie and Kenny had run off to Vegas together and tied the knot at an Elvis chapel while they were both three sheets to the wind. My mother had been devastated and bitter as all hell about not being able to host a wedding. As the youngest daughter, I was the only girl left to fulfill her dreams. Which made me even more apprehensive to turn her loose.

I lifted my chin in defiance and pulled my hand from his. "She won't like it, but it's not up to her. It's our wedding."

"Yes, it is. But I'd like to have our families' support. I know it would mean a lot to both our moms for us to have a wedding they could attend, and"—he brought my hand to his lips for a soft kiss—"it would mean a lot to me."

He was right, of course. It would crush both our moms if we got married without them, and it appeared to be as important to him as it was to them. I was the only holdout.

I can think of any number of girls who would kill to have a fiancé begging them to have a wedding and telling them they had plenty of money to spend on it, to boot!

It wasn't like I *didn't* want a wedding. Like I didn't have ideas in my head over the years of how I'd like to do my own event when it came time.

If I could plan a wedding without having everyone else's input I'd probably be excited about it, too. But I knew how difficult Mama was going to be about having it done her way, and Maggie would probably have some ideas to contribute as well. Then everyone at work would be pitching in their two cents, and… aargh.

It was exhausting already and we hadn't even begun.

I struggled to put it all in perspective as Cabe watched me, his eyes filled with uncertainty and questions I couldn't answer.

I didn't want to hurt his feelings. Or anyone else's.

They weren't asking me to hike to the top of a mountain barefooted.

It was a wedding. Something I knew quite a bit about. Undoubtedly, I could pull this off.

For Cabe. For Mama. For Maggie.

Aye-yi-yi. I was going to need a lot more wine.

Monday, June 23rd

Just when I thought we had everything out in the open, I got blindsided. By a judge, no less.

Cabe finally had his court appearance today for his little altercation at the airport. He was nervous and eager to get it over with, so I offered to go with him for moral support.

I worried if the judge didn't know about the crapload of family drama prior to the incident, he might not understand.

But it turns out the judge didn't need to know any of that. He had another piece of information that I didn't have. A clue as to why my fiancé was on edge that day. Not just that day, but for weeks leading up to Paris. It even factored into his rift with Maggie.

That one little revelation would have been ever so helpful for me in trying to figure out what was going on with him while he'd ripped my heart out and twisted me into knots.

Cabe was so nervous he almost knocked the chair over when the judge asked him to stand, catching it with his hand just before it tumbled. He cleared his throat and smoothed his tie, first putting his hands in his pockets, then immediately removing them to clasp them behind his back.

"Mr. Shaw, I understand you felt the rules the TSA has set forth don't apply to you?"

"No, sir." Cabe cleared his throat again. "Uh, I mean, yes sir, they apply to me. I understand they apply to me."

"But you didn't think they applied to you on March 6th. The rest of the traveling population obviously did not need to reach their destination as urgently as you did. Or at least they didn't see fit to assault an officer in order to do so. Now it says here you were in such a hurry because you had an engagement ring in your pocket, and the lady you intended to offer the ring to was already on the plane?"

My stomach turned a complete flip and my mouth dropped open. It's quite possible I gasped audibly because Cabe shot a quick glance my way before answering the judge.

"Yes, sir, that's correct."

What the hell? He had an engagement ring in his pocket? For Paris? Cabe had been going to ask me to marry him in Paris?

"And is it safe to assume this is the lucky lady here in court with you today?" The judge peered over his glasses at me, and I struggled to close my mouth and acknowledge him in some way. To smile. To swallow. To manage a nod. I think I made some movement, even though my mouth still hung open slightly. Quite the attractive picture, I'm sure.

"Yes, sir, that's correct," Cabe said.

"She said yes, then? After the delay of your detainment?"

"Yes, sir, she did." Cabe smiled at me and turned back to the judge. I attempted a delayed reaction smile as my brain screamed, *"Wait! You had a ring in your pocket?"*

"May I ask how the two of you became separated and caused you to find yourself on the wrong side of the security line?"

Cabe shifted his weight from foot to foot as he answered. "We had a disagreement, sir. I had walked away to cool off and didn't realize I passed the restricted area."

The judge removed his glasses. "Well, there will be many a disagreement over the course of a marriage, son. I've been married forty-two years this October, and while I applaud your intent to walk away and cool your temper, I would advise you to hold your tongue in the disagreement to keep it from escalating. If you displayed with this young lady here the level of frustration you demonstrated with the TSA agents, then she may regret saying yes. You have no prior arrests, no trouble with the law before. I'm going to waive further jail time but I'd like to suggest you find more effective ways of dealing with your emotions. I think you'll both benefit from that." The judge turned to me. "Ma'am, I wish you my sincerest congratulations on your engagement, and I hope this is the last time you need to accompany him here."

My jaw relaxed enough to close, and I managed a nod.

I stayed silent while we walked to the parking garage with the attorney, but my car door had barely closed when I blurted out the question stuck on repeat in my mind.

"You had an engagement ring in your pocket at the airport?"

"Yep." Cabe grasped my hand in his and planted a huge kiss on the ring I wore. He was still so elated about not going back to jail that he hadn't even noticed my mood change.

"This ring?" I asked.

"Well, yeah. You think I have a supply of engagement rings?" He chuckled, but I didn't.

"I don't know what you have. Why did you have a ring in your pocket that day?"

He sobered as he picked up on my mood. "Because I was going to ask you to marry me. In Paris."

"So what happened?"

He stared back at me. "What do you mean?"

"Why didn't you ask me?"

"We didn't go to Paris."

My thoughts were spinning so fast I couldn't think straight.

Cabe twisted in his seat to face me.

"Look, Ty, I didn't know the judge would mention that. I didn't think about it being part of the police report. You're obviously upset. I don't know what to say. What can I do?"

I looked away. Yes, I was upset, but I didn't know what to say either. I couldn't help but replay it all in my head. The hot and cold mood swings. The on and off relationship. Getting close. Backing off. He'd said it was stress from the family problems. But he'd also alluded to a fear of committing. So to learn he bought a ring in the midst of all that confused the hell out of me.

"When did you buy the ring, Cabe?" I asked the question without even looking at him, scared I would cry if I turned away from the window.

He exhaled deeply and turned off the car. "January."

I turned as my mouth dropped open again. "January? You bought me an engagement ring in January?"

Paris was March. We had barely crossed the line between friends and lovers in January. He had disappeared and come back all weirded out at the end of January. Was this why? What changed his mind? Had he gotten cold feet?

"So what happened?"

He shrugged. "What do you mean?"

Anger rose within me as insecurity, fear, and new doubts crept in. Kind of ridiculous, I suppose, since I was sitting there wearing the ring, just as engaged as I could possibly be, but something had changed.

Now it felt heavy on my finger.

Hot.

Itchy.

Uncomfortable.

I twisted it as I struggled to find words and sort feelings.

"Did you buy the ring for me?"

He laughed, a rather scoffing laugh filled more with disbelief than humor. "Of course. Who else would I have bought a ring for?"

"What made you decide to buy me a ring?"

The disbelief spread across his face as he widened his eyes and raised his eyebrows. "I wanted to marry you. Duh."

"Then what changed your mind?"

"Nothing changed my mind. We're getting married. Help me understand why you suddenly seem all pissed off. Why does it matter when I bought the ring?"

"Because you're telling me you bought it in January. Which means that *after* you bought the ring, you freaked out and backed off and got all scared of commitment. Am I right?"

He placed his hand on my thigh and squeezed. "That's not a question I can answer with an easy yes or no. But we're together now. Isn't that what matters?"

I laid my head back and put my hands over my eyes.

Maybe I shouldn't have cared when he bought it. Maybe the fact that we'd persevered through everything and ended up together in the end was what mattered the most.

But I'd been given new information regarding one of the most painful times in my life. Feelings of anger, hurt and bewilderment had bubbled right back up to the surface.

I've never fully understood why he backed off the way he did, and this new piece of the puzzle left me more confused than ever. I rubbed my hand across my forehead and stared out the window.

"You sat in your mother's pool house and told me you were happier than you'd ever been before, and then the very next day you fell off the face of the earth and didn't want to see me anymore."

"That's not what I said. I said I needed time to sort through everything. To be sure. I'm sure now. I've been sure for a while. Can we not just focus on where we are now?"

A groan escaped my lips. "I'm happy with where we are now. But that doesn't mean I don't want to understand what happened then. I need to know how we went from you being happier than you'd ever been to needing time to decide whether or not you were happy. When exactly did you buy the ring?"

He sighed and looked away. "The day after I told you that in the pool house."

I gasped. "You're kidding me!"

"Look, Ty, I meant what I said that night. I'd never been happier. I didn't want to waste another minute. We'd already planned to go to Paris, and I thought that would be the perfect romantic moment to pop the question. Obviously, that didn't turn out like I had planned."

My eyes filled with tears as I struggled to understand his actions and my own reactions. I thought briefly of how freaking incredible that would have been. To have Cabe with me in Paris. To experience that magical city together. To have him propose under the twinkling lights of the Eiffel Tower. Instead, I'd stood there with another man. My heart wept for what might have been.

Something didn't add up, though. The snafu with Paris and the TSA had happened long after our relationship went haywire. He still wasn't telling me everything.

"So the same day you bought me an engagement ring, you decided you didn't want to marry me? And if so, why were you carrying that ring in your pocket at the airport?"

"Wow, you're not going to drop this, are you?" He looked away from me and exhaled with a low huff.

Every muscle in my body tightened with anger at the question. "I think I dropped way too much already. If I'd pressed you for answers, if I hadn't kept my mouth shut trying not to push you or upset you, then we wouldn't have had such a hard time getting to where we are now. I'd have known about what was going on with Galen, your mom, and your other family and maybe Paris would have turned out a lot differently. Not to mention the months we've spent apart since then."

I opened the car door to get out, but he put his hand on my arm.

"But don't you see? We're better off on this end of all that. Yes, I should have been open and upfront with you about what was going on with my family. We've already established that. Of course I wish Paris had turned out differently. I would much rather *not* have gone to jail and *not* have you see my favorite city with *Jack*." He spat Jack's name with such venom I flinched. "But we both grew up a lot during the time since that happened. I know I sure did. So when I did ask you to marry me, it was with no doubt whatsoever. Does it really matter when I bought the ring?"

I stared at it on my finger, sparkling there as he held my hand in his. It looked different to me. Tainted somehow. I didn't want it anymore. Instead of a symbol of a bright future, it reminded me of the painful past and all its uncertainty. I pulled my hand from his and twisted the ring, over and over again. Trying to rewind the clock, I suppose.

The sane part of my mind argued that there was only a problem if I created one. Cabe loved me. Cabe had asked *me* to marry him. Cabe wanted to spend the rest of his life with me.

The crazy-making part of my mind would not shut up, though. If he'd changed his mind before, he could change it again. This was another example of him not being open and upfront with me. Something had changed his mind. Knowing that had changed something in mine.

I slid the ring from my finger, its heavy weight dragging across my knuckle with a heat like fire. I picked up his hand and turned it over, dropping the ring in his palm. He looked down at the ring then up at me, confusion seeping into the clear blue of his eyes. His brow furrowed together for a brief moment, and then the confusion morphed into anger as the full realization of what I'd just done dawned on him.

"Are you freakin' kidding me? Seriously?"

The hurt in his eyes punched my gut, and my heart caught in my throat. I swallowed to force it back down and raised my chin.

"I don't want it. You bought it, and then you changed your mind. You decided you didn't want me." The river of tears surged forward, and I got out and slammed the car door. I leaned against the car and crossed my arms. I cried because I was sad, feeling all hurt and rejected, and I cried because I was frustrated at myself for feeling all hurt and rejected when the man I loved had gotten out of the car and was standing right beside me, pledging his love and negating any reason for me to feel the way I did.

"Baby, baby, baby. Listen to me," he said as he stroked my hair and my back, planting light kisses along my forehead and cheeks as he spoke. "There has *never* been a time I didn't want you. *Never.* So get that out of that beautiful head of yours."

I pushed him away and stepped toward the front of the car, trying to put distance between us. "Then why did you shut everything down? Why? You left me crying on my living room floor, and I never understood why. I just want to know what happened. What happened the last weekend of January that changed everything? And if you say to me it's because of your anniversary with Monica, I may hit you."

He sighed and walked a few steps away, clasping his hands together on top of his head. He stood there for a few seconds before turning back to face me. "Buttercup, I never meant to hurt you. I swear that's true. How can I explain everything now without hurting you again?"

I tensed, suddenly unsure I wanted to hear his explanation. I might have just taken the ring off, but let's be honest. I had no intention of breaking up with him or being un-engaged. I simply wanted answers and wanted him to open up about what had transpired. But if that was going to hurt and cause more problems between us, did I really want to know?

"Ty, I didn't lie to you that night in the pool house. That was the happiest I'd ever been. I didn't want it to end. You say *you* were scared? I was terrified. I'd waited five years to hold you in my arms. I didn't want you to change your mind and say we should just be friends again. So I decided to strike while the iron was hot. Pop the question. Get something in place to make sure we were together."

He stopped talking for a moment, and I thought perhaps he had finished, but then he cleared his throat and continued. "Now, this is where it gets a little complicated, and I want you to promise me you are only going to hold me responsible for my actions and not be mad at anyone else."

Fear and apprehension exploded within my chest. "What does that mean? Who else was involved?"

"Settle down. It's nothing like that. I just don't really know how you're going to react to this, which is the reason we haven't discussed it before."

My knees wobbled and I leaned against the car for support, wary of what would come next.

"I bought the ring that morning and showed it to Mom, which definitely caught her off guard. I mean, in my head, I'd been waiting five years to give you that ring. But to Mom, it had only been a couple of weeks since our relationship had changed. She worried about us moving too fast and it blowing up in our faces."

He shrugged and paced a couple of steps, running his fingers through his hair.

"She reminded me that it had only been a year, almost to the day, in fact, since I'd stood in front of someone else and pledged marriage vows. The date hadn't even dawned on me. I'd been so caught up in us finally being together that the timing didn't register."

He sighed and shoved his hands in his pockets. "As much as I didn't want to, I had to admit everything was happening too quickly. So I backed off. Or tried to at least. Obviously, I sucked at it."

My mind spun as I tried to process all he'd just said and what it meant in relation to that weekend and to us now. And to me and his Mom.

Hurt and rejection twisted my stomach as I realized neither of his closest relatives supported our relationship. I swallowed down the ache in my throat so I could speak.

"So is this why you haven't told her we're engaged? Because you know she doesn't want us to be together?"

He turned to face me and shook his head. "I haven't told her because our schedules have been crazy and I want us both there. I have no doubt she will be happy for us. Mom loves you."

I arched my eyebrow and cocked my head to make it clear I wasn't buying that. "She loves me, but she didn't want you to marry me?"

"That's not it, babe. She never said I shouldn't marry you. She said if you were worth the wait all that time, you'd be worth the wait to take it slow."

He came and stood inches from me. His fingers brushed my cheek and dropped to caress my neck. "She was right. You were worth the wait. I can't go back and change how all this happened. But I can tell you that I've always loved you, and I always will."

I didn't resist when he pulled me to him or when his lips touched mine. Tentatively at first—asking, seeking—then more demanding.

"So why'd you have the ring in your pocket at the airport?" I said when he lifted his head.

He leaned back with his arms still around my waist, shifting his weight away from me a little.

"When you told me the night before our trip that Mom had tried to talk you out of Paris, it pissed me off. I was fed up with her and Galen interfering and decided to hell with it. I figured I'd ask you in Paris and show them they didn't have any say-so in my life. But I knew that wasn't the right reason to ask you." He looked past me, and I could tell he was seeing a different scene in his mind. "I wanted to, though. I had this vision of how that would be. Getting engaged in Paris." He looked back down at me, his eyes cloudy with painful memories. "I wonder what it would have been like if I'd made that flight. If we'd seen Paris together. If I'd asked you then, without everything blowing up the way it did."

It was my turn to shift uncomfortably. We both knew what happened when he didn't make that flight, and the choices I made stung even more in the light of this new information. I took in a deep breath and considered all that had happened between us. I needed space, and I pushed my weight off the car and out of his arms.

"How do I know you're not going to change your mind again?"

He pulled the ring from his pocket and knelt before me. He lifted my hand to his lips and kissed my ring finger before sliding the diamond back in its place. "Because when I gave you this ring, I promised you that I'm all in. I told you I'm committed to do whatever it takes to make this work. To spend the rest of my life with you. Please tell me you haven't changed *your* mind."

What could I say to that? I was pissed. I was hurt. But I also knew that at the end of the day, I loved him with every fiber of my being. I had no desire to walk away. Our past is what it is, and I can't change any of it. I just hope I can let it go and focus on our future.

Wednesday, June 25th

Some people are gluttons for punishment.

Priscilla called today. It's been five months since her groom, Neal, caught a cab to the airport and left her stranded at the altar. Well, it wasn't an *altar* really. It was a man-made beach on a lake, and she was waiting in the ladies' room for him to arrive. But she was left stranded all the same.

Seems Neal has had a change of heart and a burst of renewed commitment. They've decided to try again.

"So do you offer any kind of repeat customer discount? I mean, technically, we paid for a bunch of stuff last time that we didn't get to use, so I was just wondering if maybe we could get a break?"

To be honest, I'm a little shocked she called us again. I mean, I'm thinking if that happened to me, I would've found a different coordinator the second time around. For one thing, it'd be a wee bit embarrassing to come back after getting jilted.

I also don't think I'd want to do anything the same way the second time around. Wouldn't want to jinx it.

But not Priscilla. She's making it easy for me to pull it together by using the same songs, same flowers, and same officiant. The only change she's making is the location. This time she'll have the ceremony at the hotel where they're staying, eliminating any need for a getaway car—I mean, limo.

So we just have to make sure the groom makes it down the aisle this time.

I guess I'm not the only one who believes in second chances. Hopefully, Priscilla and I will both get our happy ending.

Thursday, June 26th

Cabe had asked Maggie where she wanted to go for her birthday, but she insisted she'd rather have us over to her place and cook for us.

I was a bundle of nerves just thinking about seeing her now that I knew how she felt about us. I wondered what her reaction would be when he told her we were engaged. Would she be happy? Would she pretend to be happy? Would I be able to tell?

I changed outfits ten times. Maybe twelve. Nothing seemed to fit well. Everything felt too tight. Too constricting. Too short. Too provocative.

"Babe, what are you doing? What happened to the purple dress?" Cabe rolled his eyes at the pile of clothes on the bed as he leaned against the door frame.

"It just didn't feel right. I have nothing to wear."

He walked over and slid his arms around me, pulling me up to him as he planted a kiss on my lips that left me breathless. Or maybe that was the skirt.

"Hold on," I said, pushing him away. "This skirt's too tight. I gotta change. I'll be out in a minute."

He caught my hands and chuckled. "The skirt's fine. The dress was fine. The last ten were fine. We're just going to Mom's for dinner. Why are you stressing?"

I closed my eyes. "I don't know."

Cabe leaned down until our foreheads touched. "Hey, look at me, babe."

I opened my eyes and struggled to focus at such close range.

"Mom loves you. She's going to be happy for us."

"Yeah, right." I shoved away from him and unzipped the skirt, adding it to the pile of discarded clothing. My shirt quickly followed.

He moved behind me and slid his hands around to the front, his hips grinding against me in unbridled appreciation for my nearly nude body. "I

47

could call her and tell her we're running late," he whispered against my neck as he trailed kisses behind my ear and tasted his way down to my collarbone.

Goose bumps rippled across my skin, and the familiar ache stirred deep within me, the tingling burning like fire on my frazzled nerves. I swayed back against him, arching my back to give his hands full access as he caressed my breasts.

"Baby, you have no idea what you do to me," Cabe groaned.

He pushed me forward slightly, pulling my hips back against his as he bent to trace his tongue up my spine. He slid his fingers inside the edge of my lace panties as he licked tiny circles across my back, his hips nudging me forward onto the bed. He wasted no time in sliding the black lace down my thighs and off, rolling me over and pushing me further into the pile of discarded clothes as his knee nudged my legs apart. Sensations exploded within me at the flick of his tongue between my legs and his teasing pinches on my nipples. I moaned into the white silk shirt I'd been wearing moments before.

All thoughts of his mother and any condemnation on her part disappeared from my consciousness. Any stress over clothing issues or dinner conversation completely evaporated as he worked his magic to push my body to climax, my muscles contracting and releasing as the tension ebbed away.

Cabe kissed his way up my bare stomach as I lay there trembling, and he fit his body beside mine on the bed. The swelling in his jeans was hot and hard against my hips.

"Damn, girl. Whose crazy-ass idea was it to wait?"

He sucked at my earlobe as I laughed and moved against him in what I am sure was pure torture.

"I believe that was your idea, Mr. Shaw. But I'm ready and willing if you want to change your mind. I've told you I think it's silly to wait if we're going to fool around in every other way." I rolled to face him, chuckling at the groan that escaped his throat. "Whaddya say?"

"I say you're evil. Here I am, trying to save myself for marriage, and you're like a temptress, leading me astray." He bit my lower lip as he said it, and the kiss we shared proved without a doubt he was not the innocent being he was making himself out to be. "I could so easily plunge right into you and be in heaven. Maybe we could do just one. Just one thrust. One good thrust." He playfully slammed his hips into mine as he spoke, his left hand back at work between my legs and his right hand cupping my rump to pull me tighter against him.

"Are you waiting for me to say no? 'Cause this is not the way to make me say no. This is the way to make me scream your name and beg for more." I laughed as he exhaled sharply.

"I can't wait for you to do just that. But right here, right now, on top of your clothes while my mother is watching the clock, is not the way I want to do it. I wanna take my time and make it last. No one-time shot when we finally give in."

He got up and offered his hand to pull me to standing. His voice deepened to a more serious tone. "You're okay with us waiting, right?"

I nodded. "Yeah. Sometimes, no, but for the most part, yeah." I smiled at him and slid my arms around his waist.

He held me and kissed my forehead. "I just want us to have something…special, I guess. You know, to mark the occasion. It's not like either of us are virgins, but I want there to be something when we get married that makes it different."

"I know. You've explained this before, remember?" I stood on tiptoes and kissed him.

He pulled back and smiled down at me. "I know it probably doesn't make much sense, especially since we're already intimate in so many other ways. It's just a crazy notion I have. Something to look forward to on our wedding night."

I moved my arms from his waist and curved one hand around his neck as I teased inside his waist band with the other hand. "I think it's sweet. A little weird. Unconventional, to be sure. But sweet. And it is something I most certainly look forward to."

He inhaled sharply as I dipped my fingers a little deeper within his waistband. His voice dropped to a whisper against my ear. "As do I, my love. As do I."

Nerves of steel, that man, I swear. We were more than a few minutes late by the time he'd sent me into spasms again and then received his own release, but his silly vow to save intercourse for marriage was still intact, and I really didn't give a shit about my outfit at that point. I went back to the purple dress I know he likes and prayed it wasn't too wrinkled from being beneath the amorous activity.

When we pulled into Maggie's driveway, Cabe reached for my hand and pressed his lips to it. "She loves you, baby. And I love you. She wants us to be happy. She never spoke against you or against us. She just wanted us to succeed, okay?"

I nodded and stepped out of the car, squaring my shoulders against the unknown inside.

In hindsight, I should have known what to expect. Maggie was Maggie. Just like she's always been. She hugged me to her when she flung the door open and kept her arm around me as she walked me to the kitchen. I prayed we didn't smell like sex.

She spotted the ring within minutes of us arriving, almost like she'd been watching for it.

"You said yes! Oh honey! Welcome to the family." She nearly knocked me over with an exuberant hug, and then she hugged Cabe with tear-filled eyes. She dabbed at them with her knuckles before taking my hand to inspect the ring.

"It's beautiful. Brilliant. He did good, didn't he?"

I nodded, forcing myself to smile and enjoy the moment without concentrating too much on her reservations about him proposing. She was either putting on a really good act or she had changed her mind about not wanting him to marry me.

"Come, come. We need to open a bottle of champagne and toast this wonderful news!"

Cabe put his arm around me and kissed my hair, whispering just above my ear, "I told you."

Maggie toasted our engagement, toasted our future happiness, and any future grandbabies we'd like to provide her. In turn, we toasted her birthday.

We talked and laughed through dinner, the conversation easy and unforced like no time had passed. I tried to set aside any thoughts of her disapproval, but I couldn't forget it completely. It was eating at me, and I knew I had to say something. Get it off my chest and out in the open somehow.

I took the opportunity as she and I cleared the dinner dishes while Cabe took out the trash.

"So Cabe says you had some reservations about us getting married." My heart pounded in my ears so loud I worried she may be able to hear it. The red wine and clam sauce churned in my guts.

Maggie paused her hands in the dishwater and turned to me, her face unreadable.

"Well, yes, I did. When he first showed me the ring, I worried that the timing was wrong." She started scrubbing again and handed me a plate to put in the dishwasher. "You saw him when he came back from Seattle. He didn't eat. Didn't sleep. Drank all the time. I never want to see him that way again." She looked at me then, her eyes holding pain and anguish. "I told you when we met for lunch that I was worried about him, didn't I?"

I nodded, unsure of what I wanted to say now that I'd brought it up and she'd acknowledged it. I wanted to defend our decision. I wanted to assure her that I had no intention of hurting her son. But none of that came spilling out in words.

She grabbed a towel and dried her hands before turning to face me, her eyes glistening with tears again.

"You have my full support, Tyler. I already view you as a part of this family. Any concerns I expressed were from a place of love and a vested interest in Cabe's well-being. The relationship you have now is not the same one you had then. You seem different now, and I know my son has matured." She reached to put her hand over mine. "I wish nothing but the best for you both, and I'm very happy if you've found that in each other."

I looked up and met her eyes. "I love Cabe. With everything in me."

Maggie nodded and smiled. "We have that in common. I just didn't want either of you to make a mistake."

Cabe's voice rang out across the kitchen before I had the chance to say anything else.

"Marrying Tyler is not a mistake," he said as he moved to my side.

"I never said it was," Maggie said. "I actually was just telling Tyler that I consider her a part of the family and that you have my blessing."

Cabe nodded. "I appreciate that." He extended his arm to pull his mother into a hug with us. "I love you, Mom, and I know you've always looked out for me. You've worked hard and given up a lot for us."

Maggie looked up at him and smiled. "I've told you before. I didn't give up anything. I gained you and your sister, and that's everything." She put her arm around him and then draped her other arm around my shoulders. "Now I'm blessed with a new daughter. My life grows richer." She smiled through her tears.

Maggie reached up to kiss Cabe on the cheek and then took a deep breath. "You asked what I wanted for my birthday, and I told you I'd think about it and let you know."

The tone of her voice suggested he wasn't going to like it, and she was right.

"Galen is coming home this weekend to celebrate, and I'd like to have both my children in the same room together without all this fighting."

The air in the room changed in an instant, suddenly charged and crackling.

Cabe exhaled and released his hold on Maggie. "Not happening. You know how I feel about this. Galen crossed a line, and she needs to apologize."

Maggie sighed. "I've already said she had no business springing them on you without your knowledge. She needs to respect your wishes, and I've told her that. But you have to respect hers. Growing up without a father affected each of you very differently, Cabe. I understand your desire to be disconnected, but your sister needs to connect. She needs to know who they are and feel like she fits in the puzzle somehow. She wants to know her family."

Tension rolled off Cabe's body and washed over me. I could feel him holding back emotion, and I increased the pressure of my arms around him to try and physically support him.

"Those people are not her family!" Cabe's voice raised in volume, and his jawline clenched hard.

"But honey, they are," Maggie said, her voice thick with emotion. "Whether you want them to be or not. Gerry Tucker is your father, and there's nothing you or I can do about that. His other children are related to you."

Cabe scoffed, but he stayed. He didn't walk away. I tried to telepathically send him calmness and strength along with a little love.

Maggie leaned back against the counter and crossed her arms over her chest. "Do you really think I don't understand your feelings? That I don't see what he's done to you? To both of you? I hate the pain he's caused you and your sister, but I can't wind back the hands of time and make it all turn out differently for you."

She glanced at me and turned away as tears filled her eyes. I could see her trembling as she struggled to maintain her composure.

I stood there watching, feeling a little like a bright green alien standing naked in a crowd. Out of place and awkwardly obvious.

Cabe groaned softly and released me to go to Maggie. "It's not your fault, Mom."

He lifted his arms to embrace her, but she pushed back from him and wiped at her eyes. "But it is. Unfortunately, it is. I chose him, and I can't regret that choice because it gave me you and Galen, but oh my God, how many times I've wished you'd had something different. I'm sorry."

Cabe dropped his arms and looked helpless for a moment, unsure of how to deal with the emotional woman in front of him. A woman who was normally the epitome of calm resolve.

She turned to me then, her shoulders set as some semblance of grace and composure returned. She looked tired. Haggard. Older, somehow.

"My daughter's headstrong and outspoken. Which you already know. But she had no right to speak to you the way she did."

I hesitated, but Cabe spoke before I had time to say anything.

"Galen needs to apologize, Mom, not you."

Maggie lifted her chin to him. "I agree. But she's not twelve, Cabe. I can't force her to apologize. I've already told her she needs to and that her actions were wrong. What more can I do?"

He sighed and his body relaxed as he chose to surrender.

"I'll go to dinner, *for you,* but she still needs to apologize."

Maggie nodded. "Thank you. It means a lot to me."

Cabe and Maggie shared a big, huge, mama bear-baby bear hug, and the mood shifted. We ate cheesecake with light conversation and sprinkled laughter and ended the evening on a good note.

All things considered and tense moments aside, I guess the evening went well. One mom down, one to go. Oh boy.

Friday, June 27th

Well, I couldn't put it off any longer.

Cabe stuck to his guns about going back home to meet Mama so we could tell her our news together. We found a July weekend when we could both get away and made arrangements for Cabe's buddy, Dean, to come and stay with Deacon.

All that was left to do was call Mama and tell her I was bringing a boy home.

It could have gone better. It could have gone worse.

The first fifteen minutes of the conversation revolved around Floyd White's arrest for tax fraud and his wife Jackie having to give up her position as president of the Junior League. Big time scandal in a small town.

Mama was all but foaming at the mouth to tell me, what with her and Jackie being lifelong sworn enemies since Jackie and my daddy supposedly dated in the eighth grade before he and Mama became an item. Everyone in town knew that Mama and Ms. Jackie couldn't walk on the same side of the street without one of them having to cross. People had been known to plan seating arrangements and holiday guest lists around Patsy Warren and Jackie White's feud. They didn't even pay their respects at the funeral home on the same nights unless there was only one night of visitation, and even then Mama always went late and Ms. Jackie went early.

When Mama finally slowed down to take a breath and a swig of coffee, I jumped at the chance.

"Mama, I was thinking I'd come home for a visit in July."

"Awww, well, I suwannee, that would be just lovely! That makes me happier than a tick on a hound dog. Everything alright? Did something happen? Did you get fired?"

"No, Mama. Why does something have to be wrong for me to come visit?"

"That's what I'd like to know."

"Everything's fine."

"You're not messing around with Dwayne Davis, are you? I heard him and Ellain split up again. Is that it? You coming to see him?"

I groaned and moved a bit farther from Cabe, hoping he didn't hear her. Dwayne Davis was not his favorite topic of conversation by any stretch.

"No, Mama. Nothing like that."

"Oh, Lord, did you and Gabe break up? Are y'all having problems?"

I started to correct her pronunciation but decided it was wasted effort. "Actually, I thought I'd bring *Cabe* home with me. He wanted to meet you, and I thought you might like to meet him."

Cabe leaned closer to me, listening intently, and I hoped Mama didn't say anything insulting.

"Oh. Well, that would be nice! I don't know why you ain't brung him home sooner. So it's going good, then? Y'all getting along good?"

I smiled in relief. "Yes, ma'am. We're getting along just fine." Her enthusiasm emboldened me, and I almost blurted out that we were engaged, but I knew how much it meant to Cabe to tell her together in person. Which will probably tickle her to no end and go a long way in scoring brownie points for him.

"Well, good. I'm glad to hear it. You still using protection? You're not pregnant, are you?"

Cabe covered his face to stifle a laugh, and I pushed him away so she wouldn't hear him.

"Mama, good grief! Please!"

"I'm just saying I'd rather know now and have some time to prepare. Don't you spring something like that on me, you hear me?"

"No, ma'am. I won't."

"Wait a minute! Are you getting married? No, don't tell me. I don't want to know. I want to be surprised. That's why you're coming home, isn't it? You're getting married. I can't believe this. I can't wait to tell Marjorie. Oh my Lord! You and Marlena can have a double wedding! Lordy-be. Do your sisters know? You told me first, right? You didn't tell anyone else, did you? I won't say a word. My lips are sealed. I am so excited. I'll act surprised, though. Do you want me to invite everybody over?"

"No, just calm down. Can't I bring a boy home to meet you without you immediately thinking I'm either pregnant or getting married?"

"You never have before! You've been gone off down there six years and I ain't seen hide nor hair of anyone you've dated. You've been doing God knows what with this Gabe fella for years now, and I ain't never even met him. Didn't he already get married? Is his divorce final?"

I closed my eyes and pictured how easy it would be to elope.

"It's Cabe, Mama. His name is Cabe, but you already know that. And yes, his divorce is final."

Cabe raised both hands and both eyebrows in a clear "what the hell?" expression but I turned away and ignored him.

"Alright. Well, don't be thinking y'all are gonna be shacking up in the same bedroom while you're here. You may be living a heathen life down there in Orlando, missy, but when you're in this house, you will follow the rules of the Lord. Do you hear me?"

"Yes, ma'am." How on earth she could justify telling me to use protection and admonishing me for being a heathen in the same breath, I don't know.

"Now when are you coming? Because I've got bingo duty at the VFW, and I've got choir practice, you know, and on the eighteenth I'm taking some of the older ladies from church up to Callaway. Although why they want to go in the middle of July beats me. Hotter than Hades, and half them needing walkers as it is. But I don't ask the questions. I just go where the Lord says I'm needed."

"We wanted to come on the eleventh and stay for the weekend. Is that okay?" (Is it a horrible thing that I silently prayed it wouldn't work?)

"Let me just look at the calendar. Well, shoot. I'd planned to go shopping with Jan that Saturday, but I can see if we can go another day. You know how hard it is to schedule anything with her and her always busy with the theater. You'd think she was on Broadway instead of our little community playhouse. If she's not in rehearsals, she's in auditions, and if she's not in auditions, she's reviewing plays. I swear I don't know how she remembers if she's coming or going with her schedule as busy as it is."

"Don't cancel your plans. We'll find something to do while you shop with Mrs. Jan. I want to show Cabe around anyway."

"Tyler Lorraine! You bring home a boyfriend for the first time in six years and you think I'm going to traipse off to Target with Jan? Are you crazy? I will be sitting right here between the two of you getting to know Gabe."

Fear gripped my heart at the thought.

"You don't have to do that. Gabe and I—," I gritted my teeth in disbelief, "—*Cabe* and I will be just fine on our own. Don't change your plans."

"Nonsense. Let me off here so I can call your sisters and your Aunt Clementine. I'm sure she will want to have you over for dinner."

"Please don't do that. I don't want Aunt Clem going to any trouble. Let's just keep this low-key, okay? Don't make a big deal out of it."

"I gotta beep. Lemme see who it is. Oh! Oh! I gotta go. It's Samantha, the vice-president of the Junior League. Bless her heart. All this has taken such a toll on her. I saw her in the Piggly Wiggly yesterday, and she'd nearly chewed her nails off. Poor thing was in desperate need of a manicure. Call me later."

She hung up, and I sat back against the couch exhausted.

"You have an Aunt Clementine? Really? That's her real name?" Cabe asked as he rubbed the tension in my neck.

"Yeah. Are you sure you don't want to elope?" I leaned my head back into his hand and turned to face him. "It's not too late."

He smiled and touched his lips to mine. "I'd still have to meet your mom eventually, Ty. Might as well get it over with it." He kissed me again and then pulled back to look at me inquisitively.

"Your mom asked if you were using protection. Does she think we're...? I mean, have you told her we...?"

I shook my head and sat up. "No. I haven't discussed our sex life with my mom, nor do I intend to. She's just on this protection kick for some reason. My sister Carrie said she thinks it stems from my brother Brad and how much time he and Kelly are spending together. Mom's paranoid about me or Brad getting pregnant before we're married."

"Ah. So should I tell her we're waiting until we're married to fully engage? Would that score me more brownie points with her?"

My stomach blanched at the thought of Cabe discussing our sex life with my mother. "No. Absolutely not. Do not even mention sex to her."

"Why not? I'd think she'd be happy to hear we're waiting."

"Maybe so, but I don't think your definition of waiting for marriage and hers are the same. All the naked games we play might disqualify you."

I got up and plugged my phone in the charger and grabbed a Diet Coke from the fridge. "Want something to drink while I'm up?"

"No thanks." He stood and walked to the kitchen, stopping just in front of me and stroking my arms with his hands. "You know I want you, right? You know I question the sanity of waiting every single day. You drive me wild with every touch. Every kiss. That look in your eyes. Yep, that one."

He pressed his lips to my neck and sent shivers down my spine.

I tilted my head back and bit my lip as he pulled my collar aside to kiss my shoulder.

"So maybe we should engage in some wedding night planning? You know. Just to get an idea of how this is all going to work. When we do finally go there." My voice was barely a whisper but he heard me loud and clear.

He lifted his head and grinned as he touched his forehead to mine. "I suppose we do need to plan. It's always best to have a plan."

I slid my tongue between his lips and pushed them open, sucking his tongue into my mouth as he moaned a little. He lifted me up and sat me on the counter, his own tongue demanding mine as I released his.

It didn't take long for me to forget all about Mama and any stress I may have had minutes before. I can't imagine it will be better than this between us after the wedding. If he's holding back now, I may die of bliss when he pulls out all the stops. Oh, how I love that man of mine.

July

Friday, July 4th

I have never understood the people who get married on July 4th. Kind of ironic, don't you think? To relinquish independence on Independence Day? Yet every year, they book it. I get that it's a holiday weekend. Which means their guests will have time off and be able to travel. Not to mention that you're pretty much guaranteed to have your anniversary off every year. But it just seems odd somehow.

For me, today was yet another step forward in setting boundaries for myself. Mainly because today's wedding further proved that we need clearly defined job responsibilities for this position.

Looking back over my career, I truly feel I've gone above and beyond for our brides.

I've taken boudoir photos of a bride wearing nothing but her garter, heels and veil. I've written more than one poignant love letter to a bride from a groom who found himself at a loss for words but knew he was expected to pony up something for the big day. I've climbed up under I don't even know how many gowns and encountered sweaty hou-has and rumps in order to bustle complicated trains and adjust garters or thigh-highs.

I've even put pantyhose on another human being, for Christ's sake.

But today, I drew a line in defense of decency and personal boundaries.

Adriana was a sweet bride. Nice. Courteous. Four bridesmaids, all nice as well. Her closest friends, I would presume.

When I retrieved her maids to line them up for the processional, I asked if she wanted her maid-of-honor, Gabrielle, to stay with her. Adriana's father had passed away when she was ten, and she was walking down the

59

aisle alone.

She thanked me and assured me she was fine to wait by herself.

I lined up the girls, sent them down the aisle to join the guys at the altar, and came back to get Adriana. It couldn't have been more than three or four minutes. Tops.

When I entered the dressing room, I knew we had a problem.

Adriana was nowhere in sight, but the sounds coming from behind the closed bathroom door left no doubt as to her whereabouts. The smell hit me like a ton of bricks, and I immediately turned to go back outside and give her some privacy and me a breath of fresh air.

The clock didn't stop ticking, however, and when I heard the organist start the bridesmaids' song again, I knew everyone inside must be wondering why the bride hadn't entered.

I gave her a few more minutes, probably two in all honesty, but it felt like an eternity while the familiar notes of the song played on and my carefully-planned timeline slipped through my fingers.

My hand hesitated on the dressing room door as I took one last gulp of clean air and steeled my senses for the inevitable assault.

"Adriana? You okay?" I tried to exhale as little as possible when I spoke, fighting to preserve the air in my lungs and avoid inhaling at all costs.

It didn't help. The smell of her distress hung heavy in the air like a poison cloud. My gag reflex betrayed my outward demeanor of nonchalance, and I clamped my hand over my mouth praying she wouldn't hear my reaction. That killed two birds with one stone, since my hand covered my nostrils as well.

"My stomach's upset," Adriana replied. Her voice cracked a bit, though I couldn't tell how much was embarrassment, how much was emotion, and how much was the strain of her situation. Literally.

I bit my tongue to keep from saying "*I know!*" and instead I asked, "Is there anything I can do?"

What a stupid question. What on earth could I possibly do to help her with intestinal explosions?

"I think I just need a minute."

"Right, okay. Let me just go tell the organist to stall a bit."

"Thanks, Tyler. I'll be fine. Maybe I had too much to drink last night."

"No problem." I forced enthusiasm into my voice, eager to put her mind at ease. Adding more stress would only complicate the situation further.

I cannot begin to imagine how mortified she must have been. Some things in life are meant to be private affairs. Not only did this poor girl have to converse with me while on the toilet, she also had one hundred wedding guests and her future husband waiting while her body rebelled.

I opened the door to the sanctuary just enough to make eye contact with the organist. He'd been watching for any sign of entry, and his hopeful smile sank in disappointment when I motioned for him to keep playing.

Time slowed down to a crawl as I waited what I thought was a reasonable amount of time before going back into the war zone. Adriana hadn't emerged from the bathroom when I returned, but the sounds had ceased. The aroma still lingered, though, burning my nostrils to the point that my eyes watered in an attempt to put out the fire.

"Doing okay, Adriana?" I cringed as I waited for her response.

"Um, yeah. I just can't . . . well, I can't figure out how to . . . with the dress, I mean . . . I can't, um, I think I need help. I can't hold up all these layers and wipe at the same time."

I took a step backwards in horror. Oh no. Oh hell no. Ain't gonna be a day. Nope. No way. I spun on my heel without even responding to the poor girl, and without a moment's hesitation I opened the sanctuary door and marched my happy ass down the aisle in front of all those guests to get the maid-of-honor and the bride's mother.

Consider the line drawn.

There are some things I will not do for a bride.

Sunday, July 6th

Going out to dinner with Cabe's family was the last thing I wanted to do after working pretty much around the clock the last three days. I was exhausted and irritable, needing sleep, mindless reality television, and a gallon of ice cream. I couldn't very well bow out, though, since Maggie had insisted they wait to go to dinner tonight because it was the only night I wasn't working.

Not that I would have bowed out anyway. Galen and Tate had flown in from New York to celebrate Maggie's birthday, and I hadn't seen Galen since the night she verbally assaulted me in the bathroom of the comedy club. No way would I duck out of dinner and make her think I was intimidated by her. Not a chance.

Besides, Maggie's parents were driving up from South Florida, so we were not only celebrating Maggie's birthday but also telling Cabe's grandparents about our engagement. I'd met Peggy and Bill a couple of times before, and they were sweet people, much like Maggie.

So despite my desire to stay in bed all day, I forced myself to roll out late in the afternoon so I could take a shower and be a presentable fiancée by the time Cabe picked me up at five.

"You look adorable," he said as he kissed me hello.

"Why, thank you. You're looking quite dapper yourself."

His suit was fitted perfectly to his broad shoulders before tapering down to hug a little slimmer at his waist, the pale gray highlighting his eyes and turning them almost the same exact shade. He had slicked back his long curls so that his square jawline and high cheekbones were prominently showcased. He'd also trimmed his goatee, thinning the mustache a bit and tapering his chin almost to a point. I marveled anew at the fact that this man had been by my side for so long without me truly noticing his hotness.

I must have been blind then, but thankfully, my eyes had since been opened.

"You nervous? About Galen, I mean?" I asked as we exited the car at the restaurant.

"No. She won't make a scene in front of Nana and Pops. She'll be the epitome of nicety," Cabe snarled. "You?"

I shook my head. "Not at all." If anything, I welcomed the opportunity to show little sister that I was not only still here, but sporting a ring that said I wasn't going anywhere any time soon.

We were the last to arrive, and the only seats available were between Maggie and her dad. I'm sure that was purposeful on someone's part, although I don't know if it was Maggie or Galen. Bill stood and hugged me and his grandson, and Cabe and I both hugged Maggie and Peggy before taking our seats. We didn't acknowledge Galen and she didn't acknowledge us, but Tate did shake Cabe's hand. I had to wonder where he stood on all the family drama as the other outsider, although I'm sure he'd side with Galen no matter what.

Maggie had me show off my ring pretty much right off the bat, which resulted in another round of hugs and loud exclamations of excitement. Bill ordered a bottle of champagne and toasted our engagement as well as Maggie's birthday. I could feel Galen's eyes boring a hole through me during the hoopla, but I chose not to make eye contact with her.

"Have you decided on a date yet, dear?" Peggy asked as we ate.

I shook my head. "No, ma'am."

"We'll have to plan it around her other weddings, Nana." Cabe smiled at me as he said it.

"I see," Peggy said. "What about a location? Do you have a place in mind?"

Well, wasn't that the million dollar question I'd hoped to avoid!

"Not yet."

Maggie turned to me. "You'll get married here, though? Orlando? With all your work, you're familiar with all the best vendors and locations, I'm sure. Of course, if you wanted to host it at the Performing Arts Center, I'd be happy to help however I could. Being an executive director does have some perks, I'd hope."

She and Peggy laughed, and I smiled, uneasy about the topic.

"Thanks, Mom," Cabe interjected to my rescue, "but we haven't made any decisions yet. We're not in a hurry." He took my hand in his.

Galen remained silent, but I could still feel her eyes on me. I finally stole a glance in her direction and almost recoiled from the venom directed my way. Almost, but not quite. I'd been caught off guard with her once already. I wouldn't do it again. This time I was on the offensive.

"So, Galen, how's New York?" I said in my sweetest voice possible.

Her eyes widened a bit, surprised that I'd asked. "Fine."

"She was just telling us about her new role. Isn't it wonderful that she and Tate got parts in the same show?" Peggy beamed at her granddaughter, who beamed back with a much warmer expression than the one she'd given me.

Conversation proceeded throughout dinner with Bill and Peggy catching up with their grandchildren and Maggie updating us on upcoming events she was planning at the Performing Arts Center. We'd finished our entrees and several glasses of wine when Galen excused herself to go to the ladies' room, and bolstered by everyone's enthusiasm for our engagement (and I'm sure, in part, the wine) I decided to take a stand.

"Excuse me. I'll be right back." I smiled to the table as I dropped my napkin on my chair. Cabe and Maggie both looked at me with either question or alarm, but I didn't acknowledge their concern. The raging tempest inside me had built to a head and had to be dealt with.

Galen had already entered a stall by the time I got to the ladies' room, so I did a quick peek underneath the other doors to make sure we were alone before locking the bathroom door. I didn't care to have an audience for what I intended to say.

I plopped myself up onto the bathroom counter, immediately regretting the decision as water soaked through my skirt. Galen opened her stall just as I realized my mistake, so I sat up straight and decided to play it cool.

"We need to talk," I said, forcing confidence into my voice despite the butterflies in my stomach and cold wetness seeping across my butt.

"Do we? About what?" Galen asked in a clipped tone as she washed her hands in the sink beside me.

"I think you know."

"Okay." She crossed her arms and took a stance that I knew would give her a height advantage, but in my wet seat on the counter, we stayed eye to eye.

"I understand you were trying to protect your brother when you attacked me that night at the comedy club—"

"Attacked you? Oh, please. Don't be dramatic." She tossed her hair over her shoulder and shifted her weight to one foot.

"And since I have a brother, I understand how you'd want to look out for his best interests. Keep anyone from hurting him. I know if anyone purposely hurt *my* brother, they'd have to answer to me. So I get where you're coming from. But here's what you need to realize."

I hopped off the counter, not even caring if my ass was wet or I was at least four inches shorter than Galen. "First, your brother is a grown man, and he doesn't need you to protect him. He can make his own decisions. Second, I love your brother, and I'm not going anywhere. So unless you want me and you to have beef from here on out, we need to come to some kind of agreement. First of all, I will never tolerate you talking to me the way you did that night."

"Oh my Lord, how many times do I have to hear about this?" Galen tossed her hands in the air and grunted. "I'm sorry, okay? Everyone has crawled all over me for this, and all I was trying to do was look out for my brother. He wants you? He can have you. Be my guest. Everyone seriously needs to get off my back about this."

She stomped to the door and broke a fingernail trying to jerk it open without realizing I'd locked it. She turned to me, mouth wide open as she grasped her finger in her hand. "You locked the door?"

"I'm not finished. I got one more thing to say. Like I said, we both got brothers, and we know how protective we feel about them. So if I'm willing to kick someone's ass over my brother, imagine what I'd be willing to do to someone who hurt my future husband. If you ever blindside him again or make even the slightest decision on his behalf without his knowledge, I will be all over you like white on rice."

I got up in her face—well, as much as possible with the height difference—and tried to look intimidating. I'd never been in a physical altercation in my life, but I wanted her to believe I could be if she hurt Cabe again.

Her jaw set tightly in a move I knew so well, and it dawned on me that it was one of the few physical similarities she and Cabe shared.

"Understood?" I had my hands on my hips, adrenaline coursing through my body like wildfire. I felt like I could whip somebody's ass, even if it was highly improbable that I actually would.

Galen stared at me for a long pause and then nodded.

I twisted the lock on the door and strode out past her with much more confidence than someone with water all over the back of their skirt should have.

Cabe's eyes were on me the minute I came into sight, and I flashed him a smile and a wink.

"Everything okay?" he whispered as he stood to pull my chair out for me.

"Fine. Just fine." I locked eyes with Galen and smiled, and she forced a smile back to me.

Whether I'd made an enemy or an ally would remain to be seen, but at least she knew this dog'll bite.

Thursday, July 10th

Tomorrow, I will introduce the love of my life to my family and announce our engagement.

Holy crapola.

He's excited beyond belief and I feel like I'm gonna throw up. It's like my worlds are colliding. The life I lived back home, the person I was there, and the life I live here as the person I've become. The two worlds are actually very different in almost every way. Culture. Lifestyle. Language. Food.

I think underneath the excitement, Cabe is a bit nervous, too.

He walked in tonight wearing cowboy boots. He doesn't own cowboy boots. Or at least he didn't before tonight.

"Look what I bought," he proudly proclaimed as he sauntered in my apartment with an exaggerated swagger.

I looked at the absolutely gorgeous boots on his feet and cracked up laughing. "What are those?"

"Cowboy boots!" He picked each foot up and turned it left and right to give me a better view.

"I know that. But why are you wearing them? Why did you buy them?"

He shrugged and grinned at me, the silly boyish grin he wears when he's a little embarrassed. "I dunno. I guess I wanted to fit in."

"Honey, you're not going to fit in just because you put on a pair of boots, and that's perfectly fine with me." I slid my hands up his chest and around his neck. "If I wanted a cowboy-boot-wearing redneck, I'd have stayed back home. I like that you're different." I stretched up on my toes to kiss the handsome man who would go to any lengths to make me happy.

"But I kinda like 'em," he said, looking down at the boots and shifting his weight from foot to foot. "They're comfortable. They're cool. Maybe this will be my new fashion statement."

I smiled and backed up to take another look. They were really nice boots, and he looked damned hot wearing them. I'd forgotten how sexy boots can be when they're worn well. Which, I must say, he was certainly doing with his faded jeans and black T-shirt.

"You don't like 'em? Really?" He scrunched his nose a bit and looked down at the boots.

"They're growing on me. Take a walk across the living room without the cowboy swagger."

At first, he played up the exaggerated sway to the hilt, but when he relaxed and walked normally, I realized how much I'd missed seeing a man in boots.

"Ah, see? I can tell you like 'em now," he said when he turned to walk back toward me. "You got that look in your eyes like you're picturing me wearing nothing but the boots."

I threw my head back in laughter, and he picked me up and twirled me before setting me back down with a kiss that left me breathless and dizzy, although that may have been partially caused by the twirling.

He pressed his forehead against mine and spanned his hands across my lower back. "I can't wait to meet your family and tell everyone you're gonna be Mrs. Cable Shaw."

I smiled at the sound of it rolling off his tongue. I'd never thought of myself that way. I'd said Tyler Shaw a few times. To him. To Melanie. I'd even written it on scrap paper at the office. Practicing the S. Figuring out the curl of the W at the end of the name rather than at the beginning like I'd always had with Warren.

But I'd never considered Mrs. Cable Shaw. It tickled me inside. It was old-fashioned, to be sure, and not something I'd probably ever use or have printed anywhere. But I liked it. It sounded like I belonged to him somehow. Like I was *his*. In that moment, I realized how much I truly wanted to be *his*. To go home on his arm and begin the next chapter of our lives together. As an engaged couple. Soon to be married couple. Soon to be Mrs. Cable Shaw.

Friday, July 11th

Worlds colliding, indeed.

I suppose the first night went really well, all things considered.

We pulled into Mama's driveway a little before eight, so it was still light out. I looked at the old house through different eyes knowing Cabe would be seeing it the first time.

The house had belonged to my grandparents, built in the thirties and added onto throughout the years. The front porch slanted to the right a little where a dog had dug a huge crater too close to the corner support. It was a year or two after Daddy died, and Mama never had gotten somebody to come out and fill the hole and shore up the porch.

I don't think the place had been painted since before Daddy passed, and the yellow, which had once been so bright it almost seemed to glow in the sunshine, had since faded to look more cream in the waning light of day.

The huge oak tree on the front left corner still stood tall and proud like a sentry guarding the house, but I noticed its heavy limbs stretched precariously close to the porch roof and needed to be trimmed. A couple of shingles were hanging loose on the roof, and there was still duct tape on the dining room window from where Brad had sent a Frisbee crashing into the house years ago. I made a mental note to give my brother grief about not taking better care of the house for Mama. I wondered if he even noticed all the imperfections and disarray when he drove up every day.

Probably not. I never had before I brought someone home I wanted to impress.

"Wow. It's a lot more property than I pictured in my head. How many acres do you have here?" Cabe asked as we were unloading the car.

"A little over fifty, but most of it is wooded back that way behind the pond." I scanned the surrounding landscape with my new Cabe-eyes. It truly was a picturesque piece of property, dotted with oaks and pines throughout the expansive front yard to the road, and then a solid wall of woods behind the house. The long, winding driveway curved around the large pond my grandfather had dug when they first built the house and then came to a stop in the parking area to the right. A smaller drive shot off the parking area to lead out to Daddy's shop, a large metal shed that almost dwarfed the house. He'd run his mechanic business on the side out of that shop, and I'd spent many an hour sitting cross-legged on the dirty cement floor, watching him work and handing him tools as he taught me the purpose for each one.

The shop sat abandoned now. Brad kept a hot rod in there and tinkered on it from time to time, but my uncles had all ransacked Daddy's tools and machinery after he died, and the ghostly building looked lonely in the twilight.

"There she is! Y'all made it!"

The screen door flew open, and Mama ran out on the porch, followed by her cocker spaniel, Boo. "I still got supper on the stove in case y'all didn't eat. Did ya eat?"

My sister Carrie came out behind Mama, and I ran up the steps to hug them both.

"Carrie! You're not working?" I had thought we might not see Carrie at all since her job as a server required her undivided attention on weekends.

"I got someone to cover for me tonight. Mama said you were bringing someone home. I wanted to see if he passed muster."

I had left poor Cabe at the car in my excitement, and I turned to find him standing right behind me with our suitcases and a tentative smile.

"Hello," he said, looking more shy and uncertain than I'd ever seen him. I guess in my own mental turmoil about the weekend I'd never considered how nerve-wracking this might be for him. Coming to meet my entire family all at once, not knowing a soul or what to expect, and asking for my hand in marriage to boot.

"Mama, Carrie, this is Cabe."

Cabe put the suitcases down and extended his hand to shake, but Mama armed him up in a huge hug instead.

"We do hugs here," she said. "Handshaking is for strangers and folks we don't take a liking to. You're family." She pulled back and looked him up and down while holding onto his arms.

He'd worn his new boots and a pair of jeans with a pale blue button-down shirt. Even in the dim light, the blue of the shirt made his eyes pop, and the smile he flashed her could have melted a heart of stone. His long hair was combed back behind his ears and my chest puffed up with pride at how handsome he was.

"We been hearing about you for so long and just dyin' to meet ya,"

Mama said as she released him. "Come on in the house and getcha something to eat." She looped her arm through Cabe's and swept him across the porch and into the house, leaving Carrie and me to bring in the bags.

"Damn, girl. He's a hottie," Carrie whispered as they left. "Good catch!" She high-fived me and grabbed my suitcase. "Mama's been about to have a heart attack waiting for y'all to get here. I think she's called everyone in the county to tell them you were coming home and bringing a boy. A man, I guess I should say. And what a man he is! Way to go, baby sister."

We laughed as we climbed the steps and entered the house. Carrie leaned in close and whispered again once we were inside. "Just so you know, she's been telling everyone she thinks you're getting engaged. The expectation has been set, so if someone asks you about it while you're here, thank Mama."

I rolled my eyes and thanked Carrie for the warning. Everyone would know soon enough.

"Where's Brad?" I asked when I noticed my brother was nowhere in sight.

"At Kelly's," Mama spat out. "If he ain't sleeping or eating me out of house and home, he's at Kelly's. Can't get him to lift a finger to do a thing here, but he can't do enough over at her mama and daddy's. And me here as a single woman, his own mama, and them both over there working and healthy and her with a brother to help. Beats all I ever seen."

She handed Cabe a plate full of food and a glass of tea.

"Mama, we ate on the road. He may not be hungry." Cabe caught my eye and shook his head, telling me not to bother.

"That's fine. I just gave him a little bit of what we had and if he don't want it, he ain't gotta eat it."

He dug in with gusto, doing his duty to be a polite guest. Luckily, Mama's a good cook, so he didn't have any trouble cleaning off the plate. Racking up the brownie points already.

"Tanya and the kids will be here tomorrow," Mama said as she cleared Cabe's plate and poured him more tea. "They had something going on with Tom's folks that evidently couldn't be missed. Ain't like they don't see them all the time. I mean, you're here for the first time in six months and you'd think she could have told them she had to be here, but who am I to judge what somebody does?"

I tried to keep my hand out of sight as much as possible because Cabe had told me he'd like to ask Mama for my hand in marriage before we showed her the ring. By the time he finished eating and we all moved to the living room to sit down, I was about to explode and blurt out the news. I literally had to sit on my hands to keep from flashing the ring.

All this time, I had dreaded telling Mama but now that I was here and the moment was upon us, I couldn't wait to share our news. I slapped against Cabe's leg and nodded, sure that if he didn't speak up I was going to spill the beans.

He cleared his throat and reached to take my hand in his. "Um, Mrs. Warren, I thank you for welcoming me into your home, and I'm real happy to meet you and Carrie. I look forward to meeting the rest of the family." He looked to me and smiled before swallowing hard and looking back to Mama. "Tyler has told me so much about all of you that I feel like I know you already."

Mama laughed and clapped her hand against her chest. "Shoot, there's no telling what she told you, so promise me you won't hold any of it against us 'til you get to know us, okay?"

I nudged his leg to make him get on with it. He squeezed my hand in response and cleared his throat yet again.

"Cabe, do you need more tea?" Carrie looked at me and winked as she said it, obviously aware of his discomfort and perhaps guessing the reason for it.

"No, thank you, I've got some here." He smiled at Carrie and scooted forward on the couch, pulling me with him. "Mrs. Warren, I know this may seem sudden with us just meeting tonight, but I've known your daughter for quite some time. I can't imagine my life without Tyler, and though you don't know me yet, I can assure you I'm fully committed to her and would give my life for her. With your permission, ma'am, I'd like to make her my wife." He exhaled when he was done, as though he'd been holding his breath as he talked.

My heart raced to hear his words and to know that this was real. This was happening. I'd already said yes. I'd been wearing the ring for weeks. But this made it all seem more valid somehow.

Cabe and I were getting married!

I bounced off the couch and flung my hand in Mama's face, flashing my ring finger and squealing like a little kid who's just gotten the thing she's most wanted on Christmas morning.

Mama immediately burst into tears and clapped her hands together. She grabbed my hand and whooped and hollered, hugging me tight to her before shoving me aside to arm up Cabe.

Carrie took my hand and inspected the ring, nodding in approval as she hugged me. "Congrats, little sister. That's awesome."

I wiped tears of joy from my eyes as Mama let go of Cabe and hugged me again.

"Welcome to the family," Carrie said as she hugged Cabe. "Wait! Mama! You didn't give the boy an answer. Are you gonna let him marry her?"

"Oh Lord, yes! Yes! I thought I said it already. Yes, sir. You can have her! Take her!" Mama hugged me again, laughing and crying simultaneously.

"Oh my goodness. I gotta call Marjorie. She's just not going to believe this. You and Marlena engaged at the same time. Your Aunt Clementine is gonna faint and fall out in the floor. Where's my phone, Carrie Ann?"

Anxiety crept in at the mention of Marlena's wedding, but then I saw Cabe's face, and my heart melted. His grin spread from ear to ear, and his eyes danced with excitement. He closed his arms around me and lifted me in a hug, whispering against my ear. "I love you, baby."

Our lips met as I echoed his statement, but only briefly since Brad came through the front door at that moment. I released Cabe and ran to hug my baby brother, thrilled to have someone else to share my news with.

Carrie had long since gone home to her husband by the time Mama made all her phone calls, pulling me onto the phone to talk to each person and accept congratulations. It was almost midnight by the time we headed upstairs for bed.

"Now, Cabe, you'll be in Carrie's old room. We ain't got central air upstairs, so I'll show you how to work the window unit if you get hot. I had it on earlier this evening to cool the room off a bit, so you may not need it." She showed Cabe into my sister's room and turned the covers back on the bed. "Down the hall here is the bathroom, and there's towels and washcloths under the sink."

A large creaking groan bellowed out from the floorboards as Mama walked across the hall to the bathroom. "You hear that?" She grinned. "That's my alarm system. These boards are older than me and you put together, and they creak if you put the least bit of weight on 'em. So don't be getting any ideas about sneaking into each other's rooms." She wagged her finger at us, but her eyes and mouth were smiling.

"No, ma'am. I wouldn't dare," Cabe said.

"My sister Tanya tried for years to figure out a way to grease those boards," I said as Mama rolled her eyes and grinned. "That's her room on the end, across from Carrie's. She'd try to sneak out at night and she couldn't get past Mama's room without the creaking waking Mama up." I laughed at the memory while Mama shook her head.

"She made it past me a few times. A few too many. I still say she must have been tiptoeing on the baseboards."

"And then Carrie would climb out the window onto the porch roof and shimmy down the old oak, right Mama?"

"Yes, Lord. These girls were nearly the death of me, Cabe. That's why I'm gray. I wouldn't look nearly this old if they had just behaved." She swatted me playfully on the bottom.

"What about this one here?" Cabe asked, nodding toward me. "Was she a rascal, too?" He winked at me and grinned.

"No," I said. "By the time I came along Mama already knew all the tricks and schemes. I couldn't get away with nothing!"

"Oh, she got away with plenty. Don't let her tell you that, Cabe. She's a good 'un, though. You got you a good 'un." Mama hugged me and turned to go to her room with a wave of her hand. "Y'all say your goodbyes and get on to bed." She turned back and hugged me again, planting a kiss on my cheek. "I'm so happy for ya, honey. Mama loves you."

"Love you too, Mama."

We watched her until her door closed and then Cabe pulled me in close and covered my mouth with his. All the emotion and happiness of the evening coursed through us, and my body was suddenly burning all over, begging to be touched. I pressed him back against the wall, ignoring the protests of the boards beneath our feet. He slid his hands beneath the hem of my shirt and teased his thumbs across my bare skin, leaving a trail of goose bumps everywhere he touched.

"How do you think it went?" he whispered, his eyes curious with anticipation for my answer.

"Good. Very good. She must really like you if she's gonna let you run the air conditioner at night. She *never* does that."

I heard Mama's feet cross her bedroom floor, my ears trained for years to hone in on that very sound. I sprang apart from Cabe and wiped at my mouth, pulling my shirt down as I skipped a couple of steps from him just as she opened her door.

"Hey, I forgot to tell y'all that the Lions Club is having a pancake breakfast in the morning. I thought we might head over there and show off your ring. Night-night." She closed the door again, and I looked back at Cabe, my body longing to connect with his.

"So is there any way around this floor alarm?" He grinned and flashed his eyes, cracking me up with the mischievous expression he wore.

"None that I ever mastered. Only Tanya could get past it, and that was many years ago." I tiptoed across the space between us, pausing as a particularly noisy board cried out. I covered my hand to stifle a laugh just as Mama's voice rang out from behind her closed door.

"Go to bed you two. In your own rooms."

"Yes, ma'am!" I called out and then turned back to Cabe. "Good night, Cable. Sleep tight. Don't let the bed bugs bite."

He kissed his fingers and extended them to brush against my lips, setting my skin aflame again. Somehow knowing I couldn't have him made me want him even more.

Now I've been lying here for nearly an hour, acutely aware that the man who drives me wild and takes my body to the grandest heights of ecstasy is in the room next door but might as well be a hundred miles away.

I've spent the time getting reacquainted with my bedroom, which still looks exactly the same as when I left it years ago. It's funny that the room never changes, but each time I return, I've become someone else. Last

Christmas when I came home, I was coming to terms with my past and letting go of a relationship that had held me captive far too long.

Now I'm here on the cusp of a huge life decision, blending my past and future as I introduce my soon-to-be husband to the people who shaped me into the woman he loves.

Someday soon, I'll return to this room as someone's wife. Of course, then he'll be lying beside me, so I'm pretty sure I'll be too busy for all this introspection.

Saturday, July 12th

"Up and at 'em! Get up, get up. You've got hundreds of years to sleep in a coffin, but here you are laid up in the bed."

Mama's voice invaded my dreams with a rude awakening. I plunged deeper under the quilt and pulled the pillow over my head.

She turned off the window air conditioner blasting cold in my room, and without that white noise humming, her voice was even louder. She popped my bottom through the covers and then whipped the quilt off me.

"You're lucky you didn't freeze to death with that thing cranked down so low," Mama said as I clutched the end of the quilt and pulled it back over my goose-fleshed skin. "I'm willing to bet you don't keep it that cold at your house where you pay the power bill."

"Good morning, Mama," I moaned as she pulled the cover from me again.

"You should get up and go take a shower in my bathroom so Gabe can use the hall bathroom. We don't want to be late for the pancake breakfast or we won't get seats together."

I sat straight up in bed and glared at her. "You called him by the correct name all night last night. You never once messed up, and now you're saying Gabe again. Do you do this just to irritate me?"

"Cabe, Gabe, I don't know what I'm saying. Get your rump outta bed and in the shower. You gonna wake him up or you want me to?"

"I'll wake him up," I said as I rolled to the side of the bed and tried to wake myself up. It *was* freezing in the room, but I refused to shiver and give her the satisfaction of telling me not to run the air conditioner tonight.

I shuffled down the hall and knocked on his door. Cabe mumbled something incoherent, and I opened the door and went in to sit on the bed next to him. It cracked me up to see my huge, strapping fiancé all curled up in my sister's old pink sheets and comforter, his messy curls splayed across a pillowcase covered in hearts.

"What are you laughing at?" Cabe cocked one eye open and squinted at me.

"You look adorable." I leaned forward and kissed his forehead, laughing again as he suddenly wrapped both arms around me and pulled me across his body on the bed.

As if on cue, Mama immediately admonished me from the hall as she headed downstairs. "Tyler Lorraine, you need to get in the shower if we're gonna get pancakes."

"You don't want to miss out on pancakes, Tyler Lorraine," Cabe whispered in an exaggerated Southern drawl. "You better get yo butt in the shower, gurrrl."

I slapped at his chest and planted a quick peck on his cheek before crawling off the bed. I turned at the door and looked back at him. He had rolled to his side and propped up on his elbow, and the sleepy fog of his eyes pulled at my heartstrings and awakened other sensations deep within me. Oh, how I wish I could have just crawled under the covers with him and snuggled back to sleep. I never realized how lucky I was to get to sleep next to him until it became forbidden fruit last night. It made me long for the warmth of his body pressed against mine and the sound of his steady breathing on my neck. The touch of his hands as they caressed my skin. The little sounds he makes with his sighs and groans as we tease and pleasure each other.

That thought process would get me nowhere while we were at Mama's, so I shook my head and grinned at Cabe. "I'm gonna use Mama's bathroom so you can get in the hall shower."

"What? You're not going to join me?" His voice teased and insinuated everything my mind was already thinking.

"You have no idea how bad I want to, but—"

Mama's voice bellowed from the bottom of the stairs. "Tyler Lorraine! Did you get in the shower yet? I don't hear water running. Do I need to come up there?"

"I gotta go."

Cabe laughed and flung back the covers, and at the sight of his muscular body in nothing but boxers, I almost decided it was worth risking my mother's cardiac arrest to jump back in bed with him. But fear of her climbing the stairs overwhelmed my carnal desires, so I blew him a kiss and left to get ready.

When we'd had our fill of pancakes and met more people than Cabe could possibly remember in one day, we left Mama to chat at the pancake breakfast and took off for a little exploring on our own. I showed him a few landmarks and drove him around the perimeter of the town, the entire tour taking probably twenty minutes with such a small area to cover.

"We used to have a red light when I was growing up, but they took it out a few years ago. Carrie said there's not enough traffic since they built the bypass, so now it's just a flashing caution light." We'd parked at the small gazebo between the courthouse and the river and gotten out to sit on a picnic table for arguably the best view of the massive waterway that curved around our town.

"Wow. I don't think I've ever heard of a place growing backward and losing their traffic light. I knew you came from a small town, but I had no idea it was this small. Weekends must have been a blast."

"Yeah. Not so much. I mean, Atlanta's an easy drive, so we went there sometimes for a concert or a baseball game or something. And there's a movie theater about a half hour west of here, so it's not like we were completely out in the boondocks, but nothing like growing up in Orlando, either."

The breeze lifted my hair across my face, and Cabe tucked it behind my ear. "I can't picture you here," he said. "I don't see you in this environment."

"Me neither." I threw a small pebble someone had left on the picnic table. "I couldn't wait to leave. Now, it feels so weird to be here. Like it's home, it's familiar, and I know what it is and what to expect. I know the people here, and I can fit in for a few days. But at the same time, it's not home anymore. It's not who I am or who I want to be. When I'm here, I get flooded with memories. Sensations. Sounds. Kind of like going back in time, I guess. I enjoy the journey, and I like feeling that nostalgia, that connection, but the whole time I'm antsy to get back to present day. To my life."

He tucked his finger under my chin and turned my face to his, pressing his lips together with mine in the softest of kisses. He pulled back after a few seconds, but only far enough for us to breathe and look into each other's eyes.

"Thanks for bringing me here," he said. "Thanks for showing me this part of you. For sharing your past and your background. I like learning new things about you. Getting new pieces in the puzzle of Tyler." He kissed me again, and as the kiss deepened I was awkwardly aware of where we were.

I pulled away and hopped off the picnic table with a quick glance around to see who might be watching, but the area was pretty bare.

Cabe laughed. "We gonna get arrested for PDA?"

"No, but tongues wag. I don't want Mama on my ass for being indecent in the middle of town. Let's go get a drink."

"A drink? At ten in the morning? I wouldn't think bars would be open here so early." He slid off the table and dusted the back of his jeans with his hand.

"There's no bars here!" I cracked up laughing as I considered his preposterous statement. The notion that there would be a bar in my tiny little Southern Baptist-dominated town nearly doubled me over in laughter. Especially to think that anyone would dare drink in broad daylight on a Saturday morning.

"No bar? Seriously? Like in the whole town?" He stopped in his tracks and stared at me in amazement.

"Babe! You've seen the whole town. It's like five blocks. Did you see a bar?"

"I just figured we hadn't gotten to that part of the tour yet. So no one drinks?"

We got in the car and I backed out, still laughing at the mental image of Patsy Warren and the ladies of the Junior League having their monthly meetings in some dimly-lit bar tossing back shots of whiskey with their Caesar salads.

"Oh, they drink, I can assure you. But not out in public. I meant we'd get a Coke or something."

I passed the big, new convenience store on the right to head over the hill and around the curve to the small store on the way out of town. The newer store had been built after I left, so it never occurred to me to go there. I went where I knew to go.

My brain did a double-take when I saw the large red pick-up truck parked beside the empty space I pulled into. What are the chances that out of all the people in our town, the one person I'd hoped to avoid seeing just happened to be in the same tiny, little store I had driven to at the same exact time as me?

"Something wrong?" Cabe asked as we got out of the car.

"Dwayne's here."

"Dweeb Dwayne? Awesome." Cabe picked up his pace and almost passed me in his haste to get inside. He held the entrance door open for me, already scanning the store interior for his long-time nemesis.

"Behave, please," I pleaded as I scanned the store on my own. At first glance, there was no one there but the cashier, a distant cousin on my daddy's side. I exchanged pleasantries with her, and she had that look people back home often get where they think they know me but they can't quite place who I am. Cabe and I walked to the back of the store and grabbed drinks from the cooler, both of us looking for any sign of my ex-boyfriend.

He came out of the men's room just as we headed back to the cash register.

"Well, I'll be damned. Tie me up and call me tongue-tied. If you ain't a sight for sore eyes, darlin'." Dwayne Davis stood face to face with me, his silly grin spreading even as I felt the tension roll off the man behind me.

Dwayne extended his arms for a hug, and I twisted to do a side-hug and an introduction at the same time.

"Dwayne, this is Cabe. My fiancé." I stammered a little bit on the word, and I realized it was the first time I'd ever introduced him as such. How ironic.

Cabe had drawn up to his full height with his chest and shoulders expanded in that peacock move men instinctively do. He extended his hand to shake Dwayne's, and I noticed as I looked back at Dwayne that he had pulled himself up and out too. It didn't do a lot of good, though. Cabe towered over him as they exchanged greetings.

Dwayne took a step back to a more appropriate distance for someone who is engaged and has her fiancé standing *right there*, and I chuckled at the overwhelming essence of testosterone filling the air.

"I heard you was getting hitched," Dwayne said, casting sideways glances toward Cabe while looking at me. "Congratulations."

"News travels fast in this town," I said as Dwayne reached for my left hand.

"May I?" he asked, though I don't know if he was asking me or Cabe.

I extended my hand and he took it, turning it to catch the reflections of light dancing off the diamond.

What a surreal moment. Here stood the man who had captured my heart so long ago, ripped it to shreds and held the remnants captive for so many years. And next to me stood the man who had helped put the pieces back together, despite the fact that the damage caused had left my heart unavailable to him. He now held my heart and my future.

I felt fortunate to have revisited my relationship with Dwayne last year. To have worked through the faded imprint of heartache he left behind and released any lingering hold he had on me. Standing before him now, I felt nothing but warm memories of him as connected to my past. I leaned deeper into Cabe's hand on my back and knew no one held any place in my heart except him. I belonged to Cabe now, completely and utterly. No longer restrained.

"You're a very lucky man," Dwayne told Cabe. "I'd say this little lady is about the best catch on the planet. Treat her well."

Cabe nodded as he circled his arm around my waist and pulled me against him. "You're not telling me anything I don't already know. And don't worry. She'll be treated very well."

Dwayne swallowed hard, and I noticed he looked even older than the last time I'd seen him six months ago. At one point in my life, I saw him as my destiny. Thank God for unanswered prayers.

"He's shorter than I imagined," Cabe said as we got back in the car. "Skinnier."

"Well, he's lost a lot of weight over the years." I don't know why I felt the need to defend Dwayne, or my choice of Dwayne, more like it.

"He's not your type. It never would have worked."

"Oh really? And what, pray tell, is my type?" I popped open the soda and took a swig as I waited to hear his description.

"Tall. Blonde. Surfer. Computer geek. Music aficionado. Closet romantic. Passionate kisser. Video game addict. Skilled masseuse. Great chef. Extraordinary lover. Compassionate animal owner."

I laughed as his list went on and on, growing more complimentary and outrageous as he went. Though I can't say any of it was really an exaggeration. Cabe was all that and more.

"Well, lucky for me, I found a guy who fits just that description." I braced my weight on the console as I leaned in for a kiss. "You're my perfect match."

He cupped my face in his hands and demonstrated some of the skills he'd just described. When he pulled away from the kiss, I was tempted to discover if any of the old backwoods haunts were still great places to go parking. A quick glance at the clock told me Mama would be tapping her foot waiting for us to pick her up, though, so I cranked the car and shelved passion for another time.

Still Saturday –
Afternoon

We made a few more stops once we picked up Mama, mostly to visit people so she could show off my ring and share her big news. I didn't mind. It was fun to finally be excited about the engagement after dreading this trip so long. Mama was in a great mood, and it felt good to make her happy for once. Of course, it didn't hurt that I had the most handsome man in the world by my side. Showing him off was even better than the ring.

He made a great impression on Mama. I don't know what she was expecting me to bring home, but she gave me her stamp of approval as we made lunch while Brad and Cabe horsed around with the basketball outside.

"He's sweet," Mama said. "Real polite. Well-spoken. He's got good manners. I haven't had to open a door all day, and he seems real attentive to ya. The way he looks at you, I swear. He's smitten, for sure."

My heart swelled, and my cheeks blushed warm as my smile widened across my face. In part because it made me all gooey inside to hear someone else tell me Cabe was smitten with me, and in part because Mama doesn't lavish praise often. I was soaking it up like a sponge.

"Where's his family from again?" Her question seemed nonchalant, but I'd be willing to bet she was looking for a chink in the armor.

"He was born in Florida."

"I know that, but where's his family from? You can tell a lot about how a tree will grow by its roots. He's got good family? You've met 'em?"

"Yes, ma'am. You would love his mama. She's so nice. She used to be a ballerina. What are your plans for dinner? Want to just go out somewhere so we don't have to cook? We'd love to take you out. Treat you somewhere." I had hoped I could distract her from asking about Cabe's dad. I didn't have answers to those questions, and I didn't want her asking Cabe about him.

"We'll see. What about his daddy? What does he do?"

She was undeterred.

"Um, I don't know much about his daddy."

"What do you mean you don't know much about his daddy? You haven't met him?"

I sighed and told the truth. "He left when Cabe was three. His mama raised him on her own."

"So what then? His daddy didn't see him anymore? Why not?"

I debated how in depth to answer her, but before I could decide, Brad and Cabe came busting up in the kitchen, hot and sweaty and needing refreshment.

"We're gonna take off on the four-wheeler. We'll be back in a few. When's lunch?" Brad asked as he tossed Cabe a Gatorade bottle from the fridge and opened one for himself.

"Not long. How far ya goin'?" Mama asked.

"I'm gonna take him up to the creek and back." Brad grabbed a banana and motioned to Cabe to ask if he wanted one.

While I was certainly happy to see Cabe and my brother bonding and getting along so well, I suddenly felt like Cabe was one of Brad's buddies and I was the outsider.

"I wanna come." My voice sounded a little more like a whine than I had intended.

Brad looked at me like I was an annoying little sister. Probably exactly the same expression I had given him as the annoying little brother over the years. "There's no room. We'll be back in a few minutes. I think you can live without him that long." He rolled his eyes and scowled.

"Oh, you're one to talk," Mama chimed in. "I'm surprised you're taking in oxygen without Kelly attached to your hip. I thought for sure your lungs didn't function if she wasn't sharing your breathing space."

"Where is Kelly? Are we gonna see her while I'm here?" I asked.

"She's shopping with her mom today, but she'll be at Aunt Clem's tonight."

"Why? What's happening at Aunt Clem's?"

Brad's eyes widened and he broke out into a mischievous grin before darting out the door. "See ya later. Sorry, Mom."

"Bradley David, I swear you couldn't keep a secret if your life depended on it. Loud mouth young'un." Mama shook her head and continued chopping potatoes.

"Mama? What secret? What's happening at Aunt Clem's tonight? Please tell me you didn't go and plan something after I asked you not to." Visions of my entire extended family swarming all over Cabe, asking him questions, and embarrassing the living daylights out of me flooded through my mind and unsettled my stomach.

"C'mon, honey. You got engaged, and you're home to tell us. Everybody wants to celebrate with you and meet your fella. Don't be stingy with him."

"Aw, Mama! I don't want to go over to Aunt Clem's and have fifty million people talking all at once, asking Cabe a bunch of questions and making fun of me."

She dropped the potatoes in the fryer and wiped her hands on her apron.

"Tyler, you can't always just think about yourself. Sometimes you have to consider other people. There's a lot of folks up here who don't ever get to see you and certainly don't ever hear from you, but they love you just the same. Now you have some news to share and you're bringing a complete stranger into the family. None of us knows him or knows his family. People want to meet him. Check him out. Tell you congratulations. Can't you just let folks be happy?"

I pulled the condiments from the fridge, my body on auto-pilot remembering how to set the table and argue with my mother at the same time.

"I'm all for people being happy. But why can't we have dinner here? Or maybe just visit with Aunt Clem and let her tell everybody about him? I think it's going to be overwhelming for Cabe to meet everyone all at once." There were a few choice family members I knew would be overwhelming even if he met them all by themselves, but to put all the crazy in the same room at the same time was a little much. Even for me, and I already knew them.

"So you'd rather me work myself to death and spend a ton of money hosting an engagement party here when Aunt Clem has graciously offered to do it without me lifting a finger? Well, thank you very much, but no." She flipped the burgers and rattled the fryer basket with the fries.

"We could go out to eat. Invite everyone to come to a restaurant or something. Maybe the diner?"

"Money might grow on trees down in Orlando, but ain't nobody here gonna take their entire family out to dinner just because you're too high-falutin' to have potluck at your great-aunt's house. Besides, if he meets everybody tonight, then when y'all come back for the wedding, he'll already know 'em and it'll be more fun for him."

I immediately went silent. The location of the wedding was not a topic I was ready to delve into. I wasn't about to tell her I was considering getting married in Orlando. Or the Caribbean. Or anywhere except here.

She mistook my silence for further dissent and sighed heavily as she spooned the grease-laden fries onto a plate full of paper towels.

"I suwannee, Tyler. Can't nobody do nothing for you without you ruining it. People been working hard all day trying to put together a nice surprise for you and Gabe—with no time to plan, I might add, since you sprung this on all of us last minute—and could you be the least bit grateful that folks are willing to give up their Saturday night plans for you? Nooo. Not one bit of gratitude. I don't know where I went wrong with you."

"Cabe."

"What?"

"His name is *Cabe.*" I turned and bolted up the stairs, my go-to move growing up for escaping once she started in on me. But when I got to my room, I remembered I wasn't a teenager anymore, and suddenly flopping across my bed and turning the stereo up loud didn't seem to be a viable solution to the problem.

I stood at my bedroom window and stared out across the pond and the drive toward the road, aggravated at the turn of events, but fully aware that the machine was in motion and there was nothing I could do to stop it.

Like it or not, we'd be spending the evening at Aunt Clementine's, surrounded by my loving family.

Still Saturday–
Evening

We had an impressive turnout, I suppose. A little over fifty people came and went at various times throughout the evening, with about thirty there the whole time.

I'm sure Cabe was a bit shell-shocked at the number of people and the level of noise, but bless his heart, he never once lost his smile. He stayed gracious as could be throughout the evening and did pretty well at remembering names and getting the family connections linked in his brain.

"Now who does she belong to?"

"My cousin Lloyd."

"And Lloyd is Raymond's brother?"

"Yep."

"Okay, and Raymond is the welder with one arm, right?"

"Yep."

I saw cousins I hadn't seen in years before I left for Orlando, much less the time since I'd been gone. Everybody who had ever known me—and a few people I swear I never met—turned up at Clementine's to wish us well.

"Cabe, every one of my siblings live right here on this side of the river," Mama explained as she sat down next to him. "Then every one of my mama and daddy's brothers and sisters live within this tri-county area. We know our cousins out to tenth, but of course, by that far out you got so many married and interconnected it gets hard to keep up with." Mama beamed with pride as she pointed out key family members to him.

"That there is my sister Sally Jo, and she's the oldest of us. She's married to Claude over yonder in the den watching the TV. They got two daughters, Zula and Zona, over there playing cards in the dining room. Them girls have five kids between 'em, all grown with babies of their own. Next in line is Pearl. She's over there cutting pies. She's got four young'uns grown and married and two grandbabies, but none of them could make it tonight.

Then there's Frank, but he's offshore. Hopefully, you'll meet him at the wedding. He didn't know y'all was coming home with this news, and it's near impossible for him to take off." She glared at me with that comment.

"Then comes me in the lineup, and after me was Robert Clyde, but we lost him at thirteen. Tractor accident. And my baby sister is Marjorie. She's outside with the little ones. Her daughter Marlena is getting married in the spring. I told Tyler y'all should talk to her about doing a double wedding or maybe using some of her stuff. It would save you a ton of money."

Cabe stayed engaged through the entire conversation, nodding where appropriate and seeming genuinely interested in her family tree. God bless him. I'm sure his eyes were about ready to glaze over, but he kept on smiling and nodding. Good-natured as ever.

Mama had to make a big deal out of his name every time someone new came in, explaining that it was Cabe with a C, not Gabe with a G. That it may sound like Gabe, but it wasn't. That it was short for Cable, and he was named after his daddy's brother, who had died in Vietnam. Lord rest his soul.

I was shocked she remembered all those facts I'd given her time and time again over the years. I truly thought she never listened to me, which was the only explanation that made sense considering she mispronounced his name all the damned time.

No one else seemed as fascinated by it as Mama, and if Cabe minded being put on display like that every five minutes, he didn't let on.

"You doing okay?" I'd ask every now and then when the planets aligned and we got a brief moment alone.

"Yeah, yeah. I'm fine. This is a trip. You're really related to all these people?" He widened his eyes as he laughed.

I nodded. "Yeah, somehow. By blood or marriage. Sometimes both."

Aunt Donna, Uncle Frank's wife, ended up being the one that took us down the path I'd tried to avoid.

"So where's your family from, Cabe?"

I swear the entire room dropped a couple of notches in volume as every ear strained to hear his answer.

"Florida. My mom was born and raised in South Florida, and my sister and I were both born in Miami. We moved to Orlando when we were little, so that's always been home."

Aunt Donna leaned in, and I suspected she'd been nominated by the others to be the investigative reporter. "And what about your daddy? He's from Florida too?"

I cringed at the mention of his dad and opened my mouth to step in, but he answered without missing a beat.

"He was born in Ohio."

Donna nodded. "So he moved to Florida and met your mama?"

Cabe nodded back. "They met in Florida, yes."

Aunt Sally Jo came in from the kitchen and joined the interrogation. "Patsy said your mama used to be a ballerina. What does she do now?"

I glanced up to see more people moving in closer to listen, sort of like vultures circling fresh meat.

"She's an executive director at the Performing Arts Center in Orlando. She coordinates all the fundraising and social events at the Center."

I heard a few "aahs" in the growing crowd surrounding us, and I knew that one of the hot topics had been checked off.

"And your daddy? What does he do?" My cousin Callie had joined the discussion, perched on the arm of Donna's chair.

Cabe's eyes met mine for a brief moment, and I could sense his apprehension. "He's a show producer."

"What's that?" This from another cousin who had joined the fray.

"Um, he finances productions. Ballets, Broadway shows, concerts."

"Tyler, what's your last name gonna be?" That came from my cousin Jarod, watching TV in the den with Uncle Claude, who pretty much spent every family gathering in the recliner watching Andy Griffith reruns.

"Shaw."

"Tyler Shaw." Several in the crowd murmured the name, repeating it over and over again. I smiled, listening to my future name and liking the sound of it.

"I knew some Shaws in Toledo. Where did you say your Daddy's family was from?" Uncle Claude asked. I honestly thought he was asleep and didn't know he'd heard the conversation.

Cabe shifted his weight as he spoke, and I wondered if he knew any members of Gerry's family or where they lived. I was somewhat surprised he had known where his father was born.

"I just know they were from Ohio. I'm not sure exactly where."

The room grew quiet.

"You don't know where your family's from?" Aunt Sally Jo asked the question in an accusatory tone.

Uncle Claude bellowed out from the den, his deep voice rising above the quiet murmur in the room over Cabe's last answer. "These Shaws were from Toledo, but I think they had some relatives in Canada. Your daddy got any Canadian relatives?"

"Um, actually my father's last name is Tucker. I have my mom's last name."

It was like one of those moments on the school bus where just as you say something completely inappropriate or humiliating, the entire bus goes quiet and your voice rings out in the unexpected silence.

Every person in the house seemed to shut up at once, and I could almost hear the sound of a needle skipping across a record as their heads swiveled around to gawk at Cabe.

"Really? Now why's that, honey?" Aunt Pearl said as Mama avoided my eyes.

Cabe shrugged, wondering I'm sure how much he should answer and how in depth he was expected to go.

"Are y'all writing a book?" I said. "Leave the poor man alone. Y'all gonna run him off and I won't ever get him down the aisle. Come on, Cabe. Let's go play cards." I grasped his hand and pulled, and he hopped up to accompany me, obviously happy to be out of the hot seat.

I saw Mama and the aunts exchange glances with raised eyebrows, and I knew I'd only postponed the line of questioning. There was a story there, and their little noses itched and burned to get to the bottom of it. I didn't want Cabe subjected to their judgment or their analysis, and I'd be more than happy to tell them all to mind their own business if it came to that.

When I saw the other card players at the table, I paused for a moment, not sure I hadn't just taken him out of the kettle only to throw him into the fire.

My daddy's youngest sister was the first to look up and see us. "Y'all wanna play? Scootch over and make room for Tyler and her beau, honey."

"Thank you," Cabe said. "Helene, right?"

Aunt Helene nodded. "That's right! Good memory. I'm Tyler's daddy's sister. God rest his soul."

I struggled to fit onto the bench seat with Cabe, cursing my ample backside for the millionth time in my life. Of course, my fat rump wasn't the only reason I was having trouble fitting on the bench. On the other side of Cabe and Aunt Helene was Helene's husband, Rodney. Uncle Rodney's butt was as wide as mine and Cabe's put together.

"Please tell me he's actually an Elvis impersonator, and he doesn't just dress that way for no reason," Cabe had whispered when Rodney and Helene arrived.

Rodney had been an Elvis impersonator my whole life, so I didn't really notice it anymore. But looking at him tonight through Cabe's eyes, I have to admit it seemed a bit strange.

His hair was dyed so black it was almost blue, and the large swoop of bangs hanging over his eyebrows looked suspiciously like a wig. What man that age would have so much hair?

His pudgy face was lined on either side with thick, bushy, black sideburns, groomed to a straight line that cut across just below his earlobe. He was never without a pair of gold aviator sunglasses—rain or shine, indoors or out—and a thick gold chain sparkled in the nest of black curls bursting out the top of his ever present button-down silk shirt, which was always unbuttoned at least three down. He'd partnered tonight's white shirt with a pair of royal blue silk shorts and some gray suede loafers.

"I don't mean to be critical, but shouldn't his shoes be blue instead of the shorts?" Cabe had whispered as I playfully slapped his arm and shushed him.

When we'd finished a round of cards, Rodney leaned around Helene and addressed Cabe.

"Son, I'm here to tell you. Coming into this bunch as an outsider is a hard row to hoe, but it can be done. You may not guess this as well as I fit in with them, but I'm not from around here."

Cabe raised his eyebrows and dropped his chin with a nod as my cousin Todd snorted across the table. "Really, Rodney? Way to state the obvious."

"Rodney's from New York City," Helene said with pride. "He's an Elvis impersonator."

"No kidding." Cabe managed a straight face as he said it, but the rest of the table cracked up.

"Don't mind these people," Rodney said. "They wouldn't know entertainment if it walked up and hit 'em between the eyes. But from one outsider to another, I welcome you to the family." He raised his tea glass to Cabe and saluted.

Cabe nodded and smiled. "Well, thank you, sir. I appreciate that."

"In fact, I'd like to make a toast for your engagement. Everybody listen up!" Rodney's voice rang out across the house and was immediately answered by numerous people crowding into the dining room to see what he wanted.

"I'd like to make a toast," Uncle Rodney said as he stood and pulled his shorts from his butt crack without even trying to be discreet about the movement.

Mama and my sister Tanya both came in and stood beside me.

"A toast?" Mama asked. "It ain't their wedding yet, Rodney. What we gonna toast with? Iced tea?"

"You don't have to be at a wedding to toast, Patsy. You can toast any time."

Mama had never liked Rodney, and the feeling was mutual. Everyone knew there was no love lost between those two and never would be.

He raised his glass of tea high in the air and cleared his throat, releasing a little bit of gas under the cover of the sound. "To Tyler and Cable, may your love always keep you warm at night and send you to bed without a fight."

"Ah, honey, that's so romantic." Aunt Helene rubbed her hand across Rodney's back and smiled up at him like an adoring groupie. She stood and planted a red-lipsticked kiss on his cheek, leaving a smear that came across more sunburned than sexy.

Rodney smiled back at her and then continued his speech. "As a gift for their special day, I'm offering to sing at the wedding."

Aunt Clementine choked on her cornbread and motioned for my cousin Micah to slap her back.

Aunt Helene clapped her hands together and squealed in delight. "Oh honey, that's so sweet of you. My brother would be so honored. God rest his soul."

I locked eyes with Mama and silently pleaded with her to do something. Anything. There was no way in hell I wanted Rodney belting out *Love Me Tender* in a satin jumpsuit at my wedding.

Rodney turned to Cabe and smiled as the gold medallion around his neck caught the light from the globe above the table and flashed like a strobe light as he spoke. "You, sir, are in for a treat. I'm not one to brag"— I heard at least three people cough—"but I once sang back-up for the band that opened for Kenny Rogers. Voice like an angel, my ma always said."

"The Angel of Death," Tanya whispered behind me.

"He did," Aunt Helene chimed in. "I was there. Right up in front. Proudest moment of my life to see the man I loved up on that stage."

They both looked to Cabe as though they anticipated a grand reaction. Cabe looked startled, unsure what to say. He gave a polite smile, and I elbowed Mama.

"That's real nice of you, Rodney, but I'm sure the kids have their own plans of what they'd like to do. Dance music or something. They can't dance to you crooning Presley and Sinatra."

"Well, I didn't plan to sing while they danced, Patsy. Maybe I'll sing at the ceremony. Be their soloist."

Aunt Clem had finally coughed up the last chunks of cornbread and chased down what was left with tea. As the oldest surviving member of Mama's family, she was the reigning matriarch. "Rodney, it was a music festival. You sang back-up at ten o'clock in the morning for a local gospel band, and Kenny Rogers took the stage at eight o'clock that night. Call a spade a spade. Hmmph. Up here puttin' on airs like you and The Gambler was hanging out playing cards after the show." She clacked her false teeth and swished tea around her mouth to rid it of any stray cornbread crumbs.

"I never said we was," Uncle Rodney protested. "The fact remains, I shared a stage with Kenny Rogers."

"You did, baby doll, you did," Aunt Helene patted his arm. "I was there."

"Well, either way, I'm sure they have their own plans. Cabe's family might have a singer as well," Mama said.

"Any singers in your family, boy?" Uncle Claude asked. I jumped at the sound of his voice, shocked to see him out of the recliner and in the midst of the others crowded into the dining room entrance.

"Um, no sir. Not any that I know of, sir." Cabe leaned around me to make eye contact with Uncle Claude, who nodded slightly in reply.

"Cable doesn't know his father's family, Claude. His daddy left his mama when he was a young'un," Mama explained.

I gasped and slapped at her arm. "Mama! Everybody doesn't need to know that."

"Well, Lord, child, who do you think is everybody? This is family. He's joining the family, ain't he?" She rubbed her arm and shot me a look under her eyebrows that would have put the fear of God in me when I was younger. But now she was messing with Cabe. I refused to back down.

"Yes, he is, but that doesn't mean he needs his business laid out for everyone to see."

"It's okay, Ty," Cabe mumbled, but his hand was hot when I reached for it. Embarrassed at being the center of attention on behalf of his daddy, I'm sure.

"That ain't nothing to be ashamed of, honey." Aunt Pearl came in from smoking on the front porch and joined the conversation like she'd been there all along. "I've had three husbands leave me. Ain't heard hide nor hair of 'em since the day they crunk their trucks and pulled out the driveway."

"That gives you a forty percent success rate, Pearl." Rodney laughed and sat back down.

"The other two ended with them dead. I wouldn't call those successes," Aunt Clem said.

"I just haven't found the right one yet." She smiled at Cabe and left the room along with most of the others.

We played a couple more rounds of cards in peace and then people began to leave as the hour grew late. We helped with the clean-up and hung around until almost everyone had gone.

"I thought it was sweet of Rodney and Helene to come and represent your daddy's family," Aunt Donna said as she finished drying the dishes.

"Hmmph," Aunt Clem said. "Rodney ain't gonna pass up a free meal." She hobbled over to me and hugged me tight against her chest. "Y'all had a real good turnout, honey-girl."

She'd never had any children of her own, and she looked at each of us as her babies. I breathed in her ever-present peppermint scent and thanked her for throwing the party for us.

Cabe bent down to hug her too, and she cupped his face in her wrinkled, twisted hands. "You take care of my honey-girl, and she'll take care of you. You have kind eyes, son. I see a kind heart. You're welcome back anytime."

"Thank you, ma'am. I'll certainly take you up on that."

And just like that, Cabe was officially welcomed into the family. Thank God he survived.

Sunday, July 13th

I'd just finished writing last night and turned off my lamp when something tapped against my window. At first, I thought it was a limb from the oak scraping the glass. But when it happened again at the same evenly spaced intervals, I sat straight up in bed and stared at the closed blinds.

My heart beat so loudly in my ears that I couldn't tell if the sound was still there, but then it happened again, a little louder and more insistent.

"Psst. Ty."

I threw back the sheet and went to the window blinds, cringing as the floor boards creaked beneath me. I peeked between the blinds and there stood Cabe, on the porch roof, shirtless and in his boxers.

The ancient old window probably hadn't been opened since I lived in this room, and I began to think it wasn't going to budge at all and we might have to remove the A/C unit from the other window instead. Finally with Cabe working one side and me on the other, we got it open.

"What are you doing?" I whispered as he climbed through the window and inside my room. I threw both arms around him and pressed myself against his bare chest, feeling the humidity of the night air on his skin.

He tilted my head back and took possession of my mouth, his other hand lifting the back of my T-shirt and pulling me tight against his hips. I slid my foot up his calf, looping my own leg around his. The fire between us ignited it so quickly I wanted to climb up his body and wrap myself completely around him.

We inched our way back to my bed, pausing slightly when the boards creaked, but never parting lips. I fell backward across the bed with his full weight on top of me, his kiss overtaking me as his hands roamed and plundered with a fevered urgency. The bed groaned as we moved, and I pushed against his arms and separated my mouth from his.

"Turn on the air," I said, motioning toward the window. "It'll drown out the bed springs."

"Are you speaking from experience?" He lifted one brow and tilted his head to the side.

I laughed softly. "No, just using common sense."

He lifted off me and went to the window, and he'd no sooner gone than my body ached to feel his weight against me again. I parted my legs as he lay down, wrapping my ankles around his hips and pulling his mouth back to mine. I ran my fingers into his hair and mussed it, fluffing it out. He'd kept it slicked back since we got here and I longed to see those curls wild around his face again.

Cabe tore away from my mouth but his lips never left my skin. He made his way along my jawline and down my neck, leaving hungry kisses and sucking just enough to make my blood pulse hard beneath the surface.

"Don't you dare leave a mark, Cabe Shaw. My mama will whip your ass," I whispered, arching my back as he lingered across my collarbone and dipped lower.

A slow creak whined in the hallway outside my door, and I grabbed Cabe's head with both hands and held him still. He looked up at me from my navel and grinned.

I motioned for him to be quiet and strained to hear any further sounds from the hallway. My breaths were coming so fast I was basically panting, and I struggled to quiet my breathing so I could hear.

Cabe laid his head on my stomach and waited in the silence with me as I twisted his hair around my fingers. After a few minutes, he lifted his head and propped his chin on his hands across my ribs.

"Think the coast is clear?" he whispered.

I shrugged and turned my head toward the door, praying I wouldn't hear anything else. I really wanted to get back to where we'd been headed before.

He slowly crawled up my body quiet as a mouse, pausing to give me tiny feather-kisses as he made his way to my lips again. He rolled to his side and I stretched against him, tucking my knee between his knees and nestling my head underneath his chin.

"You're extraordinary," he whispered as he kissed the top of my head so softly I could only feel the wind of his breath against my hair.

"What? Why do you say that?"

He pulled me closer to him and moved his lips to my ear to keep his volume as low as possible.

"I can't even explain what I feel for you after this weekend," he said. "I feel like I've seen a new side of you. I thought I knew you so well, but here's this whole other aspect I never saw. It's expanded my view, and I'm even more fascinated than I was before."

"Wow. Why?"

He traced a figure eight on my back over and over again with his fingers while he talked, sending a series of chills that resulted in tiny muscle contractions rolling over my body.

"I've heard you say several times that you don't want to be average. Ordinary. And you don't see that there's nothing at all ordinary about you. I see this place, where you came from, and I see the way you interact with your family, and my heart is full. Your family is sweet. Crazy. Bizarre. But warm-hearted. Entertaining, for sure."

"Sounds like you nailed them." I chuckled and buried my face deeper into his neck, breathing in his cologne and enjoying the rumble of his voice against my cheek.

"You're like the best parts of all of them, wrapped up in a beautiful package. You can fit in here in the woods and the rural environment, but you also fit in with the most exclusive clientele at the Ritz Carlton. When we're with Dean and my buddies, you can hang with the best of the boys, yet you are feminine and soft and every bit a lady."

His hands ventured further down my back with their figure eight, and I pulled my knee up higher to get even closer to him as he talked.

"Your body drives me insane. I can't touch you enough, can't kiss you enough. Can't wait to bury myself inside you and find paradise. But at the same time, you're my best friend. My favorite hang-out buddy, and I feel completely at ease with you, no matter where we are. Your love and your support makes me feel like I can take on the world. So I just look at all that and think you're extraordinary. I'm the luckiest man alive, Tyler Warren."

"Did you, like, watch a cheesy movie after you went to bed or something?" I tilted my head back so I could meet his eyes. The love I saw there melted my insides and turned them to goo. He cupped the back of my head and pressed his lips to mine as he closed his eyes.

He held the kiss for an extended pause with no movement, no sound, and then he opened his eyes and parted from me to speak. "I know this sounds stupid when we're going home tomorrow, but I don't want to be away from you. What if we set your phone alarm and I'll get up and go back to the other room before anyone else wakes up?"

So that's what we did. We fell asleep intertwined in each other and we didn't move from that position the entire night.

My alarm vibrated at five o'clock, and Cabe stumbled back out the window and made his way across the porch to Carrie's room. My bed was lonely without him, but I was too tired to miss him long.

When I woke up, sunlight filled my room and I was shocked to see it was after nine.

I walked down the hall to Carrie's room, but the door was open and Cabe was nowhere in sight.

Mama's laughter rang out downstairs, and as I made my way down and across the kitchen, I followed the sound of voices to find her and Cabe sitting on the porch drinking coffee, Mama in her rocker and Cabe on the swing.

"Good morning, beautiful," Cabe said as I came to sit beside him. He kissed my cheek and nestled his nose in my hair, wrapping his arm around my shoulders as I intertwined my fingers in his.

"Morning, sugar. Want some coffee?" Mama asked. She stood and went inside to pour me a cup, and I smiled at Cabe as he leaned forward to kiss me.

"What time did you get up?" I asked.

"I couldn't go back to sleep without you," he said. "I watched some TV on mute upstairs, but then I heard your mom downstairs around seven-thirty, so I came down and we've been sitting out here talking. Waiting for the love of my life to awake. I was beginning to think I was going to have to come upstairs and rescue you with true love's kiss."

"Damn, I don't know if the country air is good for you. You're getting all sappy on me." I wrinkled my nose and winked at him.

We drank coffee with Mama and then ate breakfast with her and Brad before packing up our stuff and hitting the road.

The trip went much better than I had imagined it would. Amazingly, it somehow made Cabe and I even closer. More bonded. More deeply rooted in each other. Maybe I was wrong to dread the wedding so much. I forget sometimes what a romantic guy Cabe is. How could I have ever thought he would be okay without the pomp and circumstance?

Maybe it won't be so bad. Maybe Cabe and I will be able to enjoy planning. Researching together and deciding what we want for our wedding. We talked some details as we ticked off the miles on the way back home, and I honestly think I may be able to get excited about planning this wedding. We'll see.

Monday, July 14th

It's a damned good thing Deacon is so cute.

Cabe dropped me at my apartment when we got back in town and then he went home to Deacon. Dean had called on our way back to say he was leaving Cabe's house and would put Deacon in his crate.

I guess somehow he failed to latch it, though, because when Cabe got home after dropping me off, Deacon was running loose and Cabe's living room was destroyed.

I'm talking, it looked like an explosion had gone off.

He'd torn off huge chunks of the couch, scattering whatever pieces he didn't swallow all over the room.

The window blinds were completely destroyed and hanging in threads.

The mail left on the dining room table was shredded and partially ingested.

The couch toss pillows were annihilated. Nothing left but remnants of cloth and a few puffs of stuffing.

One leg of an end table looked like it had been attacked by a chain saw, and two dining room chairs were turned on their sides and dragged across the room. (Quite possibly to hide the broken lamp from said end table.)

I think it's safe to say Deacon has some separation anxiety.

I'm also thinking Dean will not be my first choice for dog sitting the next time we go out of town.

"Do you think he left Deacon by himself a lot this weekend?" I asked, trying to justify the dog's behavior in any way I could.

Cabe shook his head. "No. Dean slept here both nights, and I talked to him a couple of times Saturday. He hung out here all day, playing video games. I called him yesterday on our way home, and he was here until like three in the afternoon."

"So Deacon did all this in a few hours? Busy boy."

I walked amid the destruction dumbfounded. It was even worse than Cabe had described it on the phone. I could only imagine how he must have felt when he walked in last night after our trip and found his home in ruins. I'm sort of glad he dropped me off first and I didn't see it without time to mentally prepare.

"So I guess we'll be going furniture shopping sooner than we thought," Cabe said as he lifted what was left of a sofa cushion and tossed it in a trash bag.

"Well…" I started and then stopped. I don't know why I hesitated. I'd been thinking about it for days, and I knew it made sense to do. I mean, we're getting married. So obviously I'll be moving in here eventually. We spend almost every night together as it is, which is often a pain in deciding whose place to stay at and making sure we have clothes and whatever else we need at the right house. Not to mention carting Deacon back and forth between the apartment and Cabe's place, always worried someone is going to report me for having a dog in violation of my lease. So it made all the sense in the world for me to go ahead and move in here.

But giving up my apartment was hard. It was the last shred of independent life before I merged my decisions, my goals, and my life with another person. From here on out, Cabe and I would make our path together, taking each other into consideration on matters big and small. At my apartment, it was just me. I could do whatever I wanted. However I wanted.

Not that I thought Cabe wouldn't be on board with whatever I wanted to do in the future, but it's different when you need to consider someone else. I guess that's part of what makes marriage so hard. It's not all about you anymore. You have someone else's feelings, habits, likes and dislikes interfering with your own stuff. And if you love them, and you want it to work, you kind of have to be open to compromise and taking their wants and needs to heart.

Whew.

I took another deep breath as I surveyed the damage and weighed the next step in the commitment I'd already made. It wasn't like I had any intention of backing out of that commitment. Hell, with every passing day I was even more sure I wanted to marry Cabe. The sooner, the better. It wasn't like I didn't already take his wants and needs into consideration when making decisions, or that I didn't feel certain he did the same for me.

So why was giving up my place so hard? Was that my "all-in"? Was giving up my apartment the last stumbling block in me being completely onboard with becoming one with Cabe?

I watched him move among the remnants of his living space and pick through the scraps, determining what was trash and what could be salvaged. Deacon sat by the door, tongue wagging without a care in the world. If anything, he looked proud of his accomplishments. Like, *hey, look guys! Look what I did! Isn't it awesome?*

Cabe absentmindedly reached to pet Deacon as he walked past him with the full garbage bag and a bent lampshade.

I smiled at Cabe's ability to roll with the flow. To go with whatever the situation was. Whether that was a room full of wedding industry people fawning over table linens, an animal shelter with us knee-deep in suds and mud, a house full of people quizzing him about his past and his future intentions, or an expensive lesson in dog ownership.

We'd have times where we didn't agree. I knew that. We'd have days when what I wanted didn't align with what he wanted or what we'd envisioned didn't match up. But this was my guy. My future. My life. I had no doubts. It was time to go the distance.

"Well, what?" Cabe asked when I didn't continue my sentence.

"I was gonna say that my lease is up at the end of August. I have to give thirty days' notice if I'm not renewing. So I was thinking maybe I'd just go ahead and move in here. We could use my furniture for the time being. Take our time shopping for new stuff so we can make sure we get something we want."

He turned and smiled at me, the grin on his face lifting my heart and swelling it to near bursting. He dropped the trash bag and the lamp shade at his feet and rushed to me, picking me up in a big bear hug. I jumped and put my legs around his waist and he twirled me around until we both got dizzy.

"When? Tonight? Wanna move in tonight?" He held me effortlessly with his hands tucked under my rump and my legs circled tight around him. I pushed his hair behind his ears and kissed him, first his forehead and then his soft lips.

"I'm thinking I might need a little time to pack." I slid down him and he kissed me again, this time only lifting me a few inches off the ground before setting me down and releasing me.

"Okay," he said, his enthusiasm like that of a kid who's just gotten a new toy. "Let's *do* this. Tell me what I need to do to help you."

I laughed with a mixture of joy and nervous apprehension. I dreaded packing up everything, moving and unpacking. I wished I could just cross my arms and blink hard and magically transport my stuff like a genie.

We finished the clean-up and stared at the aftermath. A ruined sofa with no cushions and one end gnawed. One end table destroyed and no lamp for the living room now. One dining room chair with a rickety leg, and another that had more chew marks than we'd first realized.

"You wanted a dog," Cabe said with a sigh.

"You picked him," I replied with a grin.

"Let's sleep at your place tomorrow night. We can get started packing."

So here we go. Full commitment commencing now.

Wednesday, July 16th

It has begun.

Mama called today three times in a twenty-minute period. I try not to answer her calls at work because I never know what kind of tangent she's gonna go off on, or what kind of mood she's gonna put me in, but the frequency conveyed an urgency I thought I shouldn't ignore.

"Hey Mama. What's up?"

"I'm at the outlet mall and I found baskets on sale sixty percent off."

For this she called me three times in twenty minutes?

"Okay. Why are you telling me this?"

"We've got a wedding to plan, honey. You can always use baskets. We could do baskets for centerpieces. We could have a basket on a table for when people bring cards. You could have a basket for your rice."

"I'm not doing rice, Mama. It's bad for the environment, and it hurts when you get pelted with it."

"Well, then a basket for birdseed or whatever you're gonna do."

I sighed. "I don't know if I'm going to do anything like that. I think it's overdone. I kind of just want us to leave without all the hooplah."

"That's ridiculous. People want to throw rice. Or birdseed. Or something. It makes 'em happy."

"Does it really? Make them happy? Or is just a pain in the butt to get everyone lined up and make sure they have whatever they're supposed to throw and then hope the photographer gets a shot without your eyes closed or someone's arm in front of your face?"

Long pause.

"I'm gonna buy twenty baskets. Do you think that's enough?"

"What kind of baskets are they? I don't need twenty baskets. I don't know if I need any baskets. Just hold off."

"If I hold off, they may not have them when you want them. It's an *outlet*, Tyler. Close-out."

"I don't think we need baskets, Mama."

"What about taper candles? They've got boxes of white unscented taper candles ten for a dollar. Ten candles, not ten boxes. Want me to get those? How many? Fifty? A hundred?"

My pulse began to pound at my right temple.

"We don't even have a guest count yet, Mama. I don't know how many people, how many tables. Just don't buy anything. Wait until we've made some decisions and I have a better idea of what we're doing." *Or better yet, don't do anything at all and let me handle it.* I wanted to say that so bad, but I refrained.

"Okay, but you wait until the last minute to do all this and you're going to have to settle for what's left. I may go ahead and get these candles. If you don't use them, I can give them to the church. I was in the craft store yesterday and they've got satin on sale. We could get your cousin Wanda to whip up some bridesmaid dresses if you pick a color. She's such a good seamstress. You can't tell her stitches from Pete when it comes to store-bought."

My mind blanched at the thought of satin bridesmaid dresses at the same time it analyzed where that saying came from. Who was Pete and why on earth is he referenced in conversation?

"I gotta get back to work. I'll let you know as soon as we make decisions. Don't buy anything yet, okay?"

She called again an hour later. I knew it would do no good not to answer it; she'd just keep calling until I did.

"Yes, Mama?"

"They have nice silk flower stalks dirt cheap. Want me to buy a bunch and me and Pearl could make centerpieces? We could put them in the baskets."

Both temples were pounding now, so hard it hurt my head for her to talk.

"I think we'll probably go with fresh floral, but thanks. Don't buy anything."

"Fresh floral? Good Lord, child. Did you win the lottery? You keep in mind we don't have the kind of budget those brides you work with have. We need to be cost-effective. I may go ahead and buy some of these silks. I mean, they're on clearance. You'll use them somewhere."

The train had left the station, and it was dragging me unwillingly behind it. I rubbed my forehead and squinted to shut out the light.

"I don't want any silk flowers. Do not buy any silk flowers."

"You'd like these. They're high quality."

"I gotta go. I'll let you know once we've made decisions. Don't. Buy. Anything."

Friday, July 18th

We all cringe when we get a groom doing the planning. More often than not, a man planning his own wedding is controlling, nit-picky, hard to please, and more than a tad bit anal.

It certainly rings true with Richard.

I don't get what Laramie sees in him. He has vetoed her choice of colors, every song she's suggested, and her ideas for the menu. He picked her dress and ordered it online, and he chose the photographer, the DJ, and the flowers.

Most of his decisions were strictly budget-based, and if it came down to a choice between items, the cheaper one won out almost every time.

He's not rude, and he's not unpleasant on the phone.

But it's his way or no way. Every time.

Which I guess must work for them, since she never protests his decisions and she agreed to marry him.

I watched Laramie tonight at the rehearsal. I looked for any signs of fear. Of regret. Of whether or not she doubted the union. I didn't see any, so if she has them, they're well-hidden.

All I can say is, I would probably kill that man in his sleep if I had to live with him.

"As we've been planning this and I've pictured this moment in my mind," Richard said as we stood in the sand beside the lake rehearsing their ceremony, "I always thought her veil and her hair would blow that direction, away from her face. I always pictured her veil trailing out from her to make for a great picture with the lake and the palm trees in the background. But this is all wrong." He pointed to Laramie's face.

The wind was blowing from behind her, a none too gentle breeze in the afternoon heat and an indicator that our customary afternoon thunderstorm was fast approaching. Her long, brown hair whipped around her face, covering most of her delicate features and forcing her to close her eyes.

"This won't do," Richard said. "You can't even see her. She can't open her eyes. Will it be like this tomorrow?"

I stared at him and swallowed every sarcastic response that came to mind. Was he actually asking me to predict the wind twenty-four hours from now?

"All I can tell you is the forecast for tomorrow is only a twenty-percent chance of precipitation, which is good. As I explained, here in Central Florida, we are tropical enough to contend with the daily afternoon storms, but we've planned your ceremony later in the evening to hopefully avoid that."

"But what about the wind? Is it going to blow the wrong way?"

I bit my tongue again. "Richard, I can't say what the wind will do tomorrow afternoon."

"Well, you've done weddings here before, right? I mean, you guys set up the ceremony in this spot, so I'm assuming this is where it typically happens. What does the wind do? I find it hard to believe you've never had someone complain if the bride's veil covers her faces in photos."

Surprisingly enough, in the myriad of complaints that people issue regarding weddings, I had never heard from one of my clients or through any of my colleagues about a veil complaint due to wind. I think most people are intelligent enough to know that no one can predict or control the flippin' wind. I tried to figure out a way to say this to Richard without sounding condescending.

"This is the ceremony site, yes, but the wind is different each day depending on weather patterns. And no, I have not had that complaint."

"Well, isn't there someone you could call? Like a weatherman or something?"

He wasn't getting it.

"Richard, the wind depends on a number of variables. I think they can predict which general direction the wind will come from due to fronts and barometric pressure and other weather stuff. But I don't think they can say what direction a breeze will blow between seven and seven-thirty tomorrow."

He put his hands on his hips and scanned the lake. "This is ridiculous. We've spent all this money and planned for all this time, and you never thought to mention that this could be a problem?"

"I don't see where there's a problem. The wind may or may not blow in several directions during your ceremony."

"I thought the whole reason we hired a planner was so the event would be planned down to the very last detail and there wouldn't be any unpleasant surprises." He crossed his arms and widened his stance in the sand.

I looked at Laramie, who was watching us both now that the breeze had changed directions. I searched her face for any inkling that she knew her fiancé was an insane jackass. Nothing. She stared blankly at him. I began to think maybe she was hypnotized or under some form of mind control.

"Richard, we have planned your itinerary to take into consideration a wide variety of circumstances, including rain or inclement weather. The direction of an afternoon breeze is beyond the scope of our planning." I tried to say it politely. I don't think I succeeded.

Marriage is a lifetime commitment. Why on earth would someone willingly sign up to partner with him for life?

I normally pray for no rain on wedding days. I guess tomorrow I need to pray for no wind as well.

Saturday, July 19th

Well, the wind cooperated today, which is more than I can say for Richard.

He micromanaged every detail of every aspect of the wedding. Standing over everyone's shoulder and counting each penny as it floated out of his pocket. And I mean the shoulder part literally. He watched over the bartender's shoulder for about twenty minutes after he disputed the amount of the pours.

He kept asking to see the photographer's photo count so he would know how many pictures were being taken per hour. He even counted the number of cake slices the catering staff cut to ensure he'd been given the correct amount of cake by the bakery and that the staff was serving it correctly to optimize the number of servings.

I don't know how he could have possibly enjoyed anything at the event. He was too busy auditing it and worrying about whether or not he got his money's worth. I never saw him and Laramie standing together talking and laughing with guests, enjoying their day. Other than the first dance and the last dance, I never saw them together on the dance floor. In fact, I didn't see them together very often at all.

Laramie seemed to enjoy herself, though, and if she was concerned about his behavior, she never let on. I guess she knows how he is. She willingly signed up for this journey, after all.

It was exhausting for me, though. Me and everyone else working the event. It was like being under a microscope. Like we were being inspected and scrutinized every minute.

I would rather not even have a wedding than to have one and be so paranoid about every penny spent that I couldn't enjoy myself.

I feel like every wedding I've been doing since I got promoted has been bare bones budgets. It makes sense. The larger weddings with the deeper pockets are going to the more experienced planners with more seniority. I get that. But it sucks. I want a budget I can play with. I want to go over the top and plan extravagant things. With someone else's money, of course. Not mine.

Cabe and I have been talking budget, head count, and some details. So far, we seem to be in agreement on what is reasonable, which is nice. Neither of us wants to go overboard and spend a bunch of money on stuff that isn't necessary, but I also want to go in with the mindset that whatever we spend, we spend without obsessing over it.

What's the point of having a wedding if you don't enjoy it?

Sunday, July 20th

My family must have made a big impression on Cabe. He's mentioned them at random times throughout the week.

"Where did they come up with these names? Zula? Zona?"

"I have no idea," I said. "Why?"

"Don't you think they're odd?"

I shrugged. "Coming from someone named Cable with a sister named Galen? Ha! You're one to talk. I guess I never really thought about them as odd. They're just my cousins' names. We've got a Zolon, too, but on my daddy's side. You didn't get to meet all them."

"Yeah, I noticed most people seemed to be your mom's family. Any reason?"

"Some of that's on me," I said. "I didn't call a bunch of people and tell 'em I was coming. But some of it is small-town politics. Who doesn't associate with who."

"I think it's awesome that so many people came to your aunt's just to see you and congratulate us. I've never had that many people related to me in one place at the same time. I don't think I even know that many relatives."

I laughed and propped my feet up on the dashboard in the sun as Cabe sped down the highway toward the beach. "Yeah, I guess. But most of those people would have come to Aunt Clem's for any reason, not just because I was there. Plus, you were big news. Everybody was curious to see what you looked like and who I'd brought home. If it had been just me, the turnout might not have been so big."

"Why does Aunt Clem call you 'honey-girl'?"

"When we were kids, we went to Aunt Clem's every Sunday after church and spent the day. It was always a huge crowd, people coming in and out.

The adults took up all available space in the house, so us kids would run around in the woods all day or play in the yard. Aunt Clem had bee houses set up back behind her barn, and I was notorious for sneaking back there and stealing honey. I loved the stuff. Couldn't get enough of it."

"You stole honey from the bees? Didn't they sting you?"

I shook my head with my chin held high with pride and defiance. "Nope. I was the only one who never got stung. I could walk up and pull out a rack of honey and eat my fill. They'd swarm a little, but they never bit me. I even got honey from a wild hive once when I was thirteen. Climbed up a tree and got me a snack. Daddy always said my blood was too sweet for the bees. Aunt Clem said it was a gift, and she called me honey-girl."

My heart smiled at the memories. A strong longing for home clutched at my chest and tears sprang to my eyes.

"I wish you could have known my daddy."

Cabe switched hands on the steering wheel so he could reach and take my hand in his. "Me too, babe. I would love to have met him."

I swiped at the tears and swallowed the lump in my throat, remembering Daddy's laughter and the strength of his big bear hugs. I rarely let my mind focus on his memories, knowing that when I do, it can send me in a funk that lasts for days. But riding to the beach on such a sunny day with Cabe by my side and the sunroof open made me feel like it was safe to let Daddy creep into my thoughts.

I told Cabe about our fishing trips, and how Daddy always laughed at me because I loved to catch the fish but couldn't stand to touch them and get them off the hook. Or how he tried to take me duck hunting, but since I couldn't be still or quiet, I scared all the ducks away. So Daddy started calling it our early-morning-sit-in-the-woods instead of hunting.

We laughed about the mule dragging Daddy across the yard when his foot got tangled in the rope, and I sent Cabe into fits of laughter describing Daddy's multiple failed attempts at teaching me how to shift a standard transmission.

By the time we'd reached the beach, my heart was as warm as the sand beneath my feet, and I could feel Daddy's presence surrounding me. I really should talk about him more. Set him free every now and then.

Monday, July 21st

I think the wedding gods were listening to my plea, and they've granted my wish to have a huge budget wedding to play with.

Laura called me into her office as soon as I got into work today. If I get called in by one of my bosses, I'd always rather it be Laura, but it still makes me a bit nervous. Even when I know I haven't done anything wrong. It's kind of like that 'called to the principal's office' feeling in your gut.

"As you know, part of your promotion to a senior planner involved an internship with another company to expand your experiences and help you gain new practices. I was at a social event this weekend and bumped into Reynalda Riley, and she mentioned she has a large event coming up and is short-handed."

I sat up a little straighter in my chair. When I'd offered to intern as a solution to my lack of experience outside our company, I figured it would be with one of the other planners in town that we normally conversed with. I never dreamed it would be with Reynalda Riley.

She's probably the most well-known planner in Florida. One of the best known in the Southeastern US. If anyone getting married is even remotely statused as a celebrity in these parts, Reynalda does their wedding. Lillian says it's not because she's a great planner, but she's a master at self-promotion.

Reynalda has made the cover of pretty much every wedding-related or event-related magazine. She's consistently quoted as an expert on weddings in various magazines and newspapers across the country—not just in Florida. Her television appearances and radio interviews have grown too numerous to count, and she is a permanent fixture at any cocktail gathering or party of note in Orlando.

To be assigned to intern with Reynalda was a pretty big deal, and a little tingle of excitement fluttered in my belly at the prospect.

"It's pretty close in," Laura explained. "I would imagine most of the planning has been done, but she'd love to meet with you and answer any questions you may have, and then you would be onboard for any remaining planning sessions or meetings with this event and to help out the weekend of."

"Whose wedding is it?" I asked and then immediately stammered a recovery so I didn't look starstruck. "I mean, I'm just wondering the scope of the event and how involved it might be, that's all. It doesn't matter whose it is."

"Some hip-hop star? Marrying a swimsuit model, I think? Not anything that's on my playlist so I couldn't tell you for sure, but here's her cell if you want to call and set up an initial meeting."

I went back to my office and dialed her number with a little more gusto than necessary, all the while telling myself to play it cool and not act like a groupie.

"Reynalda Riley." She answered the phone with her name only. No hello. No how can I help you. Just a clear statement of who I'd reached.

"Um, hi, Reynalda? This is Tyler Warren with Lillian & Laura? Laura asked me to give you a call to set up a meeting about interning there for one of your events?" I couldn't believe how nervous I felt. I'd turned every sentence into a question without meaning to.

"Let me get my assistant."

She placed me on hold without any sign that she knew what I was talking about. I wondered if maybe Laura had misunderstood.

"This is Heidi. Tyler, right?" A much younger voice came on the line, and relief lowered my shoulders a bit when she actually knew my name without me telling her.

"Yes, Laura told me to call about interning an event?"

"Right. Can you be here tomorrow at nine o'clock to meet with Reynalda?"

I checked my calendar and mentally went through my wardrobe at home to figure out what was clean and presentable for a meeting with Reynalda Riley.

"Sure. How long should I plan to be there?"

"Block out an hour. Do you know the address?"

I dutifully wrote it down as she said it, but I already knew the address. Everyone in the industry knew the address. Reynalda's office was located inside the Ritz Carlton. I wasn't sure how exactly she'd scored that coup since she wasn't a Ritz employee, but it certainly helped her get the majority of their wedding clientele.

I walked to Laura's office to update her. "I set up a meeting with Reynalda for nine in the morning."

"Into the den of vipers they sent her," Lillian called out from her office adjacent to Laura's. I leaned around the door frame and peeked in.

"I'm sorry, were you talking to me?"

Lillian removed her glasses from their perch on her nose and sat back in her chair, crossing her hands in her lap and grinning quite the sinister smile.

"You have no idea what you're in for. I told Laura she'd lost her mind sending you over to that twit."

Lillian never spoke favorably of Reynalda.

"Calm down over there!" Laura yelled.

"Agggh. She's a media whore, nothing more. Couldn't plan her way through a covered bridge in broad daylight. She chews up people and spits them out. Has no use for them if they don't serve her purposes, and uses them up if they do. If the purpose of this folly is for you to learn, I'm not sure the lessons you get there will be of much benefit to you or us."

"Now, now. Let's not put notions in Tyler's head," Laura answered from her own desk. "Let her meet Reynalda and come to her own conclusions. Her work style notwithstanding, she does book complex events, and I think Tyler could learn a lot with the right frame of mind."

"Ha. She surrounds herself with the best vendors money can buy. Those events have nothing to do with her, and everything to do with the people holding her up."

"That in itself is a lesson. Let's just see what Tyler does with this, shall we?"

Lillian rolled her eyes and winked at me as Laura spoke, then she returned her glasses to their perch and waved me out.

I don't know what they've gotten me into, but I can't see why I wouldn't enjoy working on a wedding that's not counting how many servings of cake get handed out.

Tuesday, July 22nd

I got up an extra hour early so I wouldn't be stressed out before the meeting, but after changing clothes twenty times, I ended up barely making it out the door on time.

I wanted something that said professional without being dowdy. Fashionable without being trendy. Modern without being pretentious. Nothing in my closet seemed to make all those statements.

Traffic was a little heavier than I expected, and by the time I pulled into valet at the Ritz and got directions to her office, it was nine o'clock on the dot without a minute to spare.

The door was closed and locked with no lights visible through the glass panel. I checked my watch and my phone in case I'd screwed up the time, but both confirmed it was nine.

It was clearly the right location. Hers was the only office in the narrow hallway off a small courtyard on the side of the convention center. The glass panel was etched with her double "R" insignia with her name below the design in a scrawling cursive. Two lush armchairs sat in the hallway just outside the door with a stack of magazines on the table between the chairs. Reynalda stared at me from the covers.

When fifteen minutes had passed with no sign of anyone, I began to worry that I had misunderstood where to meet. I checked the address I'd written down, which was clearly the Ritz.

I gave it another five minutes and called Reynalda's number, which went straight to voice mail.

When a half hour had passed, I stood and walked to the end of the hallway, trying to decide what to do. Should I just leave? Should I ask at the convention services office or front desk if they knew her whereabouts? I opted to go to the restroom first and make decisions if no one was there when I returned.

The light was on when I got back so I opened the door and went inside. It wasn't an office space in the traditional sense. It had originally been conference space. A nice area for a breakfast room or a small breakout lunch. The ceilings were low but lit with two exquisite chandeliers. The back wall was filled with windows overlooking manicured gardens and the lake with its massive spray fountain beyond the grass. The rich tapestry walls in soft peach tones were complimented by the upholstered sofas and chairs she had placed in a vignette to the right of the entrance. Two large mahogany desks dominated the nearest half of the room with copy machines and file cabinets lining the walls on either side. An ornate double screen in mahogany had been erected behind the desks, and through the design I could see another desk banked against the windows.

A young girl—well, younger than me—emerged from behind the screen and greeted me. She wore a pale pink skirt with a snug white sweater, which looked great on her petite frame, whereas on me it would have looked like it didn't fit.

"You must be Tyler," she said, extending her hand in greeting. "I'm making coffee if you'd like some. Reynalda will be here shortly."

"Yes, coffee would be great. I'm sorry. I thought I was supposed to be here at nine?" I glanced down at my watch. It was nine-forty.

"Yeah, nine. Reynalda's just running a couple minutes late. She'll be here soon." The girl I assumed was Heidi turned and went through a door I hadn't noticed before. The telltale red soles on the bottom of her nude pumps shone like a beacon as she walked away, and I immediately had shoe envy.

I took a seat on the nearest sofa for lack of anything better to do and wondered if I'd stepped into some weird alternate time zone. Since when was forty minutes late considered a couple of minutes? Lillian would have had my head on the chopping block if I'd been forty minutes late to a meeting. And with no apology? No explanation? No call to let me know she was on her way? My first impression wasn't a good one, and I hadn't even met her yet.

It was almost ten when Reynalda finally glided into the room.

Her perfume preceded her entrance. It was heavy and floral, and it stung my eyes and burned my nostrils.

She was hardly a size zero. I don't know if they make negative sizes, but if they did, that's what she'd wear. Even though she was tiny, she had curves, and her crimson red wrap dress hugged every one of them in all the right places. She wore strappy stilettos that I recognized as Jimmy Choo, and she carried several designer shopping bags in both hands.

She didn't make eye contact with me or greet me in any way, despite my obvious presence in the room. Instead, she breezed past me and continued behind the mahogany screen, depositing her packages on the floor with a huff.

"Heidi!" she yelled. "Do something with these bags."

I could see Reynalda through the carved design on the screen, rummaging through papers on her desk.

The girl came out and scooped up the bags, taking them with her back into the other room.

"Heidi!" Reynalda yelled again. "Who's here?"

Heidi reemerged and disappeared behind the screen, still visible, as was Reynalda.

"That's Tyler Warren. Your nine o'clock. She's here about interning the wedding."

"Right. Okay. Tell her I'll be a minute."

Was she actually under some delusion that I couldn't hear every word she was saying? We were in the *same room*. Separated only by a piece of wood with holes in it. I could *see* her.

Heidi leaned out from behind the screen and gave me a smile. "Reynalda will be right with you."

I nodded at her before she disappeared again and I turned my attention back to watching Reynalda behind the screen. She went and looked out the window for a few minutes. She rummaged through paperwork again. She popped open a compact mirror and checked her hair and makeup. Reapplied the blood-red lipstick on her obviously injected pout.

It actually seemed like she was stalling to meet me, though for what purpose I have no idea.

When she finally told Heidi to show me in, the hour I'd blocked out for the meeting had already passed and then some.

I followed Heidi behind the screen, more than a little irritated and under-impressed. Reynalda stood by the window turned at an odd angle which suggested she'd posed in just that spot awaiting my arrival.

"Tyler, this is Reynalda Riley," Heidi said in what may as well have been a pre-recorded message for all the pomp it conveyed.

Reynalda turned slightly and appeared startled, as though she hadn't realized she had company and was surprised to see us standing there. "Oh, well hello, Tyler. Welcome, welcome." She extended her hand, but it was turned over. I don't know if she expected me to kiss it, but I grabbed hold and shook it anyway.

"Sit, sit." She indicated the upholstered zebra print fur chairs across from her desk, which clashed so badly with the muted and elegant surroundings that they almost seemed a joke.

"So how long have you been with Lillian and Laura?" she asked as she sat on the edge of her huge desk, one leg braced against the floor on her Jimmy Choos and the other slender leg swinging slowly back and forth in a contrived movement that in no way looked casual or without effort.

I got the feeling everything this woman did was calculated for the effect it would have, and I had to wonder what she was like when she was all alone with no one to watch her.

"Going on four years now."

She crossed her arms and tapped a long manicured finger against her sleeve. "So. What brings you to my door? Why would you want to intern if you've already been doing weddings for four years?"

Her stare was so direct and so bold that I found it hard to maintain eye contact. Her make-up was impeccable. She must have someone do it for her. Her eyelashes were gargantuan. A long, thick black fringe framing her dark chocolate eyes. Her hair tumbled in waves around her shoulders but was pulled up away from her face in a small hive atop her head. Probably one of those bun things you see on TV. Her hair was almost the same color as her eyes, a rich, dark brown with subtle hints of auburn. I guessed her to be mid-thirties, but she obviously went to great lengths in self-care so it's possible she was older.

I kind of thought Laura would have already explained to her what we were trying to accomplish, but based on her question, I guess not.

"I've recently been promoted, and I wanted to visit other event planning companies to expand my knowledge base."

Reynalda didn't reply. She just stared at me through those ginormous lashes.

Heidi came in with coffee and handed us both a cup. Reynalda stood as she took hers and went behind her desk to sit.

I noticed the zebra chairs were a little lower than her desk chair, so that even though she was a petite lady, she still appeared taller than me as we looked across the desk at each other.

"Have you ever heard of a yard sale?"

The question caught me off guard. What the hell did that have to do with anything?

"Um, yes. I have."

"So in theory, people take stuff out of their homes they no longer want, and set up a shop in their driveway to sell it?"

I'm sure my expression betrayed my bewilderment. "Yes, that's basically how it works."

"People buy it, though? They actually come into someone's driveway, rummage through their castoffs, and then hand them cash for it?"

I nodded.

"How crude. So how much money could be made?"

I scrunched my brows together in confusion and uncertainty. "I'm not sure. I suppose that depends on what was being sold."

"My housekeeper tells me she and her sister are having a yard sale this weekend to help pay for her daughter's wedding. Is this something people do?"

My brows scrunched tighter. "I don't know. I haven't heard of it, but I guess they could? Again, it would depend on what they had to sell."

I couldn't for the life of me imagine how on earth this pertained to the event I was supposed to help with. Were some hip-hop star and his swimsuit model going to have a yard sale to pay for their event? For real?

"Heidi? Ring the usual list of media and tell them I have an idea for an article. Then research yard sales and get me some statistics on how many happen annually and what income they generate. See if you can find anyone who has actually done this to pay for a wedding and get me a quote. I'd like to see this in an issue somewhere next month to get publicity before the Woodcock wedding, so get on it pronto. Bring me the file for Donaldson."

I heard the file cabinet open and close as Reynalda stared at me over her coffee cup.

"Here you go." Heidi placed a thick binder on the desk in front of Reynalda, who set down the cup and opened the binder. Paper-clipped to the inside was a manila folder of papers, which Reynalda handed to me.

"I'll keep the original file here, of course, but Heidi has already made copies of the most pertinent information you'll need. You're to meet with the clients on Friday at eleven. They'll expect an update from you on their vendor proposals, especially the floral orders. You'll need to get from them a definitive song list for the band and a payment method for the furniture rental. I also need you to come up with a projected timeline and itinerary for them to sign off on. Heidi can get you letterhead to print that on. Welcome aboard."

With that, she stood and walked away. No goodbye. No parting handshake. Not a single sentence of discussion about the wedding, the clients, what my role would be, or how any of it pertained to a freakin' yard sale.

Now I have three days to memorize all I can in the limited details they copied for me and come up with updates from *her* vendors on *her* event with no prior knowledge of what's going on.

So needless to say, I told Cabe I wouldn't be packing tonight. Instead, I'll be studying the file and firing off emails while Cabe heads to Dean's for gaming. Oh lucky me.

Wednesday, July 23rd

This is ridiculous. Absolutely ridiculous.

The paperwork they gave me is minimal. Pretty much nothing has been done for this wedding, and now I've got to somehow pull a bunch of plans out of my rump in order to meet with the bride and groom on Friday and present myself as having my act together.

Is Reynalda Riley really this clueless or is she just malicious enough to compromise her own business to set me up to fail?

I've tried to call her several times today but her phone always goes straight to voice mail. How on earth does someone run a business without ever answering their phone? (Okay, come to think of it, Lillian does the same thing and seems to be successful, but whatever.)

Six messages on Reynalda's phone and three messages on the main company line later, I finally got a call back from Heidi as Cabe and I were on our way to dinner.

"Heidi? Thanks for calling me back. Look, there are several things that Reynalda wanted me to report on with the client on Friday that haven't been put in place yet. I've sent emails and made phone calls, but I'm waiting to hear back from vendors and I may not have what we need before Friday. I'm not sure what she wants me to do."

I heard Reynalda talking in the background as Heidi paused. "She said just do the best you can and be ready Friday."

"Oh, is Reynalda there? That's great. I've been trying to reach her all day."

Another pause, and distinct whispering in the background. "Reynalda has stepped out, but she said just do the best you can with what you have and send her an update Friday morning before the meeting."

My temper flared hot at the very idea that this woman would put me in such an impossible situation with *her* clients and refuse to talk to me. Then have someone lie to do so.

"Heidi, I can hear her talking. I know she's there. Can you please put her on the phone?"

Another long pause. My phone beeped its low battery warning. A quick glance showed me the battery had barely any red left, which meant my phone was about to die. Aargh.

"Heidi? Can you hear me? My phone's about to die, but I need to talk to Reynalda. I can't go in and meet with her clients without talking to her. Decisions need to be made. I need more information"—my phone beeped again—"so can you please put her on the phone?"

When they paused again, I couldn't hear any whispering in the background, and I thought my phone had died. I reached for Cabe's phone in the console between the seats but then heard Reynalda's voice in my ear.

"Tyler, hello! Sorry I haven't called you back. I had meetings and interviews back to back today and it's been brutal."

"Reynalda, hi. Look, my phone's about to die, but I really need to talk to you. Can I please call you right back from my fiancé's phone?"

"Actually, I need to run right now, but listen. I realize the file hasn't had much attention. We've been shorthanded here in the office, and Heidi and I haven't been able to focus on these clients, which is why I thought our arrangement would be perfect. Laura spoke so highly of you, and you mentioned your recent promotion. I know Lillian Graham would not promote anyone she didn't have full confidence in. So just take it and run with it. I'm sure any decision you make will be fine. We'll talk later."

"Wait! Reynalda! I need to talk to you with specific questions. Can I please call you back from my fiancé's phone? I'll be brief, but I need—"

"I've got to go. I'll see you at eleven on Friday."

"Wait—can we talk before then?"

Whether she hung up first or my phone died first I'll never know, but she was gone. I tried calling her number and the office number from Cabe's phone and got no answer at either.

"Ugh!" I growled, tempted to slam my phone into the dashboard but realizing that would do nothing to solve the problem and would only leave me without a phone. "What a bitch! How does she do business this way?"

"Have you talked to Laura? Can they do anything?" Cabe asked as we exited the car at the valet stand.

I shook my head. "I haven't. I spent all day trying to go over what each of the vendors sent to see what I could match up with the file. I swear they didn't give me everything. There has to be more in the file that I'm not seeing, but none of the vendors had complete profiles either. I don't know what I'm supposed to tell these people on Friday. Hi, I'm Tyler, and I have no information for you? Oh, and by the way, can you give me a credit card for the furniture order I've never seen?"

The seating hostess led us to a table right away, and Cabe asked her to bring me a glass of wine to tide me over until our server arrived. I didn't even pause in my rant.

"I thought this was going to be this great experience, ya know? Working such a high-profile wedding with such a high-profile planner. But from what I've seen so far, she's a joke." I accepted the glass of wine with a forced smile and drained it about halfway down. I wiped my mouth with the back of my hand as Cabe chuckled. All kind of ladylike manners on display tonight.

"Will she be there Friday?"

I nodded. "She said 'See you Friday' before she hung up."

"Then let her run it. You're not her employee. You're an intern. Sit in the meeting and keep your mouth shut unless she specifically asks you a question. Let her look unprepared to the client, not you."

"But I don't want to be unprepared at all! I want to have this all pulled together for them, and if she would just answer my questions I could probably get quite a bit done tomorrow. What reason could she possibly have not to take my calls?"

We placed our order and got a refill for my wine, but I couldn't let it go. I couldn't unwind and no matter how hard I tried, I couldn't stop thinking about it.

How terrible would it be if I told Laura I don't want this opportunity?

Thursday, July 24th

"Get done what you're able to do within the time frame you've been given, but I'd let her do the talking with the clients tomorrow. You've been sent there as an intern, not a workhorse," Melanie said as she waited for the microwave to beep.

I'd laid the whole thing out while we were all eating lunch in the break room.

"I'd suggest you be ready to talk to the clients. Even if Reynalda is in the meeting, you don't know what her input will be. If she's willing to drive it, let her. But if she turns and puts it in your lap, you want to be prepared," Laura offered.

"Mark my words," Lillian said as she pointed at me with her fork. "If Reynalda shows up, and I wouldn't even count on that, but if she shows up—probably with a camera crew—she'll just smile and you'll still be stuck doing the working part of the meeting. So don't plan on her lifting a finger. Protect yourself. Be prepared."

"I'd love to, but she gave me almost nothing to go on as far as what the clients want and what they've already discussed. I called the florist, the photographer, the band, and the catering manager at their hotel. None of them have spoken with the clients directly, and none of them have enough details to piece together proposals. And she won't give me the clients' contact info. She says she wants to wait and introduce me before I contact them." I poked my fork at my salad, really wishing I'd ordered a cheeseburger and fries instead. Greens might be the healthier choice, but they did nothing for my stress levels.

"Then you have a blank slate." Laura smiled. "Propose whatever you want. Take the few details you have and come up with ideas. If the clients like your ideas, great. If not, you'll have a basis to work with for them to tell you what they don't like and what they'd rather see."

"So her office is basically a banquet room?" Mel asked.

I nodded.

"She's *close* with the GM," Lillian said with a wink. "Take that however you'd like it and you'll probably be correct. That room's been taken out of the system and blocked for remodeling for two years now. She uses it rent-free. And the resort's internet, electricity, and power, too."

Mel whistled. "Dang. That's quite an arrangement."

Laura shook her head at Lillian, though I'm sure she knew after all these years the admonishment would do no good. "Let's not resort to gossip. Tyler has asked for help with the situation, and we need to stay focused on guidance."

"I'm not the one who sent her to sleep with the enemy." Lillian tilted her head with a smirk.

"Reynalda said she'd been shorthanded," I said. "Is it really just her and Heidi? I thought she would have a huge team of people."

"She recruits volunteers from the hospitality schools for the actual events. She describes it as her effort to give back to the community and help train the next generation of planners," Laura said.

Lillian slapped her hand lightly on the table. "She uses free labor because the woman has no money! She runs around all over town wearing Gucci and Prada. She jet sets all over the place and name-drops like crazy. Puts on airs like she's the Queen of Sheba, but she's flat broke." Lillian shook her head. "Bloody hell, she can't afford an office, much less a staff."

Mel piped in. "I thought she had a full-time coordinator, though. Mindy? Mitzi? What was her name?"

"Maritza," Laura answered.

Mel nodded. "Yeah, Maritza. That was it. What happened to her?"

Lillian placed both palms on the table and leaned forward. "She's been through seven coordinators and-or assistants in three years. No one wants to work for her."

"Heidi's been there almost a year," Mel said between bites. "That's who you should talk to. Get in with Heidi. She obviously knows what's up."

Laura sighed as she cleaned up her lunch area. "Ladies, I don't think this is really helping Tyler. Look, I didn't send you there to hang you out to dry. I sent you there because Reynalda asked for our help, and because we had already agreed you'd spend time with another planner. So it seemed to be a win-win. Now, I certainly don't want you mistreated, and I will not abide a client's wedding being mishandled, even if it's not our clients."

Lillian scoffed with a loud harrumph.

Laura ignored her and continued speaking. "I firmly believe we can learn something from every situation we're put in. So I suggest you do all you can for the clients, be prepared to the extent you're able with what's available to you, and look for every opportunity to learn. We may not agree with her tactics, but she has been in business for almost ten years. She maintains a roster of the highest level clientele. She's doing something well. Figure out what that is. Even if you're learning what not to do with your own clients, you're still learning."

I nodded, unsure of how to achieve what lay ahead of me but not wanting to fail in the task Laura had given me.

I left the kitchen in a bit of a funk but determined to be prepared for tomorrow. I spent the rest of the afternoon on the phone with vendors, constructing what I could of proposals without input from the clients.

At the end of the day, I do have something to present them tomorrow. Whether it's good enough or not remains to be seen, but at least I don't feel like I'm going in empty-handed.

Friday, July 25th

Mama called as I was on my way to meet Reynalda's clients. I didn't want my phone ringing off the hook in the meeting, so I went ahead and answered.

"Hey Mama. What's up? I'm heading to a meeting so I've only got a few minutes."

"How many people are you inviting to the wedding, and have y'all picked a date yet?"

"I don't know and no. Why? What's up?"

"Well, y'all need to decide. We can't do much of nothing 'til you know the answers to those two questions. That needs to be your top priority."

I groaned and tried not to scream. I had a meeting in fifteen minutes with high-profile clients I'd never met and a half-assed proposal I wasn't sure they would like. I had completely neglected my own brides for the past week dealing with Reynalda's lack of planning and jumping through hoops to try and get today settled. My wedding was all the way on the back burner as far as I was concerned.

"When Cabe and I make decisions, you'll be the first to know."

"I was talking to Marjorie last night, and I think you should seriously consider doing a double wedding with Marlena. Y'all could split the costs of the music and the flowers and any kind of decorations, and then each of y'all could pay for whatever your guests ate and drank. You could even use the same invitation and put both names on it. Everybody in our family would only need one invite for the both of you, so that would save you money right there. Marjorie said y'all could split the costs of our family members rather than both of y'all paying to feed them at separate events."

I seriously had no mental capacity to deal with my own wedding in that moment.

"Mama, I may have seen Marlena once in the past six years. We don't keep in touch. I can't imagine that we would have a lot in common or that we would have the same tastes. I appreciate your efforts, but I think we'll stick with separate weddings."

"That's the silliest thing I've ever heard. Who cares if y'all have seen each other or not? Y'all are cousins. Blood-related. You could have a much nicer wedding if you go in with her. Marjorie said Marlena is looking at a place that holds two hundred. You said Cabe ain't got much family, right?"

I pulled up to the guard shack at the clients' hotel and gave them my ID as I explained where I was going and who I was meeting.

"Are you talking to me? I can't hear you. What are you saying?" Mama's voice chattered away in my ear the whole time I conversed with the security guard. Like a buzzing mosquito you can't do anything about.

"I was getting a pass to go to a hotel, Mama. I wasn't talking to you. I gotta go. Please stop making plans. I will let you know once we're ready."

"Alright, but I'm gonna tell Marjorie you're getting your numbers together and not to count you out yet, okay?"

I saw Reynalda get out of her Mercedes at the valet and sped up to try and catch her before she went inside.

"Okay, I gotta go. Bye, Mama."

It wasn't until after I hung up that I realized I'd just told her okay, which I'm sure she took as an okay for telling Aunt Marjorie not to count me out. I'd have to correct that later, though, because right then I needed to catch Reynalda.

"Reynalda! Reynalda!" I stepped out of my car and snatched the valet tag from his hands. I cursed the cobblestone drive as I tried to run in my heels, yelling her name as I followed her inside.

The doorman held the door for me, and I knew she had to have heard me as close as we were, but she never turned around until we were both inside. She slid off her Prada shades and pushed them on top of her head.

"Tyler, you're making a scene. What is so urgent that you need to run around shouting like there's a fire?"

I gulped air and tried to catch my breath and restore some measure of dignity. "I need to talk to you before we go in. I have questions."

"Well, calm down and get yourself together while I let the reception desk know we're here."

I watched her sashay her way over to reception, her emerald green dress swishing back and forth in rhythm with her rump.

My frustration and stress of the week rolled into just being pissed. Why was I so freaked out and blowing up my blood pressure when she seemed so calm and collected? They were her clients. I'd never even met these people. I decided to take Cabe's advice. I'd just sit back in the meeting and let her do all the talking. If a question was asked and I didn't have an answer, then oh well. I'd done all I could do.

By the time she made her way back over to me, I had calmed down and assumed what I hoped was an air of cool indifference. I planned it all out and pictured it in my head. How she'd come walking back up and finally ask what my questions were after avoiding me for days, and I'd just casually say 'never mind' and then let her be the one with mud on her face when we got into the meeting and she had no idea what was going on.

But I forgot everything I'd learned so far about Reynalda Riley.

She never even asked what my questions were. She didn't care. She came walking up, adjusting her hair on her shoulders, and said, "You mentioned a fiancé on the phone. I didn't know you were engaged. Let me see your ring."

I lifted my hand and she took it in hers, twisting it from side to side to peer at my ring.

"Two carats?" she asked as she lifted my finger and squinted at the ring like she had to look hard to see it or something.

"I don't know. I didn't ask." From the rings I'd seen in my career, I'd agree it was about two carats, but it didn't matter to me what size it was, only who it was from. So I hadn't asked.

"What does he do for a living?" she asked without looking up from my ring.

"He's a program development manager. Computers."

"Oh," she said, releasing my hand and stepping back. "Then don't worry. He'll be able to upgrade it at some point. At least you're not like Heidi—dating the hired help."

The clients arrived before I could tell the smug bitch that I wasn't worried at all, nor did I need an upgrade.

She didn't even bother to introduce me until we'd been seated in the bar area set aside for our meeting. I tagged along behind them like a puppy dog, pissed at the situation, fed up with her pompousness, and wanting to just turn and walk away. But some little part of me wanted to see the look on her face when I left her hanging to run the meeting without the information she'd thrown in my lap to retrieve.

"So Chris, Jayah, this is Tyler," she turned to me with a flourish of her hand and flashed a smile larger than any I'd seen on her since we met. "Tyler is my right hand, and she will be handling all your planning meetings from here on out. Now, don't worry, because I will still be a phone call away if you need anything at all, but Tyler is more than capable of taking care of whatever you need. You can call her anytime, day or night, seven days a week and she'll be there for you." She patted Jayah's hand as I struggled to keep my mouth from flying open.

"Will you still be there on our wedding day?" Jayah asked, looking as nervous as any bride who's just been told a complete stranger will suddenly be taking over all their wedding plans with no warning at all.

"Oh girl," Reynalda playfully slapped at Jayah's hand. "I wouldn't miss it for the world! Are you kidding me? This is just the most effective way to make sure you have someone's undivided attention. My time is in such high demand, and I have to be in so many places, often all at once. I can't be everywhere. Tyler will handle all your details, which gives you full access whenever it's needed. But I'll be in constant contact with Tyler throughout the planning, and then I'll be there for your entire event."

Reynalda flashed another smile, and I resisted the urge to slap it off her face. How dare she set me up like that? I wasn't willing to be available seven days a week any time day or night for my own clients who were paying top dollar for my services. I was Reynalda's intern. Free labor. No way was I available around the clock. Plus, I had other brides. Other priorities. This bride would need to understand that.

But before I could argue the point or slap Reynalda silly, she stood and said, "Speaking of trying to be everywhere all at once, I have a ribbon cutting across town I must attend. So I'll leave you to it because I know Tyler has a lot to share with you. Ta-ta!"

She left.

She left me there with *her* clients knowing I didn't have everything they needed.

The two of them had visibly stiffened with her announcement, and it took every bit of charm I possess to get them to relax and talk to me.

The only reason I even tried was my deep belief that Laura was right. The clients were the top priority. It wasn't the clients' fault they had chosen Reynalda and gotten me. I resolved to do the best I could by them instead of focusing on plotting revenge against the media monster they'd hired.

Sunday, July 27th

We've been staying at my house pretty much every night since Deacon turned into Mr. Destructo at Cabe's. He went ahead and got rid of what was left of the couch, and he tossed the damaged dining room chairs and end tables since I have matched sets of both. So until I can get my crap all packed up and move everything to his place, it's more comfortable for us to be here.

Unfortunately, Deacon's not easy to hide. He barks, and he needs to be walked multiple times each day. So I knew it was only a matter of time before my management company said something about me having a dog on the premises.

When I got home from the wedding last night, there was a note on my door telling me I have to pony up a three-hundred dollar pet deposit or remove the dog.

Now, I'm obviously not going to pay a three-hundred dollar deposit when I'm in the process of packing up to move out. Nor am I going to send Cabe and Deacon home to an empty living room and dining room while I stay here alone.

Here I thought I had the whole month of August to take my time packing up and moving out without much stress, maybe purging some stuff and tossing what I don't need. But now the timeline's been moved up a bit.

I gotta move *now*.

Cabe rented a truck for him and Dean to take the big stuff next Saturday while he's off work, but I need to spend every spare minute this week packing and taking stuff over as I get it done.

The problem is I have no minutes to spare. On top of dealing with Reynalda's jacked-up wedding, I have my own brides who have been pushed aside the last couple of weeks and are now demanding my attention because of it. On top of that, August begins the build-up to the busy fall wedding season at work. Oh, and then there's the matter of my own wedding, which we have yet to even nail down a date for. Or location. Or any concrete details other than the color purple.

Oh happy happy joy joy.

Tuesday, July 29th

I took the boxes I'd packed over to Cabe's tonight, and after we unloaded them, we sat down to eat dinner. It started out as a normal, ordinary dinner. I'd just finished my salad and was savoring my first bite of Cabe's famous chicken fricassee.

"By the way, Monica called today," Cabe said, just as casually as he might have said *I bought ice cream for dessert.*

The chicken lost all its flavor and became a rubbery mass in my mouth. I attempted to swallow it, but it refused to go down. I coughed and tried to drown it down with water, but the lump in my throat remained.

"You okay?" Cabe asked, reaching over to pat me on the back.

I nodded, draining my water glass and staring at his back as he went to get me more.

"What did she want?" I hoped my voice sounded normal. Little tremors danced across my skin and flittered through my stomach. Monica. The woman he left me for. Yeah, I know. I told him to go, but that was because I thought it would make him happy. It was before I knew he was in love with me. Or that I was in love with him.

Cabe filled my water glass and sat back down. Was I imagining it, or was he avoiding eye contact with me?

"She's going to be in town next week. She wants to get the rest of her stuff."

Her stuff. The boxes of pictures, letters, and mementos the landlord sent to Cabe from Seattle when she couldn't find an address for Monica. The boxes I packed up to keep Cabe from slipping further into his depression. The night I held him as he cried himself to sleep under the weight of failure.

"So is she just going to go by your mom's and pick them up?" *Please say yes. Please say yes. Please say yes. Please don't tell me you're going to see her.*

"She wants to meet for dinner." Still no eye contact. I wasn't imagining it at all.

"What? Why?"

He shrugged.

"She wants to clear the air. Talk about what happened. We left things on pretty bad terms. I think maybe she wants to get some closure."

"Really. Maybe she should have thought about that before she walked out and left you for Kristen or whatever her name was." He looked away, and I realized even though it was directed at her, the comment struck him, which I hadn't intended.

Anger tightened my throat, making it hard to swallow. How dare she just call him up and ask him to dinner. Contact him out of the blue and expect anything from him after all this time. It wasn't fair to him.

Yeah, okay. Perhaps my feelings leaned a little more toward me feeling threatened and outraged than being concerned for him, but I didn't want to admit that at the time. Easier to think of myself as noble and caring. Putting him first.

"Babe, I think there's a lot that was left unsaid." He finally made eye contact as he spoke. "It would probably be a good idea to put it all on the table. I know I didn't do a great job at taking responsibility for my part in the marriage failing. I wasn't willing to admit what was really going on."

I was well aware he meant the part about him being in love with me the whole time he was with her, but somehow, that didn't make me feel any better about her dinner offer.

Cabe reached and took my hand. "I won't go if it bothers you. I'll tell her no, and I'll have her go by Mom's and get her stuff without me being there. All you have to do is say the word. But if you're okay with it, I do have a few things I'd like to say to her."

I stared back at him and fought the tears that tickled and burned at the back of my eyes. I blinked a couple of times, hoping they wouldn't fall and betray my turmoil.

On some level, I felt like it was petty and insecure on my part to tell him not to go. After all, not only had he already told me the marriage ended in part because he was in love with me and not her, but there was the little matter of the engagement ring on my finger that clearly said we were together now.

So why on earth should I feel threatened in any way by him having dinner with his ex-wife? (Wow. I don't think I've ever written that title for her before. It just went all over me as I wrote it. I don't want to think of Monica as his wife in any way whatsoever, not even ex. I know she was. That can't be changed. But it doesn't mean I have to like it. Or ever write it again.)

I guess my reaction was rooted in the knowledge that Monica was the only woman he ever felt strongly enough about to even consider leaving me. He had dated other girls over the years, but he never got serious. Not even close. Monica was different. Something in her appealed to him like no one else had. So even though he said their marriage failed because he was in love with me, I couldn't ignore the fact that he had severed all ties with me for her. He *married* her. Add to that the fact that in the end, *she* left *him*. He didn't leave her.

"Aw, Ty, you look like you're gonna cry. Don't cry. Please don't cry. I don't want you upset by this. Not at all. There is absolutely nothing for you to worry about. You have me, Ty. Heart and soul. Body and blood. I'm yours."

I nodded and attempted a smile. I think I managed a weak one of sorts. He returned the smile and continued to talk.

"I just feel like I wasn't fair to her, you know? It was easy for me to blame her for leaving, but she checked out because I wasn't checked in. I know I really struggled with the whole divorce thing. The sense of failure and what caused it, and I'm sure she did, too. I wasn't the only one affected. It was her life. Her marriage. Her marriage failed because of me. I didn't fulfill the vows I made to her. I feel like I owe her an admission at least. An apology, I guess."

"What am I supposed to say to that, Cabe? Obviously I don't want to tell you no. To keep you from doing what you feel like you should. How petty would that be? I know you love me. It's not like I think you're going to go to dinner and suddenly call off our engagement and go back to her." I'd been looking at our hands intertwined, but I looked up to meet his eyes then. "You're not, are you?"

A soft chuckle rumbled under his breath. "No, baby. I'm not. Not a chance." He lifted my hand and kissed it.

"I just don't like it, Cabe. I don't want her back in town. I don't want her anywhere near you. I don't want to even think about you being married to her, much less know that you're out to dinner with her discussing it all. I know I should be supportive and mature enough to say, '*Yeah, sure, no problem.*' But I'm a little freaked out right now."

"Come 'ere." He scooted his chair back and pulled me up and into his lap, putting both arms around me. I laid my cheek against his curls as he nestled his face into my neck.

"Tyler, how do you think I felt when you drove three hours to see Dweeb Dwayne? Your freshly-divorced, on-the-prowl ex-boyfriend who I'd watched you grieve over for years when we met. Years! I didn't have a promise of anything from you. Not even a hope of any kind of admission of your feelings for me. But I'm here telling you that I love you with everything in me, far beyond what I've ever felt for anyone else. You have absolutely nothing to fear."

I kissed the top of his head and sighed. "I know, and I appreciate you saying that. I know it wasn't easy for you when Dwayne and I were talking again, and I can see the similarities with getting closure. I just...well, I just don't like it."

He leaned back to look at me. "Then I won't go. Done. End of discussion. If it bothers you, I won't do it." He gently cradled the back of my head and pulled me toward him. Our lips met and held together, a quiet strength behind the physical connection.

I didn't want him to go.

It wasn't that I didn't trust him or that I thought he'd go back to her. I just didn't want him to go. But I also didn't want to be *that girl*. I didn't want to be the reason he didn't go. I wanted to be the reason he came back home, for sure. But not the reason he couldn't go. I pulled away from his kiss, but only far enough to speak, our noses and foreheads still touching.

"Why dinner? Couldn't you guys just meet up at your mom's and talk while she's packing her stuff in the car?"

"If that's what you want me to do, I will. I think she feels uncomfortable going to Mom's. Embarrassed, maybe. I don't know. But your feelings matter far more than hers."

I rolled my eyes and swallowed again to try and dislodge the stubborn lump in my throat.

"Okay, fine. Whatever. Go to dinner with your ex-wife."

"No. You're upset."

"No, I mean it. I want you to go and say what you need to say. I'll be fine. Just come home to me, Cable." I kissed him then, using every tool in my kissing arsenal to remind him of our passion, our connection, our love. I wanted to burn an impression on him to leave no doubt in his mind where he belonged.

He responded wholeheartedly. It didn't take long at all for me to forget who was leaving an impression on whom. Our meal had long since turned cold before we detached from each other long enough to clear the dishes and resume the physical part of our conversation in his bedroom.

But now I'm lying here while he sleeps and little tiny words of doubt and resentment keep burrowing into my brain. Why on earth did I tell my Cabe he could go to dinner with his ex-wife?

Wednesday, July 30th

Tonight was the night. My fiancé's closure dinner with his ex-wife.

I felt sick all day. Nauseated and anxious. Angry and insecure. Irritable and jealous. A bundle of nerves ready to explode.

He called three times today. I sent him to voice mail every time and then as soon as the notification buzzed I'd grab that phone and play his message like I'd been holding my breath and his voice was oxygen.

The first two messages were just *"Hey, call me."*

His last call conveyed some frustration in his tone and a bit more urgency.

> *"I have a strange suspicion you're not picking up the phone because you're upset with me. If so, you need to tell me what's going on. We're supposed to be honest with each other, remember? So if there's a problem, you need to tell me. Call me back."*

I didn't call him back. There was a problem all right, and the fact that it was a problem was a problem. I wanted to be confident and carefree. I wanted to be perfectly fine with it. I wanted him to get whatever closure he needed so we could move on with our life together without any lingering guilt or remorse skulking in the recesses of his mind.

But I wasn't fine with it. I didn't want my fiancé going to dinner with his ex-wife. I didn't want my fiancé going to dinner with *any* woman, much less some woman he'd slept with, pledged his life to, and given his last name. By four o'clock, I was useless at work, so I left. I went through a drive-thru for fries and a milkshake, and then I picked up a pint of cookie dough ice cream from the convenience store by my place. After all, it was a small milkshake and I'd almost drunk the entire thing by the time I reached home. I needed a larger supply.

I turned my phone off and sank into a hot bubble bath, dripping tears into the ice cream container as I scraped it clean. I had cranked the music up loud before running my bath, but not even Adele's powerful pipes could drown out the chatter in my head. My mind churned through an angry diatribe as my stomach rebelled against the onslaught of dairy and greasy fries in an already hostile environment.

Damn him and his closure. Damn his ex-wife for showing up to rain on my parade. He should have just thrown all that stuff away when the landlord sent it to him. It would serve Monica right for leaving without a forwarding address. Who does she think she is, waltzing back into his life a year later and asking him to dinner? She has no business being here. No business going to dinner with him.

And what about him? What is he thinking? He's engaged. You don't go out with other women when you're engaged. Especially not other women you were married to. Other women you slept with.

Images of Monica popped into my head. Skinny little Monica. Size zero Monica. Monica with the dancer's legs and the perky little breasts. I don't think she even owned a bra. God knows she never wore one if she did. And her high-pitched, obnoxious little laugh. The way she looked up at him when she laughed. God! It pissed me off just to remember the two of them together. Funny how it didn't make me mad at the time it was happening, but to look back on it now that everything had changed was infuriating.

Against my will, my mind conjured pictures of the two of them together. Cabe kissing Monica. Caressing her. Going down on her. My stomach lurched. I chucked the ice cream container in the trash can by the toilet and sank lower in the water, shaking my head to dispel the sickening movie reel in my mind. The sound of her laughter morphed into a seductive mating rumble, a triumphant chuckle at my expense as their naked bodies intertwined in passion. I slapped the water with my hands and shouted *No!*, but my brain refused to stop the train from racing down the track. I couldn't unsee the thoughts as they continued to assault me.

The two of them having sex. Consummating their relationship in the most intimate of ways. Sharing an act so personal. Going beyond what the two of us had even shared.

I held my breath and slid beneath the water in an effort to change my mental scenery. This was ridiculous. It was the past. I was his present. His future. He was having dinner with her. Nothing more. The sordid scenes in my head were of my own creation. My own fears. Based in the reality of their past relationship, but not something I needed to worry about or torture myself with.

The pressure in my lungs demanded attention, and I started to release the air a little at a time, focusing on the bubbles as they rose up through the water so I could redirect my haunted thoughts. When no air remained and my body was screaming for oxygen, I resurfaced, scattering bubbles across the tiles as I reached for the sides of the tub to pull myself up.

"There you are!" Cabe's voice in the bathroom scared the crap out of me, and I sloshed water all over the floor as I fought to wipe the soap from my eyes.

"What are you doing here?" I coughed and sputtered as bubble bath suds slid down my face and into my mouth.

Cabe knelt on the floor beside the tub and wiped my face with the towel I'd left on the toilet lid. "Why are you covered in suds? Are you swimming or bathing?" He grinned, and my heart leapt inside my chest at the sight of his blue eyes. His dark blonde curls hung softly against his cheeks and fell over his forehead in disarray. He'd ridden with the windows down and his unruly hair had suffered for it.

"Why are you here? Why aren't you there?" I asked again, hoping beyond all hopes he was here to stay and not just dropping by on his way to meet her for dinner. Whatever I'd convinced myself and him of earlier, I knew now how much I didn't want him to go, and there was no way in hell I'd be able to pretend it was okay again.

"Let me turn this music down so I can hear what you're saying and the neighbors can hear their TV sets." He kissed the top of my wet head as he stood, and I wanted to grab him and pull him into the tub with me rather than watch him walk away.

Adele's voice disappeared, and I listened for the sound of Cabe's steps in the hallway.

He stopped in the doorway and stood there, his elbows against the door frame as he leaned his weight forward. His gaze traveled slowly over my body, and I looked down to see that the once frothy bubbles had mostly melted away, leaving me pretty much on display. My nipples protruded up from the water, surrounded by little tufts of suds floating around them like cushioning pillows. I crossed my arms over my chest and sat up higher, the suds falling away from me as tiny bubbles swirled and popped.

"So, why are you here?"

"Because there is absolutely no place on earth I'd rather be right now," Cabe said. "Unless maybe it was in that tub with you, or across the hall on that bed with you."

He walked slowly toward me, the mischief in his eyes replaced by a darker, more sensual tone. He bent to kiss me as his fingers slid over my wet shoulders and along the tops of my crossed arms, his kiss and his hand working together in convincing me to drop my arms away from my chest and give him the full access he wanted. I obliged him and moved my hands into his hair, moaning a bit as he slid one hand down to do some underwater exploration. He released me from our kiss to bend and take my nipple between his lips, and my fingernails raked across his scalp, his curls wet from my dripping hands.

I lay my head back against the cold tile, and my seated angle placed the small pillow attached to the tub perfectly behind my upper back to lift my breasts to him. He traced a path with his tongue from one to the other, leaving a trail of gooseflesh across my skin despite the heat of the water. He bit down with the slightest of pressure, just enough to prick a tiny stab of pleasure-tinged pain that coursed directly from my nipple to the epicenter of sensations deep within me.

Somewhere in my mind I knew I was supposed to be upset with him, but I couldn't make myself care why. My hands were wild in his hair as he brought me to the brink of madness and blissfully over the edge.

I sank back down into the water afterward and softened my grip in his curls, moaning his name softly before he closed his mouth over mine. My limbs trembled, every bit of tension gone from me as I came back down from the heightened state he'd taken me to.

Cold air brushed across my skin in a swoosh as he moved away from me, and I struggled to open my eyes in the hazy fog of my dreamlike state, wanting nothing more than to sink further into the water's warmth and melt into the trance he'd put me under.

He sat on the side of the tub, watching me with an intense gaze heavily shrouded in desire. He smiled at me, a confident grin that conveyed an impish mixture of cockiness and sexuality. He knew what effect he had on me, and he reveled in the knowledge that he could leave me speechless and unable to move.

"How you doin'?" He reached forward to push my hair back, and I thought about how frightful I must look after dunking myself under water. I lifted my hand to my hair, cringing at the tangled wet mess I felt. I moved to sit up, but swirls of lights danced before me and I lay back against the small pillow, woozy but content.

"Here," Cabe said as he extended his hand for me. "Let's get you out of there before the water gets cold and you shrivel up like a raisin."

"Isn't it a prune?" I pulled myself up to standing with his help, still seeing stars and feeling aftershocks. "Isn't the saying shriveled like a prune?"

"I don't know," Cabe answered as he lifted me from the tub and set my feet gently on the floor, wrapping me in the towel. He patted me dry from head to toe, his lips occasionally lighting upon my skin and sending shivers down my spine. By the time he'd tucked the towel tight around me, I'd pretty much completely forgotten there was ever a time he wasn't here with me or that I had nearly driven myself crazy with mental images of him and Monica only a short time earlier.

But when he took my hand and turned to lead me from the bathroom, I noticed he was fully dressed. Like, more than his normal jeans and T-shirt attire. The deep midnight blue form-fitting slacks hugged his muscular thighs and buns in all the right places, and the gray and white paisley shirt was one I hadn't seen in quite a while. A favorite of mine he rarely wore. He'd rolled the sleeves up to a tight cuff near his elbow, but I could see his left arm had gotten soaked for a few inches due to our bathtub encounter.

It all came flooding back to me. The reason he'd put thought into his outfit. His plans for the evening. His ex-wife.

I stopped walking and dropped my hand from his.

"Why are you here? What time is your dinner?" My stomach immediately went back to its nauseated state and any remaining shreds of weightless ecstasy fled. My body tensed in preparation for his answer.

He turned back to me with a look of confusion and then recognition.

"Oh, I didn't tell you. I got a little distracted, didn't I?" He smiled and cupped my face in his hands, kissing me lightly.

I pulled back. "Tell me what?"

"I'm not going to dinner."

Relief flooded through me, and I resisted the urge to clap my hands together in glee. I didn't know why yet, so any celebration would need to be internal until I had more info.

"Why not? What happened?"

He tilted his head to one side and smiled, and I couldn't help but smile back. He melts me. Every. Damned. Time.

"Why'd you turn your phone off?"

I shook my head. "Nope. I asked first. You gotta answer first."

He chuckled, low and deep, and kissed me again. "I will, but I wanna know why you turned your phone off."

Heat filled my cheeks, and I wished in that moment I wasn't standing there in a towel feeling all vulnerable. I stepped around him and went to my closet to grab a robe.

"Tyler? Why did you turn your phone off?"

He had followed me to my room, and he stood there lounging against my door frame, looking all casual with just a hint of smug tickling the corners of his smile. Probably as sexy as I've ever seen him look.

"I was getting in the tub." I tied the robe and went past him to the bathroom to get a comb. "I didn't want to bring the phone in and risk dropping it in the tub. Besides, I had the music up loud and I wouldn't have been able to hear it ring." I fought with the tangles in my hair and resisted making eye contact with him in the mirror when he came and stood behind me.

"No, you definitely wouldn't have heard it; that's for sure. You didn't hear me ring the doorbell, or knock, or use my key to let myself in."

"You're right, I didn't. You scared the crap out of me."

He took the comb and began to work through the tangled knots in my hair with much more patience and kindness than I'd shown toward it. I have a short fuse with my thick mess of hair, which was even more uncooperative than usual since I'd gotten all soapy without using conditioner afterward.

"You gonna answer me? With the truth this time?" He stared at me in the mirror as he separated strands of hair between his fingers and the comb.

I met his eyes in the mirror and held his gaze, my heart fluttering under his scrutiny.

"I told you the truth," I lied. "I was getting in the tub."

He slid his arms around my waist and rested his chin on my shoulder so that our faces were side by side. My wet, brown web of tangles mingling with his dark blond curls. His clear blue eyes almost transparent next to the deep green of my own. His square jawline so masculine alongside my soft cheeks. What beautiful babies we would have. I smiled at the thought.

"We promised each other we'd stop hiding what we're feeling." His voice reverberated inside my head as he spoke pressed up next to me. "That we'd get it out in the open, no matter what. I think you're not being entirely honest with me."

I looked down at my hands on top of his where they rested on my tummy. My baby train of thought briefly imagined me being swelled out pregnant underneath his hands, and my heart tugged at the thought of our future. I met his eyes again.

"I didn't want you to go tonight. I told you to go, but I really didn't want you to."

"I knew you didn't. So why'd you tell me to go?"

"Because I felt like it was the right thing to do. To say. You needed to talk to her and get things off your chest, and I felt like I should be okay with it."

"You don't have to be okay with it. I wouldn't be okay with it. Hell, I wasn't okay with it when it was Dwayne. So why not just tell me you don't want me to go? Why avoid my calls, not return my messages, and turn off your phone?"

I took the comb from him and started yanking it through my hair.

"Tyler, listen to me." He turned me to face him and lifted me up to sit on the sink's counter. He nestled his hips between my knees, and I placed my arms around his neck as he spoke again. "We have to be honest with each other. You don't want me disappearing? Running away from my feelings? Avoiding you? Well, it goes both ways. I want you to tell me what you're thinking and what you're feeling, and then we work through it. Like we agreed to do."

"I know. But you had things you needed to say to her, and I don't want you living with guilt or regrets or whatever it is you still have with her. I'd rather you go ahead and get it said so we can move on and leave her in the past. So why aren't you going to dinner?"

He sighed and rubbed his palms along the tops of my thighs.

"Because no one's feelings are more important to me than yours. I knew last night you didn't want me to go, so I called Mom first thing this morning to make sure she was okay with Monica coming there, and then I texted Monica that I wouldn't be able to make dinner and she could meet Mom to pick up her stuff."

Relief and elation surged within me, peppered with guilt and apprehension.

"But see, that's what I didn't want," I said. "You're not gonna talk to her because of me so you won't get the closure you needed. Now it's always going to hang over our heads and it's my fault. You should've just gone." I yanked through my hair with the comb again, wincing at the pain I caused myself.

"I said what I needed to say. I wrote her a letter and left it with her things."

I stopped torturing my hair and stared at him. I wasn't sure how to feel about that. On the one hand I was thrilled that he wasn't going to dinner. But another part of me felt funny about him writing his ex-wife some long, heartfelt letter. Before I could put any energy into getting all worked up about it, he took his phone from his pocket and flipped through it.

"Here, I took a picture of the letter so you could see exactly what I wrote. I didn't want you obsessing over what was in it or what I may have said to her."

He handed me the phone and took the comb from me, working through the strands again with his tender touch.

I yelped as he hit a tough tangle and pain shot across my scalp. "Ow! No, take this." I tried to hand him back the phone, but he didn't take it. "I don't need to see the letter. That's personal."

"Sorry," he said as he rubbed my head where the tangle had pulled. "Yeah, it's personal, but we have no secrets, remember? I don't care if you see what I wrote her. I know you, Tyler. It will eat you alive wondering what's in the letter. You might as well just read it and be done with it. I'm starving, and you still have to get dressed."

"Why do I have to get dressed? Where am I going?"

"We're going to dinner. I tried to tell you this afternoon, but you wouldn't answer your damned phone. I even wore this ridiculous paisley shirt I know you like and I've got Dean coming over to walk Deacon for us. Now get dressed, girl. I think I have all the tangles out."

"Wait, why are we going to dinner? Did you, like, make reservations for Monica or something?"

He laughed and pulled me to him until our faces were just inches apart.

"We're going to dinner because you are the love of my life, and I don't want to waste another minute worrying about anyone other than you. You are my heart. My light. My girl. I want to wine you, dine you, dance with you. Make sure you know you're my one and only."

He kissed me then, and the world was a wonderful place.

Of course, I read the letter after dinner. He's right. It would have driven me nuts wondering. It turned out to be short, simple, and to the point. And though it still pricked my heart in little twinges of jealousy and possessiveness, I know how lucky I am to have the man he has become. And I'm grateful.

Dear Monica,

I didn't feel like dinner would be appropriate under the circumstances, but I did have something I needed to say. An apology, if you will.

I'm sorry I blamed you for my unhappiness. I wasn't willing to take responsibility for my own decisions then, and I found it much easier to focus on you than to face my own shortcomings.

I know how hard you tried to make our relationship work, and I'm sorry for what I put you through. You were right when you said I was never really in it. I couldn't see that then, and seeing it now makes me realize how unfair I was to you. I was running from something I couldn't escape, and I'm sorry I dragged you along for a portion of the painful journey.

I never meant to hurt you. I never meant to make such a mess of things. I can't go back and erase it, but I can tell you this. Although I regret the pain I caused you, and I regret the circumstances I unwittingly put you in, I cannot regret our time together. Because of you, I have learned invaluable lessons about myself and about relationships. The experience has forever changed me and made me, I hope, a better man. Maybe one day you will be able to look back and find value in what we had as well.

Please know I wish you only happiness as you move forward with your life. I hope you can find it in your heart to do the same for me.

Best Wishes,
Cabe

August

Monday, August 4th

I never knew how much stuff I had crammed in my apartment. It took us all weekend to get everything out of there and moved in here, and I haven't even begun to unpack any of it. I'm exhausted. We may live here the rest of our lives just so I don't have to move again.

Cabe woke me when he left for work with the intent that I would get up and get busy, but I didn't budge.

Until Mama called.

"I need a date and I need a guest count. Today. You cannot possibly expect me to plan a wedding without those key pieces of information."

I groaned and flipped back the covers. I needed coffee if I was going to be civil to my mother.

"Mama, no one's asking you to plan a wedding. Just relax."

"Relax? Relax, she says. Here I am, elbow deep in baskets and silk arrangements, fielding calls all day every day from family members wanting to mark their calendars, and you tell me to relax?"

I silently thanked the Lord above for my fiancé's foresight in leaving coffee in the pot as I poured a cup and put it in the microwave.

"I told you not to buy baskets and silk flowers. I don't know what we're doing yet, so there's no reason for you to buy anything. Can you please just wait until we've made decisions? We'll let everyone know as soon as we do."

"Tyler Lorraine, people have lives. They need to make plans. I would think you would know these things since you do this for a living. Arrangements have to be made in advance. You can't dilly-dally around with this. You want this to be a wedding we can be proud of or something that looks like it was thrown together in the middle of a storm? Lord, help me, I don't need all this stress. I been getting the indigestion on a daily basis since we started planning this wedding and I can't even lay down flat for the burning."

I rubbed my eyes, burned my tongue on my coffee, and tucked my feet under me on the couch next to Deacon. I wasn't awake enough to deal with my mother or my wedding.

"You gotta calm down, Patsy."

"Don't you call me 'Patsy'. I hate when your sister Carrie does that. Don't you start."

I leaned my head back on the sofa and closed my eyes.

"We haven't even talked dates yet, Mom. We've been busy." I hoped she didn't ask with what because I definitely wasn't up to explaining that I'd made the big leap to full-on living in sin over the weekend.

"Too busy to figure out your own wedding date? What could be more important than that? I talked to Sharon in the church office yesterday, and she's got folks already booked through the spring and even into summer. Those people all figured out their wedding date. Now, what exactly is the hold-up? I told Sharon I'd let her know as soon as possible. Could you at least give me some tentative dates she could hold? I can't sleep until I know we have the church booked."

"I'll talk to Cabe tonight." I took a deep breath and dropped the bomb I'd been holding. "I don't know if we're gonna have it at the church."

She sucked in an intake of air with a simultaneous screech that pierced my ears and made Deacon lift up and peer at the phone with his head cocked to one side.

"Not use the church? Oh, Sweet Jesus. Oh, Heavenly Father. What do you mean, not use the church? Oh, I feel faint. Heaven, help me. Tyler Lorraine, I have been through this with both your sisters and their disregard of the sanctity of marriage. I won't stand for it again, do you hear me? I still have heart palpitations every time I think about Carrie Ann traipsing off to Vegas with Kenny and getting married in an Elvis chapel. She could've had your Uncle Rodney perform the ceremony here if cheap and trashy was what she was going for. If you think you're gonna follow in her footsteps, you got another think coming."

I stared at Deacon and he stared back at me. I sighed, and he nudged my hand with his nose until I complied with his request and rubbed his ears.

"Look. I'm not going to get married in an Elvis chapel in Vegas, okay? But we're still tossing around ideas. I don't know if we're going to get married back home or maybe somewhere down here. Maybe even an island somewhere. Who knows?"

She pulled out all the stops and burst into tears.

"Why do you not care about my feelings?"

She sobbed.

"I'm getting older by the day, and what do I ask of my kids?"

More sobbing.

"One day I'll leave this world. Dead and gone I'll be, laid to rest by your daddy's side. Lord bless his soul."

Louder sobs.

"But while I'm breathing, couldn't just one of my children think of me and my feelings? Just one?"

Incomprehensible mumbling and sobbing.

I knew from years of experience there was really nothing I could say when she got like this, but since I couldn't just hang up the phone with her crying, I searched for a way to appease her without making any promises.

"Mama, I know this is real important to you. I'll talk to Cabe, and we'll make decisions this week, okay? I'll get you an answer by Friday. Okay? Mama? C'mon. Please stop crying."

She huffed and puffed a few more times and then blew her nose before speaking.

"Oh Lord. I feel a migraine coming on. I gotta find my pills and go lay down for a while. Obviously, you're gonna do what you're gonna do. My feelings don't mean a thing to you and neither do your daddy's."

"Oh, come on. Don't bring him into this." I groaned and flopped across the couch, nudging Deacon out of my way. He grumbled and curled up on the floor.

"He'd want you married in a church with a proper wedding. You know I'm right."

I rolled my eyes and closed them against the stress. "I'll talk to Cabe tonight, okay? I'll call you before the end of the week."

We hung up, and I stared at the boxes scattered across the living room. I had zero motivation to crack them open, so I leashed up Deacon and went for a walk.

It's not that I don't care how Mama feels or that I want to upset her. But I don't know that going back home and getting married in that church is what I want for our wedding. Cabe's not even Baptist.

Which Mama doesn't know yet.

That place holds no value for him and no meaning for the two of us together.

As much as the idea of a beach ceremony on some island appeals to me, I know that realistically, that would pretty much exclude most of my family from attending. Which may not be a bad thing. However, Cabe's already said it's important to him for our families to be there, so I guess I need to scrap the whole escape-to-the-tropics idea.

There are several locations here in Orlando I really like, but I don't want to have the wedding some place I work. I want it to be special. Unique. Not like just another wedding I'm at.

Maybe we should look at a beach on the East Coast. Cocoa or Melbourne. Maybe even head up to St. Augustine or Amelia Island. We both love the beach, and he pretty much spends every spare minute he has on the sand or in the water. That could be a great compromise of my tropical paradise but still being close enough for family to attend.

Aargh. So many decisions to make, and no way to make everyone happy.

Tuesday, August 5th

Weather forecasters have placed Orlando in the cone of uncertainty for an approaching hurricane this weekend.

It's not that uncertain at all over here. We're in the midst of a wedding hurricane, and the wind is starting to blow from all directions.

Maggie called this morning to ask if Cabe and I could meet her for lunch. Considering that she's never asked us that before, I was a little nervous.

I called Cabe as I drove to meet him downtown. "What do you think she wants?"

"I think she wants to take us to lunch."

"But why?"

"Um, because she loves us and wants to spend time with us?"

"She's never asked us to lunch before."

He laughed. "She asks me to lunch all the time. Maybe now that we're engaged she wants to spend more time with you. I wouldn't worry about it. It's a free lunch and you get to see me."

"Both fabulous prizes, to be sure, but I'm just a little apprehensive. I've already got my mama dragon breathing down my neck. I'd prefer to stay on good terms with yours."

It was a lovely lunch. Maggie had recommended a little Thai cafe, and it didn't disappoint. The dumplings were delicious and the Panang curry was one of the best I'd ever eaten.

We'd finished our meal and were waiting on the check when the climate shifted.

"I thought I'd ask you two downtown so we could take a look at the Performing Arts Center. I'm not sure how familiar you are with our space, Tyler, and though we aren't known as a wedding location, there are a couple

147

of terraces and alcoves that would be just lovely. You may already have locations, but I'd like to at least show you a few things for your consideration."

My stomach tightened and my Panang went sour. This was what I had dreaded. The counter-attack. The last thing I wanted was to be in a tug-of-war between my mom and his.

We walked the space with her, and she was right. There were some beautiful locations to consider. The venue was centrally located and the atmosphere was pure elegance. Several key hotels were within walking distance, and there were many options for both ceremony and reception at the Arts Center.

Had I not been faced with such tension and turmoil regarding our wedding location, I probably would have been intrigued.

It definitely interested me that I had never done a wedding there, nor had Laura or Lillian. Maggie mentioned they had an in-house coordinator who had handled a couple of small events, but weddings were not a business they desired or pursued. So it definitely fit the unique qualification I was seeking.

Maggie was the consummate tour guide, pointing out all the amenities and benefits of the location without ever pushing a hard sale.

Several times she would say, *"Of course, it's up to the two of you,"* or *"it's your event, so whatever you feel is best"* or even *"it doesn't matter to me one way or another. I just want you to have options."*

I appreciated her saying those things, and I appreciated the time and effort she put in. She was not in any way applying the tourniquet my mother uses. But at the same time, it added more pressure. Here was someone else's opinion to take into consideration and someone else who might be disappointed or let down depending on our choice, despite what she said.

Cabe asked what was wrong as I picked at my dinner tonight.

"I don't know. I just feel like everyone has a stake in where we have the wedding, and I kind of want it to be up to us."

"It is up to us. It's our decision."

"Ha! Right. Our decision. And as soon as we make it, everyone will let us know how we let them down." I stood and took my unfinished plate to the kitchen.

"You can't let that bother you, babe. It's our wedding. It's our decision."

"You already said that." I walked past him and flopped down on the couch.

He finished eating and followed me to the living room.

"So what is it you want to do? If no one else was involved?"

I covered my face with my arm and swallowed against the tears of frustration I felt stinging my eyes.

Cabe lifted my feet and pulled them into his lap. He began to rub the soles and my toes, which normally tickles so badly I can't stand it. But I was in no mood to be tickled tonight.

I moved my arm to look at him.

"I don't know what I want. Part of me thinks it would be cool to get married in my hometown church with all my family there and have the big party afterwards. But I can't begin to think how much of a pain that would be to plan from here and how much Mama and her sisters would take over. Besides, that's not your church. It's not your home. I want our wedding to be about both of us."

"It will be. No matter where it is."

"So you don't care if we have it there?"

He shook his head. "Nope. If that's where you want it, that's fine with me. You tell me where to show up and I'll be there. Locked and ready. Any time. Any place."

"But then another part of me wants to have it here. I have photographers and DJs and people I work with and I've seen what they can do. I'd kind of like to have them involved, ya know? I know if we have this back home, I'm gonna get some god-awful DIY project that Mama and Aunt Pearl throw together under Aunt Pearl's carport. She wants my cousin Wanda to make the bridesmaids' dresses. Ugh!"

I covered my face again, unable to keep my pouty tears at bay any longer.

"So have it here somewhere." Cabe stated it so matter-of-factly that I wanted to throw something at him.

I sat up and pulled my feet from his lap. "You don't get it. You just don't get it. These people aren't going to be mad at you or hurt and offended by your choices. You're the groom. You get to just show up and look hot in a tux. Grooms have it easy."

"Okay. What can I do to help? How can I take some of the pressure off you?"

I stood up. "You can't. Don't you see? The groom doesn't have to pick flowers and music and linens and dresses and make sure everyone's feelings are being considered and no one's left out."

"I'm willing to, if that helps. I can go with you to pick flowers and linens. I'd love to pick music. Just tell me how to help you, and I'll do it."

I paced a couple of times and sat back down. "I appreciate your help. I do. And I want your input and I want you involved. I just feel like no matter what I do, someone's not going to be happy. I spend every day of my life making sure other people's weddings are what they want them to be. That they're beautiful and orchestrated well. That they reflect the couple and who they are. I feel like I can't do that for us. Which is why I wanted to elope."

Cabe sat quiet for a few minutes and then reached and took my hand in his. He rubbed his thumb across the back of my hand as he stared at our fingers.

"Then let's elope," he finally said with a big exhale. "Let's just say screw it and take off. Just the two of us. We won't even tell anyone."

I held my breath for a second, unsure if he was serious. "But I thought you didn't want to elope. I thought you wanted the big wedding."

He shrugged. "I guess I didn't know what I was getting into. The last thing I wanted was for you to be all stressed out and unhappy. If this can't be fun for you, then I don't want it. Let's elope."

"You mean it? Really? You're not going to regret it?"

He answered me with a kiss, and I felt like a weight had been lifted from my shoulders. I felt lighter than air.

This feels right. This is the answer. We're gonna elope!

Thursday, August 7th

I can't believe how excited I am to plan now that we're eloping. I've been doing some internet searches for locations and I've requested a few brochures. My heart has felt lighter and the sun has shone brighter since we decided to elope. Well, okay, the sun's been peeking between clouds from the impending storm, but still.

My bride for this weekend is surprisingly calm about the whole hurricane thing. They arrived yesterday from England and were greeted at hotel check-in with a letter advising guests of the projected path bringing the hurricane right over Orlando.

They'd traveled here with twenty-four of their closest friends and family, and the excitement of an approaching hurricane only seemed to add to their festive spirits.

I spoke with the catering manager at the hotel, who has assured me they have procedures in place for back-up in case of a storm, but I'd still feel better if the forecast models shifted it out into the Atlantic.

Cabe went to Home Depot last night to buy shutters for our house, and then he took the day off today to put up Maggie's shutters and install ours. We brought in the patio furniture from the porches yesterday and stacked it all in the living room, which has confused poor Deacon something bad. He was just beginning to calm back down from the shock of having my furniture moved in along with my myriad of boxes all over the house.

More than once I was worried he was going to lift a leg to mark his territory with so much upheaval.

I called Cabe from the grocery store this afternoon, amazed at what I was seeing. "Honey, evidently this is serious. There's no water. No bread. No soups. I keep looking around at other people's carts and going *oh, pop-tarts. That's a good idea. Ravioli. That doesn't have to be heated.* But then when I

151

get to that aisle, all the non-perishable stuff that could be eaten without electricity is gone. I never knew how many food items depend on electricity."

"I picked up water and batteries at Home Depot earlier, so don't worry about those. Be sure you stop and get gas, though. They're saying some stations are running out."

"Holy crap. It's like the apocalypse. Do you think it's going to get that bad?"

The sound of his hammer pounding in the background was almost deafening.

"I don't know, babe. We've ridden out hurricanes before, and usually by the time they get to Orlando, they've crossed enough land to weaken. But they're saying this is a big one. So we'll see. It still could turn."

I told him goodbye to answer Laura's incoming call.

"Your wedding still on?"

"Yep. So far," I said.

"Okay, that means all four ceremonies for Saturday are still on track. Let's regroup later this afternoon and see what the forecast is. We can always cancel tonight if need be. Unless, of course, your bride and groom choose to cancel before then. Keep me posted."

The line at the gas station was ridiculously long. It took me over forty-five minutes to make it to a pump and get gas. A couple of people were even fighting over pumps and who had gotten there first.

I felt like I had been transported to a different place and time. Everything around me felt foreign and unfamiliar.

"What did you end up getting?" Cabe asked when I came through the door several hours later.

"Some cheese in a can, crackers, and some bags of pepperoni. Oh, and snack cakes."

He looked at my haul as I poured it out on the table.

"Powdered donuts? Awesome. We may survive the hurricane and die from an overdose of junk food."

"It was all they had left. I went to three different stores before I could find Doritos or cinnamon buns. It was crazy insane out there."

My phone rang as I was trying to find places in the pantry for our junk food feast.

"Hey, sugar. Are y'all about to blow away down there?"

"Not yet, Mama. The news said it would probably start to get bad later this evening when the storm gets closer."

"Your apartment's on the top floor, right? Is it safe?"

I cringed. I still hadn't told her I'd moved in with Cabe. Nor did I plan to if I could help it.

"Actually, I'm gonna ride out the storm here at Cabe's house. Probably safer."

"Good. That's good. I feel better knowing you'll be in a house and not by yourself. What about his mama? Where's she gonna be?"

"Maggie's on the rideout crew at the Performing Arts Center. I think they're opening some areas for shelter for some of the residents downtown. So she'll be safe."

"Good. Good. Well, I just wanted to check on y'all. Keep me posted. I'm watching the news here and it looks bad heading your way. I'll be on pins and needles 'til you call me."

I hesitated, unsure if now would be the best time to tell her our decision. I'd told her I'd give her an answer by the end of the week, but with the storm coming and her being all worried about us, it didn't seem fair to destroy her wedding dreams on top of it.

She brought it up before I could mention it, though.

"Tyler, honey, I been thinking a lot about this wedding, and I want you to know I'll support you with whatever you decide. I know I've put a lot of pressure on you to come here and have it like I want it, and of course, I'd be thrilled if you did that. But it's your wedding, baby. Yours and Cabe's. I already had the only wedding I'm ever gonna have. You deserve to have yours the way you want it."

I was astounded. Caught off guard. Speechless. Immediately brought to tears.

"Well, thank you, Mama."

"You don't have to thank me. Just be happy. That's all I've ever wanted for any of my young'uns was for y'all to be happy." Her voice broke with emotion. "I guess I can understand why none of you girls would want me involved in your wedding. I know I'm not always the easiest mother to deal with, but everything I've done—everything I do—is because I love you. Want the best for you."

"I know, Mama. I know that. We all know that." I cried right along with her.

"So do your wedding like you want it. I'll abide by it."

"Thank you, Mama. That really means a lot. You have no idea—"

"That's what your sisters did. They did what they wanted and didn't worry about what I might want. And I'm sure your brother is going to end up marrying Kelly, and her mama and daddy will be doing their wedding. I probably won't be included then either. I just never thought when your sweet daddy and I birthed four children—oh Lord rest his soul—that I wouldn't even get one wedding, not one wedding, out of the four to plan."

I got quiet. Somewhere along the line, her kind gesture had morphed back into typical Mama.

"I'll let you go, sugar. But keep me in the loop, okay? I'll feel better if I can at least be in on your plans. Love you. Stay safe. Call me."

She hung up and the lump settled back into its comfy spot in my stomach. My shoulders tensed and drew back up closer to my ears. The entire room darkened, which I know was due to Cabe covering the last set of windows with a storm shutter, but it matched my mood.

I hadn't escaped the hurricane after all.

Saturday, August 9th

The sky turned dark yesterday long before night. Once the rains started, it seemed they would never end.

Luckily, I think we dodged the worst of it, but it was definitely not pleasant.

Cabe had made dinner early so we would have a good meal before the storm began. We walked Deacon when the wind picked up and the sky began to darken, not knowing for sure when he'd next be able to go out.

The power went around seven and still hasn't come back on. Once it blew, there wasn't anything we could do but ride it out. Sleeping was out of the question with the wind howling incessantly and the constant battering of rain against the house. So Cabe opened a bottle of wine, and we played Scrabble by candlelight for hours, listening to the wind and trying to keep Deacon calm.

Poor baby shivered and shook, whining as he paced back and forth from me to Cabe in a steady pant. Cabe had bought him one of those thunder things that's supposed to calm dogs in storms. I think maybe if it had been a normal Florida rainstorm it might have helped, but it was no match for a category three hurricane.

We kept the battery-operated storm radio nearby in case of tornado warnings or any other imminent threat, but all in all, it was a pretty uneventful night. We finally got to sleep sometime after four.

When we woke around nine, the storm had passed, and the sun even popped through the clouds every now and then.

I tried to call the hotel to reach my bride, but I kept getting an *'all circuits are busy'* warning. The wedding was scheduled for two in the afternoon, so I decided to go ahead and drive to the hotel a little before noon.

It was like driving through a war zone. Traffic lights were out. Power lines were down. Tree limbs littered the streets and debris was scattered everywhere. The highways and interstate were deserted, and I wondered if the curfew from last night had been extended.

When I reached the hotel, the front drive was almost unrecognizable. The huge stately palms had been stripped of their fronds, which lay like a carpet covering the road. The lush landscape looked, well, like a hurricane had torn through there. Plants and bushes were tossed every which way and everywhere I looked appeared disheveled and battered.

The buildings were intact, though, and the bell services manager who took my car at the valet stand assured me all guests were safe and sound inside.

My wedding party greeted me in the lobby as soon as I walked in. Katerina, the bride, rushed across the marble floor to embrace me.

"Tyler, you're safe! Are you alright? I've been trying to call your phone but it won't go through. Is your home safe?"

I nodded and assured her we were fine.

"Is the wedding on then? Are we okay?" Gottfried, the groom, asked.

"I think so," I replied. "Let me check with the hotel and see what's going on with the ceremony site."

From the looks of the front hotel grounds, I had a pretty strong suspicion that the gardens in the back where we'd scheduled the ceremony might not be in any shape to host us. My suspicion was correct.

"We can't even get there right now," Mike, the catering manager, told me. "The little stone bridge that crosses over to the gardens from the hotel was knocked out by a fallen tree, and coming in from the other way is impossible due to debris across the walkway. We'll have to move the event indoors."

I used the hotel's land lines to try and reach the florist, officiant, violinist and pastry chef. Reverend Markham had never lost power or cable and was planning to be on time. The florist had a huge tree down across her street, which had pulled several utility lines down with it. The police and fire rescue had blocked off the area from both directions, so she was basically trapped at home. I kept getting the busy message with the violinist, and the pastry chef said she had no power and had been storing all the cakes in her refrigerated truck, but was uncertain how deliveries were going to go with unknown road conditions. The cake would get delivered eventually, but no guarantee as to when.

Amazingly, Katerina never batted an eye at any of it. No flowers? No problem. No violinist? No problem. Possibly no cake? No problem. No garden ceremony? Who needs it.

"Thank you so much for taking this so well," I told her as we walked to the new ceremony site. "I can't imagine how I would feel in your shoes, and I really appreciate you being so easy to work with."

"Tyler, there may be people who lost their lives last night, or their family members, or their homes. We are all here. Together and safe. Gottfried and I will be married. We will celebrate. The rest of it is just details. It doesn't matter."

I smiled at her, relieved at her attitude and wishing beyond all wishes that I could repay her kindness with something magnificent. My hands were tied, though. A state of emergency surrounded us, so there was very little I could do to go above and beyond.

Mike and his staff came through in a big way by procuring some fresh floral from hotel arrangements for a makeshift bouquet, and the chef in the main restaurant offered to bake a cake as back-up. They moved in greenery from all over the hotel to create a lush backdrop for the ceremony in a richly-appointed lounge area. It was a splendid room with velvet curtains and an expanse of windows overlooking the pool. The hotel even rigged up an MP3 connection so we could play music for the ceremony based on what Katerina and Gottfried had chosen.

It was amazing to see everyone pull together to make it happen, especially since most of the staff had been there all night on ride-out crew and had yet to go to their own homes and survey possible damage.

It was, all things considered, a lovely event for lovely people.

I congratulated them again before I departed and thanked them once more for being so gracious under trying circumstances.

"The marriage takes place here," Gottfried said, motioning to his heart. "The wedding is a way for your family and friends to celebrate what happens here." He motioned again to his heart. "So as long as you have your family and friends with you and you take your vows together, that is what truly matters."

Aargh. Stick me in the heart and leave me to bleed, Gottfried. He couldn't have known the effect his words would have on me or the inner turmoil it sparked.

He was right, of course. It would be easy to elope to some remote destination and keep our marriage all to ourselves, but the most beautiful weddings I'd ever participated in had all been events where the couple was surrounded by love. The love and support of those closest to them as they celebrated the commitment and the union.

"I know you're gonna think I'm crazy and wonder what the hell you've gotten yourself into," I told Cabe as we ate powdered donuts and cheese with crackers by candlelight tonight, "but I think I've changed my mind."

"About what?" he asked as he tilted his head back and filled his mouth from the squeeze can of cheese.

"I want to have a wedding. Like, a real one. With our families."

He opened his eyes wide and swallowed the cheese. "What changed your mind?"

"Love. I was reminded today that it's meant to be shared. I think I fell into the trap of being a bride. Of believing it's all about me and my feelings and what I want. I see brides with that mindset all the time, and I hate it."

Cabe shook his head. "I don't see you like that at all. I don't think you were being selfish. I think you were trying to have your wedding be your own."

"Thank you for that, really. I know I haven't been a barrel of roses to deal with since we got engaged, and I'm sorry. But I think I need to get out of my own head and allow this event to belong to more than just me. I realize I can't please everyone, but I don't have to focus on pleasing just me either."

He stroked his palm against my cheek and leaned in to kiss me. When he pulled away, the candlelight flickered across his eyes and illuminated his smile.

"You're sure?" he asked. "Because I'm fine with eloping. You just say the word and we're on a jet plane. Or in a car. Boat. Plane. Whatever you want. I will marry you any time, any place."

"I'm sure," I told him with a smile. "Now, you may need to remind me from time to time that I'm sure. Like, every time I talk to my mother for instance. Or when we're buried up to our necks in place cards and seating arrangements. But I'm sure. I want to share our celebration with the people who love us." I took a deep breath and sighed. "Which means, we need to choose a location and set a date."

Cabe arched an eyebrow and grinned, "Is tomorrow too soon?"

I laughed. "I'm thinking we want to give people more notice."

"True. So how far out do you want to push this?"

I thumbed through my phone's calendar, thankful again that Cabe had bought us portable chargers prior to the storm. "Not too far. Let's get the show on the road. I'm thinking before the end of the year. You?"

He smiled. "I already said tomorrow would work for me."

"Okay, I have, like, no weekends after this month. September and October are insane. November 11th is crazy because of the whole eleven-eleven thing. Looks like my first weekend off is November 22nd. That's the weekend before Thanksgiving, and my bride for the Saturday after canceled. That would mean a honeymoon Thanksgiving week, but if we spend time with our families at the wedding, maybe that's okay? We could take off after my wedding on the fifteenth and head up there to get everything tied up that week? "

"So we're definitely doing the hometown thing?"

My eyes darted up from the phone to meet his. "Is that okay?"

He pushed his chair back and leaned toward me, his arms braced on his knees. "Tyler, I already told you. I will marry you any time. Any place. You tell me when and where, and I'll be there. Stop worrying about me in all this. As long as I've got you, I'm happy. Do whatever you want to do or whatever will cause you the least amount of stress."

I rolled my eyes and groaned a little. "I don't think getting married back home will cause me the least amount of stress, but I think it means more to Mama than it does to anyone other than us. Maggie's already said she will support our decision no matter what. Your grandparents have the means to travel. Our friends from work can come as long as they have enough notice. So getting married back home seems to be the best way to do it with all things considered."

"Okay. That's decided. What's the date again?"

"November 22nd. Does that work for you?"

He brushed his goatee with his fingers and gazed toward the ceiling. "November 22nd. November 22nd. Hmmm. I think I'm available."

I poked my finger in his stomach and laughed as he doubled over and wrapped me in a bear hug.

"We have a wedding date and a location!" He sounded more excited than I could feel.

Okay. Here we go. Start your engines.

Monday, August 11th

We spent all day yesterday cleaning up the yard from the storm and removing the storm shutters. Still no power, although Cabe said he talked to a neighbor who'd heard it would be back on later today.

Neither of us were in the mood for foraging in the pantry for more junk food last night, so we drove to an area of town that had power to get something to eat.

I got up when Cabe left this morning to concentrate on getting my stuff unpacked and put away. The plethora of windows in this house came in handy as far as letting the light in, but they also let in the heat. I think that's what I miss the most about having electricity—air conditioning. Or maybe the coffee pot. And the microwave. Okay, yeah. I need electricity.

By noon, Deacon and I were both panting in the stifling house, and I was beyond done with unpacking. We loaded up and went out for ice cream. I got Deacon a vanilla cone, his favorite thing in the whole world. He wolfed it down in about two bites and then zeroed in on my milkshake. We'd gone to the park to sit on the bench in the shade. Normally he runs and plays as soon as he's out of the car, but today his milkshake fixation kept him right at my feet.

When I had about a fourth of the shake left, I held out the cup for him and he ran his nose all the way down in it, licking and slurping like there was no tomorrow. When it was close to empty, he turned his face up with the cup still on his nose and let it drip into his mouth. Well, his mouth, his eyes, his snout. He was covered in pink.

I took a pic and texted Cabe.

Deacon has a new favorite color.

He texted right back.

Looks like he got in a fight with Pepto Bismol. And lost.

I was about to text him another picture when Mama called.

"Hey sugar! I ran into Teri Casanova this morning, and her daughter just got married. She said we can use whatever they've got left. She's even got tablecloths she bought over in Dallas somewhere. How do you feel about lemon yellow?"

"Ummm, I'm not feeling it. Cabe and I want to use purple."

"Purple? Well, purple goes with yellow. Have the girls wear purple dresses or something and then decorate with yellow. That would be real pretty together for a spring or summer wedding."

"Well, actually, I had planned to call you later tonight to tell you that we picked a date." I took a deep breath and exhaled as I spoke. "November 22nd."

"November 22nd? Of next year?"

I braced myself. "This year."

"Have you lost your cotton-pickin' mind? That's three months away. How on earth do you expect me to plan a wedding in three months?"

"That's plenty of time."

"Tyler Lorraine! It's coming up on pecan season. Not to mention muscadines and pears. You know how much work it is for me to make my jellies and preserves. How am I supposed to plan a wedding if I'm up to my elbows in muscadines? Oh Lord in heaven, I can't believe you would put me in this situation. I've gotta sit down. Oh, I feel faint. Hold on and let me put my head between my knees."

I had no real fear that she would faint. I'd never known the woman to faint at any point of her life, but she loved the drama of the threat and used it quite regularly.

"Mama, I don't expect you to plan anything. I'm a wedding planner, remember? I can plan my own wedding."

"I can't hear you right now, Tyler. I've got my head between my knees to keep from fainting."

I rolled my eyes and walked Deacon over to the doggie fountain to try and get the pink off his face before it dried.

"Okay. Call me back when you calm down."

"Don't you dare hang up on me! Make me mad enough to cuss and then think you're just gonna end the conversation? Oh, no ma'am. Ain't gonna be a day. I've caught my breath now. You'll just have to change it."

"Change it? My date?"

"Yep."

Deacon shook with great gusto and splattered water all over me, which felt quite refreshing in the unrelenting heat of the day. I walked him back to the car and grabbed the Deacon towel from the backseat. "That's the date, Mama. It'll be fine. Please don't get so worked up about it. We have plenty of time."

"It's freezin' cold in November. Who wants to go to a wedding in the cold? This is ridiculous. You gotta move it. Why can't you pick a nice day in the spring or summer?"

"We don't want to wait until next year. November will be fine. I'm thinking I'll do a winter theme."

"Oh my Lord. Sweet Jesus, call me home. A theme? You *have* lost your mind. You've done gone off down there and been around all these high-falutin' rich folks and now you're thinking you can do a wedding in the dead-cold of November with three months to plan. I've never in my life heard of such."

"We only want a simple event so we—"

Her sharp intake of air cut me off even before she shrieked into the phone. "Oh Lord. Oh no. Oh no, no, no. Are you pregnant? Is that why you're rushin'? So help me heaven if you are pregnant after I've begged you to—"

"No, I'm not pregnant! If I was, then I think waiting three months to have the wedding would kind of defeat the purpose, don't you think?"

"Oh, thank you, Jesus. I gotta sit down. I feel like I'm gonna faint again. Let me put my head between my legs."

"Okay, I gotta go." Deacon danced dangerously near the water's edge, and the last thing I wanted to do was go in the lake after him. That, plus I really wanted off the phone.

"Wait, wait. Tyler, don't hang up yet. What about the yellow? Want me to get it just in case? You can figure out what to do with it later."

"I'm not seeing yellow, Mama. We'll figure something else out."

"But it's free." Free basically meant the holy grail to her. If something was free, we needed it. Even if we had no use for it at all. Free was a beacon that called to my mother and caught her in a tractor beam. I knew no matter what I answered, by the end of the day the back of her car would be filled with anything yellow Teri Casanova wanted to unload from her garage. If that hadn't happened already before she even called me.

Deacon pounced into the lake in pursuit of a duck, forgetting that his abnormally short legs would sink in the mud almost immediately. He turned back to me with a look that was part terror and part embarrassment.

"I gotta fish Deacon out of the lake. I'll call you later. No yellow."

I got the silly dog dried off as best I could and put him in the back seat on the Deacon blanket. When we pulled into our driveway, I was thrilled to see the front porch light on, which was great since it meant the air was back on, but not so great since I'd left all the windows open.

I led Deacon to the back yard and unleashed him, then went in the house to shut the windows before heading back outside to bathe him. The heat inside the house was suffocating, and it did nothing to help my irritable mood.

Pretty much the main reason I'd decided to get married back home was so Mama could be involved. Now I just had to figure out how to navigate those waters without sinking the whole ship.

Thursday, August 14th

Heidi called on Monday to ask if I could stop by Reynalda's office today to go over some new proposals for Jayah and Chris's event. She stressed that Reynalda had a three o'clock appointment immediately following our meeting, so I'd need to be there promptly at one so we could go over the files and allow her to get out and across town on time. I was tempted to be an hour late just to give Reynalda a taste of her own medicine, but my schedule was pretty packed so I didn't have time to waste.

I got there about a quarter 'til one. I was relieved to see the lights on and Heidi at her desk, and I must admit I wasn't surprised to find Reynalda absent.

"She's just running a little late coming back from lunch, but she'll be here shortly. I've made copies of the new proposals for you if you'd like to read through them before she gets here."

"You know, Heidi, this would be so much simpler if I could just go back to having all the vendors email me directly. They could still copy you and Reynalda so you get everything, but then I'd have it right away and we could accomplish these meetings over the phone."

"Reynalda doesn't feel comfortable with you having them email you since you work for another company."

"But all the vendors know me! They already know I work for Lillian and Laura, and that I'm just interning here for this event. It's adding more time in the process for you to get the proposals and then me coming here to get them. Even if you emailed them to me when you got them. Then I could review them and call Reynalda to discuss." Not that there was much discussion anyway. She'd yet to actually discuss the event in any detail, almost like she couldn't be bothered.

Heidi shook her head slowly. "Reynalda wants you to come here."

"But that makes no sense. It's not efficient. Especially not if she's going to be late every time I come."

Heidi shrugged and handed me the copies she'd made. Reynalda's double-R insignia was watermarked across all the pages. "Really? Does she think I'm going to somehow *steal* the proposals and use them for my own brides? Or woo Chris and Jayah to follow me?"

I stared at Heidi as she looked at the ground. I felt bad for raking her over the coals. It wasn't like she'd made any of the decisions.

When I'd finished reviewing all the proposals and Reynalda still hadn't arrived, I stood to go. "Please tell her I had to leave. She can reschedule or she can call me to discuss." I held the copies up. "Am I allowed to take these with me, or do I need to leave them here?"

Heidi stood up and wrung her hands together, dancing from foot to foot like she had to pee or something. "Please don't leave. Just a few more minutes. She'll be here, I swear, but she'll be so upset if you leave. Please stay? A couple more minutes? Okay?"

The girl looked like she was near tears. I felt like I'd wandered into the den of the Wicked Witch and found a lowly servant girl who'd been put under a spell of torment. "Okay, I'll give it a couple more minutes. Are you alright?"

She shook her head and dabbed at her eyes as her chin trembled. "I'm sorry. My boyfriend broke up with me last night. He's seeing someone else." As the words tumbled out, her tears fell and her voice broke. I started toward her, wanting to instinctively comfort a fellow human being in pain. But before I had taken two steps, Reynalda's voice rang out behind me.

"Oh, please. Are you still sniveling?"

She swept past me without so much as a word. She wore a solid black sheath underneath a long pashmina wrap in zebra print. A scarlet red wide-brimmed hat sat atop her dark brown locks, a perfect match for the red pumps she wore and the leather Prada bag she carried in the same shade.

She made her way behind the screen to fling the purse on her desk, removing her hat to toss it across the desk as well. She reemerged and stood behind Heidi with her hands on her hips.

"You've got to get over this," Reynalda said to Heidi. She still hadn't acknowledged my presence.

Heidi sniffled and wiped her eyes, drawing her shoulders back with a deep breath.

"Her boyfriend broke up with her last night," I said in her defense.

"Yes," Reynalda said with the arch of a drawn-on eyebrow, "and that's what she gets for dating the hired help. She's much better off without him."

Heidi gulped and her shoulders shook, but no tears escaped.

"The hired help? What does that mean?" I looked back and forth between Reynalda and Heidi.

They both remained silent for a moment, and then Reynalda spoke.

"I've tried to explain to Heidi that you can fall in love with a rich man just as easily as you can fall in love with a poor man. So why would you choose poor?" Reynalda turned and went back to her desk, and I weighed how awkward it would be to wrap my arms around the poor girl and rescue her from the Witch.

Heidi's eyes met mine, and a twinge of pain struck me at the wounds I saw there. She'd been betrayed and abandoned, which was painful for any girl in love, but then to have someone rub salt in it the way Reynalda had was just cruel.

I extended one arm to offer a hug, but she shook her head and left the office.

"Where's she going?" Reynalda asked from behind the screen. "I have to leave for an appointment in the next twenty minutes. I need her in here to go through these files with you. Will you fetch her please?"

Fetch her? Oh my Lord, it was taking all I had not to go off on this crazy lady. I stepped to the edge of the screen and peered at Reynalda, wishing I could melt her with my gaze.

"She seems upset. Maybe we should give her a minute."

"I don't have a minute," Reynalda clipped back. "I have somewhere to be."

I held the copies up in front of me and waved them. "She gave me the proposals, and I've looked over them. Do you want to just go through them quickly while she's composing herself?"

The startled look on her face told me she had no idea what was in the proposals and needed Heidi in order to conduct the meeting. I sighed and went to find the servant girl to deliver her to the Witch.

She was standing at the end of the hallway, crying quietly as she stared out the glass doors into the courtyard.

"Hey. You okay?"

Heidi nodded but didn't look at me.

"Why do you work for her?" I probably shouldn't have asked, but I really wanted to know.

She glanced over her shoulder at me and then looked straight ahead through the doors again. "Every assistant that has worked for her has been offered a job somewhere better. If I can do my time here, I can get somewhere. These events she does, she works with everybody who's anybody. It's great exposure. If I can just hang in here and meet a few people, I can walk out with a great opportunity."

"But she's mean and nasty. Why do people let her get away with it?"

"Because she gets stuff done. She makes things happen. She has the connections, and she always comes out on top." Heidi sighed and faced me with her arms crossed. "Besides, she doesn't act that way in front of everyone. Only the *hired help* like you and me." Her lips twisted as she stressed the words, her mouth spitting them out as if they tasted bad.

"What does that even mean? What was she talking about?"

"My boyfriend was a photographer's assistant. I met him when he worked one of our events. Reynalda never approved."

I shrugged and grimaced. "Why does she have to? She's your boss, not your mom. Why should she care who you date? And I'd say if he's gainfully employed, that's a plus, not a negative."

"We better get back in there," Heidi's shoulders slumped as she walked past me and down the hallway.

Reynalda met us at the door to her office, purse in hand, hat on head.

"I've got to go. I can't be late for my meeting because the two of you are out here boo-hooing over spilt milk. We'll have to reschedule."

My pulse started pounding and my hands shook. "I've been waiting here over an hour for you."

She ignored me and directed her attention to Heidi. "If you aren't going to be able to function professionally, I suggest you go home. But forward the phones to your cell so we don't miss any calls due to your personal baggage."

With that she slid her sunglasses on and left us dismissed as she exited the building.

"What a bitch," I muttered under my breath. I swear I saw a slight nod from Heidi, but it could have been my imagination.

I told Heidi I'd call her to reschedule and gave her a quick hug. "Don't let her get to you. Life is tough enough without letting mean people walk all over you. Go home like she told you, but don't forward the stupid phones. They can leave voice mails."

She smiled a teensy bit and swung open the glass door as I turned to go.

I'm not sure if I can finish this wedding. I might just end up on TV or in a magazine for punching out Reynalda Riley, Wicked Witch of Central Florida. I can see the headlines now.

Monday, August 18th

We picked a date. We picked a color. We picked a location. Eventually, we'll get around to picking everything else, but we're not moving fast enough for Mama.

"Hey, baby girl," she said when she called this evening, just as we were sitting down to dinner. "I wanted to let you know I picked up all that stuff Teri had—good, quality stuff by the way. I figured I'd get it since it was free, and you can go through it when you come up for the bridal shower."

I knew when she said it was free that she would—wait, did she just say bridal shower?

"Whose bridal shower?"

"Why, yours, silly. Who else's?" She laughed like I'd just said the funniest thing.

"I'm having a bridal shower?"

She stopped laughing. "Did your aunt Marjorie not call you? Well, I suwannee. Marlena is coming home Labor Day weekend for a shower, and I told Marjorie we should go ahead and have yours at the same time. Kill two birds with one stone. Marjorie was gonna call and give you all the details."

I slapped the palm of my hand against my forehead. "Okay, first of all, as you should know from this being my job for the last several years, I am slammed busy Labor Day weekend with weddings. It's a holiday weekend. People get married on holiday weekends when it's easy for their family to be off work. Secondly, I don't wanna infringe on Marlena's shower. That's rude."

"How do you figure? This way people will only have to come to one shower. Of course, your sister Tanya said that probably means you'll get less expensive gifts since they're shopping for both of you. So that's something to consider."

I groaned as Cabe took the peeler from me and finished the salads while I stood there stunned by the conversation.

"You know what? I don't even need a shower. Count me out."

"Don't be ridiculous! This is one of the few times in your adult life that people actually buy you stuff. Well, some of these old coots are gonna buy you junk no matter what. But getting married and having a baby is pretty much it once you outgrow childhood. You need to get the nice stuff while you can. Go to Target and Walmart and register for whatever y'all need."

Oh, the irony that my mother wants us to go register at Walmart to get the only nice gifts offered in adulthood.

"We already have our own stuff, Mom. We've both been living on our own a while, so we pretty much have two sets of everything." In fact, we had boxes of duplicate items sitting by the door to go to Goodwill, but she didn't need to know that.

"Well, that don't mean you can't get new stuff or better stuff. Just go register. It ain't gonna hurt nothing and some people don't pay no attention to it anyway. They just give you what they want you to have or whatever they have sitting in a closet to regift."

"But Mama, I can't come home for a shower Labor Day weekend even if I wanted to. We have seven weddings that weekend."

"Alright, I'll see if Marjorie can move it, but I don't think so. Marlena's job is very important and she can't take time off real often. She saves lives, you know."

As compared to my job, where I ruin lives by facilitating marriages?

"Don't move Marlena's shower. I don't want to have a shower at all, much less invite ourselves to be part of someone else's. Promise me you won't bully Aunt Marjorie into hosting a shower for me."

"Oh, I won't ask Marjorie. She's busier than a one-armed paper hanger trying to get Marlena's wedding planned. And she has nearly a year to plan. Her daughter didn't throw a wedding in her lap and expect her to get anything worth attending arranged in two months."

"Two? It's three—"

"Oh! Before I forget, I told your cousin Bonnie she could be a bridesmaid. She ain't never been a bridesmaid, and she's just dying to wear a fancy dress and walk down the aisle."

Cabe took my hand to lead me to the table to sit, but I was too keyed up to even look at dinner. I waved him off and went to the living room.

"Mama, no. I haven't even asked anyone to be a bridesmaid yet. You can't be asking people."

"Well, I didn't ask *people*, Tyler. I asked your cousin Bonnie. She ain't never been a bridesmaid before."

"She's fourteen. She has plenty of time to be a bridesmaid. When she's older and has some concept of what it all means. I don't even know who I'm asking, so could you just chill and let me figure out my own wedding party? Please?"

"Well, obviously you'll ask your sisters. And you might want to include a few more cousins, depending on your numbers. How many is Cabe asking?"

I rested my forehead against the living room wall and relished the cool strength of it. Then I bopped my forehead against it a couple of times in frustration.

"We. Don't. Know. We haven't discussed it yet. Let me worry about our wedding party, okay? Now, Cabe's sitting at the table all by himself and my dinner's getting cold. I'll call you when we've made decisions. Don't do anything else, please?"

He'd pretty much finished eating by the time I joined him.

"What's Patsy up to now?"

"She's picking my bridesmaids. She told my cousin Bonnie she could be in the wedding. If I have Bonnie in the wedding, there's about twenty other cousins who will want to be in the wedding, I'm sure. I don't want this all blown up to a huge event. I want something small and simple. You?"

"Small and simple works for me."

"Have you thought about who you want for groomsmen? I'm assuming Dean will be your best man?"

Cabe nodded and poured me more wine. "Yeah, I guess. I was thinking Dean, my cousin Danny. Your brother. Is there some magic number I'm supposed to have?"

I shook my head. "No, not at all. Traditionally, they match the girls with the boys, but there's no hard-fast rule. None that we're following anyway."

"What about you? Who you asking?"

"Well, I pretty much have to ask Tanya and Carrie, because they're my sisters, so that's a given. I was thinking maybe to ask Mel to be my maid of honor? Well, matron. I'd ask Carmen, but I know it would be hard for Omar to take time off from work and I don't think she'd come by herself with the baby. I can't believe Lila's almost a year old. Wow."

So much had happened since Carmen left work on maternity leave last year after having Lila. Cabe and I weren't even in contact then, and now here we are getting married.

"You don't want Lila in the wedding? Flower girl or something?"

I shuddered. "Lord, no. There is no way I would ever put a baby or a toddler in a wedding. It's unfair to them. The energy level is all elevated and they have no idea why. They're off their normal schedule and being passed around to people they don't even know. Everyone's staring at them and expecting them to walk in front of strangers without crying. No. I love Lila too much to do that to her."

"What about Eric and Erin?"

Cabe had gotten along fabulously with my niece and nephew in the short time he had with them while we were home, and he'd even talked to my sister Tanya about them coming down to visit the theme parks sometime soon.

"Yeah, I'd consider that, if Tanya was up for it. It's a big expense to have your kid in someone's wedding, especially since she's gonna be in it, too. I know she and Tommy struggle with her staying at home and them living on his teacher salary. I mean, he gets a stipend to coach, but still. I'll ask her, though."

"What about Galen?" Cabe had been looking at his plate, but he looked up as he asked the question. His eyes searched mine, his expression unreadable.

"You want me to ask Galen?" My eyes opened wide at the thought and both eyebrows shot up. "Really?"

"Not if you don't want to. But she is my sister. You're planning on her coming to the wedding, aren't you?"

I sat back in the chair and searched for my answer. "I guess? Yeah? I don't know. Do you want her to come? I kind of thought you were still waiting on the apology that may never happen. So I guess I'm a little surprised to hear that you'd want her in our wedding party."

Cabe shrugged. "I don't know what to do with it. I still think she owes us both an apology, but it's our wedding. Kind of a big deal. I don't know that I want to shut her out completely. She's my baby sister. Even when she's being a pain in my ass. Let me chew on it a little. I just wanted to know how you felt about it, you know?"

I nodded. I'd assumed Galen would be at our wedding. I couldn't imagine telling Maggie or Bill and Peggy we didn't want her there. I'd not given any thought to her being *in it*. Of course, if Cabe wanted her to be, then it's his wedding, too, and I wouldn't stand in the way.

So many decisions. No wonder brides are bitchy. I think I have a whole new understanding now.

Thursday, August 21st

Lila was not feeling well today, so Carmen stayed home with her. Which meant Charlotte was on the main phones. Happy happy joy joy.

Mel and Laura were both out doing site inspections with clients, and Charlotte is terrified of Lillian, so guess who got stuck answering her questions every time she didn't know what to do? Which was pretty much every time the phone rang.

My favorite had to have been when she told me she had a bride on the line who asked if we could do scallops rumaki without the bacon. It was about the twentieth time she'd been to my desk and it was not even noon yet. I stared at Charlotte for a moment and willed myself to answer nicely.

"Charlotte, you've never had scallops rumaki, have you?"

Her eyes widened. "No. Why? Have you?"

I nodded. "Yes, I have. Scallops rumaki are scallops wrapped in bacon. So no. We wouldn't be able to do that. She can have scallops by themselves if she'd like."

She was back twenty minutes later. "I have a bride on the phone who wants to get married underwater dressed as a mermaid. Do we do that?"

I rubbed my temples. "No. I'd have to say we don't. I can't think of an underwater facility off the top of my head."

I'm sure there's probably some place in Central Florida that it could happen, but at that moment, I was happy to pass on it.

Charlotte was intrigued, though. "They have mermaids at that Weekiwachee place, and they live underwater. Maybe we could have it there? Like, maybe the real mermaids could help with her wedding."

I glanced up from the budget in front of me, expecting to see a teasing smile, but no. Charlotte was dead serious.

"Honey, you realize those aren't *real* mermaids at Weekiwachee, right?"

She shook her head in protest. "Oh, no! I saw them on television in a special. They live under the water. They showed them swimming around, and they didn't have tanks or anything."

I nodded and weighed whether or not it mattered enough to correct her. Would it really harm anyone if Charlotte went on believing there were real mermaids living underwater at a Florida attraction?

"Tell her to call Weekiwachee and see if they can help her. We don't have a facility to accommodate it."

Her interruptions were non-stop throughout the day. It wasn't really her fault. I've been on the phones up front before, and they ring non-stop. People ask the craziest things, too. So it wasn't like I had no sympathy for Charlotte. It takes a special kind of person to man the phones. I think the reason Carmen does it so well is because she walks the line between providing over-the-top customer service and "*I don't give a damn so bye-bye.*" I certainly couldn't do that all day every day.

I tell you someone else who doesn't need to be doing it, and that's the church lady at the church across from the old manor house. It's the cutest little chapel. Stunning stained glass windows. Stone walls. Rich, wood floors. It's well over a hundred years old and quite well-preserved. Its proximity to the manor house would make it the perfect ceremony location for a reception at the old house, and that's just what my bride Ingrid had in mind to do.

She and Kyle saw the church from the outside during our initial walk-thru of the manor house yesterday, but they had to fly back to Michigan today, so I told them I'd find out what we could make happen at the church.

Mel and Lillian both said I was crazy for even trying. The church lady there is legendary among planners as being the most ferocious of her kind. Church ladies are often quite fond of their position of power, and they wield their hold on their churches with undying loyalty to the rules. Woe be unto anyone who infringes upon their authority.

I get it, to some extent, anyway. When I was in charge of the chapel at Lakeside Gardens, I had a routine. A method to my madness. We had rules in place, and they were there for a reason. You couldn't let anyone come in and take over without setting precedent for all weddings to be chaos. Rules exist to keep order and make things fair.

Undaunted, I thought perhaps I could use our common ground and shared understanding of the need for order to make some headway where others had failed. I also planned to lay on my Southern charm as thick as I could smear it. I'd be so sweet sugar wouldn't melt in my mouth.

She, on the other hand, answered the phone about as chipper and happy as a rodeo bull before the eight second bell. Where my accent was syrup, hers was vinegar.

"Good afternoon! How are you today?" I asked.

"Fine," she said, followed by the most awkward silence possible right where all of society knows you're supposed to say "and you?" or in some way return the nicety.

It unnerved me, and I stammered.

"I'm um, a, uh, wedding planner, and I have an out-of-town bride who was interested in, um, perhaps, uh, having her ceremony at—" I didn't get to finish.

"Is she a member of this church?"

"Um, no, she's—"

"We do not cater to non-parishioners. We cannot simply rent the Lord Jesus Christ by the hour. If you want to have a personal relationship with the Savior, then you can attend our church on a regular basis to worship him and engage with him."

Then she hung up on me!

Without waiting for any response, explanation or question, she just yelled into the phone that her church is not a Jesus-Rent-A-Center and hung up.

I'd love to know who nominated her to be the person answering the phones and making first contact with any unlucky caller.

It would have been fine for her to say no. I half-expected that anyway, and we get that from churches all the time. Even though you'd think a church would have somewhat of an open door policy where all who seek are not lost.

That lady would probably turn away the angels. She's probably descended from the innkeeper who told Joseph there was no room at the inn. I bet if Jesus himself came walking up in a robe and sandals, she'd asked if he was a member and then send him away.

Sunday, August 24th

Cabe's birthday is this Wednesday, and since his grandparents won't be able to come to Orlando, they invited us to come down to their house in Delray Beach today to celebrate. Maggie had mentioned that a few extended family members would be there and were eager to meet Cabe's new fiancée. I figured fair is fair, and it was my turn to sit in the middle of a room full of strangers and have everyone inspect me and ask me questions.

I got off much easier than Cabe, if I do say so myself.

Let me say, first of all, that I had no idea how wealthy Cabe's grandparents are. I mean, I knew they had money. I've met them, after all. I knew Maggie grew up in the upper echelon of society and had attended the most elite schools. I also knew that even though Cabe and Galen had grown up in a single mom household, they'd never hurt for anything materially. Maggie's parents had taken those kids traipsing all over the world. Of course, Maggie herself had a high-paying position at the Performing Arts Center and had held her own as a provider.

But Cabe never told me the extent of his family's wealth.

"It just never came up, I guess," he explained as we drove back to Orlando late tonight. "I don't look at them as being rich. I just look at them as Nana and Pops. They're my grandparents."

"Cabe! They live in a freakin' mansion on the beach. Like, you could put four of my mother's house in that house we were just in."

"It's not right on the beach. It's a couple of blocks over."

I sighed.

I had realized as we got close to his grandparents' neighborhood on the GPS that the houses were getting bigger and more elaborate. The palm trees were getting taller and the landscaping more lush. The guard gate at the entrance of their neighborhood was impressive, and my mouth probably hung open from the time the guard cleared us through to when we pulled up in front of the massive white house surrounded by palms. Almost the entire front of the house was filled with windows, which when coupled with the two-story ceilings inside the living area, made it feel huge when you entered. The entire house was done in a palette of dove gray, white, and black with occasional pops of color brought out in throw pillows, framed art or fresh floral.

The sleek, modern lines blew me away. The curved white iron free-standing staircase. The clear globes suspended from the high ceilings hanging low over the long black table set for ten with clear acrylic chairs, then a bit higher over the low gray sofas in the den with the clear octagonal table in the center, and in a variety of heights over the black leather sectional that took up almost the entire living area.

Pretty much the whole first floor was an open floor plan opening onto the patio with its rectangular lap pool and hot tub along with a large seating area and an additional table for ten out on the lawn. The tall, lush greenery blocked the view of the beach and neighboring houses, but you could hear the sound of the waves crashing nonetheless.

I walked around in a daze as Peggy gave me a tour of her home. I must have looked like country girl gone city with star-crossed eyes. I've never in my life been in a house anywhere near that large or that luxurious. I mean, my grandparents' house, where Mama lives now, is pretty big, but it's up on cinder blocks and creaks when you walk. Pa Pat used to joke that Granny had remodeled with so many new floors and ceilings that eventually he was gonna have to crawl around for lack of height in the rooms.

Never in my wildest dreams did I picture Bill and Peggy stumbling across their shiny white marble floors to make coffee on their gray marble countertops and sit down for breakfast in acrylic chairs. They just didn't strike me as ultra-contemporary. I mean, they weren't stodgy or anything. But I don't think of grandparents being so…modern.

I met Bill's sister and brother-in-law, and their daughter Bree, who is Danny the drummer's mom. Peggy's brother Rich was there with his husband Skipper and Peggy's niece, Kathryn. There was a neighbor there as well, Suzann, but I don't think she was related to the family. Just a friend close enough to be counted as family.

Everyone was so *nice*. They asked questions about my job or where I was from, but they maintained a polite distance and didn't pry. They asked about the wedding, and we all laughed at how much we haven't decided on, but they didn't jump in with suggestions or offer judgment on any of it.

I guess I hit the jackpot of families to marry into without even realizing it.

"I feel kind of inferior now," I said as Cabe and I walked across the tennis courts and down to the beach.

"What? Why?" He held my hand while we walked across the uneven sand.

"I don't know. I feel like the country bumpkin. Like one of these things is not like the other, and it's me."

"Oh my gosh, Ty. Don't be ridiculous. My family's not like that. At all."

"No, I know. I'm not saying it's them. They've been nothing but welcoming to me. But I had no idea they were so…I don't know. I look at where I come from, where I just took you to, and I want to crack up laughing. We have very different backgrounds."

"Yes, and each of those backgrounds has their benefits and their drawbacks. I told you I loved seeing you in the environment you grew up in. That small town. Everyone knowing each other. So many family members all together in the same place. It's comfortable. Cozy. Beautiful. The trees and the hills. The landscape is so tranquil. I grew up in the city, constantly surrounded by noise and activity. I never knew my father's family, and my mom is an only child, so her family is limited in size. Except for a couple of people, you pretty much met my entire extended family today. I think together we merge the best of both worlds."

"I guess. Does your family know my family's not wealthy? 'Cause if they don't, they're gonna find out at the wedding."

He stopped and took my face in his hands. "Ty, my family knows that I love you and that you make me incredibly happy just by being by my side. That's all that matters to them. You don't think I was worried about your family accepting me? Coming in as an outsider and not dressing like them or talking like them? I couldn't understand what people were saying half the time. Then when everybody starting asking me about Gerry leaving us and me not having his name? I thought I was gonna be run out of town or something. Declared a bastard or illegitimate or something crazy like that. We are who we are because of our backgrounds, babe. Now together we build our future. Just think. Our kids will have a little bit of both."

I smiled at the thought as he kissed me.

"We've never really talked about kids," I said as he released me and took my hand again. The sea air whipped my hair around my head and made an unruly mess of Cabe's curls.

"So let's talk. What about 'em?"

"You want kids?" I scrunched my nose and squinted against the sun as I looked up at him, wishing that I'd remembered to grab my shades from the car.

"Sure. Don't you?"

"Yeah, I guess. Someday. Like, how soon do you want kids?"

"Oh. I dunno. Whenever we get ready. Let's get Deacon trained first and see how we do with him before we start experimenting with human beings, okay?"

I laughed and squeezed his hand.

My heart nearly burst with the happiness of the day. The view. The water. The sand. The clear blue skies. The breeze rolling in off the waves as they crashed against the shore.

Most importantly, Cabe by my side and the future laid out before us. The warmth and acceptance of family surrounding us.

Back at the house, Peggy brought out a huge ice-cream cake for Cabe's birthday and we all sang to him. They gave him a new surfboard. It was Bill who had first introduced his grandson to the sport when Cabe was only four. Bill was a lifelong surfer and an avid fisherman as well. Cabe had clearly inherited his love of the water from his grandfather.

Maggie gave Cabe a new guitar with a condition that he promised to start playing again on a regular basis, something he hadn't done much since he returned from Seattle.

He hugged everyone and thanked them for their gifts. Peggy clapped her hand on his back and said, "We have one more surprise before the end of the festivities, and I hope you don't mind that we tagged this onto your birthday. It's actually part of your wedding gift, but we needed to go ahead and give it to you so arrangements can be made." Her eyes sparkled with joy and mischief.

Bill slid an envelope across the table to Cabe.

"Congratulations Cabe and Tyler" was scrawled across the front.

Cabe opened it with a grin and flipped it around so I could see it—an all expenses paid honeymoon to Costa Rica.

"You have to read the brochure, Tyler," Peggy gushed. "It sounds just heavenly. The rooms are little bungalows on the side of a mountain surrounded by the jungle. Every room has a hammock and an outdoor shower, and one of those mosquito nets over the bed. It looks awfully romantic!" She winked at me and patted my hand.

I smiled back at her, trying to absorb that someone had just given us a honeymoon. The best I could hope for from my family was a matching set of cookware that hadn't already been used. A honeymoon. All expenses paid. How does one casually say thank you for such an extravagant gift?

Excitement and curiosity bubbled up in me as I considered Cabe and me on our honeymoon. We hadn't talked about where we might like to go or what that would entail. I mean, I'd considered and ruled out several places for eloping, but I'd been so freaked out about the actual wedding that I hadn't really thought about the two of us taking a trip afterwards.

Costa Rica, huh? I knew nothing about it, but the brochure Peggy slid in front of me looked beautiful.

"Some of the best surfing in the world right there," Bill said. "I've tested those waters myself when I was younger. I think you're gonna love it."

Cabe grinned from ear to ear and hugged both his grandparents and his mom, and then we shared our goodbyes for the evening.

To think it was not so long ago that I felt like Cabe's family hated me and I'd never fit in. Suck it, Galen!

Wednesday, August 27th

"Okay, Mr. Shaw, this is the final birthday of your twenties and your final birthday as a single man. So is there anything in particular you'd like to do tonight?" I kicked one high-heeled sandal off under the table and slid my foot up his calf as I asked, leaving no doubt in his mind what I'd like his answer to be.

"Well, when you put it that way, several things come to mind, but we're gonna need to leave this restaurant."

We'd just finished eating at a fabulous seafood dive on St. Pete Beach. We'd driven over earlier in the afternoon to check into our pet-friendly hotel and get Deacon settled so we could watch the sun set over the gulf as we dined. So far, everything had gone right on schedule for a pretty perfect evening.

"I thought maybe we could go back and get our boy, and then take a walk along the beach under the moonlight before retiring to the room for the night." I winked and nudged my foot a little higher under the table, laughing at the sparkle of his eyes and the sharp intake of breath as he grabbed my foot and held it.

I had his gift waiting back in the room, and I'd also packed a sexy black negligee, though I didn't intend to wear it long.

The hotel was only a couple of blocks from the restaurant, and we walked back with our arms around each other's waist, nuzzling and kissing as we reveled in the high that good love brings. He stopped just short of unlocking the door of our room, claiming my lips as he pulled my body against his. Sparks of electricity coursed through me, increasing the intensity of the deep throbbing that had been building all night.

Suddenly, something slammed the window by the door with enough force that I ducked for fear the glass would shatter. Cabe instinctively drew me behind him just as the window was hit again.

"Dammit, Deacon!" Cabe scrambled to get the door unlocked and was nearly bowled over by Deacon when it opened. "What the hell?"

"But he was in the crate! How is he out? He was in his crate. I latched it. I swear."

My eyes took in the room with amazement and horror. The comforter had been stripped almost completely from the bed, and the pillows had been reduced to puffs of foam scattered all over the room. The painting that had hung over the bed had been knocked off the wall, its glass shattered all over the nightstand and mattress. The lamp was on the floor, its shade crushed and torn. The window blinds were destroyed and half-eaten, hanging by a thread and almost torn free on one side. The window itself had originally been covered in a thick, dark tint, but that had been shredded by his nails as he scratched the window repeatedly in our absence.

The small sofa underneath the window had one of its two leather cushions torn open and its guts removed. The back of the sofa was shredded almost as bad as the window.

To say Deacon looked happy to see us would be the ultimate understatement. I don't know if he thought we'd dropped him off and left him forever, but the pure joy and relief on his face was unmistakable.

"Okay, buddy. Okay, calm down. Sit down. Okay, buddy. Okay." Cabe stared at the room almost in a daze as he stroked Deacon's head and worked to settle him down.

"I swear I latched the crate," I repeated as I replayed the evening in my head, clearly seeing my fingers slide the latch in place before we left for the restaurant.

"Well, if you swear you latched it, and Dean swears he latched it when we went out of town to visit your mom, then I think our boy may have figured out how to open the latch."

I examined the latch and looked back and forth from Deacon to the crate, stunned and bewildered. "Are you serious? But how could he do that?"

Cabe dropped to his knees and petted Deacon as he began to settle down. "I guess he's just really intelligent."

"And suffers from really bad separation anxiety."

"Yeah, he's only done it when we'd been gone for the weekend and when we left him here in a strange place."

I sank down on the chair, the only untouched piece of furniture in the room it seemed.

"Sooo, what? We're not ever going to be able to go anywhere?"

Cabe examined the crate as Deacon came over to beg my affection.

"I think we need to secure the latch somehow so he can't slide it."

We cleaned up the glass and the foam, removed the destroyed blinds and threw away the damaged pillows.

"I wonder if housekeeping would give us a vacuum cleaner to make sure we got all the glass out of the bed." I stood looking at the mattress with my hands on my hips, dreading the possibility of rolling over in the night and getting stabbed with a sliver of glass.

"Babe, did you see the size of this place? There's only, like, twelve rooms. They don't have housekeeping staff on at night. You'd be lucky to find a front desk clerk."

"So what can we do?"

"I'll go see if there's anyone at the desk, and if not, I'll look and see if I can find a supply closet with a vacuum cleaner." Deacon immediately started dancing in circles at the mere suggestion that Cabe was leaving.

"What's up with him? He doesn't act like this when you leave at home." I sat in the floor and pulled Deacon in my lap, trying to calm him without much success.

"Deacon got surrendered to three different shelters before I got him. He's a little skittish about being left again. I think the fact that it's a new place and he's not familiar is probably freaking him out. Hold onto him, and I'll be right back."

Deacon nearly busted a gut trying to get out of my lap and follow Cabe. His nails, which were jagged from ripping through window tint, blinds, and a leather cushion pretty much ruined my skirt and left nasty red marks all over my legs.

Cabe returned within minutes with a vacuum cleaner. "Found one! There's a janitor's closet right by the ice machine. Wasn't locked."

He vacuumed the bed and the floor, and I carefully inspected the sheets for any sign of glass. No matter how many times I looked them over, I kept seeing little tiny sparkles in the light.

"Alright, well, looks like we're gonna have to go get new sheets and some new window blinds," Cabe said as looked over my shoulder at the contaminated bedclothes.

"Are you serious? Where?"

"There's an all-night Walmart over on the mainland, not too far from here. One of us can go in and the other can sit with Deacon in the car. We're obviously going to lose our deposit when they see the room, but at least with sheets and blinds we can get some sleep tonight."

So instead of taking a nice, romantic walk along the water's edge under the pale glow of the moon, we made a trek to Walmart, Mecca of the strange and unkempt at eleven o'clock at night. I don't know which shift was scarier, staying in the parking lot with Deacon or going inside.

Needless to say, by the time we finished our late night purchases, put the fresh-new-still-smelling-like-chemical sheets on the bed and installed the new window blinds with the screwdriver he found in the janitor's closet, we were both too exhausted to even think about amorous activities. I didn't even pull the negligee out of the suitcase and opted instead to sleep in the swimsuit cover-up I'd brought for the beach tomorrow.

Deacon curled up across our feet as soon as we climbed in bed and was asleep within minutes. Poor baby had quite the workout tonight. Physically and emotionally.

We hadn't been laying there in the dark long when Cabe sighed. "What a way to end my birthday, huh?"

"Oh crap!" I said, throwing back the covers and sprinting across the room.

"What? What's wrong?" He sat up and turned on the flashlight on his phone since the lamp was inoperable.

"Your gift. In all the excitement of Capt. Deacon Destructo, I forgot to give it to you." I flipped on the overhead light and handed him the box as I folded my feet beneath me on the bed, suddenly excited to see his response.

He opened it slowly and read the front of the packet inside, his mouth widening in a grin that spread across his face.

I wish I could freeze frame the expression on his face when he looked up to meet my eyes. I never want to forget it. The light in his eyes. The way the blue seemed to swirl in his excitement, the pupils moving in response to his emotion as I watched. The transformation of the stressed and tired set of his jaw to a relaxed smile, mouth open wide to expose his perfect white teeth.

"Are you kidding me? Is this for real?" He waved the piece of paper and laughed, a deep belly laugh that tickled me down to my very being. "Oh my god, babe, how did you do this?"

"Laura had a groom come in last month who was a music producer, and I asked if he'd ever heard of the band Running with Scissors. I told him they were your favorite group, and I'd love to get you some kind of signed memorabilia. He not only had heard of them but he asked if I knew they were working on a new album to be out next year. They're planning on touring when the new record releases."

Cabe whooped another big belly laugh and looked down to read the paper again.

"So he contacted me a couple of weeks ago and said he could get you access into a recording session so you could meet the band. I told him you play guitar a little as a hobby, and he said bring it and you can jam with them. I guess he's close with their manager or something? So yeah. We're flying to Dallas in February to hang out with your band for the day. Your VIP passes are in there, along with our plane tickets and hotel reservations. That's the studio pass you're holding." I grinned almost as big as he did. I knew it was a kick-ass gift, and I knew how much it meant to him.

He pulled me against him and expressed his appreciation well into the wee hours of the night.

His birthday had a happy ending after all.

September

Monday, September 1st

My phone rang first thing this morning. I have to remind Mama that I don't have Mondays off now that we're moving back into the busy season. I think I've talked to her more in the last two months than I have in the past six years.

"I can't really talk right now, Mama. What's up?"

"I talked to Tanya and Carrie both this weekend and neither one of them have heard boo from you about being a bridesmaid. Are you gonna ask your sisters to be in your wedding?"

"Yes, I'm going to ask them. Work's been crazy. I'll call them tonight. I gotta go."

"Have you asked anybody? How many people are we talking? What about Gabe's sister?"

"Cabe. And I don't know."

"You don't know if you've asked anybody?"

I pinched the bridge of my nose and shut my eyes against the stress. I had a pile of paperwork to do, an inbox full of unanswered emails, and a phone conference with Reynalda's bride in twenty minutes. I had no spare time or energy to deal with Mama and my wedding.

"No, I don't know if Cabe's sister will be a bridesmaid. I need to go, though."

"Well, why on earth wouldn't she be?"

"We had somewhat of a falling out, so I don't know what's going on there. Can we talk about this later? I'm buried at work and I have—"

"What? What sort of falling out? Won't she be a bridesmaid?"

I glanced at the clock and the stack on my desk and sighed. I needed all the time I could get to prepare for the call to Reynalda's bride.

"I don't know. We haven't decided yet."

Mama's voice rose an octave in distress. "But that's his *sister*. She's *family*. She has to be in it. You can't leave out his sister."

I cursed myself for answering her call knowing I had no time to talk. "I didn't say we weren't gonna ask her; I said we haven't decided yet. She's pretty much not speaking to either one of us right now."

"Look here, Tyler Lorraine. When the train has left the station and you got nowhere to go, family is family."

"That makes no sense. What does that even mean?"

She sighed. "You have to forgive family no matter what. You marry this man, you marry his family. This girl's gone be your sister-in-law the rest of your life, Lord willing and this marriage works out. Don't exclude her from the start, 'cause she won't forget it if you do. She'll be madder than a wet hen and she'll remind you every anniversary."

"But you don't know what she's done."

"Now, you listen to me. Your daddy's sisters have done plenty to me over the years, and I reckon I've done my share to them. Your aunt Donna and me didn't speak to each other for nigh about five years when you was little. No need to get into the whys, but I'm just telling you this stuff happens in families. You ask this girl to be your bridesmaid. You bury whatever hatchet you got to get through the day. Go on being mad at her if she's done something deserving of it, but don't keep her out of the wedding. Y'all gonna make up at some point, but this can't be undone. I gotta go. My hair's drying and you know what a rat's nest it'll be if I don't do something with it while it's damp."

Oh, never mind that I'm at work and have asked to go multiple times. God forbid her hair be frizzy.

"Bye, Mama."

"Wait! How many dresses should I tell Wanda she's making? She wants to get the material and she needs measurements."

"I've already told you I don't want Wanda to do the dresses. We'll buy dresses. Don't plan anything with Wanda for dresses."

"Look here, Miss High-Falutin', your sister Tanya lives on a very tight budget, and I'll not have you putting her in debt buying fancy outfits she and those kids won't ever wear again. Wanda is willing to make them without charging you a cent out of the kindness of her heart and dedication to family. So you need to think about your sister and do what's best for her."

I looked up to see Mel in my doorway and I pressed my hands together in a silent plea for prayer.

"It's not that I'm not thinking of Tanya, Mama. In fact, Cabe and I talked about not having Eric and Erin in the wedding so that it wouldn't be such an expense for her."

"What? Not have your only niece and nephew in your own wedding?

Have you lost your mind? She'll have to get something for them to wear either way. Or are you not going to invite them at all? I mean, if they don't mean enough to you to be in your wedding, your *only* niece and nephew, then I guess it doesn't matter to you if they're even there. Your sister will be thrilled to hear her family is not even important enough to be included."

"Oh, Jesus, I didn't—"

"Don't you dare take the Lord's name in vain! It's one thing for you to disrespect us, your own flesh and blood. But I will not stand by and allow you to disrespect our Lord and Savior."

I pulled the phone away from my ear to protect my eardrum as Mel grimaced and tiptoed out of my office.

"I'm not trying to disrespect anybody! Or be inconsiderate of anybody. But I do think that I should be allowed to make decisions on what I want for my own wedding. It's not like I'm asking for some extravagant, over-the-top event. If anything, I'm trying to tone down what you're cooking up. But I do have certain things that I want and don't want, and I think I'm within my rights to say that. I haven't asked you to plan anything, Mama. *Nothing.* I haven't asked you to spend one penny. And I appreciate what you've done and what you're doing, and I appreciate that you care and you want to help, but it's *my* wedding. I feel like when you ignore my requests and don't listen to what I'm asking, you're being inconsiderate of me and disrespecting me."

"I did not raise you to speak to me that way. Your poor daddy, Lord bless his soul, is spinning over in his grave out yonder behind that church, and he's likely to burrow his way to China listening to you talk to me like that. I'm hanging up and you can call me back when you're ready to apologize."

Well. At least I got her off the phone so I could work. Jeez. What was I thinking? Why didn't we just elope?

Tuesday, September 2nd

I didn't have the energy or motivation to call back and apologize last night for something I think I had every right to say.

I see brides all the time who yell and scream and demand exorbitant extravagances from their parents. I didn't raise my voice. I didn't act ugly to her. I simply stood up for myself and what's important to me.

If we're not asking her to pay for the wedding—to pay for anything at the wedding—then why is it rude for me to say what I want?

I called Tanya this morning after my second cup of coffee and blubbered out the whole mess, ruining my make-up in the process. I knew my sister would understand.

"You're preaching to the choir, honey. Why do you think Carrie and I both chose not to have weddings? You can't let her railroad you into doing what you don't want, but you also need to realize this is all she's got right now. My kids are getting older and now that I'm staying at home, I call her a lot less to pick them up, babysit, run errands for me. Carrie hasn't needed Mama since the age of two, and Brad is off in college and head over heels into Kelly. What do you think of her by the way?"

"She's nice, I guess. I didn't get to spend much time with her. You?"

"Eh. She's okay. But back to the subject at hand, this is all Mama has going on right now. She's bored and feeling unnecessary, and I think pouring all her energy into your wedding keeps her occupied and makes her feel good. Which we all appreciate by the way."

"So glad I could help. You couldn't tell she's feeling good by the way she talks. She's doing all this stuff that I never asked her to do and then complaining about the time and expense of doing it."

"That's just Patsy, and you know that. Mama ain't happy unless she's got something to complain about. Daddy used to say Mama's philosophy was the more misery, the merrier. You gotta ignore that."

"She keeps telling me how rude I'm being to everybody. So where do I draw the line between wanting what I want and not being selfish? Because I see selfish brides. Brides who are so nasty to their mothers and their fiancés that I don't know why anyone would even come to their wedding. I don't feel like I'm being that way at all. I just don't want silk flowers in baskets and Wanda's attempt at bridesmaids' dresses."

I wiped at my eyes and blew my nose, ignoring the call coming in on my desk phone.

"Oh, please tell me she is not trying to convince you to have Wanda make dresses. Bless her heart, that girl couldn't sew a straight line if she had a yard stick glued to the fabric. You need to say no."

I rocked my chair back to an upright position and slid under the desk.

"Wait a minute. Mama told me I need to let Wanda make the dresses because you can't afford to buy one and that I'm being inconsiderate of you. So you don't want Wanda to make the dresses?"

"Of course not! I ain't wearing anything Wanda makes."

"Oh my gosh! I am so relieved. I don't want Wanda to sew the dresses, but I didn't want to put you out. Cabe and I even talked about not asking Eric and Erin to be in the wedding since I know that's a huge expense. Um, by the way, will you be my bridesmaid?"

Tanya laughed. "Of course, sweetie. You know that. Look. If you want the kids in the wedding, ask the kids to be in the wedding and let me know what you want them to wear. If I can come up with it, I will. If we can't, I'll tell you. Just be reasonable with what you pick and I'm sure it'll be fine. We're living on a budget but we're not destitute."

"I don't care specifically what you choose for them. Maybe just something white or silver for Erin to go with the winter theme, which Mama also says is stupid."

"Really? Because she's been bragging all over town about how her daughter the wedding planner has chosen a winter wonderland theme for her wedding. So she may be giving you crap about it, but to everyone else she's singing your praises."

"So what do I do about these silk centerpieces? I really don't want them. I'm not knocking it for anyone else who likes it. If it works for them, that's great. But it's just not my taste, you know?"

"You don't have to apologize for what you want, Ty. It's your wedding. Hopefully the only one you'll ever get. I never had one, so I didn't get any say-so at all. This is your opportunity. Take it. Make it your own."

"What do I do about Mama though?"

"Apologize to Patsy and mend the fence. Why don't you give her a job? Like, think of some task you don't care that much about, and tell her to run with it. That way she has some control and can make some decisions, and you get to focus on the stuff that's important to you."

"That's actually a great idea. Thanks, T."

"You're welcome. Little T."

I dreaded making the call all day. I even waited until after dinner and a glass of wine. Finally, I bit the bullet and called my mother. I told her I was sorry I'd lost my temper and that I was sure it was due to the nonstop work schedule and pressure I'd been under. I bit my lip and said a prayer that my sister's suggestion would work.

"There's something I'd like to ask your help with." My voice sounded more uncertain than I had intended.

"Oh, really? Do tell. Because it seems like you don't want my help at all. You've criticized everything I've tried to do, and no matter how hard I try to make you happy, all I get is attitude and ungratefulness."

Her voice broke in between her guilt-inducing pleas.

"No one in the world loves their children more than I do."

Sob.

"But ain't nobody that gets treated with more ungratefulness than I do."

Sob.

"From all four of you. Ain't a one of you appreciates all I do for you."

Sob.

"One of these days I'll be dead and gone. Buried out yonder by your daddy—" She couldn't continue for the sobbing.

I gave her a minute or so to regain her composure before continuing.

"Mama, I appreciate all you're doing. I really do. There's just some things I want to handle on my own, and I have ideas in my head of what I want. But I was thinking since you and Aunt Pearl are so crafty and so artistic, maybe the two of you could come up with an idea for a favor."

"A what?"

"A favor. You know. Something you give everyone that attends the wedding."

"Well, why are you giving them gifts? It's your wedding. They need to be giving you gifts."

"It's a token, Mama. Something that says you appreciate them coming. Some folks do a little bag of chocolate kisses or Jordan almonds."

"Oh, I hate those things. I cracked a crown off my tooth eating a Jordan almond at Earleen's granddaughter's wedding. It's given me fits ever since."

"Well, we're not doing Jordan almonds so that won't be a problem. I was thinking maybe y'all could come up with something that fits the winter theme, or maybe something that reflects our family's heritage."

"Our heritage? Hmmph."

She was silent a moment, and I waited to see if she was building up steam to blow again or just mulling over an idea.

"Okay. Let me talk to Pearl and see what we can come up with."

Hallelujah. Peace on earth. For a moment at least.

Thursday, September 4th

Charlotte came running into my office today clapping her hands and hopping up and down like a hyperactive Energizer bunny.

"Guess what? Guess what? Guess what?" Her voice bubbled over the top with enthusiasm.

"What? What? What?" I asked with no enthusiasm at all.

"It's happening. We did it! We actually did it!"

"What are you talking about, Charlotte?"

"The mermaid wedding! I told the lady to call Weekiwachee like you said, and she did. She called me back just now and said Weekiwachee is willing to let her have the wedding there. Underwater. So now she needs you to get the contracts or whatever it is that we do next. She wanted to come in and meet me, but I told her she'd need to work with you. I mean, I said I'd help out, of course. I can, right? I can help, right?"

"Slow down the horse and cart, Nelly! What are you talking about?"

"Remember? Two weeks ago this lady called and wanted to do an underwater wedding dressed as a mermaid? But you said we don't have any places to do that and you told me to have her call Weekiwachee? And you're not going to believe this, but remember you said those weren't real mermaids? You were right. It turns out it's just regular people like you and me except they train to hold their breath for, like, a really long time. They're gonna train this bride. Isn't this exciting?"

"Wait. Whoa. Someone wants us to do a mermaid wedding up in Weekiwachee? Are you serious? I told you to tell her we couldn't do her wedding."

"No, you told me we didn't have a place to do it, and then you suggested a place for her to call. So now we're good to go. I can help, right?"

I buried my head in my hands and cursed myself for not taking the time to deal with this when the call came in. Now I'm doing a mermaid wedding underwater.

Just when I think I've seen it all, another crazy bride shows up and proves it's a never-ending parade.

Saturday, September 6th

My morning wedding was done by one, so I headed over to help Mel with her ceremony and reception before visiting Lillian at her late-night dessert party.

"So are you definitely doing a winter theme?" Mel asked as we waited for her reception to begin.

I nodded. "Yeah. As much as I can call it a theme with my mother involved. It's probably going to look more like a flea market grouping. Let's say I *want* a winter theme. What I get might be another story. For some reason, I'm liking snowflakes. I found some invitations with a snowflake on vellum over a purple background, then you lift the snowflake up and details are in silver on the purple. Mama's stroking that I'm sending out invitations. She wanted to put an ad in the paper and a picture of me and Cabe with a notice that said '*friends and family of the bride and groom are invited to attend via this medium.*' I told her I didn't want half the county in attendance."

"Do people do that?"

"All the time."

"But how do you know how many will come? How do you prepare food or plan seating?"

I laughed. "Potluck and lots of folding chairs."

"Nice. I'm thinking you're right to go with invitations. Know what you're getting. You're sticking with the purple then?"

"Yeah. We both really like purple, and I think it goes well with the white and silver winter wonderland look."

"You gonna do a purple wedding dress?"

Memories of a tattooed derriere floated in front of my eyes and I shuddered. "Uh, no. Definitely not."

"Oh come on," Mel teased. "You could do a purple veil and maybe put some snowflakes on it. You could buy some glittery snowflake Christmas ornaments and hot glue them to the skirt and the train."

"As fabulous as that sounds, I'm gonna pass."

She laughed. "Have you found a dress yet?"

"I haven't had time to go look. Considering I don't have another day off for like six weeks, I was thinking maybe you and I might go one night after work. When are you available?"

"Any night Paul is watching car shows on TV. So basically, any night! Don't you want to go with your mama though?"

I drew back and looked at her like she'd lost her mind. "Lord, no! Are you crazy? My mother and I have vastly different tastes in clothing. I could never shop with her for school clothes or prom or anything. My wedding? No, thanks!"

"What about your sisters?"

"I'd love to have them with me, and I'm sure they'd love to be there, but logistically, it's not possible. I don't want to shop for a dress up there and have to go there for fittings and stuff. Plus, there's such a wider selection here, and I know all the seamstresses and shops. I figured I'd just take my matron of honor with me to get a feel for what's out there. Make a fun evening of it. Then maybe once I narrowed it down, I could show my sisters and Mama and maybe let them cast a vote or something."

Mel scrunched her nose and forehead in confusion and looked at me. "Who's your matron of honor?"

"Well, I was hoping you'd be!"

"Oh my gosh! Oh wow!" she shrieked, which caught the attention of everyone in the convention center hallway. She then grasped both my arms and hopped up and down as she giggled, which definitely got her some more quizzical looks. "Are you serious? Are you asking me? Are you sure?"

I laughed along with her and nodded. "Yep? Will you be my matron?"

"I've never been a maid of honor before, or a matron. Sounds so old, doesn't it? Can't we just tell people I'm the maid of honor? Most people don't know the difference anyway."

"You can give yourself whatever title you'd like."

"Oh, I'll have to think about that."

"You've got a little over two months to come up with it. But right now, we have to get your reception underway so I can go help Lillian with dessert."

Many hours later, I was leaving Lillian's event and hobbling on the pins and needles in my feet.

"What time are you back tomorrow?" Lillian walked alongside me without any indication of the number of hours she'd been on her feet. I don't know if her feet went completely numb years ago or if she hides the pain like a Spartan warrior.

"I told Laura I'd check her reception since she needs to be at the ceremony and Charlotte can't go unsupervised."

"Useless twit," Lillian said with a roll of her eyes. "I don't know why Laura insists on keeping her. We're not a charity."

"She's been doing a little better," I said with a smile, though in reality I agreed with Lillian wholeheartedly.

"Oh yes. She's done splendid. She told someone on the phone they could have a reception in the chapel at Lakeside if they brought their own food, and I'm sure you heard that she broke one of Mel's toasting glasses last weekend."

"Hey, at least she unwrapped the glasses. That's progress."

We reached our cars and were about to get in and go our separate ways when she turned to me. "I don't think I've said congratulations."

She had not. Though there had been several conversations at work regarding my ring, my wedding, the date I'd set. She'd never spoken up or acknowledged it in any way.

She looked at me for a moment, and the expression in her eyes saddened me. It was wistful. Like she was remembering something painful. Something far away. Then she focused again and fixed her eyes directly into mine.

"Be happy. Be in love and rejoice in all it has to offer. But do not ever lose yourself to it. You cannot ever fully depend on any other person. They're flawed. We all are. I know I've told you this before, but people look out for their own best interests. In a marriage, you must look out for each other. Care for one another. But don't ever forget to take care of yourself. To protect yourself. Congratulations, Tyler. I wish a lifetime of happiness for you and Cabe both."

With that, she drove away into the night.

Monday, September 8th
Labor Day

I hobbled into the house on numb feet after participating in some way in seven weddings over four days. I swear whoever came up with the idea of women wearing heels had to be a master of torture devices.

My wonderful fiancé, who had spent the day relaxing and surfing at the beach, greeted me at the door with a Pina Colada. My surfer boy was shirtless, tanned beyond belief, and sporting some sexy tousled beach curls. It's a testament to how tired I was that he looked that good yet I had no desire to do anything but take a bath and sleep.

He had run a lavender bath for me and bought me the latest issue of Cosmo, and he even popped in and refilled my Pina Colada when my glass was half full.

If I hadn't already promised to marry this man, I would have signed up tonight without question.

Mama had called twice during the day, and I let it go to voice mail both times. So as soon as the water had gotten too chilled to be comfortable and my drink had melted, I decided it was time to face the music and call her back.

When I stepped out of the tub, sharp pains shot through my heels and up into my calves. I winced and tried to step lightly, which didn't help in the slightest.

When I'd gotten my jammies on and limped down the hallway to the couch, I settled against the pillows to call her. Cabe lifted my feet like he was going to rub them, but I waved him away in fear of the pain any physical contact would cause.

"It's about time you called," Mama said. "I needed you to make a

198

decision but couldn't get a call back, so I decided for you."

Oh no. What on earth had been picked for me now?

"You said you wanted a winter theme, and I found some programs with snowmen on them. But Tanya said she thought you'd like the snowflakes better. I tried to call and ask you—"

"Don't get programs! We don't need programs. That's a waste of money."

She didn't miss a beat. "—but you didn't answer your phone. I called twice. What do you mean you don't need programs? How on earth will people know what's going on if you don't have programs?"

"Weddings are pretty self-explanatory, Mama. People come in. They say the vows, do the rings, they kiss, and people go out. When have you ever been at a wedding and thought, '*oh, I'm lost. What's happening next?*' You don't. I'm telling you, it's a waste of money."

"But it's a keepsake. People like to keep them."

"Tell me how many wedding programs you have in your house right now and where they are. You know what? Never mind. You're a bad example. Ask Tanya how many wedding programs she has and where they are. People don't pay attention to them, and they toss them out after the wedding."

"Now's a fine time to tell me. Why couldn't you tell me that before I bought two hundred and fifty cards?"

"Two hundred and fifty?" I sat up and scared the crap out of Deacon who'd been sleeping at Cabe's feet. "Why did you buy so many?"

She yelled her response in my ear so loud that me, Deacon, and Cabe all jumped. "*Because you haven't given me a number and you didn't answer your phone.*"

Deacon crawled behind Cabe's legs and Cabe stared back at me with his eyes wide with shock.

"I was *working*," I answered back with all the attitude of a fifteen-year-old called out on her behavior.

"I've been asking you to tell me how many people are coming since you first told me you were getting married. I've been working nonstop to try and pull this together on your behalf with very little input or work on your part, missy. I'm about ready to throw my hands up in the air and tell you you're on your own."

Oh, that I should be so lucky.

"Remember, you were sure," Cabe whispered as he rubbed my calves where I'd draped them across his leg.

"Thanks," I mouthed and then stuck my tongue out at him.

"Mama, I appreciate how hard you've been working on this. Cabe and I both appreciate it." He nodded dramatically with his lips puckered out. "I've told you I'm happy to handle the planning on my own, but I know it means a lot to you to help out."

"Help out? Name one single thing you've done."

She might have a point. I hadn't actually done a lot. Yet. I planned to do a lot. I just hadn't gotten around to it. But I hadn't asked her to do all she'd been doing either.

"I picked out invitations."

"Really. Did you order those invitations? Because in order to do that, you'd need to know how many people you're inviting."

I moved my legs off Cabe's lap, his well-intentioned touch too irritating in light of the conversation I was having.

She wasn't close to being finished.

"I got a carport full of yellow stuff you've decided you don't want, I can't see my dining room table for all the silks I bought that you don't want, and now I am the proud owner of two hundred and fifty snowflake cards that you're saying is a waste of money. Why should I bother doing anything else?"

Now, in all fairness, I didn't ask her to do any of that. In fact, I specifically told her not to do the yellow or the silks. But I knew good and well that Patsy Warren wasn't gonna hear that. Just like I knew she wasn't going to back off and let me plan my own event. So I took a deep breath and blew it out real slow and reminded myself what Cabe had said. I was sure I wanted a wedding back home even though that meant dealing with Mama.

"We can use the snowflake cards. The invitations I picked are snowflakes too, so maybe that will match somehow. Can you take a picture of them and send it to me, or maybe have Tanya take one and send it?"

"When are you gonna decide who's invited? Folks need to make plans, Tyler. Unlike me, they don't have nothing but time on their hands to be at your beck and call."

I groaned and glared at Cabe. Not because he'd done anything, but just because he was there and the person I wanted to glare at was not. "Tomorrow. We'll decide a count tomorrow."

Cabe's head popped up from his magazine and his eyes widened again. "Tomorrow?"

I put my hand up and turned away from him.

"Okay. I'm on hold until I have that number. I can't do centerpieces. I can't do programs. I can't figure out tablecloths. So I guess maybe I might get something done in my own life while I'm waiting on you."

"All of which I've asked you not to do."

"Well, you need to get going. You're not taking this seriously enough. People need to know. Things need to be arranged. You need to come up with who you're inviting and how many. Stop putting it off."

"I'm not putting it off! I'm busy. You want a count? A hundred. I don't think it will be that many, but say a hundred. There. You have a number."

"Does that include all your cousins?"

I almost threw the phone. "Mama, I can't afford to invite every cousin we have. I'll invite your brother and sisters, and Daddy's sisters but I can't do all the cousins."

"I declare, Tyler. You're gonna insult half the county if you do that."

"That may very well be, but unless half the county wants to pay for their meal, they're not invited."

Mama clucked her tongue. "We'll just have a potluck and have everybody bring a dish. Then it won't cost you and you can invite as many as you want."

"But I don't want to invite the whole county. I want a small, intimate event with my closest friends and family. And it would still cost me money because of linens and centerpieces and all that goes with it. So no. I'm not inviting all those people."

"I got you free linens you could use, and I have a carport full of silks for centerpieces. How is that gonna cost you a dime?"

It was like talking to a brick wall. No matter how many times I said the same thing, she wouldn't listen. It was exhausting and I was already beyond exhausted from the weekend I'd just had. I was done.

"I gotta go. I'll talk to you later."

"I wanted to ask—"

"Mama, I'm hanging up. I can't talk about weddings any more. I'll call you tomorrow. Bye."

My shoulders sank as I turned to face Cabe, tears tickling the backs of my eyelids in a combination of exhaustion, frustration, irritation, and desperation.

"C'mere." He opened his arms and enveloped me in their warmth and security. "So we need to make a list?"

I nodded and swallowed hard against the burning in my throat.

He kneaded the tight muscles between my shoulder blades and up my neck. "Okay. We can do that. Why don't you give me a job? You know, like you gave Patsy a specific task? Give me one. Tell me what I can do to help you."

"You're not the problem. I don't need you to do anything. I need Patsy to stop doing things."

"Well, I can't control what Patsy does or doesn't do, but I can help you alleviate some stress on this end. Give me a job. Tell me what you want me to do."

"I don't know. What do you want to do?"

"Want me to handle the music? I could pick out all the songs for the ceremony and reception. Get playlists together. Would that help?"

"That would be good. Yeah. You do the music. And I need you, Dean and Danny to pick out whatever you're going to wear and go get fitted.

Once you've made those arrangements, let my brother know."

"Okay. We can do that. What else?"

"I don't know."

He kissed the top of my head and held me tighter as I snuggled closer to him. "Why don't you delegate some other stuff out? Put Carrie in charge of something. Or Tanya. Get someone else to deal with Patsy so it's not all on you."

"Thank you for being so supportive." I leaned back to look in his eyes and smiled at the thought of being his wife. "Sure do wish we could skip all this. Just sneak away. The two of us."

"We can."

I stretched to kiss him, and he leaned to meet me halfway.

"We can't," I said when our lips parted. "We're too far gone now. There's no way I could tell her we're calling the whole thing off and eloping. I should have taken you up on it when you first offered. We'd be done by now. I'd be Mrs. Cabe Shaw, and I wouldn't be dealing with any of this."

"So let's say for the rest of the night, you don't have to deal with it. We'll turn the phones off and watch some sappy movies, or we can play a round of Scrabble, or we could venture down the hallway and take your mind off it another way."

Hmmm. Let me see. A sappy movie that will make me cry, a round of Scrabble where I have to tax my tired brain in order to beat Mr. Word Genius, or a little romp between the sheets with my tanned, sculpted, curly-haired, blue-eyed fiancé? Not even a question.

Thursday, September 11th

Maggie called last night to ask if Cabe and I would meet her for lunch. I didn't have any apprehension this time, just curiosity and a heavy dose of guilt for leaving the pile of papers on my desk to go out to lunch.

"I wanted to talk to you both about the rehearsal dinner," she said after we'd finished the customary small talk. "Do you know of a location that would be appropriate to hold it?"

My stomach lurched. I hadn't even thought of the rehearsal dinner. Hell, I'd had so much stress thinking about the wedding itself I'd not even considered that we'd have a rehearsal or rehearsal dinner.

"What were you thinking of doing? Like a restaurant or something?" I asked.

"I'd like to reserve a private space. I have a dear friend, Sandy, who owns an event company in Atlanta. They do floral design, decor, catering. I'd thought to rent a space near your church and have her bring her team. If that's okay with you?"

I nodded. "Sure, that sounds great. I'm just not sure what's available like that. I mean, you could do the fellowship hall at the church, which is where we're having the reception. I don't really know of like a convention space or banquet hall, though."

"It's a real small town, Mom." Cabe chuckled and winked at me.

"I see. Well, I can have Sandy research it, I suppose."

"I'll ask my mom, too. She may know of something."

Maggie smiled and shifted her weight in her chair. "The other thing I wanted to mention, and I want to make it clear that I'm not trying to step on toes or take control, but I'd like to offer Sandy's services. She does amazing events, and she's already said she'd love to be involved in whatever way possible. Sandy and I danced together when we first made Company, oh, a hundred years ago when the world was young. She's known Cabe his whole life, and she's thrilled that you're getting married so near her. If you wanted to have her do the flowers or the catering, I'd be happy to put you in touch with her. I'll pick up the tab for whatever you choose in floral as my wedding gift to you."

A tiny little spark of excitement caught fire within me and spread the smile across my face. "Really? That would be incredible!"

Part of my hesitation in planning the floral and catering was the lack of options available. The only caterer in our tiny town is Bubba Dog's BBQ, which is not what I have in mind for my wedding. As far as flowers, I knew Maude Price could do a decent job, but she was no designer. She'd run the floral shop in town for over thirty years, but her forte was delivery bouquets and funeral wreaths. Not centerpieces. Unfortunately, Mama would have a hissy fit if I mentioned hiring someone from Atlanta, but if it was a gift from Maggie, surely she wouldn't refuse that!

"Great," Maggie said. "I'll text you Sandy's contact info and you can get in touch with her directly. Then just let me know what you decide and I'll work it out with her."

"Thanks, Mom," Cabe said as he leaned in to plant a light kiss on her cheek. He sat back and took my hand in his. "We really appreciate it. Tyler's been under a lot of stress trying to get everything planned, and I know it would help her a lot for Sandy to be onboard."

I nodded and thanked Maggie, trying to ignore the whiny voice in the back of my head telling me I was nuts if I thought my mother was going to be okay with this.

She had no reason not to, really. I mean, it would be a lot less work for her, right?

I watched Cabe as we walked hand-in-hand back to our cars, amused by the sly grin he wore.

"Did you do that?"

"Do what?" he asked, the grin spreading.

"Did you tell your mom to do that?"

He lifted my hand to his lips and deposited a soft kiss against it, tickling my insides and sending little waves of pleasure through me.

"She asked what we wanted for a wedding gift, and I might have mentioned to her that this would be helpful." He stopped walking and faced me. "Is that okay? I mean, if you don't want it..."

"Oh, no! I think it's brilliant. If it's a gift, that makes it a whole different issue to present to my mother. She won't want me to offend your mom or make her feel slighted. Mama would tell me no all day long on hiring anyone, but she won't say no to your mom. Hell, even if we pay your mom for it and just say it was a gift, this is amazing."

He laughed. "Whew. I didn't know how you'd take it, and I worried I was going to add more stress instead of helping. Mom was thrilled. She wasn't sure what to get us, and she would love having Sandy involved. Makes her feel more a part of things, you know? She's kind of far removed from it all since it's happening in your hometown and your mom's doing everything."

"My mom's not *supposed* to be doing everything," I said as Cabe opened my car door.

"Well, then hopefully this will work out nicely for everyone. I may go by Dean's after work and hang out for a while. What time are you and Mel done dress shopping?"

"Don't know. Depends on whether or not we find something quickly, I suppose."

"Okay. You gonna stop by home and let Deacon out, or should I?"

"I'll get him. You go to Dean's. Thanks, Cabe. I really appreciate what you did."

He kissed me and flashed me a wink with a quick pat on my rump as he walked away.

Love him to death. Could just eat him up, I swear.

Tuesday, September 16th

I don't know who was more nervous today. Me or the bride.

I originally told Priscilla that I had too many weddings in September to re-book hers, but she argued that all their details were already planned from the last time they tried this, and since they only wanted a quick ceremony and a champagne toast, it would be less than two hours out of my day. They weren't bringing her parents or the kids—to take the pressure off Neal, she said—and she'd decided to have the ceremony at the hotel to eliminate the possibility of Neal disappearing like last time.

None of that helped my nerves any. On top of my normal stress level with the number of events our office is producing this month and the underlying stress of my own wedding, the last thing I wanted to comfort this poor woman again if Neal's feet turned cold a second time.

He actually alluded to that in an ill-worded apology when I greeted them in the hotel lobby last night.

"Just so you know, I brought a couple extra pair of socks this time. You know, so my feet don't get cold or nothing. I offered to let her handcuff me to the bed to make sure I wasn't going nowhere, but she said she'd take her chances and save the handcuffs for the honeymoon. So thanks for fitting us in and sorry 'bout all that."

I nodded and tried to force a smile, unsure of how to respond appropriately.

He was sitting in the lobby again this morning when I arrived, sipping a coffee in a black suit with a white shirt and black tie.

"Don't you look handsome?" I asked with more enthusiasm than I felt. "Is Priscilla ready?"

He broke into a grin but shook his head no. I swear I could see a sheen of perspiration covering his face. His hands shook slightly on the coffee

206

cup, and I wondered if perhaps he'd taken something. He just seemed edgy. Hyper. Too tense for a man prone to skipping town. It made me wary of leaving him in the lobby alone.

I called Priscilla on my cell and asked how long she needed. Normally, I'd be headed to her room to see for myself and assist her in getting out of the room and downstairs. But I figured in this case, I was more help to her staying put on Neal-watch.

She assured me she'd be down within twenty minutes and asked if I'd seen Neal.

"Yep. He's standing here with me right now."

Priscilla exhaled. "Thank you, Tyler. Keep an eye on him, okay?"

I agreed I would and ended the call. Why does she want to marry someone she needs to guard in order to get him down the aisle? If he doesn't walk willingly, then why would she take those vows seriously? But on the other hand, why is he back here and pledging to walk with her if he doesn't want to be? Why even pretend just to run out all over again?

The conversation between Neal and me ran dry after a few short minutes, and I was relieved when the officiant arrived. Reverend Markham could talk a fence post into the ground, so I stood back and let him take over the small talk while we waited for Priscilla.

Neal grew more antsy as the clock ticked on, and the beads of sweat rolled down the sides of his face and seeped into his collar. I left him with Reverend Markham just long enough to go in the ladies' room and get tissues, which Neal accepted graciously as he dabbed at his face.

"Thanks, Tyler. Warm in this monkey suit. Not used to wearing a jacket. Florida heat. Probably sweating off a hangover a little, too."

His plethora of excuses rolled out one right after another, and I felt sorry for the man. What was his deal? Did he not *want* to marry Priscilla? Was it the kids that scared him like he'd mentioned in the letter last time? Was it her parents, who I could easily see as crossing the line into intimidating without much of a nudge? Did he love her? If not, why on earth did he come back? Because at that moment, he certainly did not look the epitome of the happy groom excited to see his beautiful bride. He looked more like a dead man walking. Breathing his last breaths of fresh air before the executioner carried out his sentence.

As much as I hated to leave him, I needed to make sure the ceremony site was set up and put the speaker in place for the iPod so we'd have music.

"You're okay here with Reverend Markham for a few minutes? I need to check on a couple of things."

Neal laughed a little too heartily and nodded. "I'm fine, Tyler. Don't worry about me. I ain't going nowhere. She'd kill me if I pulled that again."

I smiled and made eye contact with Reverend Markham, who gave me one deep nod as if to say *"I got this. Go ahead."*

The hotel's archway had been set in the courtyard area and covered in silk greenery with large pink silk hibiscus. A white column stood at either side of the aisle. The whole set-up looked somewhat out of place without any chairs, but since we had no guests, none were needed.

My phone rang as I started back into the hotel.

"Hi Priscilla, you ready?"

"Yeah, I think so. I have Neal's boutonniere here with my bouquet. Should I just bring it down with me?"

"Sure. You need me to come up?" I felt guilty for leaving her on her own, especially now that Reverend Markham was babysitting Neal, which left me free.

"No, that's fine. I'll just grab the bouquet and the boutonniere and head to the elevator. Can you make sure Neal has a key? I wasn't planning to bring my purse, so I have no place to stick a key. Unless I hide it in my cleavage, I suppose." She chuckled, and I could hear nervous apprehension in her voice. Was that due to getting married or fear about the groom disappearing?

"I'm not with him right this minute. Why don't you bring the key with you, and I can hold it or give it to Neal? In case he doesn't have one."

"You're not with him? Where is he? When did you last see him?" The emotion in her voice heightened, and I could almost feel her fear through the phone.

"It's okay! He's with Reverend Markham in the lobby. I needed to check the ceremony site and get the speaker set up. I'm headed back to them now. Unless you want me to come get you?"

"No, no. I'll come down. I'm sorry to be such a nervous Nellie. I know he'll be there. I guess it's just hard to forget what it felt like before, you know?"

I certainly knew. I remembered the angst I felt on her behalf when it all happened. Then coincidentally, the day after Neal abandoned Priscilla at the altar, Cabe went AWOL and dropped off the face of the earth, which started our downward spiral.

So yes. I remembered what it felt like all too well, and associating their wedding with our painful past was probably part of the reason for my uneasiness today. I knew that was foolish, of course. Cabe and I were engaged now. Living together. Making a life together in our new home. Planning a wedding. We couldn't be further from where we were the last time Neal walked out on Priscilla. But the heart holds onto pain and reminds you how it feels every now and then.

I swung by the lobby to tell Neal and Reverend Markham that Priscilla was on her way down, figuring I had plenty of time to alert them and still be at the bottom of the elevator when she stepped out. She'd risked him being alone in order to preserve some mystery about her dress and appearance, so I didn't want to spoil that now by having him near the elevator when she exited.

Reverend Markham stood out right away, a tall man in a fancy floor-length black robe amid a lobby of shorts and flip-flops and casual vacationers. What I didn't see right away was a short sweaty man in a black suit and white shirt with black tie. I scanned the lobby as I approached the Reverend, ever hopeful that Neal was nearby.

"Where's Neal?" I asked in a voice that conveyed more panic than I intended.

Reverend Markham looked startled and concerned by my anxiety and put his hand on my forearm to help put my mind at ease. "It's fine. He needed to use the restroom." The older gentleman leaned forward with a conspiratorial smile. "I also suggested perhaps he might want to splash a bit of cold water on his face. He was sweating up a storm. Not used to the Florida heat, I guess."

"No! Reverend Markham, you can't let him out of your sight! He's not sweating because of the heat. Oh no. This is not happening. Please go in the men's room and find him. Stay with him while I go meet Priscilla and get her tucked out of sight. I'll meet you back here in the lobby, okay?"

The poor man scrunched his brows together in confusion, but he did as I asked and headed toward the restroom to find Neal. I almost broke into a run in my efforts to reach Priscilla before she got off the elevator and wandered into the lobby alone. Or ran into Neal. Or realized Neal might be gone.

Undoubtedly not. Undoubtedly, the man would not bring this poor woman all the way back down here and do the same damned thing all over again. Not twenty minutes after assuring me he was all in and ready to go. Surely, lightning would not strike twice.

Except this is Florida. The lightning capital of the world.

He wasn't in the restroom. He didn't make it back to the lobby.

The valet stand confirmed a man in a sweat-stained white shirt carrying a black jacket had indeed asked them to call a taxi for him with a destination of Orlando International Airport. Neal had done it again.

Priscilla was inconsolable, and I was sick to my stomach. For her and for the memory of pains gone by. How many times can one man break your heart? I hope I never have to find out.

Wednesday, September 17th

They say history repeats itself. They say truth is stranger than fiction. But if anyone had told me the day after Priscilla's fiancé stood her up the second time, Cabe would disappear again, I would have told them to go screw themselves.

Things were normal this morning. Nothing amiss. We shared an egg sandwich and some coffee before we each left for work. We kissed each other goodbye and went our separate ways.

Normally, I hear from him around ten. He takes a break. Gets a coffee. Goes for stroll to stretch his legs, and gives me a call.

No call this morning.

It probably wouldn't have seemed too odd if I hadn't been on edge from Priscilla and Neal, but I was almost looking for it to happen. And it did.

When he didn't call at lunch, I tried his phone, but it went straight to voice mail. No biggie. Neither of us does lunch at a specific time each day, so I thought perhaps he was busy with a project. But when he hadn't called me back by two, I started freaking out.

Cabe reaches out to me multiple times a day. He calls. He texts. He tags me on social media or shares an email he found interesting or funny. For him to go radio silent on the day after Priscilla and Neal's "Crash and Burn: Part Two" not only repeated history but it also felt like a sick joke.

I had thought about mentioning it to him last night when I recapped the day, but I didn't want to bring up bad memories. I don't think he has any way of knowing that everything went south the day after their ill-fated wedding last time, so he wouldn't make that connection now.

My work lay in stacks in front of me untouched. My thoughts were on one track. Why wasn't he calling or answering my texts and calls? Where was he?

By the time I left the office at five, I was pissed *and* ready to throw up. No way in hell was I prepared to go through this with him again. Not after all this time. Not after everything we'd been through and how good it had been.

What the hell?

To see his car in the driveway when I pulled in provided some measure of relief, but also a huge dose of frustration and anxiety. I didn't know what to expect as I climbed the porch steps. Had he changed his mind? Gotten cold feet and decided not to marry me? Was Monica back? Had they been talking all along? Had Galen done something to undermine us? Was he inside at that moment packing my stuff to throw me out? Where would I go? Where would I live? What would I do and how would I recover again?

It's amazing how far the human brain can take things in the short distance of four porch steps. The level of my paranoia and my overactive imagination is embarrassing to write about, but it took over. If there was a depth of torment my mind could conceive, it went there.

When I opened the door to a dark and silent house, my fears multiplied and diversified. Was something wrong with him? Was he ill? Had something happened to him? Had he been abducted? Where was Deacon? Why was he not doing his customary dance between my feet and around my legs? Had something happened to them both? I even thought for a moment the gas had been left on and they'd passed out, but then I remembered all our appliances are electric. Carbon monoxide maybe?

I opened the door to our bedroom tentatively and hopefully. *Please let him be in bed asleep. Please let him be sick. Not deathly ill or anything. But too sick to call me and too sick to answer his phone. Still madly in love with me, though.*

The jeans he'd worn to work were tossed across the rocking chair in the corner. His work shoes were in the closet. His phone lay on the top of his dresser, dead as a doornail. I grabbed it and plugged it in to charge as I surveyed the room for any other clue.

The front door opened before I could solve the case. Deacon bounded down the hallway and nearly knocked me down in his post-walk state of euphoria.

Of course. He'd taken Deacon for a walk after getting home from work. His daily routine. I hadn't thought of it in my panic since he'd not followed any other daily routines so far.

I peeked out of the bedroom and down the hall but there was no sight of him. Why hadn't he followed Deacon to greet me? To seek me out and ask about my day? To tell me what was up and why he'd gone AWOL again.

Deacon took off running at the sound of the pantry door opening, ready to get his post-walk treat. I followed him at a slower pace and with less enthusiasm, not sure if I was getting a trick or treat.

Cabe stood in the kitchen in a T-shirt and running shorts, covered in sweat and dripping on the floor.

"You ran?" I asked, so shocked that it temporarily pushed all other thoughts from my head. As athletic and active as Cabe is with most other sports, he absolutely loathes running. He has often joked that if I see him running, I'd better look to see who's after him. "Who's chasing you?" I asked partially in jest, but a good deal serious. Something was wrong. Off. I didn't yet know what, and I hadn't let go of the fear it might be me.

He grimaced and drained a bottle of water before wiping his face with a towel. "I'm gonna hit the shower." He stepped around me without so much as a glance. No hug. No kiss. No *hi honey, how was your day*. Not that I wanted a sweat-drenched smelly hug anyway, but I was dying inside.

"Want to talk about your day?" I asked from the bathroom doorway.

"After dinner."

Okay, so we were having dinner together. That was a good sign, right? I mean, undoubtedly he wouldn't fix dinner and sit down to eat with me and then break up or kick me out. Right?

I hated the uncertainty. I hated feeling vulnerable and not knowing what was going on. I hated feeling scared and weak and unsure of what to do or where I stood.

I tried to get angry. To tell myself that it was bullshit for him not to call or not to text and then not to tell me what was wrong when I saw him. But fear gripped my heart and punched me in the stomach and threatened my sanity.

He came back in the kitchen freshly showered and wearing nothing but a pair of shorts, looking hotter than a man should when you need to be mad at him.

"Why don't you take a shower and I'll make dinner?" He gave me a quick peck of a kiss, but he still didn't make eye contact or hug me like he always does.

"What's wrong? What happened?" I asked.

"Let's talk after dinner. Go get cleaned up and I'll cook."

I hadn't done anything I needed to get cleaned up from, but I didn't know if I was ready to push the issue. I was scared of the answer. I shuffled to the bathroom and tried to get myself under control. No sense freaking out without knowing what was going on, right? Except my freak factor had already multiplied exponentially.

We ate in silence for a few minutes. Well, he ate. I picked at my food and tried to convince my stomach that throwing up would not help the situation.

"Deacon's in the trash," I said with a point of my fork.

"Deacon! Get out of there!" Cabe got up and put the trash can on the counter, scowling at Deacon before he came back to the table.

"We need a trash can with a lid."

"That one had a lid," he said as he sat back down. "He ate it."

"Okay, then we need to get a metal trash can. With a lid."

He took a bite of his chicken and chased it with a gulp of wine.

"You gonna tell me?" I asked.

He tossed his napkin on the table and rubbed his eyes. "I'm sorry if I'm being a jerk, but I don't really feel like talking about it."

That statement did a few things. One, it told me that he probably wasn't going to kick me out. In fact, my gut instinct told me the way he answered indicated that I wasn't the issue at all. Something or someone else was. Which led me to my next point, which was if it's not me and has nothing to do with me, why in the hell have you ignored me all day and gotten me all worked up and freaked out like a psycho for no reason?

The fear dam broke and anger flooded through.

"You don't feel like talking about it? Really? You disappear again, not calling me, not texting me, not returning my calls or texts. You turn your phone off and basically don't even acknowledge me when I get home, and all you have to say is 'I don't want to talk about it?'"

He looked at me in shock and then irritation. "C'mon, Ty. I don't need this crap. I've had enough bullshit today. I'm sorry I didn't call you, okay? I was dealing with something, and I wanted to be left alone. Can I not just be left alone sometimes without it being the end of the world or the sky falling in?" He pushed his plate away and rested his forehead on his knuckles.

"What did you tell me when you came to my place the night you were supposed to go out with Monica? You said we have to be honest with each other. You said we have to talk things through. You were upset that I turned my phone off. Sounds a bit hypocritical to me."

"I didn't turn my phone off. It died."

"And you didn't charge it?"

"Ty, I really don't want to talk right now. Can we just finish dinner without having some huge discussion?

I held up my left hand and pointed to the ring. "Do you see this? Do you remember giving me this? Because it came with a promise. Several of them actually. You don't get to shut me out and you don't get to withdraw and not talk about issues that are eating at you. This ring right here says you have to let me in."

He leaned back in the chair and stared at the ceiling. "I realize that, but you also said if I couldn't talk about something, I was supposed to tell you that I was processing and wasn't ready to talk. So this is me telling you I'm not ready to talk."

He pushed his chair away from the table and went to the back porch, leaving his plate unfinished on the table.

I cleared the dishes and filled the dishwasher, unsure of where to go with what he'd given me. He was right. I had said that. I had told him he could tell me he needed time to think. But I sort of thought that meant he'd return my calls and return my texts and let me know something was going on.

I pushed open the back door and stepped out onto the porch as I dried my hands.

"I get that you need time, but when you disappear like that it scares the shit out of me. I thought we were back where we were before."

He turned and looked up at me from where he sat on the edge of the porch. He extended his arm and I sat down beside him. He pulled me next to him, his bare skin radiating heat in the humidity of the evening along with the emotions racing through him. He kissed the top of my head and then nudged my face up to look into his.

"I didn't mean to scare you. I've told you I'm not going anywhere, and it never occurred to me that you might think otherwise. Hello? We're getting married. We're living in the same house. I'd think those commitments would attest to the fact that I'm all in and you have nothing to worry about."

I pulled back from him. "So why didn't I hear from you today?"

"Honestly, I didn't think about it. I was mad. I was pissed. I didn't want to talk to anyone. I don't mean that against you and it's not about you. I just needed to be by myself. So I left work and drove out to the beach and then I came back here to take Deacon for a run and get dinner started since I knew you'd be home soon."

"You left work? You went to the beach? What happened? Why didn't you at least tell me you were leaving?" My anger flared back up.

"I would have, but I had my phone in my pocket when I dove in the ocean. It went black. I'm hoping it will work when it dries out."

"Oh, no! I plugged it in. Should I unplug it?"

He stood and went inside to get the phone. "We need to get rice," he said when I came in our bedroom to find him inspecting the phone. "You're supposed to let it sit in rice for a few days and then hopefully it will come back on."

I sat on the bed and stared at him. Still pissed but relieved we weren't breaking up.

He came and sat beside me and took my hand in his. "I'm sorry. I screwed up. I should have called you and told you before I left the office. I didn't mean to worry you."

I looked away from him.

He brought my hand to his lips and kissed it. "Jeffrey called this morning."

"Jeffrey?" I asked.

"My *brother?*" He made air quotes with his fingers as he said it, adding to the sneer of sarcasm in his tone.

"Oh! Jeffrey. Holy shit. Why?"

"He said we need to talk and he wants to meet with me."

"What did you tell him?"

"Nothing. He left a voice mail, and I turned my phone off."

"Well, thank God I wasn't dying on the side of the road somewhere. Did it ever occur to you while you were hiding out from Jeffrey"—I used his air quotes for sarcastic emphasis—"that I might have needed to talk to you? Me? Your *fiancée?*" Air quotes again because I was on a roll.

He stood up and paced the floor like a tiger awoken. "I'm sorry, Ty. I just can't deal with them. Why can't they get through their heads that I want nothing to do with them? Why can't they leave me the hell alone? I've been more than clear about my wishes in the matter, and they all just seem to ignore that. Galen opened Pandora's box, I swear."

I didn't have anything to contribute, which was a good thing since he wasn't done.

"I didn't mean to shut you out. Or disappear, or whatever you said. I know that's screwed up on my part, and I'm sorry. I don't know what it is, but thinking about them or dealing with them sends me in such a funk. I spent my entire life trying to forget my father existed, and now I feel like everyone keeps throwing it in my face that not only is he alive and well, but the reason I needed to forget him is, too. Why should I talk to Jeffrey? Why? What could he possibly have to say to me that I need to hear?"

"You won't know until you hear him out."

He whirled around and frowned at me. "See? That's why I didn't want to talk to anyone. Right away, you're taking his side."

I gasped, mouth wide open in shock. "I'm not taking anyone's side! And if there's a side to take, I'll be on yours. But you don't even know why he called."

"I don't care why he called. I don't want to talk to him."

I took a deep breath and smoothed my hand over the comforter, tracing the wisteria flower print with my fingers. "Cabe, I know you hate this. But the fact is this other part of your family exists. Gerry exists. Jeffrey and Julie exist. You may not want anything to do with them, but you can't stop them from existing and you can't control whether or not they want to contact you."

"That's ridiculous. If I don't want to be contacted, isn't that my right? Can't I decide who I want to converse with?"

I wasn't sure there was a right answer to give him, and I certainly didn't feel I was qualified to determine what it was. But I was all he had at the moment, so I tried.

"You have the right to say what you want in your life, but they have the right to say what they want in theirs. If Jeffrey wants to talk to you about something, he has the right to reach out." I put up my hand to stop his protest. "You have the right to refuse, most definitely. But I think you need to look at this a different way."

He leaned against the door frame and crossed his arms, his pectoral muscles flexing under the tension, along with his jaw.

"You said that dealing with them puts you in a funk. Sends you in a spiral. I think if you want to move past this, you gotta take away its power. This thing with Gerry has affected you your whole life. The more you run from it, the more power you give them to affect you. Think about me, all those years after we first met. I let the pain of my failed relationship with Dwayne dictate my life." He shifted his position and grunted in obvious disdain for the topic. "Hear me out. I left home and everyone I knew because of it. I kept you at arm's length for years because of it. I even walled myself off from my own family and didn't go back home to visit because of it. But once I faced it head-on, once I dealt with it and stopped running from it, I discovered it wasn't as bad as I thought."

I stood and went to him. "I realized that what I had in my head wasn't even the truth. My relationship with Dwayne wasn't the way my memories retold it. I'd built it up to be this huge thing that was overwhelming and crippling. It didn't have to be."

I reached for him and he shrugged me away, putting up his hands in protest.

"But, Ty, you're talking about your *family*. Your home. These people aren't my family. I don't know them. I don't care to know them. There's nothing I'm missing out on here."

"You don't know that. Jeffrey could be a great guy. You'll never know if you don't give him a chance."

He scowled at me and turned to go to the kitchen. "I'm sure he is a great guy," he called over his shoulder. "He had a father and every opportunity made available to him. He had a house in the Hamptons and an Ivy League college education. He didn't grow up a bastard."

I followed him, hot on his heels. "You know what? You keep saying that like you lived in welfare housing, wondering where your next meal would come from or worried about a roof over your head. You went to college. You traveled all over the world. Your mother may have been a single mom, and I'm not knocking how hard she worked or the sacrifices she made, but give me a break. Your grandparents are basically millionaires. You wanted for nothing!"

"Except a dad. Money didn't buy me a dad, did it?"

"Oh please. You are so much better off without that asshole in your life, and you know that as well as I do. I can't begin to understand how much that must have hurt, or how it made you feel. But I can tell you this. You grew up loved and cared for. Your mom was there for you. Bill and Peggy were there for you. You were taught to surf and fish and play ball and play guitar. You had a sister and cousins and friends. You went to college and learned a profession and made a life for yourself. You turned out fine, Cabe! So get over it. Let it go. Move on and stop harboring all this resentment, this darkness, this bitterness that consumes you whenever it surfaces. The only person you're hurting is yourself. Do you think Gerry gives a damn or loses a night's sleep? Why should you?"

"You don't understand what it's like."

I crossed my arms and rocked my weight to one leg, thrusting my hip out with every bit of attitude pulsing through me. *"Excuse me?* Are you listening to yourself? I don't understand what it's like not to have my daddy? Not to be able to have him at my school functions, my social events, or something as simple as sitting at the dinner table with me? I don't know what it's like to live in a single mom household? Really? You may want to think about that before you throw it out there. Because you aren't the only person with pain in your life, and you aren't the only person who's been disappointed by how things worked out."

His eyes were sheepish when they met mine, and I raised both eyebrows and nodded. Like, *yeah buddy. That's right. You just stepped in it.*

I softened my stance and walked closer to him. "My dad didn't leave us willingly, so you're right. I don't know what that part of it does to you, and I can only imagine the pain it causes. But you have no idea what Jeffrey's life was like, or even Gerry's for that matter. It's easy to judge someone based only on our own perceptions. It's harder to listen to their side of the issue and reevaluate our own belief systems with new information. You don't know what this guy wants to say to you. No idea why he's calling."

I rubbed my hands up and down his arms, leaning in close and making sure we held eye contact. "You can either keep running and fuel the fire it sparks inside you, or you can get it all out on the table and face it. Take its power and make it your own."

He put his arms around me and sighed, his breath shaky as his body tensed and then began to relax. I squeezed my arms around his waist, burying my head in his chest and willing him to be strong enough to stand up to his demons.

He kissed the top of my head and rested his chin there.

"I'm sorry I worried you. I didn't mean to."

I nodded against his chest.

He dipped his head and whispered right against my ear. "I thought you knew I can't live without you. I thought we established that pretty clearly. So take that out of your repertoire of crazy theories in case this happens again, okay?"

I looked up at him and tried to pull off my sternest expression possible.

"*This* had better *not* happen again."

He kissed me, and I kissed him back, trying to heal his wounds in any way I could so he could fight another day.

Friday, September 19th

Maggie called and said she had received proposals for the rehearsal dinner from her friend Sandy and wanted to stop by to discuss them.

Cabe had gone out shopping for suits with Dean, so I called her on my way home from my rehearsal to have her come over.

She showed me what Sandy had suggested, and we discussed the renovated barn they'd found just outside my hometown.

"Sounds like a great location. I had Mama and my sister Tanya ride out and take a look at it, and they were both impressed. They'd never heard of it."

Maggie nodded. "Sandy said it's relatively new. Maybe within the last year or so? Some guy from Colorado moved into the area, bought the property and it had two barns. He kept one for horses and converted the other one, I guess. It's got heat and air, so the cold shouldn't be a problem."

I fed Deacon as we talked, and then I invited Maggie to come along while I took him for a walk.

"So Cabe says you're considering asking Galen to be a bridesmaid."

I tugged at Deacon's leash and glanced to see Maggie's facial expression. I assumed Galen's mother would agree with my mother and tell me to ask her. She surprised me, though.

"Has she apologized to you yet? You or Cabe?"

I shrugged a little. "Not exactly."

"Well, then I wouldn't ask her."

I looked at Maggie and back to the sidewalk ahead.

"Tyler, my daughter has many good qualities, but she is hot-tempered, outspoken, and stubborn as a mule. Much like her father in all those areas. It's my fault, too, though. I never set boundaries for her like I should. I felt bad, you know? About her dad leaving. Not having a dad. I felt bad for them both. Responsible, I guess."

"It must have been hard," I said.

We paused as Deacon inspected every square inch of bark on a nearby tree.

"They each absorbed it in different ways. Cabe with anger and bitterness. Galen with longing and an insatiable need to belong. Which is why I think she'll come to you."

"So you don't think I should ask her?"

"No, I don't. Galen desperately wants to be in a family, or her preconceived notion of a family. She feels she didn't get that, and I guess when compared to her mental concept of it, she didn't. But the tricky thing about families is they revolve around people. Relationships. Give and take. Compromise and forgiveness. Swallowing pride and putting others first. She doesn't get that part of it. She wants what she wants when she wants it, and to hell with everyone else." Maggie sighed and rubbed her hands together. "She's also very protective of her family, and she thinks that if she means well, it gives her carte blanche to do and say what she pleases. Life does not work that way, does it?"

"No, it doesn't. Look, I understand why she was upset with me. About Cabe. I know how I would feel if I thought someone was hurting my brother or one of my sisters. But I never meant to hurt Cabe. I wasn't doing it on purpose. I didn't know what was happening between us."

Maggie reached over and gave my hand a squeeze. "I know that, sweetheart. Cabe was a grown man, responsible for his own decisions. You weren't holding him handcuffed against his will." She shot me a sideways glance and a sneaky smile. "And if you were, I don't want to know about it." She laughed and it broke the tension of the conversation. "Galen overstepped her bounds, and she needs to apologize. To you, and to her brother for the position she put him in."

She sighed and looked at me, glancing back at the sidewalk every few seconds. "She wants to be a part of this wedding. I know that for a fact. Do you think someone so driven by a desire for family is going to let her brother get married and not be a part of it? Let her come to you. Let her apologize and make things right. Then if you want her in your wedding, that's up to you. You certainly don't have to ask her, and no one could blame you if you didn't. But she needs to take responsibility for her own actions. You'll do her no favors by excusing her from that. Believe me, I know. I'm speaking from experience."

Curiosity tickled my mind with a million questions. I didn't want to bring up anything unpleasant, but there was so much I wanted to know.

"How'd you meet Gerry?"

She smiled a little and looked away. Perhaps a moment's consideration of what she wanted to say, I don't know.

"He's a producer, you know that, of course. We met while working on a show. A limited run that didn't end for us when the curtains closed."

The smile lingered, and it occurred to me that this was a man she loved. Enough to risk her career and bear two children. I'd always looked at Gerry through Cabe's eyes, as a father who walked out on his child. I'd never considered Gerry through Maggie's eyes. A lover lost. A heart betrayed. Not once but twice.

"What attracted you to him?"

She paused, and I thought for a moment she might not answer. "Well, you've met his son. There's a strong family resemblance. He was a very handsome man. Very charismatic. A charmer. He could make you feel like you were the only person in a room of thousands. He was funny. Intelligent. Easy to be around."

She stopped talking suddenly and looked over at me almost like she'd forgotten for a moment that I was there. She cleared her throat and gave a stilted chuckle. "But all that glitters is not gold. Learned that lesson the hard way. I fear Galen will learn it, too. She's fascinated with him now, this fantasy father she dreamed of for so many years. He's playing into it, enjoying her adoration, but eventually, he'll let her down, too."

My heart ached at the pain in her voice, and I longed to comfort her somehow. I also longed to ask her more questions. How did they get together? Did she know he was married at the time? When did she find out? What happened when she learned she was pregnant? Why did he leave her and baby Cabe? Why did he come back? Why did she let him? And not only let him back, but conceive another child with him and be abandoned again? What did Bill and Peggy think about their daughter's change in circumstances?

My brain yearned to know more. I only had fuzzy bits and pieces of the story gathered from Cabe's childhood perspective. I wanted to know what really happened. What happened to Maggie, the woman who fell in love and gave up the life she'd planned.

I watched her as she stared straight ahead, and I weighed my own desire to get to the bottom of things against possibly upsetting Maggie or bringing her unpleasant memories.

If she'd continued talking, I would have pursued it. But she grew quiet, so I let it go. After all, this woman will be my mother-in-law. It's not like I won't ever have the opportunity to talk with her again.

Monday, September 22nd

Charlotte had added an appointment to my calendar for today with no name and no number. When I saw it pop up last week, I immediately went to ask her what was up.

"Charlotte, I can't take any more appointments this month. I told you not to book anything. Why is there no name?"

"I wrote it down, but then I spilled coffee on the note and I couldn't read her name or her number. But she said she'd met with you before and that you wouldn't mind."

"Who is she?"

"I dunno. Some bride of yours."

I groaned and returned to my desk, reminding myself that it is a felony to kill people, even if they can be declared too stupid to live.

So I spent an hour this morning racking my brain to figure out who I might be meeting with and what I might need to do to prepare for the meeting.

Had the Queen of England walked through our doors, I probably would not have been more surprised than when I saw Nadine. She was dressed in almost the exact same outfit as last time we met. Her long blonde hair was fashioned into a loose braid down her back with brightly colored ribbons woven through the plaits. She wore the same layered skirts of lace and linen, but today's were in a pale pink instead of white and ivory, all featuring multi-colored ribbons and beads. She had the same high-heeled brown boots as before, but the ribbons intertwined through the laces had been redone in shades of pink. She carried the long, black velvet shawl over one arm, a testament no doubt to the extreme heat of the day.

"Tyler!" she exclaimed as she greeted me with a hug, her vanilla and ginger scent enveloping me as I awkwardly accepted the embrace. "He's here. I told you the Universe was sending him! Look!" She released me and flung her left hand in my face. Her other fingers still carried the large stones and rocks I remembered from before, but her ring finger was adorned with a ginormous oval-cut diamond. We're talking at least four carats.

"Wow. That's beautiful. Congratulations!"

I looked from her to the man who had followed her in and who now stood with one arm around Nadine as he watched our exchange. His smile beamed, and the way he looked at her as she spoke left no doubt that he was entirely smitten with his bride-to-be.

"This is Felix. This is who I've been waiting for." Nadine swept her arm toward the man as she smiled and nodded, showing me how generous the Universe had been.

"Nice to meet you, Felix."

Felix gripped my hand like I was saving him from drowning and shook it up and down with more enthusiasm than I have probably ever felt about anything.

"Oh, it's my pleasure. I've heard so much about you, and I'm just thrilled to have you accompany us on the next step in the journey."

I nodded, unsure of what that meant or whether I wanted to take the trip.

Once they were settled in at the conference table, I went to search my file cabinet for the notes from our first meeting. I prayed the notes were there. I truly didn't think I'd ever see Nadine again, so I wasn't sure I'd even saved them. By a stroke of luck, I found them and quickly perused the details. Of course, at the time we discussed her wedding, she didn't have a groom yet and had only been told by the Universe to expect his arrival. So who knew if these details would even be the same now that the magical unicorn had appeared?

They were laughing and snuggling with each other when I returned, and I cleared my throat to announce my intrusion.

"I've got our original notes here, but of course, I'm not sure what you may want to use now that the two of you have had a chance to talk."

Nadine smiled at Felix and he put his arm around her and hugged her close to his side. "Whatever she planned is fine. I trust this woman implicitly."

Nadine giggled like a schoolgirl and twirled her braid between her fingers as she gazed at Felix.

"Isn't he just incredible?" she asked as she turned back to me, wiping a small tear from the corner of her eye. "A dream come true."

"How did you two meet?"

"Your aura is disturbed. Are you okay, Tyler? You need sleep."

"Oh, really? It's our busy season right now, so I've been working a lot." That was awkward. Was that a polite but quirky way of saying "*you look like hell*"?

She peered at me and then closed her eyes almost entirely shut as she moved her head up and down. I felt vulnerable and exposed, like she had X-ray vision or something. The whole time, Felix sat there grinning like a mule eating briers and nodding continuously. I wondered if he could channel her vision and see me too.

Her eyes flew open and her mouth split into a huge grin as she reached across the table and grasped my hand.

"Aaaah! You're engaged. You're in love. This is simply fantastic. Felix, she's in love." Felix nodded and smiled, his expression no different than before he knew my news.

Her face fell just as suddenly as it had lit up. "But you're not well. The wedding. Oh, no. You need to rest your soul. Your light is flickering."

Well, that's just what everyone wants to know. My light is flickering? Like, I'm dying? I caught myself just before I asked her. Did I really want a diagnosis from Nadine, the Stevie Nicks lookalike, bride of Felix from the Universe?

"I'm fine, really. Just busy. So how did you two meet?" I know I'd already asked, but I was dying to know.

"The Universe sent him." She smiled and patted his thigh as he kissed her cheek.

"That's amazing," I said. "Did it send him to your door, or how did you know?"

"We connected online in cosmic choreography, right, Felix?"

Felix nodded. "We were married twice before. Once in medieval times, where we lived in the French countryside. Then we found each other in the late 1800s, in Spain. We've been pulled toward each other for years this time, but the distance between our births made it difficult this time."

I nodded. I mean, I think I nodded. It's possible I stared straight ahead with a *what the hell* look on my face. But hopefully, I pulled something off that appeared to be polite.

"Thank the Universe for the internet, for it was only through that medium that we could span the distance between us and make our circle complete once more," Nadine spoke to me but looked at Felix as she spoke.

Which was fine with me because it lessened the chance they were seeing me react with "*you gotta be frickin' kidding me.*"

"Of course. I see. Now about the wedding…"

Nadine clapped her hands together and cooed. "The wedding! Yes. I'm so excited. You have the plan, right?"

I flipped through my notes.

"Sky blue…fifteen bridesmaids and fifteen groomsmen…white lillies…"

"And a chapel," Nadine interrupted. "Did you get the chapel?"

"Yes, I have that written here."

"It needs to be a small, stone chapel," Felix said. "Both of our previous weddings were in a small, stone chapel."

I almost chuckled out loud when it occurred to me how entertaining it might be to hook them up with the church lady at that small stone chapel by the Manor. She could explain how Jesus doesn't get rented by the hour, and they could explain how this was their third wedding, but the first one in this century. I stifled the humor and poised my pen to ask questions.

"Do you have a date in mind?"

They nodded and looked at each as they spoke in unison. "March 31st."

"Our anniversary."

I searched my notes for the date Nadine and I had originally met to discuss her wedding. We'd gotten together in April, but she said then she didn't know who her fiancé would be. "You met March 31st?"

"No. We married March 31st. Before."

"Ah. I see. How many guests?"

"Two hundred and fifty."

I looked at Nadine's previous answer of seventy to eighty and glanced up at her in surprise. "Wow! Felix must be bringing a lot of guests."

"We've found we have many friends to include," Felix said as they laughed and shared a kiss.

"You got the belly dancers, right, Tyler?"

I nodded. "Yep, and a band who can play disco."

Nadine's laughter rang out like tinkling bells. "Oh, yes. Felix loves to dance."

He reached up to smooth his mustache, and I gaped at the size of the ruby on his pinkie finger. It spanned his entire finger, wide enough that the pinkie actually sat separate from the ring finger at its base.

"Now, I'm not sure about the fire-eaters," I said. "It will depend on the fire code at the venue you choose. Some don't allow indoor fire."

Felix shook his hand in dismissal. "This will not be a problem. I have purchased a home here for the wedding. It has a spacious courtyard and we will be able to have the fire-eaters and belly dancers perform there. Can you get elephants?"

"Um, I can look into it." Not a request I get every day. "So did you have a caterer in mind, or should I make some recommendations?"

Nadine turned to face Felix and they held hands and hummed in exactly the same manner she had before. In perfect unison they hummed, and at precisely the same moment they stopped.

Nadine smiled as she faced me once more. "We are fine with whomever you suggest for catering and floral. Felix has a friend from New York who will be flying in to do our photos."

"Okay. Well, when did you want to set up meetings? The next few weeks are really crazy for us, but if you're planning on March, we need to get started."

Nadine shook her head. "March the year after. Not next March. No way could we get our guests pulled from the four corners of the earth in six months' time. It will take at least a year to reach all our acquaintances and let them know we've reconvened."

I wondered if the guest list would be people they'd known in medieval times, or the 1800s, or here in this century.

"Okay, then we have plenty of time for planning."

"Yes. Let's meet after the first of the year, when your schedule permits and the stress of your own wedding has passed. It will be fine if you trust your heart."

Her comment was disconcerting. Her perception of my situation could have been chalked up to seeing the ring on my finger and not seeing the exuberant reaction one might expect when she remarked on my engagement. But I certainly hadn't mentioned my wedding date to her, so how did she know I'd be married by the end of the year?

Felix spoke before I could ask how she knew. "Do you prefer a check or shall I give you my American Express?"

"Either is fine. Let me get our contract paperwork for you."

"Isn't that Steak Lady?" Carmen asked when I requested a new client packet from her.

"Yes," I hissed. "Sssh. She's gonna hear you."

"I don't care," Carmen said, only slighter lower in volume. "She knows she ordered a steak. It ain't like it's a secret." Carmen cocked her head and gave a slight shake of attitude before handing me the packet. She was an incredibly thorough office assistant and a great friend, but mild-mannered and soft-spoken she was not. Still, I preferred her sharp tongue to Charlotte's airheadedness any day.

When I returned to the conference room, Nadine and Felix sat with their foreheads together, humming and holding hands. I slid the paperwork across the table and left. They exited the room a few minutes later, paperwork and credit card in hand. We finished the business transaction and agreed on a date to meet in January.

As they left, Nadine hugged me again and then squeezed both my hands. "He loves you. You love him. This is what matters."

She left, and I turned to Carmen. "I think I need a steak. And a stiff drink."

Wednesday, September 24th

Hell may have come close to freezing over tonight.

We went out to dinner with Jeffrey.

It seems like I should write that in all caps or something. Or highlight it on the page as a monumental event.

Cabe had called him back last week after my somewhat gentle nudging. Turns out Jeffrey was going to be in town for a conference this week and wanted to meet up with Cabe. Have a conversation one-on-one, man-to-man.

Much to my surprise, Cabe agreed to go. He surprised me even further by insisting I come along.

"But he said man-to-man," I argued. "That didn't include me."

"We're a package deal," Cabe said. "If he wants to talk to me, you're coming with me."

"I don't know, babe. I don't mind coming, and if you really want me to, of course I will. But I feel like it's intruding. Like I'm tagging along without an invite. He might not like it."

Cabe glanced up at me and made a sound of annoyance in his throat. "I don't care if he likes it or not. You keep me calm. You keep me grounded. If I'm going to sit and listen to whatever this man has to say, I need you there smiling at me and reminding me how much this doesn't matter in the grand scheme of life."

I nodded and agreed to go.

I'm still reeling from my first sight of Jeffrey. We met him at a little place on International over by the convention center. We were walking toward the restaurant hand-in-hand, and suddenly I saw Cabe sitting at a table in front of me. It was the weirdest freakin' sensation. He was right beside me, holding my hand and taking his long, easy strides, but there he was, sitting right in front of me.

The same chiseled jawbones. The same full lower lip and straight nose. The thin arching eyebrows above the clearest blue eyes. The muscular neck atop the broad shoulders.

His hair was different. Short. Clipped close to his head on the sides with just a bit of a wave on top. Enough of a wave to suggest that if he allowed it to grow, it would easily twist itself into the loose shaggy curls of the gorgeous man next to me. Cabe's was lighter, the ends bleached out by his continuous exposure to surf and sun. But the base color was the same.

They could be twins.

Hell, they basically were. Born six months apart. Different moms, but obviously both inherited the stronger genes Gerry carried. Bastard. The least the universe could have done was let the boys look like their mothers. Less of a tie to the man who had created them both.

You could cut the tension at the table with a dull knife. Jeffrey stood when he saw us, and if he was surprised or displeased at seeing me there, he didn't let on in the least.

Cabe shook his hand stiffly, and then introduced me.

"Jeffrey, this is my fiancée, Tyler. Tyler, this is Jeffrey."

I smiled and shook his hand. They were the same height, and to stand there between the two of them was surreal. Being closer allowed me to see the subtle differences, though. Each man carried himself a little differently. Cabe's stance a bit more relaxed, a bit laid-back even though he was tense in this situation. Jeffrey stood tall and more rigid, his shoulders pulled back and his demeanor more professional. All business.

Their voices were similar, but Jeffrey's northern accent made it easy to distinguish between the two.

"Allow me to extend my congratulations on your upcoming marriage. Have you set a date?" Jeffrey directed the question to me as we waited for a waitress to come.

"Thank you. November 22nd."

"Coming up soon," he said with a smile. I couldn't stop staring at him. It was so weird. Like alternate universe type stuff. Like I was talking to someone I knew so well yet someone I didn't know at all.

He looked up at me and then immediately back down at the menu. He glanced up a couple more times, so I guess my staring fixation was obvious.

"I'm sorry," I said with a nervous laugh. "The resemblance is just unbelievable. I don't mean to stare."

Jeffrey looked to Cabe and back at me. "I guess we do look somewhat alike."

Cabe scoffed and gulped his water.

"You said you had some things you needed to discuss," he said, obviously eager to get the whole thing over with and struggling to keep his irritation under control.

"Okay. Let's get right to it. I wanted to let you know that I had no idea your sister hadn't told you we would be there that night."

I noticed that he said "your" sister and wondered if he considered Galen or Cabe as his siblings.

Cabe shrugged and looked away, feigning disinterest.

"I wouldn't have done that," Jeffrey said. "It's disrespectful, and I have no desire to disrespect you in any way."

"Not your fault," Cabe said with a cold glance at Jeffrey. "That was on Galen."

"It was disappointing, though, because I'd wanted to meet you for so long. A lifetime it seems."

"Meet me? Why?" I could feel Cabe's body tense as he asked, and I knew he was wary of engaging in the conversation.

"The phantom brother. I learned about you when I was ten. Gerry and my mom were arguing one night when they thought I was in bed. He'd just come back from another one of his trips, and she was giving him hell for missing Julie's recital. My Little League games. The day-to-day stuff. She asked if he'd been with his other family. With his other children. I didn't know what she meant, but it certainly piqued my interest."

The waitress came and took our orders, an inopportune interruption. I wanted to tell her to go away and come back later, but Jeffrey easily transitioned from the bitter recollections of youth to ordering a pork tenderloin and polenta without so much as blinking an eye. He struck me as a man accustomed to hiding his emotions. A far cry from my passionate, outspoken, full-feeling fiancé.

He picked right back up as soon as she walked away.

"There's another one. Another family. Not sure if you knew that. I didn't, and neither did my mother until Julie tracked them down. She's been quite the sleuth since Galen first contacted her. The two of them can't seem to talk of anything else."

Cabe sat silent, but I had to speak. "Wait, what? Another family? You mean, like, your dad left your mom and married someone else?"

"Oh no. That's not his style. Gerry's still married to my mother. But Cabe and I have two more sisters who live in Phoenix."

"They're not my sisters," Cabe said in a voice that made it clear to me he was close to losing his calm facade.

I grabbed his leg under the table, leaving my hand on his thigh as a physical symbol of support and solidarity.

Jeffrey raised his eyebrows at Cabe's remark but then directed his attention back to me. "They're both still in high school. One seventeen, one fifteen."

I nodded and tried to wrap my head around a man who would father three different sets of children, all while married to the same woman. Which then led me to try and wrap my head around why on earth Jeffrey's mother was still married to him. But I didn't think it appropriate to ask.

"I couldn't forget what I'd heard that night. It lived in my brain like a worm. Every time he left again, I pictured him with the *other family*. Everything he missed in my life, every time he let me down, I imagined he was with you. The other son. The one he loved and wanted to be with."

Cabe snarled a scoffing groan and tossed back what was left of his beer as the waitress served our food and refilled our drinks. Jeffrey waited until she was gone to continue.

"I guess I was wrong, huh? Galen said Gerry left you guys before she was even born and she never saw him again until she was sixteen. So I don't know where he was, but he wasn't with me, and he wasn't with you."

I watched Cabe's reaction to the new perspective. I thought it was pretty mind-blowing. I mean, here Cabe had thought his whole life that Jeffrey had a full-time fully-engaged dad—the dad he didn't get—and at the same time, Jeffrey spent his whole life with the same resentment directed at Cabe.

Cabe didn't react, though. Not outwardly. He maintained a cool gaze at Jeffrey, but he didn't say a word in response. He hadn't touched his food, which was a dead giveaway to me of how upset he was, but to anyone who didn't know him—like Jeffrey—they'd probably never know how dangerously close he was to standing up and walking away altogether.

Jeffrey rubbed his hand across the back of his neck.

"So look. I get it, man. I really do. Probably more than you realize. I understand you don't want anything to do with Gerry, and I understand you wanting to pretend we don't exist. I tried the same thing for years. I spent my whole life hating you. Resenting you. Blaming you. But here's what I realized when your sister called my sister and dropped the bomb on her. Our anger is displaced. We're directing it at the wrong person when we focus it on each other. We both got screwed over by the same asshole. Who just happened to create us both."

Jeffrey cleared his throat, and I could tell it wasn't as easy for him to speak as he made it appear. My heart went out to him, this man who looked so much like the love of my life and carried so much of the same heartache. I squeezed Cabe's thigh again and willed him to say something. Anything. But he just sat and looked beyond Jeffrey at the building in the distance.

"If you want me to walk away and never contact you again, I'll honor that request and respect your wishes. But I believe we have more in common than just our good looks." Jeffrey smiled as he said it, but Cabe didn't react to the humor. "I think we've both spent too much time and too much energy on Gerry Tucker and his failure as father. If we keep hating each other, it does nothing but perpetuate that negativity." He spread his hands as if to show he had nothing to hide. "I haven't done anything to you, and you haven't done anything to me. We have no reason for bad blood between us. We had no choice in our DNA, and we had no choice with how our childhood played out. But we can choose the men we want to be, and we can choose our future."

Cabe swallowed hard and I wondered if Jeffrey heard it from across the table.

"What does that mean? What do you want?" Cabe asked. I detected emotion in his voice, but he looked calm as could be on the surface.

Jeffrey shrugged and tilted his head to the side, so eerily similar to Cabe that I found myself staring again. "I'd like to get to know you. I feel like you've been in my life for years, but I have no idea who you are. What you're like. I guess I'm asking if we could be...*friends?* I don't know. I'm not sure how this works under these circumstances, but I'm willing to try if you are."

"What, like hang out and shit?"

Jeffrey chuckled, the tone of it deeper than Cabe's. Harder.

"Let's start with some conversations and go from there. Take it as it comes. No sense forcing anything."

Cabe nodded and turned to me, his eyes questioning. I slid my hand inside his and smiled, hoping it was the response he needed.

We finished our meal in stilted conversation. Sometimes it came easily, but then a topic would be raised or a question would be asked that would spark the tension simmering underneath the surface. It would take them a few minutes to recover and talk freely again. I'd try to fill in the blanks with neutrality in those moments, and by the time we'd finished dessert and stood to go, I think the two of them had forged enough to begin.

Jeffrey extended his hand to Cabe for a goodbye, and Cabe shocked us both by taking his brother's hand and pulling him in for an awkward, stiff, guy hug. The one where they're shaking hands in the middle but clap backs as they lean toward each other at a safe distance.

On impulse, I stood on tiptoes and hugged Jeffrey goodbye. His resemblance to Cabe and his shared heartbreak tugged at my emotions and I felt a connection to him. He hugged me back and gave me a grateful smile.

Cabe was silent on the way home, and I let him be. Both of us were processing all that happened. All that had been said.

We walked Deacon in silence and didn't talk as we got ready for bed. But once the lights were out and I lay intertwined in his arms and legs, he spoke.

"Thanks for coming tonight. It meant a lot to me having you there."

"Sure, baby. I'll always be there for you when you need me." I kissed his chest beneath me and snuggled in closer. "How you doing with all this?"

"Pretty much feeling like my whole life was a lie and nothing is what I thought it was."

I raised up and propped my chin on his chest, searching his eyes in the dim light.

"That's not true. Your mom. Galen. Your grandparents. Your life is exactly as it was before tonight. You just have more information and a new perspective."

"I hated him, Ty. Hated him. This invisible kid I never knew. I don't want to like him. I don't want to be friends with him. Hang out with him or discuss our common pasts. But at the same time, he's right. He's done nothing to me. He's not the one I should be angry with."

I laid my head back on his chest and fought the shivers he was causing with his fingers lightly tracing circles on my back. "Just take it as it comes, Cabe. Don't rush it. You don't have to be best friends or talk to him every day, but it could probably help you both put the past behind you to get to know each other and dispel the image you've carried in your heads."

"How 'bout Gerry having a third family?" Cabe yawned deeply, his chest expanding beneath me as his mouth opened wide and dug his chin into my head. "How crazy is that? I wonder if that's it. If there's only the six of us. What if there's more?"

"I don't know. Maybe Gerry doesn't even know. But if anything, this just reaffirms my opinion that you're better off without him in your life."

Cabe kissed the top of my head and stopped talking, his breathing steadily becoming deeper. I had more questions I wanted to ask him, but they could wait.

Monday, September 29th

It rained all weekend, which never makes for easy weddings or happy brides. Never have I ever met a bride who woke up and said, *"It's pouring out? Awesome. That's exactly what I wanted for my wedding day."*

The rain is not only inconvenient, but it adds an extra layer of tension to the goal of making everyone happy. The negative energy emanating from every single guest and family member is contagious, and it puts us on edge for the whole weekend. Especially since there's not a damned thing we can do about the rain.

I woke up this morning stopped up and sneezing with a sore throat, the result of spending all weekend in and out of rain and air conditioning, combined with being stressed out over multiple weddings, including my own.

After a quick stop by the pharmacy to buy cold meds, I dragged my tired ass into the office, but I had zero motivation to talk to any clients or crunch any budget numbers. So Mel and I sat side by side and searched the internet for bridesmaid dresses and emailed my sisters pics of the ones we liked. I told them to find dresses they were happy with and could afford and as long as they were the same aubergine shade, the styles didn't matter. I didn't care for the matchy-matchy dresses, and I knew it would be simpler for each of them to choose an acceptable price point and buy their own.

Carrie responded back with a pic she'd found of a winter wedding with white faux fur stoles, and she said she'd look into purchasing the material and seeing what she could make with it. Tanya called this afternoon to tell me she was emailing a picture of the dress she found, and we talked about what color to do for Erin and putting Eric in a gray suit to match Cabe and the boys. Which she evidently passed on to Mama, who called me tonight all in a tizzy just as we were finishing dinner.

"Brad says the men are wearing gray suits. I thought this was an evening wedding."

"It is."

"Then they need to wear black."

I'd expected this conversation, just not so soon.

"They don't have to wear black, Mama. We're not having a formal wedding."

"Well, I beg your pardon. I thought it was a formal wedding. What are we having? A picnic?"

Cabe reached across the table and took my hand. We'd talked about me staying calm the next time she called. Not letting her get to me. Perhaps the dose of cold medicine I'd just taken would help.

"Mom, it's not formal. You might say semi-formal, but not formal."

"I'm not expecting them to sport tuxes, but they need to wear black. It's an evening wedding."

I moved from the table to the couch as Cabe cleared the dishes. "It's a dark gray suit. It's perfectly acceptable."

"I've never heard of such. They need to wear black."

"Well, they're not. They're wearing gray."

"Hmmph. Alright then. Sharon at the church said Tanya called asking about linens. I could have told you what linens they had."

"You're already doing a lot. Tanya asked how she could help so I told her to call."

"We've got those yellow linens."

"I don't want the stupid yellow linens, Mother."

"You better bite your own tongue, because you're about to bite off more than you chew, missy. I'll drive to Orlando tonight if I need to. Don't get too big for your britches."

I laid back on the couch and put a pillow over my eyes. "I'm sorry, Mama. I'm coming down with something. I don't feel good."

"Are you running a fever? Have you taken anything?"

"I haven't taken my temperature but I've been drinking cold medicine all day."

"Vick's. You need Vick's Vapor Rub. Smear it all over your chest and under your lip, and then smear it on your feet. You remember me doing this when you were a kid, don't ya? You'll feel better in the morning. You got Vick's?"

"No. I'll see if Cabe can get me some." He looked up and raised his eyebrows in question. "Vick's Vapor Rub." He nodded and gave me a thumbs up.

"That's so sweet that he's there taking care of you. Tell him thank you for me. Did you ask his sister to be a bridesmaid yet?"

"No." Galen was the last thing on my mind. My head throbbed. I grabbed the blanket lying across the ottoman and covered my legs.

"You need to get it over with. She'll need to get a dress. Tanya is going to go shopping with me on Saturday to see what I can find. You're sure you want me in purple? I don't think it's a good color for me."

"You can wear whatever color you want. I just told you the girls were wearing purple."

"No, no. If you're having everyone wear purple, I'll wear purple, too. Did Tanya tell you we found some thick pillar candles at the dollar store? I picked up a few but I thought I'd get some more this weekend. How many do you think we need around the centerpieces?"

"Oh, centerpieces! Crap, I've been meaning to call and tell you." More like I'd been dreading calling and telling her. "Cabe's mom has a friend who's an event designer in Atlanta, and Maggie has offered to pay for the flowers for the wedding. As her gift to us. So you're off the hook. You can cross that off your list." I looked at Cabe and nearly busted out laughing when I saw he had his fingers crossed on both hands in support and hopefulness.

Mama was silent for a moment, a rare occurrence for her, to be sure. I didn't know if it meant she was happy, mad, or sad. "Mama? Did you hear me?"

"Does she think we can't afford to buy you flowers? Does she think we need her to—"

"No, no. It's not like that. This is her wedding gift. The lady is a good friend of Maggie's and she wants to do this. It's a good thing, right? So you don't have to worry about centerpieces or bouquets or anything. I thought you'd be excited." I gritted my teeth together and looked to Cabe for encouragement. He nodded and gave me a thumbs up.

Mama was less enthusiastic. "Do you have any idea how much money I've spent on these silk flowers and baskets? Not to mention the time Pearl and I have already put into coming up with ideas to make this crap fit your fancy-schmancy winter theme. You tell his mama that you appreciate the offer, but we'll do just fine. Be gracious, though. Don't be rude."

My hopes of having a beautiful, classy, professionally-done wedding went spiraling toward earth in flaming embers.

"I'd like to at least hear what the lady has to say. Maybe we could—"

"You wait just a minute, missy. I've not having Cabe's mama think that we can't put on a wedding for you. We'll make do with what we have, and you just make sure you thank her properly."

I closed my eyes and tried not to scream. The pressure behind my eyes continued to build, and it wasn't only because of my sinuses.

"Okay, well, what about catering? She has catering services, too. It would be so much easier on all of us to have a professional caterer. If you and Aunt Pearl want to do the centerpieces, then at least let me talk to her about the catering."

"I've already put out sign-up sheets at the church for people to make a dish. You expect me to tell all those people their hard work ain't good enough for you?"

I was exhausted, emotionally and physically spent. My body ached. My head hurt. I squeezed my eyes shut tight, but the strain of it all still escaped in big, slow-moving teardrops that trailed down my face. I didn't even bother to wipe them away. It didn't matter if they flowed.

Cabe moved to my end of the sofa and began to massage my neck and shoulders. "Calm down," he whispered. "It's okay. Don't let her get to you."

Too late.

"I gotta go, Mama. We'll have to talk about this later."

"Wait a minute. I still need to ask you—"

"I'm sick, and I need to go. Bye." My voice cracked as I said it, and I turned into Cabe's welcoming arms and let the dam break. An ugly, snotty, noisy, messy cry.

"I feel like Mama is forcing me to have a garage-sale bare-bones pot-luck wedding. Like here's the worse do-it-yourself wedding you could ever do. I don't want anyone we know to come to this. I don't even want to go. This is not what I wanted."

"So tell her," Cabe said. Which sounds so easy to say, but is not at all easy to do.

"I try. I told her not to buy the silks. Not to get the free yellow tablecloths. Not to hire my clueless cousin to make the dresses. But she doesn't listen to me!" I went to find a tissue and blew my nose as I came back to the living room. Thank God that man loves me enough to see me be a blubbering mess.

"It's like I can't even think about what I want or focus on getting it done because I'm constantly spending every spare minute fighting off her hare-brained ideas. Not to mention having the energy sucked out of me every other minute of the day by other brides whose weddings are way more important than mine. On top of which I have Reynalda Freakin' Riley and her ego the size of Texas and her crazy-ass bride who insists on talking to me every day. I have to do all these extra hoops for everything I do with her to make sure I don't go around or behind Reynalda and piss her off."

"Babe, Reynalda's nuts, so you don't need to worry about her. Once this wedding's done, you never have to talk to her again."

I tossed the tissue in the trash and flopped down on the couch beside him. "But I was supposed to be learning from her. What can I possibly learn from her? How not to be an asshole?"

"That's a valuable lesson in life." He held his arm open and I snuggled up against him. "As far as the other brides, their wedding is not any more important than yours. Than ours. Maybe focus on their weddings while you're at work, and focus on ours while you're not. Which I know is hard to do when you're working so much right now. I don't know, Buttercup. I wish I had better answers."

"I just want it all to be over with. October. November. Their weddings. Our wedding. I just want to be able to breathe."

October

Thursday, October 2nd

Galen called tonight. She talked to Cabe for a while, and then asked for me. I had heard his end of their conversation and could tell she had apologized, but the depth of her emotion still caught me off guard.

She was crying when I picked up, though she cleared her throat and tried to hide it.

"I'm sorry I haven't called to say this before, but I'm really sorry for how things got off track between us. I never meant to alienate you in any way. I was just trying to protect my brother."

"I know that."

"I'm sorry, too, that I haven't called to congratulate you and that I didn't congratulate you that night at the restaurant. I was mad at you and Cabe both. I felt like all I did was try to help my brother and do what I thought was best for him, and it seemed like no matter what I tried everybody just got mad at me. Cabe, you, Mom, Nana." Her voice broke again. "My brother means everything to me, Ty. He's always been there for me, when no one else was. He's always looked out for me and taken care of me. I would never do anything to purposely hurt him."

What was I supposed to say to that? Whether it was on purpose or not, she did hurt him.

"I can't believe you guys are getting married next month. I feel like I've missed out on the whole thing. I'm stuck up here in New York and I can't be a part of any of it. I wanted to say I was sorry and ask if I'm allowed to come to your wedding."

So she basically just made her apology all about her. What she was missing and how it is affecting her.

I swallowed a mouthful of bitterness and anger and reminded myself that ultimately I wanted us all to get along. I wanted Cabe and Maggie to be happy and enjoy the wedding without tension or strain.

"Of course, you're allowed to come to the wedding. We don't want to exclude you, Galen. We just want to be treated with respect." I motioned to Cabe and tried to communicate by hand gestures and mouthing words to figure out if he wanted me to ask her to be a bridesmaid. He shrugged and pointed back to me.

I had hoped he would make the ultimate decision. Then if it didn't work out and she ended up being a bitch, I could blame him and be off the hook. But the ball was in my court, and though I still didn't trust her or her motives, I also didn't want to hear about it for the rest of our lives if I didn't include her.

"Would you like to be a bridesmaid?"

She burst into tears and thanked me over and over again. I pretty much remained silent, unwilling to say it was okay since it wasn't. Then she asked to talk to her brother again and thanked him, apologizing one more time for all that had happened between them.

Cabe's mood was somber when they hung up.

"You okay?" I asked.

He nodded.

"At least she called. She apologized, right?"

He nodded again.

"What's up, dude? Talk to me."

"I can't stand to hear her cry. She's always been a pain in my ass, but I've always hated to hear her cry. Even when she was a baby. I used to run and get Mom any time she cried. I think I've always felt responsible for her somehow. Like I had to take care of her. Now she's an adult. I can't take care of her anymore."

I wrapped my arms around him and held him tight. "You'll always be her big brother. Nothing will change that."

Just like nothing will probably ever change her attitude, her manipulative habits, or her viewpoint that the world revolves around her alone. But she was his sister. And soon to be my sister-in-law.

At least I could check off the bridal party on my mental checklist.

Friday, October 10th

Reynalda had insisted I come to her office to go over everything before the rehearsal tonight. Funny how she hasn't attended a single meeting with Chris and Jayah–other than stopping by to introduce me the first time I met them–hasn't had a single conversation with them since I took over, and hasn't discussed boo with me the entire time I've been working with them.

She insisted I send and receive everything through her office, so I hope she has at least been keeping up with everything as it's progressed, but based on what I've seen of her and the phone conversations we've had, I have my doubts.

She announced on Tuesday that she wanted me to come early this afternoon and she would be taking over the wedding for the rehearsal and wedding day.

I came into this thinking I was going to be assisting. Shadowing her and learning what I could.

Instead I've done all the work for these clients and gotten them ready for the event, and then Glamour Girl is just going to sweep in and take over for the cameras.

If I didn't have the relationship with Jayah and Chris that I have, I'd be tempted just to say *"Here you go. Here's the file. Have fun."* Then just sit back and watch the Wicked Witch melt.

But that's not who I am and what I'm about.

So I showed up today, on time, fully expecting her not to be there.

The lights were on when I arrived, but I didn't see Heidi at her desk.

"Heidi?" I called out when I entered. No sign of Reynalda either. "Heidi? Reynalda? Anyone?"

I walked to the storage room where they keep the coffee maker and peeked in. No one there.

243

As I turned to go back toward the door, I saw a red heel out of the corner of my eye. I walked slowly to the large desk behind the screen, praying it wouldn't be a dead body or something. I think maybe I watch too many forensics shows.

She was sitting on the floor behind the desk, staring straight ahead at the window with her feet splayed out in front of her in a terribly unladylike position.

"Reynalda?" I asked, hoping she would move. She didn't look dead, but she was so still and so quiet she didn't look alive either.

She turned her head up toward me, her movements slow and lethargic. She'd been crying. A lot. Her false eyelashes had loosened on one eye and her makeup was smeared and splotchy.

I crouched down beside her. "Reynalda, are you okay? Are you alright? Do you need a doctor?"

She shook her head and looked back toward the window.

"Reynalda, are you hurt? Are you sick? What should I do?"

"I have pills in my purse. Can you get them for me?"

Her voice almost sounded like a croak, hoarse and rough.

I searched her desk for a purse but couldn't find one. I searched Heidi's desk and the storage room. No purse.

"Reynalda? Where's your purse? I can't find it."

"It's in my car."

"In your car? Okay. I need your keys. Are you going to be okay here by yourself? Should I call an ambulance?"

"No! No ambulance. I just need my pills. The valet has the keys."

"I hate to leave you here. Are you sure you're okay? What are the pills for? What's wrong?"

"Just get me my pills and I'll be fine." A huge tear rolled down her face and her bottom lip quivered.

"Okay. Okay. I'll get them."

I ran all the way to the valet stand at the front of the resort. My side cramped and the balls of my feet stung from my shoes slapping the tiles. I regretted lunch at Taco Bell almost immediately. Greasy tacos do not provide great fuel for sudden sprints.

"I need to get Reynalda Riley's car," I told the valet as I huffed and puffed and held my side.

"You got the ticket?"

The ticket. Crap. "No, I don't, but it's an emergency. I need to get Reynalda's car."

"No can do without a ticket."

My stomach churned and sweat stung my eyes. "Look, I understand, but it's a medical emergency. I have to get in her car. She needs me to bring something to her."

"You have to have a ticket to access a car. You think I can hand out keys to whoever shows up and says they want someone's car?"

Double crap. There was no way in hell I wanted to run all the way back to her office and then all the way back to valet.

"Work with me, dude. I'm not trying to steal her car. I just need to get something out of it. She doesn't feel well, and there's some kind of pills in her purse, which for reasons unknown to me, she chose to leave in her car. Can you at least take me to her car and wait while I get the pills and then bring me back?"

We debated the issue for at least ten more minutes before another valet agreed he would take me against Mr. Rule Follower's great displeasure.

Her purse was laying right on the front seat in full view. Really? Who does that?

I grabbed the bag and talked the valet guy into taking me to the back of the resort near the courtyard entrance to her office.

She was still seated in the same exact position when I returned.

"I got your purse. Here it is. Do you need water to take your pills?"

She nodded as I handed her the purse, and I ran to the storage room to get water from the mini fridge.

"Here you go." I tried to give her the water bottle but she just sat there staring. The purse was sitting in her lap where I'd left it. Untouched.

"Reynalda, take your pills."

When I got no response, I opened her purse and dug to find the pill bottle. There were five of them, ranging in size. None of the prescription labels had her name on them.

"Reynalda? Which pills?"

"Valium."

Really? I'd just risked my own cardiac arrest to get her a valium? I thought it was life or death. Like her blood sugar was bottoming out or she needed to pop a pill under her tongue for her heart or something.

I opened the bottle of Valium and handed it to her, and she popped a couple of pills in her mouth and chased it with the water. I seriously considered joining her. The bottle had several more pills in it, and I could sure use a few hours without my brain whirring at top speed.

Reynalda hiccupped and looked at me. Like, actually looked at me and made eye contact for the first time since I'd walked in.

"You think you're so much better than me." More tears flowed and she made no move to wipe them.

"Reynalda, what are you talking about? What happened?"

"I know you do. You look down at me, and you think you're so much better than me. But you don't know that I'm a star. I'm a star, and you won't ever be. They love me. They don't even know who you are."

She laughed a twisted, sick chuckle and looked back toward the window.

I stood, wondering what I was supposed to do with her.

"I think I should call an ambulance."

"No! Don't you dare call an ambulance." She struggled to get to her knees and pushed off the desk to come to standing, kicking off her heels in the process. She smoothed her huge mass of hair away from her face and grabbed a tissue from her desk to dab at her eyes. It was too little too late. Her make-up was beyond repair.

When her eyes met mine again, she had her chin held high and her shoulders back in the haughty stance she always carried. Somehow it didn't play the same with her standing there barefoot with her false eyelash flapping in the breeze and her face red and splotchy.

"No ambulance. The last thing I need is the press hearing I was taken away in an ambulance. I have a wedding this weekend. I need to be ready for the cameras."

"What happened? Are you okay?"

"Heidi quit. She left me. They all do. Bitches. They milk me for all they can, bleeding me like leeches, and then when they've had their fill, they just up and leave."

Her chin trembled and her eyes went glassy again, but she glanced at the clock and back to me, shaking her head against the tears. "We're running out of time. I have to get ready. Come with me."

She slipped her shoes on and we left the office, crossing to another section of the hotel and a row of elevators. As we stepped inside, she fished around her purse for the key card and slid it in before pressing the button for the Penthouse floor.

"You have a room here?"

She had taken out a compact mirror and was rubbing at the smudged make-up on her face. "I live here."

"In the hotel? You live in the Ritz Carlton?"

The elevator doors opened and I followed her into her penthouse suite. Which was magnificent, by the way. I guess that goes without saying.

"I need to take a shower. Wait here."

Twenty minutes later, she came out in a robe and poured herself a glass of champagne. "So tell me about this wedding. Give me the rundown. You'll run the rehearsal while I talk to the reporters. Do not give an interview. Do not answer any questions or pose for any photos. If they ask you to, tell them the client contract forbids you talking to the press."

No sooner had I started telling her about the wedding than a knock pounded on the door. Reynalda opened it and ushered in a guy with blue hair and a girl with multiple piercings. She didn't bother to introduce me or them, but it didn't take long to figure out they were there to do her hair and make-up.

I talked as they worked, flipping through the file to ensure I was recapping all the important points of the ceremony.

When I mentioned anything about the reception, she'd hold her hand up and say, "Ceremony. Focus on the ceremony."

They had her made up and back to normal within a half hour and we were at the valet.

"Are you sure you're okay to drive? You've been drinking and taking Valium," I whispered as we waited for them to bring our keys.

"Oh, please. Do you think I'm an amateur?" She slid the large tortoiseshell glasses over her eyes and sauntered to her car. Reynalda was back in business.

True to her word, she spent the whole rehearsal talking to the reporters. Occasionally, she'd call out some random-ass instruction to someone in the wedding party—I assume to make it appear she was in charge—but I basically ran the whole thing.

She never said one word about what had transpired between us. Not a thank you. Not a keep your mouth shut. Not a *"hey, sorry I said some weird, sort of crappy things."*

It was as though it had never happened.

Saturday, October 11th

What a circus. Barnum & Bailey ain't got nothing on this lady.

I arrived at Chris and Jayah's hotel around seven this morning to begin set-up for our four o'clock ceremony. Reynalda strolled in around noon.

The banquet captain had just told me the custom-designed charger plates with Chris and Jayah's initials had arrived with three plates cracked. And, of course, no extras.

In addition, the digital mapping projectors had blown out power on one side of the ballroom. When they tried to run cables to the other side of the room, the distance reduced the quality of the projection. The company's representatives were working on a solution, but there was little help to be found on a Saturday.

On top of that, the hotel had sent over a revised diagram yesterday to Reynalda requesting that they be able to drop the coffee stations and sushi stations down to one set each due to reduced labor and a shortage of six-foot tables. Reynalda or Heidi had approved the change without ever consulting me, and in all the drama that transpired, no one had told me until I got here today and realized the set was wrong.

Because they had Reynalda's signature on the change order and she was technically the signatory, I had no authority to get them to change it back.

She wasn't answering her phone, of course, so when she came busting up in the reception room in her sleek black dress and little black loafers, I immediately pounced on her.

"We have an issue with the chargers, but I've got someone from the hotel on the phone with the—"

She held up a perfectly manicured hand and shook her head. "Not now, dear. I can't. I'm exhausted from an appearance at a celebrity golf tournament this morning. I need to get checked in and catch a quick power nap before my hair and make-up appointment."

I pondered what kind of prison sentence I would get if I strangled her.

"No, Reynalda. I need your opinion to make decisions. We have charger issues, we have projection issues—"

"Tyler, please. You're a professional. You are fully capable of handling your own crises. Don't be so dependent on me."

"I'm not dependent on you! These are your clients. I need your input on how you'd like me to handle these situations."

"Do you really? Really? Are you sure you couldn't just use that brain God gave you and make some decisions on your own? I'm turning my phone off, and I'll be back down at two to meet with the press. Don't talk to them."

She spun on her heel to leave, and I trotted along behind her. "But I need your signature on a change order."

She never stopped walking. "So forge it. Tell them you're bringing it up to me to sign and then sign it and give it back. Do you think I ever actually sign any of this paperwork?"

I didn't see her again until she brought the press in a little after two o'clock to take shots of the room. She was made up to the nines and dressed in a floor-length sequined gown. You know, like all us wedding planners wear when we're *working* an event. Her hair had been swept up into an elegant chignon and her make-up was flawless. She looked stunning, and my desire to kill her grew.

The group of reporters followed her as she spoke to the banquet captain and greeted a few of the servers by name. "Did we get the charger situation resolved?" Her question was directed to the captain, who nodded and assured her it had been handled.

Hell yeah, it had. Because I had taken care of it and pulled the chargers from any seat with small children and replaced theirs with small Disney plushes from the hotel gift shops.

Reynalda's next press stop was the audio/visual booth, where she explained to the reporters that the event would feature digital projections from seven different locations around the world, which was basically the only fact I'd been able to share with her about the reception since she kept stopping me every time.

"What's the update on our projectors, Luke?" she asked the digital technician. He explained in great detail how they'd rigged the wires, and she patted him on the back and told him she'd never doubted he would figure it out.

She didn't even know what the issue was!

To hear her talk from the viewpoint of the press, you would think this was a woman in charge of the room, on top of every little detail. Despite the fact she'd only set foot in the room for ten minutes tops and couldn't be bothered to actually hear the issues then.

She never so much as looked my way while the reporters were in the room, and I didn't see her again until just before the ceremony.

I was coming out of Jayah's dressing room when Reynalda passed me on her way in.

"She's all set. We can start the ceremony whenever you're ready," I told her.

"Great. My team of helpers has arrived. I know the reception room has kind of been your baby today, so why don't you go ahead and stay in there? Make sure things are on track and put out any fires. We've got this."

A group of four young star-crossed groupies stood behind her, hanging on her every word. She snapped her fingers, and they scattered. I tromped back to the reception room, fuming. I knew she was keeping me out of the camera shots so that she appeared to be fully in control. The same thing she'd been doing all day. Fine by me. I didn't care about being photographed or interviewed or put in the limelight.

But I'd worked with Chris and Jayah for several weeks. I had helped plan every aspect of what was happening today. It bothered me not to see my bride walk down the aisle. Not to be there for my very favorite part of any wedding, in those priceless moments just before the doors swing wide and a father walks his daughter toward her future.

I hated that I wouldn't be there to congratulate them when they came bursting through the doors as man and wife. Try as I might to convince myself it didn't matter, it really bothered me and put me in a funk the rest of the night.

The best part of the evening was the very end. When all was said and done and the guests had departed, and I was walking Chris and Jayah up to their suite.

"Everything was perfect, T," said Chris. "You pulled it all off exactly how we wanted."

He slapped my hand in a weird sideways high-five that I'm sure I screwed up somehow.

Jayah gave me a huge hug and smile. "We could not have done this without you. We know how much you've done for us. We owe the success of our wedding to you, and we won't ever forget it."

That's what matters, isn't it?

Monday, October 13th

I told Mama yesterday that if she didn't send me a picture of these centerpieces she and Aunt Pearl have cooked up, I'm going to go ahead and book Sandy's floral services.

She kept telling me she couldn't figure out how to send the pictures she took with her phone, so I asked Carrie to go over and take a picture.

Oh holy hell.

A one-armed chimpanzee could have done a better silk arrangement than that, and don't even get me started on the colors.

I was aware she'd bought the silk flowers on clearance sale, (again, against my wishes) but I'd kind of thought she understood the whole winterland, white-silver-purple theme we had going. I thought she'd bought into that.

But no.

They'd done up three examples to show me. They had spray painted the baskets white and glued some kind of snowflakes on them, and that's about as winter as they got. The silk flowers were from every season imaginable and in every color of the rainbow. I'm talking red, orange, burnt orange, pale pink, hot pink, yellow. You name it, it was represented. Well, except for white, silver or purple. No, I take that back. A couple of them had purple flowers, but it was the kind of purple you'd use for a superhero costume, not the deep, elegant aubergine I had in mind. She even had one or two centerpieces with one flower in an unnatural, Easter egg blue.

I called Carrie right away.

"Are you kidding me? Please tell me this is a joke."

"I thought you knew," Carrie said. "Mama said you knew what they were doing and you just wanted a picture of the progress. I told her you were going to blow a gasket."

"I knew she was making silk arrangements in baskets, which I told her not to do, by the way, but she's hell-bent and determined to do it anyway. I thought perhaps she might *attempt* something elegant. I didn't know they were going to look like she plucked them from the Munchkin gardens of Oz. Carrie! What am I going to do?"

"You're asking me? I have no idea. I got married in an Elvis chapel wearing a rented red dress, remember?"

"Aargh. I can't believe this. I've been telling her since day one that I don't want silk flowers, or wicker baskets, or yellow linens. It's like talking to a brick wall. She does not listen to me."

"That's Patsy."

"What am I supposed to do now? If I don't use these stupid atrocities, she and Aunt Pearl are gonna be all miffed, but there is no way I'm putting that on the tables at my wedding. I'm just not."

"So tell her."

Carrie and I both sat silent for a moment as we each imagined how that would go.

"I need your help here, Carrie."

My sister laughed. "My help? What am I supposed to do?"

"Talk to her! Cabe's mom has agreed to pay for my flowers. To have a professional designer come from Atlanta and do all this for me. Not only would it keep me from having a basket of Skittles on every table, but it would also save a lot of time and stress for Mama. But she won't hear of it. She says it would be rude for me to accept the gift and embarrassing to the family. You gotta talk to her."

Carrie groaned. "Alright. I don't know that it will do any good, but I'll try."

"Thank you. You have such a way with her. Nobody can handle Mama like you do. I mean, I've tried, but you just have this—"

"Alright, alright. I already said I'd talk to her. I'll go over there Wednesday night."

"Okay, let me know how it goes."

Tuesday, October 14th

Mel and I were discussing my wedding at lunch today, crossing our fingers that Carrie can talk sense into Mama, and trying to determine what still needs to be done and what can be checked off the list.

"How's Cabe doing with the music?" Mel asked as we finished up our salads.

"Okay, I guess. He wants me to pick a song to walk down the aisle to. Said he felt like that needed to be something I chose and he'd rather be surprised. He's picked everything else for the ceremony and the reception, and we've gone over all of it except his entrance and our first dance. He wants both of those to be a surprise."

"You sure you don't want to do classical or traditional?"

"Nope. Not a chance. I'm so sick of hearing *Here Comes the Bride* and *Canon in D* that if I never heard them again, it'd be okay. Seriously, someone needs to say those wedding songs are done and we need to move on."

"Is there a song that he sings for you, or mentions that it makes him think of you?"

I shook my head. "Not really. I thought about doing *Brown-Eyed Girl*, but that's more my favorite song than anything to do with us. Besides, they don't end up together in the end, so I don't want that. You know what I did think about? He always calls me Buttercup. He's called me that for years. Pretty much since we met. There's a song where the guy calls the girl Buttercup. I know I've heard it, but for the life of me, I can't remember how it goes. I should Google it."

"Um, I don't think that one's gonna work," Mel said. She held up her hands and waved them at me. "Now don't get me wrong! I'm not telling you what you can and can't do, and I certainly am not trying to be all up in your business like your mama. But I don't think that song is what you want

253

for walking down the aisle."

"Why not? What's wrong with it? Is it sexually explicit or something? I thought it was an old song. Like back in the times when songs weren't explicit."

"Oh, honey. They were still explicit. They just hid it all in innuendo. But this song's not explicit. It's just not something you'd want played as you walk down the aisle to get married."

So, of course, I went straight to my desk and looked it up. I liked it at first, upbeat and happy. But no sooner had the lyrics started than my mouth flew open and stayed there. I didn't even wait for the whole song to finish before I called Cabe and cussed him out. I didn't even say hello.

"All this time, I thought you were calling me Buttercup like some kind of endearment. Like you were being sweet or something. Now I hear the lyrics to the song and realize it was really just a dig against me all along. What the hell, Cabe?"

"Well, hello sweetheart! And how are you today?"

"This song is about some girl who keeps screwing some guy over and treating him like shit. Is that how you felt about me? Is that who you thought I was?"

"Slow down, Buttercup."

"Don't call me that!" I screamed into the phone so loud that it even hurt *my* ear.

"Okay. I need you to calm down."

"I'm not going to calm down. You've been calling me that for *years*. The whole time, I thought it was just some sweet nickname you'd given me."

"It was. I just liked the name and I thought—"

"I know what you thought. The same thing your sister thought—that I was stringing you along and using you for my own emotional band-aid. I didn't know you felt that way."

"I didn't."

"Cabe, I read the lyrics. It's pretty damned clear what you thought of me."

He sighed, and I could hear the clicking of his keyboard keys in the background.

"Am I keeping you from working? I can hear you typing in the background. Can you seriously not just stop working long enough to explain this to me?"

"Ty, I'm looking up the lyrics so I can see what the hell you're so upset about. Once I know that, I'll figure out whether or not I can explain this to you."

He started to read the lyrics aloud.

"Cabe, I know what they say. I told you I just read them."

"Hold your horses, would you? Let me catch up to speed."

He continued to read the lyrics, and I struggled to listen patiently and failed. I listened, but I didn't achieve anything anywhere near patience.

"Okaaay. Will you give me time to speak?" His sarcasm sparked my anger even higher.

"Don't you get an attitude with me, Cable Shaw! You've been laughing at me behind my back all this time. How could you? I'm sorry I didn't know how you felt about me. I'm sorry I didn't know how I felt about you. How many times can I say I'm sorry? It's like I'll never be able to make this up to you. I can't go back and change it, Cabe."

"I'm not asking you to. I haven't asked you to apologize. Nor was I ever laughing at you behind your back or making fun of you in any way. Now I'm not sure what you want me to say, but I honestly don't know why I started calling you that. It damned sure wasn't because of these song lyrics. Although I have to admit, now that I'm reading it, the words do seem to fit us pretty well. Don't you think?"

"That's not funny." I sat back in my chair in disbelief.

"Look, obviously you saw the similarities, too, or you wouldn't have your panties all in a wad."

"I'll have you know I am not wearing any panties, and therefore they can't possibly be in a wad, thank you very much." I got up and closed my office door. Probably a little later than I should have.

"Well, damn, Buttercup. I didn't know this was gonna be that kind of phone call."

"Don't do that," I said. "Don't call me Buttercup, and don't try to charm me. It won't work. I'm really pissed."

"Baby. Sweetheart. My love. My life. I understand where you're coming from, and I can see how this looks. But I can assure you that I have meant no harm or slight in calling you Buttercup all these years. It was exactly as you thought. Simply a term of affection. If you would like for me to stop calling you that, I will do my best to cease and desist. But I can't promise I won't ever slip up."

"I definitely don't want you to call me that again, but I'm more concerned about what you've been thinking about me."

"What I've been thinking about you is that I love you and I intend to spend the rest of my life with you. You mean the world to me. But now that you've told me you're not wearing any panties, my thoughts have taken a decidedly different turn. Can we get back to that part of the conversation please? I'd like to hear more."

I was no longer sure whether I had cause to be angry. "So, you really didn't call me that because of the song?"

"Nope."

"And it really wasn't a dig at me?"

"No ma'am. It was because I was digging ya, but not digging *at* ya."

I paused for a long moment, trying to figure out what to say next. I'd gotten all worked up with my adrenaline pumping, and to find out he wasn't guilty just took the wind out of my sails. What a sad statement on my current stress levels to realize I was actually excited to be able to yell at someone.

My job doesn't allow me to yell at anyone no matter how much they frustrate me. I can't yell at my mother even though she drives me bat-shit crazy because then she just turns it around on me and makes me feel guilty. So I'd just yelled at the only person safe enough for me to unleash upon. And it turns out he wasn't even guilty.

"I'm sorry, baby. You know I'm on edge right now. I don't mean to keep taking it out on you."

"Apology accepted and situation understood. I know you're under a lot of pressure. Now, about those panties…"

I laughed. "I gotta go. Get back to work and we'll discuss my lingerie later."

"Or lack thereof?"

I smiled again, thankful for him. My calm amid the storm.

Thursday, October 16th

I'd been dreading the call all day, flinching when the phone rang and getting sweaty palms when I picked it up to see who it was. I was surprised I didn't hear from her last night since Carrie said she was going over there after she got off work.

When she hadn't called by lunchtime, I relaxed a bit, figuring maybe my sister hadn't had time to talk to her yet and I was in the clear. For today at least.

Wrong.

She jumped right into it without even saying hello.

"Carrie says you don't want to use silk flowers in your centerpieces."

"That's right." I swallowed hard and strummed my fingers on my desk. Funny how your mother's tone of voice can make you feel like you're in trouble no matter how old you are.

"Well, why didn't you say so? Pearl and I have been spending every evening in that carport making centerpieces, and now you tell your sister you don't even want them."

"I tried to say something! I told you the day you were at the store that I didn't want silk flowers, and I've told you several times since then."

"We were only trying to help you, but I guess you don't need us. You've got Ms. Pahfohming Ahts Centah to help you now." Her thick accent went nasal as she mocked Maggie's job and took it in a direction I'd really hoped to avoid.

"It's not like that. Maggie offered to pay because she wants to help with her child's wedding just like you offered to make them because you wanted to help your child."

"I don't have the money to buy you fresh flowers, Tyler. Your sweet daddy, Lord bless his soul, didn't leave me much beyond this land and this house, which is falling down around my ears. I've got your brother in college—"

"Mama, I know all that. I haven't asked you to spend a dime. I don't understand why you can't see this is actually easier on you and less stress for both of us. This lady will come in and do all the work. You and Aunt Pearl can just enjoy the day. If Maggie wants to do this as her gift, why should that bother you? You should be happy someone wants to do something nice for your daughter."

"Fine. I'll tell your aunt Pearl you don't need her help."

I rolled my eyes—grateful she couldn't see me—and propped my forehead in my hand. "What about the favors? I asked you and Aunt Pearl to work on favors."

"We can just do Jordan almonds."

Is there a possibility my phone translates my voice into another language when we talk? Because I feel like she's not hearing anything I'm saying.

"I don't want Jordan almonds, Mama. We talked about coming up with something clever. Useful. Maybe something that reflects our family or something."

"That sounds like a lot of trouble."

Says the woman who's been spending her evenings spray painting baskets and cutting stems off silk flowers and carefully gluing them into place.

"Okay, then don't worry about the favors. I'll come up with something." I took a swig of my coffee, which I immediately regretted since it was room temperature. Blech.

"No, that's alright. Me and Pearl will come up with favors. I'll send you a picture right off the bat this time, though. I ain't wasting all that time again only to have you say you don't want it."

"That's great. That way we can be on the same page. Now, just so we're clear—I'm calling Sandy today and asking her to do my flowers? Right? You're not going to keep making centerpieces or go by a whole bunch of crap and then get upset when someone shows up the day of the wedding with flowers, right?"

"You need to watch your language. I gotta go get ready for bingo."

I called Sandy as soon as we hung up and introduced myself. I explained what I had in mind and asked if she'd be able to make it happen on such short notice. She sang Maggie's praises and asked about Cabe, assuring me she'd do whatever it took to make it work. We set up a phone appointment next week to go over details.

It's too early to feel relieved. I need to see a proposal in my hand. I need to know it's not going to cost Maggie a fortune. I need to be sure Mama isn't going to make me suffer for this the rest of my life if I hire Sandy. I need to know Sandy can deliver in less than a month. What she delivers,

I'm not as concerned about. I trust Maggie's judgment when she says Sandy is talented. I mean, undoubtedly whatever she comes up with will be better than rainbow silks in white wicker.

Friday, October 17th

I couldn't focus on my rehearsal tonight for the life of me. My concentration level has been crap lately anyway. My brain is fried and my body is shuffling around in zombie mode. I called tonight's bride by next weekend's name, and I forgot they were Jewish until we'd already done the entire rehearsal before I realized the rabbi was still in the bathroom.

Luckily, they were a rowdy group, so they actually apologized to me a few times for not paying attention and throwing me off my game, but it wasn't them who had me frazzled.

Cabe went out with Jeffrey tonight.

They've been talking on the phone every few days since we had dinner together, and I've been amazed at how receptive Cabe's been. They've discovered they have an eerie amount of things in common. Not like those twins separated at birth who come together years later and find they've lived parallel lives, but too many similarities to be coincidental.

It's been cathartic and confusing for him. He harbored a lifetime of bitterness toward Jeffrey, but the man he's met is nothing like the person he hated. Their mutual disdain and disappointment in their father has certainly made it easier for them to bond, but I think they genuinely enjoy each other's company in conversation.

I'd been pleased that it was going so well, even though I admit I was sort of holding my breath when it first started, worried Cabe was going to get hurt or sent spiraling into another funk.

When he told me he'd invited Jeffrey to come down and spend the day on Bill's boat with him, I was more than a little apprehensive. It's one thing to talk to someone from a comfortable distance on a phone. It's another thing entirely to be stuck out to sea with them for eight hours. Just two men who happened to hate each other their entire lives. Yeah. Nothing bad could happen there.

He planned to pick Jeffrey up at the airport while I was at my rehearsal, then the two of them would go to dinner and meet me back at the house.

I felt like time crawled in reverse all night. I wondered where they went to eat. What they were discussing. How it was going. If Cabe regretted inviting him. If Jeffrey felt uneasy about heading out on a boat tomorrow with a half-brother who'd resented him his whole life. I really need to stop watching real-life crime shows on TV.

They weren't home when I got there, and Cabe didn't answer my text right away. I was pacing on pins and needles when my phone finally buzzed.

"Leaving the pub now. See you soon. Want ice cream?"

I responded that I didn't, but then said screw it and texted him again requesting mint chocolate chip. Stressful situations call for desperate measures. I don't have another dress fitting for two more weeks. I have time to work it off.

They came busting in the door together, laughing and talking at the same time. Their resemblance so uncanny that it blew my mind again. I couldn't stop staring at Jeffrey, even though I knew what to expect this time.

"Where'd you guys end up?"

"Raglan Road," Cabe answered, launching into a story about the band and the crowd. They shared parts of the story, and I marveled at their comfort level, so far removed from the stilted conversation at our last dinner where Cabe kept his body turned in the direction of escape and didn't utter a word without gritted teeth.

He looked happy tonight, though. Relaxed and at ease. I hoped with everything in me that Jeffrey was what he appeared to be. If he had an ulterior motive, or if he was out to hurt Cabe in some way, I'd never forgive myself for encouraging Cabe to entertain the idea of engaging with him.

I suppose there was no way to tell except time. I needed to trust Cabe's judgment. Although that wouldn't stop me from being on the lookout for any sign Jeffrey was evil incarnate.

"Tyler, thank you so much for welcoming me into your home," Jeffrey said as I showed him our guest room and pointed out the location of the towels and extra toothpaste.

"Oh, of course. You're welcome any time," I said, biting my tongue to keep from adding *"as long as you don't try to screw over my fiancé."*

I couldn't bite my tongue once Cabe and I were alone, though. "Things seem to be moving fast," I said as he pulled me into a spoon cuddle when we'd turned out the lights.

"Yeah, I guess. It's strange. I feel like I've known him for so much longer, you know?"

"Take your time, though. Be cautious."

Cabe chuckled, his breath warm against the back of my neck as he pulled my hair up and out of his face. "Are you worried about Jeffrey and I taking our relationship to the next level?"

I elbowed him in the ribs. "I'm serious. I'm happy you guys are getting along and I think it's cool that you click with him. But I'm just wary of your family after all that's happened."

He leaned over my shoulder and looked at me in the moonlight from the windows. "You're the one who told me to call him back. Who encouraged me to go to dinner with him in the first place."

I flipped onto my back. "I know that. I still think it's a good idea for you to get to know each other. Especially if it helps you both move forward and let go of the past. I just don't want to see you be hurt or disappointed, that's all."

He traced one finger down the side of my face and along my neck, curving across my shoulder as tiny shivers moved over me. "I appreciate your concern, and I love that you want to protect me. I think I can take care of myself, though. You still worried about the boat? Still thinking one of us is going to knock the other one overboard?" He laughed again and I elbowed him harder.

"Don't laugh at me. Just promise me you'll be careful. That you'll be aware of your surroundings."

"Ty, I have to do that any time I'm on a boat. I really don't think Jeffrey is a maniacal killer, but if it makes you feel better, Dean's coming with us."

Wind rushed from my lungs and my chest released its tension. "Really? Oh my gosh. That's awesome."

Cabe raised up on one elbow and looked down at me. "You're serious! You really think I'm in danger? From Jeffrey? Damn, Ty. You've got to stop binge-watching true crime shows."

"I know, I know. It's just that I can't sleep lately with my brain going ninety miles an hour, and I hate keeping you up tossing and turning. So I go to the couch and watch until I fall asleep."

He kissed my forehead and settled himself back into our cuddle. "Probably not the wisest choice of programming for lullaby, babe. Just keep counting down. It won't be long until October and all its crazy weddings are done, and then November and our crazy wedding's done, and then we'll be chilling in a bungalow on the side of a mountain in Costa Rica."

"Mmm. That sounds incredible. I can't wait." I hugged his arm around my waist and snuggled further back into his embrace, praying sleep would come and that he would be alright tomorrow.

Sunday, October 19th

They both survived. They were sunburned and had a bit of a hangover, but they got up this morning recounting tales of the fish they caught and the ones that got away. The three of us went out to breakfast together and then we drove Jeffrey to the airport and said goodbye.

He and Cabe did the man-hug thing and then Jeffrey gave me a huge hug and thanked me again for the hospitality. "I told Cabe the two of you need to come up and stay with me some weekend soon. We have a place right on the beach."

I immediately turned to Cabe, worried the reference to Jeffrey's life back home might set him off. He seemed perfectly at ease, though. Smiling and hugging me close to his side.

We had just come back in the house and let Deacon outside when my phone rang.

"It's Mama," I groaned. "I don't even want to answer it. I can't remember the last time I had a conversation with her without it ending in one of us shouting or crying. Do you think I could just not talk to her again before the wedding?"

"Sure," Cabe said. "Just don't answer the phone."

"She'll just keep calling. Over and over and over again until I answer."

I sighed and clicked *accept call*, knowing it was inevitable.

"Honey, you are not going to believe what I found. Target has these snowmen made out of white metal. They have black hats and orange noses—you know, like a carrot? You plug 'em in and they light up and the snowman waves his arm back and forth."

"Okay." I had no idea why this pertained to me.

"I was thinking we could buy some of those and put them around the fellowship hall. You know, for your winter theme? They're cute as a button, and we could return 'em and get our money back after the wedding."

"Um, no."

"What do you mean no? You haven't even seen them."

I swear I get a headache every time I am on the phone with her now. It's like Pavlov's dog but with pain. "I don't have to see them to know that I don't want light-up snowmen at my reception."

"But you said a winter theme. Oh, and before I forget to tell you, I bought the most beautiful memorial candles for Grandma, Grandpa, Granny, and Pa Pat. Then I found this photo frame for your daddy, Lord bless his soul, and it has a beautiful quote on the left side, and then there's a candleholder on the other side of the frame. It only holds a taper candle, so I didn't buy one of the memorial pillars for him."

I stopped in my tracks, halfway down the hallway. "We never discussed this. I never asked for that. I don't want that."

"What? What do you mean?"

"I don't want that. I don't want a graveyard set up at my wedding."

She laughed. "It ain't a graveyard, baby girl, it's a memorial. It's remembering those who have left us."

"I understand what it is. I see it all the time, and I don't want it."

She stopped laughing. "But it's a way to have your grandparents and your dear sweet daddy at your wedding. Lord bless his soul."

"I know what it is, but I don't want it. I'm fully aware that I've lost my grandparents and my father. I don't choose to be reminded of that on my wedding day."

"Honey, don't be upset. It's for everybody else, really. Just to show they're not forgotten."

"How on earth could they be forgotten? Do you think I somehow won't know that Daddy isn't walking me down the aisle if there's not a picture of him sitting there?"

She paused for a moment, and I gritted my teeth together. This was one issue I was not willing to back down on.

"I think you have to think about what your daddy would have wanted, sugar."

"Daddy would have wanted to walk me down the aisle, Mama. There's no doubt in my mind about that. He will be in my heart every step of the way. But I do not want to look over at any point and time and see an entire table lit up with the people I love who have died and can't be at my wedding. It's morbid, and it's depressing, and I don't want it."

She sighed. "It's not morbid. It's a beautiful way to remember them and honor their memories."

"There's other ways to honor their memory. This is a day of celebration and of moving forward. I understand that for some people, it's comforting to have those reminders there. Or maybe they feel like they're showing respect or something. I'll be happy to visit their graves and leave fresh flowers. I'll be happy to leave some arrangements in their name at the church, and I never, ever, ever forget to acknowledge their presence and send my love out to the universe. But I'm telling you that if I look up and see a table like that, I am going to lose it."

"But don't you want to include your daddy? You're the only one of his daughters to have a proper wedding. It's not fair to exclude him from it."

I continued walking down the hall, comfortable that she was at least listening to me and not fighting me on this. Wow. One thing out of a hundred. But at least this was a really important one. Choose your battles and count your victories.

"I'm not excluding him, Mama. I know he'll be with me that day, just as sure as I know my own name. I'm gonna wear the heart necklace he gave me for my birthday. Right before he died. That's between him and me. I don't want some big public showing to make everyone feel sad."

"What about your grandparents? Don't you want to recognize them? They all adored you."

"You're doing programs, right? Include their names in the programs. Put some memorial poem or quote if you want. I'm not trying to forget any of them. But I'm telling you, I don't want a memorial table. I don't want anything that's going to make me cry. If I see Daddy's picture..." I swallowed hard. I scrunched my nose and blinked rapidly, then swallowed again, gulping a huge breath of air and willing myself not to lose it.

Sometimes I could think of Daddy and smile. I could feel him around me, and it was a comfort. The memories would play in my head all in soft focus and warm light. Other times, the thought of him would make my heart clench and pause in its rhythm. The view of him lying in that casket would block out every other thought, and the loss of him would take the warmth from my body and leave ice in my veins. When grief gripped me that way, I struggled to remember the sound of his voice. The rumble of his laughter. The way he called me baby girl.

I much preferred the soft memories. The ones with the hazy yellowing of time and the home movie feel. In those memories, he was still alive. His laughter still filled a room, and his strong arms could still lift me and spin me round until I laughed and collapsed against his strong shoulders in dizzy delight.

I wasn't willing to risk the dark memories on my wedding day. I wanted to keep them at bay. If that meant upsetting my other family members or somehow slighting my grandparents, it was a risk I was willing to take.

She never really said she wouldn't do the memorial table, but she dropped the subject. That rarely happens when she digs in her heels, so I hoped it meant she could tell it was important to me.

When we'd hung up, I went to my jewelry box and pulled the tiny heart necklace from its velvet envelope. I never dared wear it for fear it would get broken or lost, but every now and then I would take it out and hold it in my hand. It helped me feel close to Daddy and see the happy memories play out in my head. I fiddled with the fragile little clasp and slid it around my neck, twisting to watch the light flash off the gold as I watched my reflection in the mirror.

Cabe walked up behind me and put his hands on my shoulders, planting a light kiss on the nape of my neck.

"You're beautiful."

I looked up to meet his eyes and smiled at the warmth I saw there. "Thank you."

He turned me to him and lifted my chin as he lowered his mouth to mine. He started the kiss tenderly, cautiously. I'd been so tired and cranky the last few weeks that I'd rebuffed any attempt he made to be intimate. Tears stung my eyes for reasons I didn't totally understand. Maybe it was thinking about Daddy. Maybe it was thinking about Cabe. Maybe it was just exhaustion and the constant weight of stress.

Cabe pulled back from me and wiped away the lone tear that escaped. His eyes clouded with concern as his eyebrows drew together in question.

I smiled. "I'm okay. I'm sorry. Just feeling a bit emotional, I guess."

He pulled me into his chest, and I buried my face there and breathed in his warmth. His scent. His masculinity. He was safe, solid, and real. I collapsed against him and exhaled a sigh.

"I'm sorry I've been such a tyrant lately. Snapping at everyone. Crying at the drop of the hat. Arguing with Mama about every little thing. I know you have to be thinking you're crazy for wanting to marry me. I've turned into Bridezilla. How did this happen?"

He stroked my hair and pulled it away from my face.

"It's okay," he said, so calm and quiet that my heart threatened to break. "You're not Bridezilla; you just have too much on your plate right now. Work is crazy. Life is crazy. You're trying to juggle our wedding and everybody else's. You're not sleeping. You need rest."

He led me to our bed and sat with his back against the headboard, pulling me down and positioning us so I laid beside him with my head on his chest. He continued to stroke my hair, running his fingers through it gently and loosening the inevitable tangles ever-present in my thick, brown waves.

"This is just not how I thought my wedding would be. Like, even when I told you I was sure I wanted to get married back home, I think I was picturing a nice, catered event with beautiful centerpieces, soft lighting, and all our family and friends surrounding us. Like singing *Kumbayah* or something. I think in reality, it's going to be a disaster. An absolute disaster. Mama is hell-bent on hosting the tackiest wedding ever in my honor, no matter what I try to do. I don't even want anyone to come. I don't even want to have this stupid wedding."

His hand halted on my head for a moment, and I felt a shift in his weight as his body tensed.

I jerked my head up and raised myself on my knees to face him. "Oh my gosh...I didn't mean I don't want to marry you. Cabe, I definitely want to marry you. I want to spend every day of my life with you. I just don't want a wedding. I wish we could fast forward. Skip right past this and be married already."

"I said we could elope," he whispered.

"I know, but that wouldn't work either, because then everyone would be mad and feel like they got cheated out of something. Like somehow, it's their God-given right to have my wedding, but somehow it's not my God-given right not to have one."

"Kind of ironic that the wedding planner doesn't want a wedding, don't you think?" He smiled and lifted his palm to my cheek, caressing and soothing.

"Yeah, right? It's my livelihood. My passion. I love doing it for other people, but being an engaged wedding planner just sucks. I have all these decisions to make, like any other bride. But because the wedding's not here with the people I know and work with, I don't know what to buy or who to hire. I've got Mama on the DIY train to Martha Stewart hell, and I feel like everything she tries to do, I shoot down and fight over. Then every day I have to plan all these other brides' weddings and get to see what they're doing and what they're having and how excited they are. I want that. I want to be excited. I want to be happy about this. But I'm not. I hate this. So much." I'd been looking down at my hands, and when I looked back up, I flinched at the hurt I saw in his eyes. "But that doesn't mean I don't want to marry you."

He attempted a smile, and I leaned forward to kiss him, not wanting any of my turmoil to cause him a moment's pain or rejection.

"I do want to marry you, Cabe. I wanna say our vows and exchange our rings and walk off into the Happily Ever After sunset. Why can't we just do that?"

"We can," he said. "We'll just go into hiding. Maybe there's some kind of marriage witness protection program where you get married and just disappear."

I laughed, more to honor his attempt at humor than because I felt like laughing. "That wouldn't work, silly. Then we'd never see our family again. I want to see them again. I just don't want to plan a wedding with them."

"So let's get married and just not tell anyone."

"I think it's a little late for that. The wheels have been set in motion. I've unleashed Patsy."

"I think you should hire Sandy and let her do the food and the flowers. When are you talking to her?"

"Wednesday."

"Call her tomorrow and tell her to put together a proposal for the menu, too."

I shook my head. "Mama would have a fit if I did that."

"So? Let her. It's not her wedding, Ty. I know you don't want to upset her, and I know the two of you have some major issues with boundaries, but when it comes down to it, it's *not her wedding*. It's yours. And mine. *Ours.* So tell her what you want to do, and do it. If she doesn't like it, oh well. You already listen to her complain every time you talk to her. How would that be any different? You want me to talk to her? Maybe have Mom call her about her offering to pay for Sandy as a gift?"

I sighed. "No. That's okay. I need to do a better job of standing up to her. It wasn't even me that got her not to do the centerpieces. It was Carrie. I hate this. All the drama. I wish it could be just you and me and a minister. Some place quiet. Some place sweet. No fuss. No stress. Just us. Maybe Mel and Dean. Maybe even your mom or my brother and sisters, but then I know I couldn't have your mom or my brother and sisters without having my mom. I feel terrible for saying it like that, because it's not that I don't want my mom there. It's just that she makes everything so damned difficult. She gets upset, and then I get upset. Or I get upset and then she gets upset. I don't know what to do. This is why I wanted to just elope, but we can't, and now it's all screwed up."

"I'm sorry." Cabe exhaled slowly as he said it.

"It's not your fault, babe."

"But it is. You wanted to elope from the start, but I talked you into having a wedding."

I ran my fingers through his curls and tousled them. "I bet you're feeling a little differently about that now, huh?"

"Whatever it takes to marry you, Buttercup. Whatever it takes."

Monday, October 20th

I'd decided to take the night off and give my brain and my body some rest. I didn't bring any wedding files home with me, I didn't check my email on my phone, and every time our wedding crept into my head, I deliberately pushed it out.

I'd just put on my pjs when the phone rang. Cabe was working late on a project, and I assumed his call meant he was headed home.

"Hey babe, what's up?"

Deacon's ears perked up when I said *babe*. I wasn't the only one ready for Cabe to come home.

"Hello beautiful! What are you doing right now?"

"Deacon took me for a walk, and I just changed into my pjs and thought perhaps I'd read a book. Or watch TV. I haven't decided. Why? Are you on your way home?"

"Not exactly. I need you to do me a favor."

I groaned inside. I'd been looking forward to curling up on the couch all day. Now that I was actually there, all comfy-cozy in my pajamas, I really didn't want to have to get up and do anything. I didn't even try to hide my lack of enthusiasm.

"What do you need?"

"Well, I just drove by our bench at the lake, and the moon is brilliant reflecting off the water. I parked the car, and I'm waiting for you on the bench. I want you to come see it with me."

I groaned out loud this time. As sweet as it was that my romantic fiancé wanted me to come and watch the moon reflect on the water with him, it was too much effort to consider. There'd be other moons.

"Aw, that's sweet, babe. But I'm exhausted. I'm comfortable. I don't want to get dressed and go out."

"You don't have to get dressed. Just throw on some jeans and join me."

I flopped against the back of the couch in protest. Deacon came and laid his head on my lap, his gaze questioning why I was agitated.

"Deacon's all settled in. I don't want to put him in his crate. Can't we see the moon another night?"

"Bring Deacon with you."

"What? No. We just vacuumed my car out yesterday. Let it be hair-free for a couple of days. Besides, he's calm and happy from his walk. I don't want to get him all riled up again."

"C'mon, Ty. I'm asking you to come sit under the moon and the stars with me. Just for a few minutes. Please?"

I shut my eyes and groaned. "Alright. Okay. But it better be the best damned moon anyone's ever laid eyes on."

"It will be. I promise. Bring Deacon, okay?"

"Yeah, yeah. We'll be right there."

I tossed the phone onto the sofa in irritation and walked to my closet. I yanked on a pair of jeans and threw a T-shirt over my camisole, not even bothering with a bra. It's not like anyone was going to see me at the lake.

Or so I thought.

There were no other cars, so I didn't realize Cabe wasn't alone until Deacon and I were almost to the bench. I'd been staring at the sky, thinking the moon looked rather ordinary and definitely not worth getting off the couch for. It wasn't even a full moon.

I'd expected Cabe to be sitting on the bench, and when I realized he wasn't, I scanned the trees to find him. My eyes began to adjust and I could make out Cabe's form in the shadows under one of the larger oaks.

"What are you doing?" I asked, irritation and frustration in my voice.

Cabe stepped out into the moonlight and walked toward me, and it was only then that I saw he wasn't alone. Reverend Hays was there, and so were Mel and Dean.

Deacon yanked the leash nearly out of my hands when he saw Cabe, and I let go partly in a desire not to have my arm torn from my shoulder and partly in confusion as to what was happening.

"What's going on? Why are they here?" I crossed my arms over my chest, very aware of my braless state and my nipples standing at attention under the thin T-shirt to announce to the world that the breeze was cool.

Cabe greeted Deacon with their normal rough-housing and then handed the leash over to Dean before standing to walk slowly to me. Even in the pale light, I could see the little half-smile he always wears when he's a bit embarrassed, and above it his eyes sparkled with mischief.

"Hello, beautiful." He slid his hands around my waist and bent to press his lips against mine.

"What is this? What are we doing?"

"This, my dearly beloved, is our wedding. Exactly as you wanted it to be. Just you and me with the minister and Mel and Dean. And Deacon, of course. I invited him. I hope you don't mind." Deacon barked at the mention of his name and pulled at Dean's grip on the leash. "Let's do it, Ty. Let's get married, just us. None of the bullshit, none of the drama. Just you and me, pledging our love and making it official."

I couldn't have stopped the tears flowing from my eyes even if I'd wanted to. I felt a million pounds lift from my shoulders, and my heart soared. My mind could barely conceive what he was saying. To marry Cabe, right there, right that moment. To have it done and over with. To be his wife. Just me and him. Without everyone else weighing in and taking over.

But then reality set in.

"We can't," I whispered, emotion choking my words. "Everyone will be so upset. Mama's done all this work and it means so much to her. Maggie and your grandparents. We can't." A sob escaped my throat as it threatened to close completely.

Cabe pulled me into his arms and kissed the top of my head. "Shhh. Listen. We'll still do all that. Patsy can have her wedding however she wants it. We'll show up and smile and jump through all the hoops she has planned for us. But you and I will know the whole time that we're already married. It's already done. This is it." He pulled back to look down at me. "This can be our wedding. The way you wanted it. We will always have this to share, just the two of us." He glanced back at the others standing under the trees. "Well, and those people over there. But you know what I mean."

It seemed to be the most perfect solution possible.

I could be married to Cabe tonight. Without any further hesitation or stress. I would be his wife tomorrow. I'd still have to deal with my mama and all my family and Cabe's family too, but I thought he might be right. It would be easier to deal with them if I didn't feel like they were stealing my experience. My wedding. Our wedding.

A smile broke out across my face as the tears flowed even more. I nodded and laughed, probably the most genuine laugh I'd been able to muster in months.

Cabe smiled back and brought my hands to his lips, kissing the ring he'd placed on my finger in this very spot.

"So whaddya say, Tyler Lorraine Warren? Will you marry me? Right here? Right now? In front of God and these witnesses? Under the light of the moon?"

"Yes, yes, yes! A million times yes. Let's do it."

"Yay!" Melanie shrieked in the background. "Here you go, love!" She stepped forward to hand me a beautiful exquisite bouquet.

I gasped. "Oh my gosh! This is it. This is *the* bouquet I picked! The picture I have on my bulletin board."

She nodded and smiled. I could see tears glisten on her cheeks in the moonlight. "The one you wanted. Now you have it. For your wedding."

We hugged each other tight as our laughter rang out through our tears. "Thank you, Mel. Thank you so much. I'm so glad you're here with me. I couldn't get married without my matron of honor."

"Yep. I get to pull double-duty now. I'll be your matron in two weddings, back-to-back."

"One more thing and we'll be good to go," Cabe said as he approached Mel and me. He held up his hand to reveal a small pendant hanging from a chain. My heart pendant. The last gift my Daddy gave to me.

"You said you wanted to wear it. To have your daddy walk down the aisle with you. I took it today and had a better clasp put on the chain."

I threw both arms around him and hugged him with every bit of strength I could muster. I hope I can somehow find a way to convey to this man how much I love him. Hopefully walking down the aisle and vowing to be his wife until death do us part would be a good start.

"Come with me, Ms. Bride," Melanie said as she led me back toward the cars.

I looked down at myself and cracked up laughing. All the time and energy brides put into choosing a gown, and here I was about to get married in a pair of flip flops, jeans, and a T-shirt over a pajama camisole.

"What's so funny?" Mel asked.

"If I'd known I was getting married, I might have at least put on a bra, if not a decent dress."

"I didn't know how to get you dressed before you came without making you suspicious," Cabe said behind me. "Do you want to go home and change? We can wait."

I turned and smiled at the man who would be my husband within minutes. "Not a chance. This is perfect."

Dean walked toward me with Deacon, and I noticed a lump on the dog's back.

"Why is Deacon wearing his hiking pack?" I looked closer to see a corsage fastened to the top of his pack and a bow tie around his neck. "Aww, Deacon, buddy. You're all dressed up for the wedding! More dressed up than me, in fact."

"He's the ringbearer," Dean said. "Just pray there's no squirrels or ducks running around this late at night."

We all laughed, and the sound of our joy rang out in the still night air.

If there'd ever been a more beautiful night, I couldn't have imagined it. The night sky twinkled with what seemed to be a million stars like diamonds sparkling against black velvet. The moon put forward its best effort to illuminate the night as it reflected off the water. A light breeze ruffled the branches around us and lifted my hair ever so slightly, the hint of coolness refreshing on my skin.

Cabe'e eyes were on me, and when I looked at him, his face lit up with a smile as bright as the moon above. He winked at me and gave a quick nod. I nodded back, an unspoken covenant passing between us. Tonight was ours. And ours alone

So many times I've stood there as a bride was ready to take that walk, and I've always wondered what she must feel in that moment. The cusp of a life change. The end of one era and the beginning of the next. Over the years I've seen brides who seemed elated, nervous, horrified, excited, and bored. In all the stress and drama of planning our wedding, I'd never given much thought to how I'd feel when I stood there. Of course, to be fair, I never knew I'd be standing *there*. At our lake. In our spot. Basking in the glow of the moon and the sweet gaze of the man I love.

That's it. The answer to the question. That's what I felt. Love. Overwhelming, all-consuming, unconditional love for this man, and from this man. We'd been through thick and thin, ups and downs, good times and bad. He's not perfect, nor am I. But as I stood there waiting to walk into my new life by his side, I had no doubts. No qualms. No questions. I have never been more sure of anything I've ever done in my life. At the end of that short walk was my destiny. I knew that as well as I knew my own name.

The strains of Israel K's *What A Wonderful World* began to play across the darkness from a wireless speaker Cabe had brought. The strum of the ukulele seemed to be in rhythm with the breeze as Dean and Mel made their way down our non-existent 'aisle' with Deacon leading as though he'd rehearsed his part to perfection.

When they'd taken their place on either side of Cabe and the minister, I touched the pendant that lay against my chest and took a deep breath. The breeze picked up and swept around me like a gentle embrace whispering a memory of a love that will never die.

I walked to Cabe, my eyes never leaving his. In some ways, it seemed every step I took represented the events of my life that had led me to him. To that very moment.

To be honest, our vows were a blur. I know what we said, of course, because we'd pulled the vows together weeks ago from several ceremonies and readings I had on file. But as we spoke, my attention focused solely on Cabe. The joy in his eyes. His sweet smile. Those perfect teeth and that strong jawline. His curls blowing in the gentle breeze. His strong fingers caressing my hands as he held them in his.

Deacon behaved so well I wondered if they'd drugged him. He sat patiently by Cabe's side, and he didn't even get excited when Cabe zipped open his pack to retrieve the rings. The mere sound of that zipper normally signals all hell to break loose since it means the Frisbee is coming out for playtime.

The whole thing went by so quickly, and when the minister told Cabe he could kiss his bride, my heart almost tightened in sadness for it ending. Almost, but not quite. Because the ceremony ending meant the most handsome man I've ever known was leaning in to kiss me and claim me as his wife. No way was I sad about that.

Cabe insisted on carrying me over the threshold when we got back to the house, which made me crack up laughing and Deacon howl in protest to what he probably saw as my distress.

"I'm gonna need you to disappear until I call you out here. I have a few more things to take care of out here, okay?" He set me down with a kiss.

"You've been quite the busy little bee this evening, Mr. Shaw." I smiled up at him.

"Yeah, turns out you're not the only wedding planner in the family, Mrs. Shaw!" He grinned so wide his cheeks looked as though they'd split wide open.

"*Mrs. Shaw,*" I repeated. "I like the sound of that." I nestled in close to him and slid my hands around his waist and below, gripping his ass in both hands and squeezing tight. He laughed, and I moved my lips against his, flicking my tongue across his bottom lip before venturing further inside. He pushed me away with a dramatic groan and a smile.

"Oh, heaven help me. Baby, please. I just need you to give me a few more minutes." He kissed my forehead and turned me toward the bedroom.

"Make it quick," I said as I made my way down the hall to our room.

I dug in my bottom drawer and made my way to the bathroom with the racy lace negligee I'd bought for our wedding night. Of course, that was when I thought my wedding night would be spent in a bed and breakfast inn in Atlanta before we took off the next morning for our honeymoon in Costa Rica.

But now? My *husband's* impromptu wedding ceremony had changed our plans in more ways than one.

Which is why I was standing in our bathroom with the water running for the second time tonight. I had no idea when I showered a couple of hours ago that I'd be back here getting ready for my wedding night.

Holy shit. My wedding night. I am a *married woman.*

Ha!

I'm *married!* To Cabe!

Oh my gosh.

My wedding night. Which means I am *finally* going to have sex with Cabe. Yes, Lord.

With my husband.

Oh wow. My *husband.*

I can't stop saying it. Can't stop writing it.

Cabe Shaw is my husband. How weird and wonderful and surreal is that?

I want to call everyone I know and tell them we're married. At the same time, I don't ever want to tell anyone. I want to stay in this little cocoon where only we know. Our own little secret conspiracy against them all.

Tuesday, October 21st

It only took me a few seconds when I woke up this morning to remember that I married Cabe last night.

My first thought was that I was nude, and I never sleep nude. My second thought was that I felt a slight tenderness in all the right places when I moved my legs to stretch, and with that realization, it all came flooding back in a warm rush of incredible memories.

He had the whole place alight with candles when I came out from my bath last night. He'd poured champagne and put on music, a slow ballad from an obscure band he loves.

He'd been looking down at his phone when I came down the hallway, and when he glanced up and saw the silky black negligee, he did a double-take and swallowed hard.

I twirled slowly with my arms held out to my sides. "You like?"

He nodded and parted his lips slightly. His tongue raked across them with a flicker, and my entire body tensed with an ache deep inside.

I took the champagne flute he offered and smiled as his eyes raked over my body. When he came back up to meet my gaze, his look conveyed in no uncertain terms that there'd be no brakes put on tonight. He bit down on his lip and reached to place his hand on my hip, pulling me toward him slightly as he leaned forward to nibble along my neck. I shuddered and tossed my head back, thrusting my fingers into his curls to hold his head and press his mouth tighter against me, wanting more, wanting all, needing his touch more than ever before.

He lifted his gaze to mine, his lips swollen and wet from the pressure of the kisses he'd burned across my skin.

I moved to set the champagne glass down so I could get both hands on him, but he paused my hand and picked up his glass to toast.

"To our future. May we always love each other as intensely as we do in this moment, and may every tomorrow be better than its yesterday."

We intertwined our arms and sipped the champagne in the traditional manner, even though no photographer was on hand to capture the scene. The cold fizz tickled and stung as it slid down my throat, the sweet scent intoxicating to my heightened senses.

Cabe drained his glass but held the contents in his mouth, smearing the moist wetness across my shoulder and allowing a tiny bit of the liquid to escape and trickle down my chest and between my breasts. He followed the shimmery, wet trail with his mouth, every lap of his tongue increasing the throbbing ache inside me.

He took my champagne glass and set it on the table next to his. One hand closed over mine as the other grasped my hip, and we began to sway in time to the music. All other thoughts left my mind except Cabe and the sensations he was causing. I closed my eyes as we moved together in rhythm with the beat, his hands firmly on my hips. He squeezed them slightly and then smoothed his hand up the soft black lace to trace the outer edge of one nipple and then the other before sliding down my ribs to span his palm across my waist. He spun me around, his other hand lifting mine high in the air to make the turn. He trailed his fingers slowly back down the inner flesh of my arm, and I shivered as I leaned back into his bare chest. A moan escaped me as he brought both his hands up under my arms and across my ribs.

His nose nuzzled behind my ear, and then his breath blew warm on my neck before he sank his teeth into my shoulder, gently but firm. His hands moved up from my ribs agonizingly slow, closing over my breasts and kneading their fullness until my nipples were taut with desire. I reached over my shoulder to sink my fingers in his hair and pull his head closer and harder against me, whispering his name like it was a healing chant.

I moaned again as his hand dipped lower, sliding the lace up over my thigh as his fingers tickled and teased across the goose bumps rippling my skin.

He spun me back around then, tilting my head back to bury his face in my neck. One hand stroked through my hair to pull gently back and open his access while the other hand down lower drove me wild and left me breathless and unable to stand.

"I've waited so damned long for this," he whispered against the hollow of my throat as he slid the thin, silky strap from my shoulder and followed its descent with his tongue.

I was about ready to scream *"Get on with it already!"* when he lifted me into his arms and carried me down the hallway to our bed. He laid me down with loving tenderness and then stood to remove his jeans, his eyes boring into mine as the tension built to an inferno.

Talk about a build-up. Six years. Six years of fighting feelings. Keeping temptation at bay. Never fully giving in.

Our physical intimacy in the months since we'd taken our relationship further had only served to increase the stakes. Every time we'd taken it to the edge and stopped. Every time we'd brought each other to the pinnacle of passion but then held back. It all made that final moment of surrender all the more special and all the more intense.

Chills rolled over my skin while he stood there looking down at me, his body magnificently chiseled and sculpted to perfection. As he eased himself down on the bed beside me, a sudden shyness filled me.

An uncertain apprehension. What if we'd waited all this time and it ended up being a letdown? What if all that build-up had blown our expectations out of proportion and the reality of what was physically possible couldn't possibly measure up?

My fears were short-lived and unfounded.

To finally be joined with Cabe was unlike anything I'd ever experienced. It moved me on so many levels. Physically, of course. That goes without saying. But it was such an emotional act. Spiritual, even, in the bond that passed between us. Completely and totally giving myself over to him and receiving his same offer in return.

True to Cabe's passion for music and his uncanny knack for bringing humor to any situation, he suddenly belted out song lyrics as we lay together in a twisted intertwining of limbs and hearts in the moments after we'd reached our goal.

"Why are you singing Boston lyrics?" I asked with a laugh that started deep within me and bubbled up and out from a place of pure bliss.

"Well, because it *has* been such a long time," he answered, capturing my earlobe between his teeth as he rolled off of me and onto his back, pulling me with him.

I laughed again, utterly relaxed and incapable of movement. "I feel like I've been drugged. Did you put something in the champagne?"

He chuckled as he caressed my back. "Nope. I'm just that intoxicating."

"Really?" I managed to lift myself on one elbow so I could see his face. "Well, consider me addicted."

He tucked his thumb under my chin and pulled me to him, his mouth soft and tentative on mine in stark contrast to the mad tempest we'd ridden out before.

He released my lips but not my chin, and I smiled as I watched his eyes look into mine.

"Was it worth the wait?" I asked, leaning back a bit to see him as he answered.

"Oh, and then some. Every painful night." He put his arms around me and rolled again, this time carrying me to lie beneath him and look up into his eyes as he spoke.

"I have never in my life loved anyone as I do you. And I will never love another."

Such a long build-up can't be squelched easily, and we spent the rest of the night allowing ourselves to freely partake of what had been dangled as forbidden fruit for so long in so many ways. It was well into the morning hours before we finally drifted off to sleep in each other's arms.

I looked over at him in the morning sunlight and smiled at his relaxed expression as he slept. I had no idea what time it was, but judging by the position of the sun on our bedroom walls, it was late. I tried to sit up and winced a bit. I twisted to see the clock, not really worried since Mel had assured me I wouldn't be expected in the office early, and Cabe had already taken the day off.

I stretched again when I stood, my body feeling like a satisfied cat who's finally got a good rubdown and a bowl of fresh milk. I don't know that I'd ever been so relaxed in my entire life. Certainly not in the hellish weeks leading up to last night. I padded down the hall in my birthday suit to get the coffee started and let Deacon out in the back yard. By the time I got back to our room, Cabe was awake, lying on his back and staring at the ceiling.

He turned his head toward me as I lounged against the door frame, admiring the image of my husband's naked body tangled in our sheets.

"Good morning, Mrs. Shaw." He smiled and lifted his arm off the bed in invitation.

I gladly accepted and crawled in bed beside him, pressing my side against his as I lay on my stomach and he lay on his back.

"Happy?" I asked.

"Blissfully so." He answered and closed his eyes.

"Ready to go again?" I teased.

He smiled, his eyes still closed. "Oh, yes, ma'am."

Needless to say, I called in sick to work. Those other brides can just wait until tomorrow. For today, I'm being the bride and enjoying my newlywed status.

Friday, October 24th

The rest of the week has been a blur. We can't get enough of each other. We're like two teenagers who've discovered the power of passion for the first time, and we just can't stop. Any time we weren't at work this week, we were in bed. We haven't done laundry. We haven't gone grocery shopping. Other than going over Sandy's proposal Wednesday night, we haven't talked about the upcoming wedding at all, and we've been letting the phone go to voice mail. It's been heavenly, but I'm running out of clean clothes and we've gone through every place that delivers food to our neighborhood.

Unfortunately, I have a rehearsal dinner and dessert party tonight, then I have a wedding plus Mel's wedding tomorrow, and a ceremony and reception with Lillian on Sunday. I swear if they don't get another assistant hired and trained soon, we're all gonna keel over from exhaustion. Laura is pretty much the only one who will take Charlotte for events, so Mel and I tag team helping each other, and then somehow I always get stuck helping Lillian.

I cannot wait for October to be over. Especially now that the pressure is totally off for our wedding. It's amazing how differently I feel about it now that we're already married. I'm not as keyed up about everything as I was before. I realize part of that is because I know Sandy will do a stellar job with the centerpieces and lighting in the fellowship hall. But a huge portion of it is because now that we've had our little wedding here, the rest doesn't matter as much. Before, I had this mindset that it was my wedding, the only one I'd ever have, and much like the brides I deal with every day, I was freaking because I wanted it to be perfect. But after experiencing the amazing simplicity of our little ceremony, none of it's worth freaking out over.

If Mama wants to print up programs for everyone to throw away, oh well. It really doesn't matter. If she wants to have a pot luck dinner and eat off paper plates, I don't care. Okay, that's not true. I will flip my lid if we get there and she's planning on using paper plates, but for the most part, I'm okay with whatever she wants to do. It's almost like this is *her* wedding. The one she never got to plan. I've made up my mind to go with the flow and let her do whatever she wants from this point.

I've already had my wedding, and to me, it was perfect in every way possible. I couldn't ask for anything more.

Monday, October 27th

I really should write these entries in pencil so they could be erased.

When I said I didn't care what she did, I didn't mean I *didn't care*. I meant I was going to try not to get so worked up over it. And I did try.

But then Mama called today to say she was having challenges with the pot luck dinner. Seven people signed up to bring banana pudding, four people want to bring buns, and at least three are making green bean casserole.

"Why don't you make a list of what you need people to bring and have a line next to it for them to put their name? Then if an item is already taken, they gotta bring something else." I gripped the stress ball on my desk and mentally counted down from twenty. I was determined not to get upset, not to battle with her, and not to put too much thought into the fact that my wedding guests will be eating banana pudding with green bean casserole and buns.

"I don't want to limit people. I mean, you can't ask somebody to sign up for red velvet cake and get somebody like Johnnie Lewis who ain't never been able to make red velvet to save her life. She might as well make a vanilla cake and put red food coloring in it. Not a drop of cocoa to be found. We've got time. It'll even out. When we get closer, we'll get more of a variety."

The whole thing churned my stomach. I didn't want to have a potluck wedding, but it seemed like I'd shot down every idea she'd had and every way she'd tried to help. I know it's important to her to be involved, but we're talking about my wedding. Not a bridal shower or a family reunion. I had people coming from Cabe's family. I had friends from the industry coming.

"I think it's important that we put together a menu, Mama. I'm not comfortable having a smorgasbord of random items. What if I send you a menu, and you can make copies and give it to the people who are willing to bring food?"

"Tyler, these are volunteers. Lifelong friends of mine who are basically providing free catering for you. They are making food out of the kindness of their hearts and from their own pockets. I'm not going to be rude and tell them what they have to bring. We'll take whatever it is. Maybe I'll call Bubba Dogs and see what he would charge me to bring some meats."

I dropped the stress ball. "Mama. I'm sorry. I love you, and I've tried to work with you. But I ain't having Bubba Dogs BBQ for my wedding. I'm hiring the caterer."

"You'll do no such thing, and I'd love to know one time in this entire process that you've tried to work with me. You've done nothing but fight me every step of the way. It's like you've got a bee in your bonnet aimed for me. Anything to hurt me."

"That's not true and not fair. I've tried harder to make you happy with this wedding than anyone else, including me or my groom. I've agreed to have it in the church, mainly because it was important to you. I've agreed to have my reception in the fellowship hall—a glorified gymnasium—because you didn't want me to look in Atlanta. I'm having programs that I didn't want, menu cards that I didn't want, and Lord only knows what else you've got planned that I don't even know about. The last thing I want to do is hurt you, disappoint you, or make you mad. But this is my wedding. I'm hiring the caterer."

"That's such a waste of money, sugar. We'll have plenty of food. I'll start calling people tomorrow. If you don't want Bubba's, I'll figure something else out."

"No. This is it. I'm done. I'm not going to spend the money to have a professional come in and add lighting and trees and centerpieces and then serve egg salad sandwiches and cheese logs."

"Lighting? Why are on God's green earth are you paying for lighting? There's plenty of lights in the fellowship hall."

"Yeah, bright fluorescents that are perfect for basketball, but this is a wedding. I want ambience. Purples and pinks. Maybe blues."

"Ambience? Give me a break. Now you're just putting on airs. It's a place of worship, not a nightclub."

Mel leaned through my open door and signaled that my clients had arrived.

"Look, I gotta go. I'm hiring the caterer. Cancel the potluck. I'll talk to you later. Bye."

I'm sure she kept arguing the point, but I ended the call and left my phone on my desk to go meet with my clients. I wanted to high-five everyone. I wanted to run through the office laughing and pumping my fist in the air while I yelled, "*Yeah! I did it!*"

But I didn't. I maintained my composure throughout my meeting, and then I called Sandy and asked if it was too late to add their catering services.

Then I left work and picked up a bottle of wine and some steaks for my husband to throw on the grill for a celebration dinner.

I thought I'd be guilt-ridden. That I'd feel anxiety and remorse. That I'd debate calling her back and apologizing. Telling her to move forward with the banana pudding extravaganza.

But no. I'm actually pretty excited to see Sandy's menus and sit down with Cabe tonight to choose what *we* want for *our* wedding guests.

I don't know if this makes me a selfish daughter or some variation of a Bridezilla, but I'm okay with it. Cabe was right. Mama's gonna complain either way. If I can't make her happy no matter how hard I try, there's no sense in both of us being unhappy.

November

Monday, November 3rd

This morning Carmen brought in bagels so we all gathered in the conference room to eat.

Yesterday was the first day the entire office was off since before Labor Day weekend. I didn't even shower or change out of my pajamas the whole day. In fact, I pretty much stayed in bed all day. Cabe would bring me food or take Deacon for a walk, but for the most part, he and Deacon lay curled up in bed with me, watching sappy movies and bad reality TV. It was the best day I've had in weeks.

When Carmen finished passing out the bagels and spreads, she flopped a glossy magazine down on the table in front of me. Reynalda's face stared back at me from the cover, her arms crossed over her sequined chest with Chris and Jayah's reception in soft focus behind her.

I tore into it, flipping the pages to find the full article. Everyone crowded around my shoulders and leaned over me to read along.

There were a few more pictures inside. One of Reynalda adjusting flowers at the ceremony. (Staged.) One of Reynalda talking with the audio/visual director. (Also staged). And one of Chris and Jayah coming down the aisle all smiles as their friends and family clapped and cheered and bubbles filled the air. (Not staged.)

Not only was there no photo of me at all, but there was no mention of me even being there. Not a single *"I'd like to thank..."* or *"Also on hand for the event was..."*

It didn't matter in the grand scheme of life. Magazine covers were not the reason I was a wedding planner. But I have to admit it was hard not to feel slighted when I'd busted my ass for that event and worked it much harder than Reynalda did, yet there she was taking all the credit.

My bagel felt thick in my throat, and my coffee soured in my stomach.

"Media whore," Lillian uttered and went back to her chair.

"What would you say are three important lessons you learned from that experience, Tyler?" asked Laura.

My first response was to blurt out *"nothing,"* but I knew Laura would never accept that. She believed we could learn something from every situation if we looked for the opportunity.

I pondered for a moment, thinking back on the whole planning chaos, the demanding expectations Jayah and Chris had (which were set forth by Reynalda), the insanity of finding her babbling on the floor, and the sheer frustration of taking on such a mammoth project by myself the day of the event.

"I'd have to say, first and foremost, I learned how important it is to treat the people working beside you with respect." I glanced to Charlotte as I spoke. Though I'd been nowhere near as abrasive and cruel as Reynalda could be, I certainly hadn't been as nice as I could have been to the poor girl. I needed to work on that.

"Second, I learned to value the teamwork we share, and the willingness of everyone here to jump in and help out. Being all alone for that event was miserable. I got pulled in a million different directions all at once. People from pretty much every aspect of the wedding needed something from me. A decision or a solution or an answer. When you're one person, it can be hard to juggle the ceremony, the reception, the table set-up, the music, the lighting, the food. It's a lot. It made me really appreciate the way we try to always have two people on each event, even if it's just for a little while to help out and lend moral support."

"Speaking of which," Laura said, "I'd like to offer a toast with my cup of coffee since it's all I have at the moment, but I'd like to toast our entire staff for getting us through another crazy wedding season. It's not over, especially with eleven-eleven coming up next week, but we're in the home stretch and the end is in sight. We will definitely have a celebration when the dust settles. And after Tyler's own wedding, of course." She smiled at me and lifted her coffee cup, waiting for us all to join her before she continued. "To teamwork, and the best and hardest-working team in the business."

We clanked our mugs together and drank to the light at the end of the tunnel. It was always short-lived, of course. We'd have a lull for November and December, but then the holidays would be here, then the new engagements, and then Valentine's and on to the spring season. It was never-ending, really, but we took our breaths where we could.

"What's number three?" Charlotte asked. "Didn't you say three? I only counted two."

"Oh, three," I said. "Let me see. I guess my third lesson would have to be that having the appearance of a lavish lifestyle and the fame that accompanies it does not guarantee happiness."

"All very valuable lessons." Laura smiled and winked at me.

I was sort of surprised to realize I'd taken anything away from it. I'd thought of it as a miserable, stressful experience that I was happy to be past. But I guess I did have a few revelations, after all. Who knew?

Wednesday, November 5th

Okay, I know I said I didn't feel any remorse or guilt and I was all excited about standing up to Mama and canceling the potluck, but that was a week ago. I hadn't heard one peep from her since then, even though I'd left multiple messages. To say I was a little freaked out about it was an understatement. We went weeks without talking all the time, even months here and there. But since the wedding planning started, we'd been talking every few days. Her radio silence so close to the wedding indicated how upset she must be with me.

My sisters assured me she was okay, and that I should give her time and space to get over it, but I couldn't help feeling like I needed to apologize or make it better. Family programming dies hard.

I'd planned to call her again tonight once I got home from picking up the bridesmaid gifts from the engraver along with the watch I'd bought and had engraved for Cabe.

My phone buzzed with a text while I was in traffic, but I didn't look at it until I pulled into the driveway.

It was from Mama's number, which was weird because she's always been fairly technologically incompetent and had never mastered the art of texting. It was a photo text, which was even stranger, because if there was anything she found more confusing about the phone than texting, it was taking a photo and sending it via text.

The picture was of a coffee mug. It was large and round, fat in the middle and slimmer at the bottom and top. Oversized a bit, like something you may see in a cartoon. It was white, but on the front it had a handpainted silver snowflake with a beautifully scripted monogram over it in dark purple, C-S-T. The mug was filled to overflowing with goodies, but it was hard to make out in the picture what they were. The phone buzzed again with a text this time.

"Favor"

I smiled from ear to ear and dialed Mama's number with tears in my eyes. She answered on the first ring.

"Did ya get it? Did it come through? It said it sent it on my end."

"Yes, ma'am, I got it. *You* sent it? I'm so proud of you."

"I did. Turns out you *can* teach an old dog new tricks. Can you see the picture good? I couldn't figure out how to zoom it, but I figured it might be best if you saw the whole thing anyways. Whadja think?"

"I love the design with the monogram. Who did it?" I put her on speaker so I could zoom into the picture on my phone and study the detail of the painting.

"Your cousin Tonya did the snowflake, and then Lisa did the monogramming. I thought they turned out real nice, but if you don't like them, we won't use them. I only had them do the one to show you, but I talked to the store manager and they can get us a hundred of the mugs if you want 'em. You just gotta let me know so I can get 'em and the girls have time to paint 'em."

Who was this calm, reasonable, nice lady, and what had she done with my mother?

"Um, yeah. I love them. I think that's a great idea. How much are they?"

"You don't worry about that. Can you see what's in them?"

I turned the phone sideways to make the photo larger on my screen, but even when I zoomed in all the way it was hard to make it out. "It looks like some plastic bags tied with ribbons?"

"Yeah. Aunt Clementine made some of her peanut brittle with the fresh peanuts of the season. Then Pearl mixed up some of her cocoa mix that she always serves at Christmas. There's wedding cookies in there, too. I made those. You said you wanted it to mean something with our family heritage, so I figured that might work. And cocoa and cookies and brittle all seemed to fit with your winter theme. Is that alright?"

It was more than alright. It was freakin' perfect. Mama had listened to me. She had heard me. Then more importantly, she had done what I wanted instead of going off on some wild tangent that was the exact opposite.

"They're perfect, Mama. I love 'em. Thank you so much." My voice broke a bit, but we both ignored it.

"I figure we'll have everybody come over to the house when you get home and stuff all the cookies and brittle in bags and then put the bags in the cups. Carrie said we should buy some of those thick cellophane bags and put the whole cup in it so nothing falls out. Maybe we could tie it with a silver ribbon?"

I sank back against the car seat in shock, vaguely aware that Cabe was looking out the window at me and Deacon was barking his head off inside after hearing my car in the drive. This couldn't be my mother. She'd never in her life been this agreeable.

"Um, that sounds good."

"So you wanna hundred?"

"I think seventy five would be fine. We've gotten most of the RSVPs I expected to get, and I have a count of people who I know are coming even though they haven't responded."

"Okay. I'm gone order eighty five in case one breaks or they mess up paintin'. Is that okay?"

My mother was asking me if what she was doing was okay. I almost cracked up laughing at the surrealness of the situation.

"Yes. That sounds good. Thanks, Mama. I really appreciate it."

"No problem, baby girl. You know Mama loves you?"

"Yes, ma'am. I love you, too."

Sunday, November 9th

We took Deacon to the dog beach today to spend some quality family time together before everything goes haywire. We're both dreading leaving him behind for our honeymoon, even though Maggie has offered to keep him. We've been taking him to her house as often as possible so he's accustomed to being there, and Cabe has shown Maggie how to wrap the rubber band around the latch on his crate to prevent another Deacon Destructo escape.

Mama nearly stroked when I told her we were bringing him home with us the week before the wedding.

"Lord, no! You can't do that! You know how Boo is about other dogs."

Boo is quite possibly the world's most aggressive and possessive cocker spaniel.

"I don't have a choice. He'll totally freak out and think we've abandoned him if I take him to a boarding place, and Dean and Maggie will both be in Georgia with us. Please, Mama?"

"I can't handle all these people up in my house if I got dogs a' fightin' underfoot."

"We'll watch him real close. We'll bring his crate so he can stay in my room when we're not home."

Heavy sigh on her end. "I suwannee, Tyler. There's no end for what you ask me to do. Been working my tail off trying to get a wedding pulled together for you, which has not been appreciated not one bit, and now you want to bring a strange dog in my house."

"He's not a strange dog, Mama. He's your granddog."

"My what? Pssht. Granddog. No such thing. Does he shed? People gonna be coming in and out. I don't want them getting dog hair on their clothes."

"Not much," I said, ignoring the fact that we have tufts of dog hair rolling across our hardwood floors like tumbleweeds no matter how often we vacuum.

She exhaled with a groan. "You're not going to take no for an answer, are you?"

"Wonder where I got that from?" I teased, but she wasn't amused.

"That ain't funny. Don't get sassy with me. What you gonna do with this dog while y'all fly off down to Costa Rica?"

Progress. She was considering it.

"He'll come back home with Maggie, and she's going to keep him while we're gone."

I think that's what finally did it. If Maggie could keep the granddog, so could she.

I turned to Deacon when I got off the phone and scrunched his face between my hands. "Deacon! Buddy! You're going to Georgia. You're going to meet Grandma Patsy and Demon Dog Boo!"

Deacon barked once in reply, and Cabe and I both laughed.

How weird that this time next week, the three of us will be at my mama's house getting ready for the wedding. Eeek!

This time two weeks from now, Cabe and I will be swinging in a hammock made for two in Costa Rica. Wow!

Monday, November 17th

Cabe and I had hoped for a calm, quiet evening at Mama's after driving seven hours with Deacon, but half the county was at her house when we arrived this afternoon. They kept coming in a never-ending stream of arrivals and departures until well after dinner, stopping by to wish us well and to meet Cabe if they'd missed his last visit.

I caught some attitude from a few cousins and community friends who were put out that they weren't invited, but it couldn't be helped. Even if we had done the potluck, I still wouldn't have wanted all the other costs that rise with the guest list.

If I hadn't been so worn out from the past few months and the drive today, I probably would have enjoyed having company a whole lot more. My cheeks hurt from forcing a smile and my patience with small talk had worn thin long before the crowd started getting smaller at the end of the night.

I had just sat down on the couch while Cabe took Deacon outside when my cousin Danielle plopped down beside me.

"Where y'all going for ya honeymoon?" Danielle had never been out of the state to my knowledge, and it was quite possible she'd only left the county a dozen times.

It was probably the fiftieth time I'd answered the same question tonight, and though I appreciated everyone's interest, I also was about ready to make a sign with all the pertinent details and hang it on the wall to keep from repeating myself. "Costa Rica," I answered with my pasted-on smile.

Her eyes widened in amazement. "Where's that?"

I'd gotten used to that follow-up question as the night wore on. Turns out a large percentage of my family and hometown had never heard of Costa Rica or if they had, they had no clue where it was located in relation to them. It is rather small, after all.

"Central America."

"Central America? You mean like, Kansas?"

I did a double-take when she said it, unsure if maybe she was joking. I'd given geography lessons to many people tonight, but those had all been about the specific location of Costa Rica within its region. This was the first confusion I'd encountered over the location of Central America.

I was tempted to tell her yes. To say that we would be ziplining, white water rafting, and surfing along the coastline of the dense rainforests of Kansas. But before the wicked soul inside me could lie to the poor girl, Cabe came back in with Deacon and I had to grab Boo to keep him from getting all territorial again. I never did make it back to talk with Danielle, so I hope she learns from someone that Central America doesn't mean the Midwest.

By the time the last people had left and we had dragged our tired asses up the stairs, I was ready to collapse across the bed fully clothed and lay there 'til morning. The temperature difference between Orlando and home was brutal, and Cabe and I were both thankful Mama had turned on the wall heaters in our rooms before we came upstairs.

"So I guess I'm sleeping in Carrie's old room again, huh?" Cabe whispered as we stood side by side in the hall bath brushing our teeth.

I nodded as I brushed and then bent to spit in the sink. "Yep. As far as the world out there knows, we ain't married yet. I'm going to freeze without you next to me."

Cabe was like a human furnace. All I had to do was snuggle up next to him for a few minutes, and I'd be toasty warm. He made an excellent foot warmer.

He rinsed his mouth and leaned toward me to whisper again. "Your mama has about twenty quilts piled on my bed. I think she's trying to suffocate me."

"Ha! What you don't realize is that Patsy don't run the heat at night. Too much electricity. She's gonna make you turn that heater off before she goes to bed, so you may be thankful for those quilts before morning." I dried my hands and playfully twisted the towel to pop him on the butt with it, which ended up in all-out war until we heard Mama coming up the stairs.

She was carrying the broom and dust pan, and she handed them to Cabe and walked away. "Night y'all," she said as she waved over her shoulder. "Get on to bed. Busy days ahead."

Cabe looked at me in confusion, and I shrugged. "Wait. Mama? What's the broom for?"

She never even turned around. She just called out the answer over her shoulder as she shut her bedroom door.

"I thought maybe Cabe might not mind sweeping all the leaves off the roof of the porch if he takes a walk tonight. I gave him a few extra quilts in case he's cold when he comes back through the window."

So she knew he'd snuck into my room on our last visit.

Cabe grinned and slid his arm around my waist. "Does that mean it's okay if I come in? So could I just use the hallway?"

"Hell no," I whispered, pushing his arm away. "She was letting you know she ain't stupid and you got caught. She wasn't saying you can do it again. Why do you think she set you up in the other room?"

He laughed and we kissed goodnight. Deacon came in my room and curled up across me on the bed. Our Florida dog isn't used to the cold!

Thursday, November 20th

Go, go, go. That's been the theme of the week. We're up early every morning and off to run various errands and settle last-minute details. By the time we get back to Mama's in the late afternoon, folks have already started arriving to visit for the evening. Luckily, they always bring food, so we've had plenty to eat and Mama hasn't had to cook dinner a single night.

She seems happy. In her element with a houseful of people laughing and telling stories. She's been in a relatively good mood all week, in fact. So far, we've only had one little spat, and it was over the menu cards and programs.

The card stock was beautiful. It was round, with silver snowflakes placed sporadically around the perimeter of the circle. Mama had sprung to pay the newspaper office to print them on their color printer so the words would be dark purple. It was really striking, and they'd done a great job with the printing.

Unfortunately, they'd spelled my husband's name as Gable.

"I'm sure I told them Cable," Mama said for the fifteenth time.

"You probably didn't, Mama. You say Gabe all the time. No matter how many times I correct you."

"Like that's my fault. What kind of name is Cable? Who would name a child that? It's a piece of equipment. Like something you'd plug into the wall to watch TV or something they string from the light poles. Who would look at a tiny baby boy and name him Cable? It don't make no sense to me."

"We've had this conversation." I had no desire to have it again.

"I'm sure I said Cable. It's unique. How would I forget that?"

"You conveniently forget it *all the time*. It doesn't really matter at this point what you said. This is what they printed, and now we can't use them."

Mama clutched her hand over her chest and dropped her mouth open with a gasp. "Can't use them? By George, we most certainly can. I spent a

298

fortune on this paper and then paid an arm and a leg and a kidney to have them printed with that purple ink. I'll get a marker and fix the G before I throw these things away."

"You can't fix it. If it was a C, you could add the little line. But you can't take the little line away."

"You hide and watch. I ain't throwing these things. Might as well ride down the road throwing money out the window if I'm gonna do that. When we go by Lisa's to pick up the mugs, I'm taking her these cards to see what she can do. She's got all sorts of little fancy pens. She'll fix it. You'll see."

Lisa didn't look so sure when we dropped them off.

"I can't take away the G, but maybe I could add another little snowflake or something silver to go over it. Make it look like it's part of the design. I don't know if I could finish 'em all in time for the wedding though. I gotta double shift tomorrow so I can be off Saturday night."

"That's alright," Mama said. "You do what you can. Not everyone needs a program anyway. They can follow along with their neighbor if need be. We could probably get away with a few menu cards on each table. I may have to throw some of 'em away, but I ain't throwing all of them away. Work your magic, Lisa."

Thankfully, Cabe had run around with my brother all day so he didn't see the cards. I didn't want him to see his name spelled wrong, and I didn't want him being all gracious and polite and agreeing to use programs and menu cards with the wrong name. I could see him doing that, and I knew Mama would probably ask him to. She saw nothing at all wrong with using the wrong name when she talked about him; why would it be a problem to see it printed it that way?

I thought we had shelved the name conversation for the day, but then Mama asked Maggie about it when we met her for dinner shortly after she got into town tonight. We'd just gotten our entrees, and Mama had already been talking Maggie's ear off.

"Cable is such an interesting name. Where'd ya come up with that one? Tyler said it's a family name?"

I glared at Mama as I sipped my tea, wary of where she was heading with her line of questioning. I'd already told her any conversation about Cabe's dad was off limits.

"Yes," Maggie answered without any hesitation. "Cabe's father had an older brother who was killed in Vietnam. His name was Cable, and we wanted to honor his memory."

"Such an odd name, don't you think?" Mama asked. I kicked her softly under the table, and she grunted and gave me a sideways glance.

Maggie was too gracious to do anything other than smile, but I swear I'm gonna go off on Mama if she brings it up again.

Friday, November 21st

Maggie had asked me weeks ago if I wanted to know the details of the rehearsal dinner. I told her I'd rather be surprised. After fighting so much with Mama over the reception, I had no desire to start a dialog with my mother-in-law about what I liked or didn't like about her event. Besides, I trusted Maggie's taste enough to know I wouldn't be disappointed.

And I wasn't.

The barn venue Sandy found was a hit, and her team pulled out all the stops to produce a fun and relaxing rehearsal dinner. They'd taken the barn theme and ran with it, using red antique lanterns with battery-operated bulbs, hay bales, red gingham tablecloths, and mason jar glasses. The menu featured several down-home favorites, including barbecued pulled pork sandwiches, roasted chicken, and a big cauldron of chili with all the fixings.

Any concerns I may have had about Cabe's family being overwhelmed by mine were unfounded. Maggie puts on parties for a living, and Bill and Peggy are the consummate hosts. By the end of the evening, I think every member of my family had invited them to come back and visit again sometime. My brother and Kelly seemed completely enamored with Galen and Tate. They hung together all night. Any time Galen interacted with me or Cabe, sugar wouldn't melt in her mouth. At the risk of sounding cynical, I don't think it was nearly as genuine as she'd like us to believe, but if it keeps her from being an ass at my wedding, I'll take it.

Even Mama let her proverbial hair down and had a good time. Much of which revolved around Oscar, the venue's owner. At first, I thought he was just being an attentive site host. He brought in extra standing heaters to boost the efficiency of his central heating system in the record cold. He helped Sandy's staff move tables. He took out the trash. He mingled and laughed with everyone. But he was most attentive to one guest in particular.

Every time I looked up, they were chatting. The first couple of times, I thought perhaps she was asking him for something. Maybe an extra chair or another heater. But as I saw them together more, it was obvious their conversations were more of a personal nature.

She tugged at her hair. She tilted her head to the side. She laid her palm across her chest when she laughed. Which was often.

She wasn't alone in her flirtation. Not by any means. He lit up when she was near, and he kept his eye on her when she wasn't.

"Carrie," I whispered as I looped my arm through hers. "I think Mama's flirting."

"What? No way." I steered her body in the right direction and pointed as discreetly as possible. "She's laid her hand across her chest at least five times already, which Cosmo says is a gesture women make subconsciously to show men the empty ring finger."

"Get out!" Carrie openly stared where I'd tried to remain nonchalant. "Holy crap, I think you're right. Patsy's gotta beau."

We made a beeline for my sister Tanya and alerted her to our discovery. "That's old news," she said with a wave of her hand. "She's been meeting him for lunch in town a couple of days a week, and they've gone to bingo together every Wednesday night for a month."

Carrie and I both struggled to regain our composure. "You knew about this?" Carrie asked Tanya. "And you didn't say anything to us? You dirty dog." She playfully slapped our sister's arm.

"I couldn't. She asked me not to! I don't tell your secrets to her, so I ain't gonna tell hers to you. We came out to look at the place when the catering lady first mentioned it. Neither of us had ever heard of it, or him, so we wanted to make sure Cabe's mama wasn't getting taken. The sparks flew from the first conversation. Blew my mind and creeped me out all at the same time."

Talk about huge news. My mama had not even so much as gone on a friendly date since my daddy died, much less engage in an ongoing relationship. I was beyond thrilled for her and a little hurt that she hadn't told me. Although, I suppose I had been a bit preoccupied.

"Weatherman's saying it could snow tomorrow," Mama said when I came out of the bathroom from taking a shower once we'd gotten home.

"Snow? Really? In November?"

She nodded. "It's happened before, but not in many a year. It won't stick, of course, but with the temperatures being so much lower than normal and a front moving in, it could happen."

"Wow. Wouldn't that be awesome, to have snow for my winter wonderland wedding?"

"No," Mama said in a matter-of-fact tone. "It would be messy and slushy, and it would make the roads dangerous. Not to mention mess up your hair. You'd better pray for no snow, honey-girl."

I smiled at the term of affection. One I rarely heard anymore. Besides Aunt Clem and Daddy, no one had called me that.

"Daddy loved the snow, didn't he?"

"He did, that. More than once, he'd load us all up in that green station wagon we had and drive us up north of Atlanta to see the snow. Craziest thing ever. We didn't have no business being on the roads, but your daddy wanted y'all to see snow. So we'd drive up 'til it got white on the ground, and then he'd drag y'all out of the car and roll around in it with you. Y'all would be bundled up so thick ya couldn't hardly move, but he'd lie beside you on the ground teaching you to make snow angels. Then he'd insist we build a snowman, right there on the side of the road or the parking lot or wherever we'd stopped. When y'all got tuckered out and the snow had turned to mush beneath your feet, he'd load us back up and bring us home. Yes, Lord, that man loved the snow."

I smiled at the thought of snow flurries tomorrow. The meteorologists could talk all they wanted about record temperatures and cold fronts moving south. I knew without any doubt I'd see snow tomorrow, and I had no doubt who would send it.

"It's gonna take your room a few minutes to warm up. Wanna lay in here with me for a while? Watch some TV 'til our eyes get heavy?" Mama patted her big king-size bed.

I nodded as I crawled under the covers and snuggled up next to her with my head against her shoulder like I'd done a million times before.

"You and Cabe had a nice turnout tonight," she said. "Especially with the weather."

I nodded. My heart missed him, even though he'd only been gone an hour. He'd stopped by here after the rehearsal dinner to get his bags. He was staying at the bed and breakfast with his family for tonight to ensure the groom didn't see the bride tomorrow on the wedding day. Never mind that we'd been secretly married a month already and seen every inch of each other from every angle.

We had stood in the upstairs hall, listening to the din of family laughter downstairs and dreading saying goodbye.

"I wish you didn't have to go." I tugged at the buttons on his shirt as I pouted.

"Me, too. But this time tomorrow night, I'll be able to tell the world you're my wife. Then we can officially sleep together with everyone's permission."

I laughed and he kissed me, a slow and methodical exploration that made promises of things to come. My body responded with a yearning that didn't want to wait until tomorrow.

"I gotta go. They're waiting for me downstairs. But meet me at the church tomorrow. I'll be the one in the gray suit."

"I'll be there. Look for me in a white dress."

He cupped the back of my head in his hand and pressed his lips to my forehead, holding me close against him. "I can't wait to marry you again, Tyler Shaw."

I walked him to the door, my heart breaking ridiculously hard for a separation that wouldn't even be twenty-four hours.

I don't know who missed him more, though. Me or Deacon. The traitorous mutt had howled when Cabe left and kept pacing back and forth upstairs in front of Carrie's door where Cabe had slept the night before. No question where his loyalty lies.

Deacon looked so depressed the rest of the night that Mama let him come in her room with us, though Boo made it very clear he wasn't allowed on the bed.

Mama and I watched TV for nearly an hour, commenting on the shows and programs and avoiding me leaving her room. It was one more separation for us, and this one meant a lot in the long run. I had wanted so badly for time to hurry up and bring it, but now that it was here, I hesitated to break the final ties for independence. I snuggled a little closer and breathed in the familiar scent of my mama. It was both comforting and sad.

We'd had so much difficulty together in reaching this point, in pulling together the wedding for tomorrow. Yet here we lay, mother and daughter, side by side. On the cusp of a whole new chapter in our lives. Me, going off into a marriage and eventually a family of my own. Her, still here but with one more daughter hitched and a son on his way out the door. My heart hurt to think of her here alone after we'd all left.

"I noticed you and Oscar talking tonight," I said with as much nonchalance as I could muster. Tanya had threatened me if I told Mama she'd blabbed, but if I could get Mama to admit it on her own, that would be different.

"What of it?" Her voice was suspicious, and her body tensed ever so slightly.

"Nothing. I just think he's a handsome man and he seems well to do. Interesting, for sure, with all his business ventures and his background. I was thinking you should ask him out."

"Ha," Mama snorted. "Don't be silly. You need to get some sleep. You gotta big day tomorrow, my baby girl. All grown up and on her way."

She patted my back and rested her hand between my shoulders. "He makes you happy?"

I nodded. "Yes, ma'am. Very much so."

"He seems to treat you well. Real fond of ya from what I can tell. Comes from a nice family, too. I was happy to meet 'em."

"Yes, ma'am. They are. Real nice, in fact."

"You did good, baby. Mama's proud of you." I heard the crack in her voice, and it nearly did me in.

"I love you, Mama."

"I love you, too, sugar."

I didn't move, and she didn't make me. As far as the world knew, it was my last night as a single girl before I pledged my life as someone's wife. I decided to spend it curled up in my mama's big ole bed, snug as a bug in a rug.

Saturday, November 22nd
My Wedding Day

It was much colder this time around than the first time we got married.

That night at the lake had been perfect. Not warm, not cold, and just enough of a breeze to stir the air.

Today was colder than a witch's brass brassiere in a blizzard.

I was so thankful Mel and I had chosen a dress with long sleeves. If I'd been in a strapless dress, I may have turned blue.

My high school friend, Kerrie, opened her salon early for us to come in for hair and make-up. She swept the left side of my hair to the back in a loose, messy braid that came around my head and back over the top, where she tucked in the ends and pinned them. Then she swept the front to the right low across my face, and started another braid that ran beneath the first one to just behind my ear, where she weaved it into the larger braid above it and pinned it with white pouf of feather and a sprig of dark purple-berry hydrangea. The rest of my hair hung in loose curls down past my shoulder on the right side. So from the left, it looked like an upswept messy braid, but the right had a Bohemian vibe with the double braids and the curls framing my face and neck. The perfect combination of my hair up, which I had wanted, and my hair down, which my husband had requested.

"Is it supposed to be all messy like that? I think she needs to spray it," Mama said when Kerrie walked away.

I laughed. "No, Mama. It's supposed to be messy. Tousled."

"Are those fake?" She stepped in close and inspected the false eyelashes Kerrie had put on my upper lids.

"Yes ma'am."

"Hmmph," she said, as she leaned back and surveyed me from head to toe. "Something borrowed, something blue, something fake, and something new. Times, they are a'changing."

Despite her joke, I did have all the traditional components. My dress was new. My heart necklace from Daddy was old, and Maggie had loaned me a sapphire ring to knock out both borrowed and blue.

We waited until we reached the church's waiting room to put my dress on, but my ladies all got ready at Kerrie's shop. I'd only asked them to choose the same deep aubergine color, but they'd all picked velvet to go with my dress as well.

Mel's had long sleeves and a deep V-neck. She'd had sheer panels of purple sewn inside the neckline to minimize the amount of cleavage and chest she had on display. The dress was more fitted through the waist, which cinched her middle in nicely when paired with Spanx underneath, but hampered her breathing and her ability to eat. According to her.

Tanya's was an elegant column dress with a sweetheart bodice and an attached cowl shawl that swooped low across her chest and then over her shoulders to hang loose down her back beyond her rump. If she could keep Eric and Erin from swinging on it, it would be beautiful.

Carrie's dress was a bit edgier, as was befitting Carrie. It was form-fitting, hugging her tall, straight body. She was built like Daddy's sisters. Tanya and I got Mama's hips and height. Carrie's dress was ruched down a center line from the V-neck to just below her navel. The ruching made small folds fan out from the center of her body like a starburst. It had short sleeves that were ruched from her shoulder with a bit of a pouf at the top. The dress was cut to a deep V in the front and back, filled with a sheer panel embroidered with intricate lace detail and accented with black and purple rhinestones that rose to a sheer mandarin collar trimmed in black stones.

True to form like the dancer and drama princess she was, Galen had chosen a dress with one long sleeve and one bare shoulder and arm. It fit her like a glove all the way down to just above her knees where the velvet gave way to a sheer skirt of the deepest purple that fell to her feet and pooled on the floor.

It was odd to see her mingle with my sisters and Mel. She was out of place, out of her comfort zone, and it gave me an odd satisfaction to see her act so quiet and demure.

My sisters had no idea of what all had transpired between us, but Mel knew, and I could sense her tension toward Galen every time the two of them conversed.

Laura greeted us when we arrived at the church. "I think you're going to be pleased. Wanna take a peek?"

"Of course!" I'd been dying to see the fellowship hall all morning to see what Sandy had been able to do with the bland gymnasium space.

Laura opened the door and ushered me into my winter wonderland. The huge rows of fluorescent lights across the ceiling weren't being used at all. Instead, Sandy had suspended a canopy of twinkle lights to create a magical, whimsical camouflage for the industrial ceiling. She also placed can lights around the perimeter of the room to light up the walls in varying shades of purple and magenta. Each corner featured a 'grove' of bare trees that had been sprayed white and dusted with iridescent 'frost.' The clusters of trees sat in a bank of what looked like snow, with small LED lights at the base of the trees to spotlight them.

She'd used digital mapping to project scenes of a snow-filled forest onto the two side walls, immersing the entire room into winter.

Each table centerpiece featured a smaller version of the trees stretching tall from a round clear glass globe filled with silver balls. An aubergine velvet ribbon was bound around the cluster of branches just above the rim of each globe, and silver pillar candles in slender glass vases of varying heights surrounded the centerpieces, illuminating the entire room with a warm, soft glow. Each place setting featured a dark purple charger with a menu card and a silver napkin.

Upon closer inspection, I could see that Lisa had added a few tiny snowflakes randomly spread across the card, making sure each G had a strategically placed snowflake over the line. It wasn't a perfect fix, and it would definitely show up in bright light. But in the dim cast of the pillars, it was undetectable. I have no idea how hard my poor cousin worked to get them all done, but every place setting had one.

As I stepped back from the table, I realized Sandy had also brought in silver Chiavari chairs with an aubergine velvet ribbon. I turned to her and blinked rapidly to try and prevent the tears from ruining my make-up.

Sandy smiled. "So do you like it?"

"Like it? Sandy, it's absolutely incredible. It's beyond what I could imagine this room transformed into, and I've seen a lot of room transformations. But it's too much. You did way more than what was on the proposal." I motioned toward the chairs, the mapping on the walls, and the canopy of lights.

She smiled and grasped my hand, her own eyes just as glassy as mine as we both tried not to cry. "Maggie Mae is one of my oldest friends. We've been through a lot of life together. I was there at the hospital the day Cabe was born, and I've watched him grow into an amazing man who I am sure will be an amazing husband. Nothing I could do would be enough to reflect what they mean to me. But I've tried."

She led me to the back of the room, where there was a custom s'mores station and hot chocolate brewery by the cake table. The four-tiered square cake featured what appeared to be icicles draped from every layer and a cluster of deep purple-berry hydrangea on the top.

Laura stood nearby, and I knew we needed to go, but I was enchanted by the room. I couldn't believe this was our church gymnasium yesterday. I hugged Sandy and thanked her again as Laura led us away.

Mama and Maggie were walking in as we were walking out.

"Well, I'll be a monkey's uncle. Tied up and tarnation, I've never seen anything so pretty," Mama exclaimed, wide-eyed and in shock.

"I told you," Maggie said with a smile. "I said you'd be blown away."

"Maggie, thank you. The room is amazing, and Sandy has done an incredible job. I can't thank you enough," I said as I hugged my mother-in-law.

"It was my pleasure."

Mama nodded. "Yes, Maggie. Thank you so much. I never could have done this for her, and I don't have the words to tell you how appreciative I am. It's truly beautiful." She took my hands and squeezed them. "You did the right thing. This is amazing."

I smiled and fought back the tears that seem to be ever-present and ready to flood at any moment.

"We need to get her in her dress, ladies. Feel free to join us in the waiting room in just a few minutes." Laura was in work mode behind us, keeping us on track.

It took Mel, Laura and both my sisters to get me in the dress. It was slim-fitting white velvet with long sleeves trimmed in rhinestones and a scoop neckline trimmed in the same. The back of the dress was completely sheer save for my shoulders and the strip of velvet that formed the back of the collar and served to join the sleeves together. A row of tiny little pearl bead buttons started at my neckline and went all the way down the center of my back to the top of the fishtail train. The sheer panel dipped low to a V at the base of my spine and then curved around under each arm to come to a sheer point across my ribs. The outline was also trimmed in rhinestones.

Daddy's heart necklace lay at the base of my throat, quivering ever so slightly as my pulse raced with excitement.

Mama and Maggie came in with Eric and Erin in tow. Eric's suit was the same dark gray as Cabe's, and Erin wore a dress of aubergine velvet trimmed around her collar, wrists, and hem with white faux fur. Carrie had gotten creative.

"Oh, Tyler," Maggie exclaimed with her hand at her throat. "Oh honey." She shook her head slightly as tears filled her eyes and she covered her open mouth with her hand. She walked toward me slowly.

"Don't you make me cry," I said as I laughed. "I've been trying all day not to cry."

She hugged me, taking care not to muss our hair or makeup or squish her hydrangea corsage. "You are the most beautiful bride I've ever seen.

You are glowing. Oh." Her voice broke off with emotion, and she laughed it away. "He's going to be mesmerized. I can't wait to see his face."

"You're a beauty, sugar. Stunning." Mama must have been really impressed. She is rarely a woman of so few words, and even more rarely are they complimentary.

"Any word from Lillian?" I looked to Laura, who frowned and shook her head. Lillian's flight this morning had been canceled due to the weather. The last anyone had heard she planned to drive here, but since she doesn't answer her phone in the car we had no way of knowing her progress.

"Thanks for being here, Laura. It means the world to me, and I can't tell you how much I appreciate it. I mean, just giving up a weekend off that you could have been with your family." My eyes welled up again. "I can't thank you enough."

"Oh, sweetie, you don't have to thank me. I would not have missed this for the world. I'm honored to be here."

I heard someone say it was time to go, and the room became a flurry of activity. All day long, time had moved so slowly it felt it wasn't moving at all, and yet the whole day sped by so fast that when I thought about it, I got dizzy.

Next thing I knew, Maggie and Mama had already gone in the sanctuary to be seated, and Tanya and Carrie were waiting to go through the double wood doors as *What A Wonderful World* continued to play. We'd chosen to use the same processional song we had before.

The glass doors behind me swung open with a blast of frigid air and a huffy Brit.

"Jesus, it's freezing out there," Lillian said as she stepped inside and smoothed her hair down. Sharon from the church staff glared at her, not only for being late, but for using the Lord's name in vain, I am sure. Lillian was oblivious. "Did you know it's snowing?"

"Snow!" Eric and Erin took off to press their faces against the glass doors, jumping up and down in excitement. I stood behind them, watching the light flurries dance and twirl as they fell from the sky. My heart expanded and filled my chest as the tears broke free and slid down my cheeks. I touched my fingers to the gold heart nestled at the base of my throat and whispered, "I knew you'd come."

"We're gonna run out of song," Laura called out as Tanya herded Eric and Erin back into place behind Mel and I hugged Lillian and thanked her for coming.

First Carrie was gone, then Laura. It was Mel's turn next and I gave her a quick hug before she went. She grabbed my arm and whispered close in my ear. "This is beautiful, but I prefer your last wedding." She winked at me and blew me a kiss. "Remember what I always tell my brides. When those doors open, take a moment to see everything."

I nodded, unable to believe that I'd heard her say that so many times before, and here I was on the receiving end today.

Eric and Erin went in next, and we could hear the crowd ooh and aah as they made their way down the aisle.

Lillian somehow nudged Sharon back so she could stand at the door opposite of Laura. How fitting for those two ladies, my bosses and mentors, to be the gatekeepers as I stepped into the new life before me.

"Only wedding I've ever been late to," Lillian said under her breath. She winked at me and said, "Knock 'em dead, kiddo. You look gorgeous."

"Thanks again for coming," I managed to say before my voice broke and tears threatened me again.

This was it. This was my moment. My favorite part of every wedding. When the bride is standing there, waiting for the doors to open. When everything behind her, every step she's taken in the path of life, has somehow led her to this choice, and after those doors open and she walks inside, her life will never be the same again.

Today, I was the bride. My favorite moment was mine.

I held tight to my brother's arm as Lillian and Laura prepared to swing the doors open. "You look beautiful," he said. "I love you."

"You too."

The doors swung wide and I saw what the planner never sees.

Family and friends looking back at me with wonder and expectation. Our mothers at the end of the aisle, smiling as they both wiped away tears of happiness.

My sisters standing side by side on the altar, welcoming me on this new journey. Mel beside them, her face filled with tears as she smiled with a love no less greater than that of a true sister.

And then, there he was. He came into my line of vision, and everything else disappeared.

My heart leapt, and I wanted to break free from my brother and run to him. To throw myself in his arms and scream, "*We made it!*"

His smile radiated out across the distance between us, as though the joy it conveyed could not be contained.

I stood a second longer, making sure I memorized everything, froze each detail in my mind to be recalled for the rest of my life.

His hair, slicked back away from his face, tousled and damp on the sides where it fell in loose curls around his collar.

His shoulders, broad and strong beneath his jacket, and his hands, so adept at caressing my skin, clasped in front of him as he rocked back and forth on his heels.

I noticed his tears flowing just as openly as mine when I gazed into his eyes. Oh, those eyes. Those beautiful eyes. I saw my world in those eyes.

And suddenly, I couldn't wait any more. I tugged at Brad's arm and stepped forward to go to Cabe, unable to stay away any longer.

He met us at the bottom of the stairs. He shook Brad's hand and then took mine, bending to kiss my cheek as the crowd laughed.

"I thought you'd never get here, but you were worth the wait," he whispered in my ear as the pastor playfully admonished him for the kiss. He held my hand to lead me up the steps to the altar, and when we'd settled in place, he looked at me and mouthed, "Wow. Hot."

I smiled at him as the pastor started his *"Dearly Beloved"* speech. I leaned toward Cabe ever so slightly and whispered in a voice so low, I wasn't sure he'd be able to hear me.

"Ready to do this again?"

He leaned back and answered me, "Any time. Any place."

Want more?
Read Maggie's Story!

You've read Cabe's side of the story through Tyler's diary entries. Now get Maggie's version of what happened between her and Cabe's dad, as well as her own account of her present-day romance.

Volume 4 in the Tales Behind the Veils series features parallel stories of Maggie's second chance at love set against the backdrop of her disastrous, career-ending first romance.

Visit www.violethowe.com to learn more.

Love Romantic Suspense?

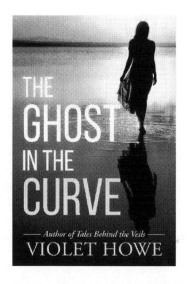

This lighthearted romantic suspense has a charming paranormal twist! Sloane Reid never believed in ghosts before she met Chelsea. Now she's trying to solve the mystery Chelsea has carried for thirteen years. But Sloane can't solve it alone, and before local deputy Tristan Rogers will help her, she'll have to convince him she's not crazy. Or a criminal. As they work together to unlock the secrets of the past, Sloane soon discovers it may be her own life that needs saving.

To purchase, visit www.books2read.com/GhostintheCurve
or www.violethowe.com.

Wanna Know What Happens Next? Sign up for my Newsletter!

If you want to know what's coming next from Violet Howe, visit www.violethowe.com and sign up for Violet's newsletter. You'll get monthly updates on new releases, upcoming events, interesting tidbits, fun prize drawings, and more!

You'll also find out how to join Violet's Facebook Reader Group, the Ultra Violets, where you can get exclusive content, book discussions, and contests. Plus you'll be in the know before anyone else on all things Violet.

Thank You

Thank you for reading! I'd love to hear your feedback.
Please consider leaving a review on Amazon, Goodreads, or whatever social media you prefer.

If you liked it, then please tell somebody! Tell your friends. Tell your family. Tell a co-worker. Tell the person next to you in line at the grocery store.

Photo Credit: Theresa Murphy

About the Author

Violet Howe enjoys writing romance with humor. She lives in Florida with her husband—her knight in shining armor—and their two handsome sons. They share their home with three adorable but spoiled dogs. When she's not writing, Violet is usually watching movies, reading, or planning her next travel adventure. You can follow Violet's ramblings on her blog, The Goddess Howe.

www.violethowe.com
Facebook.com/VioletHoweAuthor
@Violet_Howe
Instagram.com/VioletHowe

Made in the USA
Middletown, DE
20 February 2020